SANDSTEALERS

BEN BROWN

Sandstealers

Harper*Press*
An imprint of HarperCollins*Publishers*
77–85 Fulham Palace Road
Hammersmith, London W6 8JB
www.harpercollins.co.uk

Visit our authors' blog: www.fifthestate.co.uk
Love this book? www.bookarmy.com

First published by Harper*Press* in 2009
1

A catalogue record for this book is available from the British Library

This novel is a work of fiction. The names, characters and incidents portrayed in it are the work of the author's imagination, or are used fictionally, and resemblance to actual persons, living or dead, events or localities is entirely coincidental.

ISBN 978-0-00-728014-8

Set in Minion and Helvetica by
G&M Designs Limited, Raunds, Northamptonshire

Printed and bound in Great Britain by Clays Ltd, St Ives plc

For Geraldine

‘We live more in a year than most people live in a lifetime.’

DANIEL L. LOWENSTEIN, war correspondent

PART ONE

1

Post-Liberation Iraq, August 2004

Danny Lowenstein had a premonition he would die that day. It wasn't unusual for him to foresee his own death: such thoughts went with the territory. The main thing was not to take them too seriously, otherwise he'd never get out of bed in the morning.

He cursed the sun, which had barely been born into Iraq's morning sky. Already a sapping heat was rising from the tarmac and soon the temperature would hit a grotesque 50 degrees Celsius. He daren't translate it into Fahrenheit. As he stood at the petrol station, the road to Iskandariya shimmered ahead of him. Danny wondered if the surface might evaporate before his eyes.

For now he was still fresh. He had sprayed himself with so much deodorant it almost choked him, but his skin felt good beneath the linen shirt he'd bought at Heathrow and his favourite pair of chinos. They were the pseudo-military sort, with extra pockets on the thighs which bulged with a notepad, assorted pens, a small Dictaphone – another terminal purchase – his US passport and press accreditation, some scrunched-up dollar bills and chewing gum for when the day started to drag him under.

Danny knew that, before long, the same skin that was now so pleasantly clean and dry would be soaked in sweat. Little streams would crawl down the valley between his shoulder blades towards his waist, where they'd meet his tightly buckled belt and form an irritating reservoir. The fresh clothes would start to cling to him like cloying dishcloths. His rigorous dawn shower back at the hotel would be redundant and he'd wonder why he'd bothered to make the effort at all: he might as well have just put back on what he'd worn the day before. By dusk, he'd be drained of whatever energy he'd woken up with.

'God, sometimes I hate this country,' he told Mohammed, who was only half listening.

'Don't say bad things, Mr Daniel. I think you would miss us.'

'I'd miss *you*, Mohammed, of course I would, but not a whole lot else.'

'There is not another story like it, not anywhere in the world. You told me so yourself.'

'Yeah, I know, our Vietnam and all that. But Heaven help your country if that's all you've become – a story. The thing is, I'm just so ...'

'Tired?'

'No, not tired. Exhausted. Sorry if I'm kind of grumpy.'

'Woman trouble?'

'You could say. And this heat, and this war and this ... I mean, just take a look around us.'

He waved towards the sprawling strip of charmless shops just beyond them, many selling satellite dishes, fridges and all the other consumer electricals that had flooded in after liberation. Snapped power cables drooped down around them mockingly. On the road ahead, battered cars jostled one another amid a cacophony of horns, most of them unheeded. It seemed to Danny that the traffic, like everything else, was getting worse.

'You know, I remember the day I got my first visa for this place: 19th April 1990. I'd never wanted anything so much. Now? Two

Gulf wars and a fucked-up occupation later, I don't think I'd care if I never came back.'

Mohammed stood next to him and surveyed the scene, not with Danny's weariness but the alert eyes of an intelligence officer: scrutinising faces, analysing cars, studying young policemen behind their sandbags – were they really police, or insurgents in impeccable disguise? Nothing was as it seemed.

A teenage pump attendant slid in the nozzle.

'Can't believe you forgot to fill up last night,' said Danny.

'I told you, it was Farrah's birthday.'

Danny felt bad. He should have sent her a present. He'd remembered with all Mohammed's other kids.

'But even so, I mean, for fuck's sake.'

Danny hated it when things went wrong. It made him feel the whole story, the whole day, might be cursed. He glanced at his watch. They were already running late for the rendezvous with Abu Mukhtar, and he was uneasy.

'How long till we get there?'

'Twenty minutes, maybe twenty-five.'

'I hope you can find this al-Talha, or whatever they call it. It's not even on the map.'

'No problem – we ask people.'

As a rule, Danny liked to have a 'chase car', a second vehicle following behind, which could rescue them if they broke down in the badlands. Today, Saad, who usually drove it, was sick with an upset stomach – or claimed he was. Either way, it meant they were travelling alone.

First the chase car, then the petrol. Bad omens, thought Danny.

Mohammed's hawkish eyes continued their search for anything that was different or out of place. It was how he lived these days, even in his own street in Karada – always watching.

'You are sure you want to go there?' Mohammed asked Danny for at least the third time. 'You're risking your life, you know.'

'Sure I'm sure. I risk it whenever I leave Baghdad – or the hotel, for that matter. Sometimes I feel so damned incarcerated.'

'No, no! *Liberated!*'

Mohammed was a fervent supporter of the invasion and endearing in his optimism. Just look at it like this, he'd insist: we're an abused child, and abused children can be ungrateful. They need time, and a little love from their foster parents. You Americans, you must stay however long you want! Danny would reply that he didn't see them as 'his' Americans at all.

'At least when the old man was in charge I could walk the streets, day or night, without being bundled into a car and decapitated on the Internet,' said Danny.

'So why have we come here?'

'Because I guess it's worth the risk. I have cast-iron guarantees.'

Now it was Mohammed's turn to be cynical.

'You know what they say about such guarantees in my country? The cast iron is always full of bullet holes. I don't want to die.'

'Me neither, you idiot.'

Danny put an affectionate arm around him.

'You are a single man,' said Mohammed. 'Me, I have a wife and five children. Nothing can happen to me.' Mohammed had got into the habit of kissing each member of his family whenever he left home, in case he never returned.

'And nothing will, my friend, nothing will.'

'Maybe you should have some children of your own, Mr Daniel.'

Children! Why was it people were always telling him to have them? Didn't they realise a free-wheeling, fast-moving war correspondent like him couldn't be weighed down by a family? And anyway, who the hell would want to be his son or daughter? What kind of burden would it be to have a father who might come home one day in a coffin? It didn't mean Danny disliked kids – actually he rather enjoyed them. But other people's, not his own.

Danny thought about the happy moments he'd shared at Mohammed's home. His last visit there had been a journey to an Iraq that was desperate to retain the appearance of normality. In his garden, Mohammed had barbecued masgouf, the delicious fishy smoke of it wafting around him as his wife Sabeen sprinkled it with lemon juice. Soon she had the table sagging under a relentless supply of her other favourite dishes: fasolada soup, baba ghanoush, eggplant salad, falafel, pitta and houmous, all washed down with a bottle of ferocious arak. Before they ate, Mohammed had sat on a red plastic garden chair while, one by one, his offspring piled on top of him until the legs buckled and they all toppled on to the grass in a hopeless, giggling heap.

Danny had entertained all five children, especially Farrah – six years old, the youngest and cutest. Under a lemon tree, he'd held her hands and swung her round so that she flew like a plane, horizontal and in dizzying circles. She'd screamed in ecstasy, and everyone applauded but now, in his anxiety about the trip to al-Talha, he had forgotten little Farrah's birthday. It was something else to trouble him. Danny liked to lavish gifts on Mohammed and his family. Every time he flew into Baghdad, he'd bring back copies of the *Lancet* and the *British Medical Journal*, which Mohammed devoured. He was a former paediatrician who'd trained at Great Ormond Street. He'd only given up medicine because the foreign press paid him ten times what he'd been earning in his hospital, and he needed the money. Another triumph for the occupation, Danny told anyone who'd listen.

The first thing people noticed about Mohammed was his unfortunate resemblance to the fallen dictator: fatter and older, but with the same darting eyes and the signature moustache. When a bounty was put on Saddam's head, strangers would come up to him and laugh: 'Americans, we've found him. We claim our reward! Death to the despot!' Mohammed would smile along with them, but the joke became tiresome and he felt he deserved more respect.

Now he wandered away from the petrol pump, his pot belly wobbling affably. He struck up casual conversations with a couple of shopkeepers and idle, jobless men who gossiped and fiddled with their worry beads. He was trying to get a feel for the area ahead and to pick up anything they might have heard about Abu Mukhtar and his boys. Of course it might only put them in more danger, tipping off hungry wolves that tasty meat was on its way. In Iraq, there were pros and cons to every move you made and death lurked around every corner. A couple of dirty street children hawked trayloads of cigarettes and fizzy drinks. Kids like these had been known to pass word that 'foreigners' were about, and Mohammed kept an eye on them.

Beside them a goat sniffed its way through a heap of rubbish. Lamp posts lay broken and some plastic bags were caught up in fencing, ensnared like fleeing prisoners. A burnt-out vehicle was nearby, charred and cannibalised, and a pool of stagnant water stretched across the street. It smelt as if, on closer inspection, it might well turn out to be an open sewer.

Danny climbed back into the Pajero and caught a glimpse of himself in the mirror. He looked as worn out as he felt. Grey was advancing rapidly around his temples and wrinkles had multiplied around his eyes. He could almost hear the whispered questions from the twenty-somethings of the Baghdad press corps, people half his age, another generation: was Lowenstein really still the 'operator' that he had been, or just another 'veteran' past his sell-by date? Oh sure, he'd won a Pulitzer, but that was years ago, wasn't it? I mean, Bosnia – who even remembers what *that* war was all about? The doubts weighed down on him. He felt a rookie insecurity, the same draining need to prove himself as when he'd first hit the road a quarter of a century earlier.

He could have shared the Abu Mukhtar interview and all its dangers with his fellow Junkies, but in Danny's book you had to get away from the crowd to stand out from it, even if the 'crowd' included your oldest friends. Of course it could be a trap, and his general rule in Iraq was never to make appointments with people he didn't know. On the other hand, these days the concept of a clandestine rendezvous with any kind of insurgent leader – even a middle-ranking one – was intoxicating. Abu Mukhtar wasn't a celebrity terrorist like al Zarqawi; in fact, hardly anyone beyond the cognoscenti of US army intelligence would have heard of him. Even so, according to Asmat Mahmoud, Mukhtar had passionate opinions he wanted to pass on to the world. Danny could write it hard, with plenty of topspin to tickle the fancy of even the most blasé, battle-weary, war-numbed reader. My God, he thought, if I'm bored of it all, what must they be? Mukhtar's views, however mundane, would ultimately be processed into front-page news. In his head, he had already written the story's most important line: '… told me in a secret and dangerous meeting, deep inside the bandit country of Iskandariya, south of Baghdad …' It was just a case of filling in the rest. He would sell it easily to his old paper, the *New York Times*, or perhaps turn it into a wider, more rambling piece for *Rolling Stone* magazine or *Vanity Fair*. And it would make at least a couple of pages in the memoirs he was struggling to complete.

Still, the premonition returned. Mohammed had reawakened it.

'So, Mr Daniel, we go on?'

Why did he have to keep asking? Danny was already queasy with uncertainty. Even now he could call it off, he only had to say the word. He remembered all the moments in his career when he had faced dilemmas such as this, and each time he had picked the harder road. He remembered the twenty-somethings too. He couldn't afford to relax and he certainly couldn't afford to put down roots or have children. Danny breathed in deeply.

'Absolutely, we go on!'

'No problem!' Mohammed smiled unconvincingly, a chubby Saddam-smile.

'You're a good guy, the very best.'

A few hundred yards away, men in a rusting white-and-orange taxi studied them both through binoculars with a hatred that was entirely sure of itself, and open to nothing so frail as doubt.

It is another two miles before the turnoff on to a narrower road. Danny wonders if it is one of the insurgent 'rat runs', as the Americans like to call them: a phrase, he has noted in one recent piece, that implies the enemy will be destroyed – just as soon as someone can come up with the right kind of pest control.

The wheels blow up a dust cloud.

Quiet roads. Danny seems to have spent a career travelling along them, wondering what they have in store for him: the story of a lifetime, or the end of a lifetime.

A small, mangy dog emerges from nowhere and starts to cross in front of them. It is limping badly.

'Watch out!' Danny screams at Mohammed, who is driving hard and fast and doesn't see it till the last minute. His attempt to avoid the wretched animal is too half-hearted. There is a thud and slight crunch, and they carry on.

'Did you really have to do that?' Danny can't bring himself to look back at the body, yet another corpse in a country overflowing with them. Has life here got so cheap that it's not even worth the casual movement of a wrist to save a life? It's more bad karma, another jinx on his day. First the chase car, then the petrol, now the dog.

'Fuck's sake,' he mutters to himself.

The undercarriage scrapes some chunks of rock and now it's Mohammed's turn to curse aloud, though with incomprehensible Arabic expletives.

Danny notices another car up ahead. It is a Toyota, red with a distinctive white roof. Shock smacks him hard around the face. He knows this car, he'd know it from a mile away. Two people: the journalist inside, someone else – the driver – kneeling on the ground, changing a tyre. There is very little time to think. Has Asmat Mahmoud flogged the same story twice? Is the enigmatic Abu Mukhtar actually just some media tart?

'I don't believe it – they've crashed our fucking interview!'

Danny's first inclination is to drive straight on, but he can't ignore them. He leans from his passenger window and talks to the other journalist. The words are venomous, the anger mutual. Danny's foul mood has just got much, much worse, but after he has said his piece, he manages to calm himself.

'Anyhow, I'm pushing on,' he says, drawing a line under the argument. 'How's everything up there? Okay?'

The question is carefully calibrated. With this perfunctory request, Danny makes it clear he's not interested in striking some last-minute bargain on the story, he's merely seeking reassurance on what lies ahead.

His fellow Junkie says nothing, responding with … with what, exactly? Some vague movement of affirmation, or is it merely the *absence* of something – a prohibitive hand or a piercing cry that says: Jesus Christ no, Danny! We've just been shot at! Don't go up there, don't go another yard!

Whatever it is or isn't, the biggest mistake of Danny's distinguished career is to take it as a yes. Before any further complications can spoil his story, he turns to Mohammed: 'Jalah, jalah!' And obediently, Mohammed speeds away.

Still, Danny's head is dizzy with doubt. In his younger days, he was never afflicted by the curse of hesitation. The life he led then was charmed: bullet-proof, blast-proof, death-proof. Shit happens, but not to me. Friends died, fallen soldiers on the battlefield, until it seemed he'd attended more funerals than weddings, but somehow it was always *them* who fell, and always *him* at the lectern in the home-town church, delivering the Bible readings and moving eulogies, the well-judged words of comfort for the grieving parents or partner, the final tears as the coffin was eased into the earth. Danny seemed agreeably immune to death, as though it were a ritual for him to observe rather than take part in. Chechnya showed him that. Against all the odds, he had survived it, though not entirely unscathed. Death had touched him there, laid its chilly fingers upon his face as he stood by and watched a good friend's life drain away. He'd always expected that one day the gods would punish him. Perhaps part of him thought they should.

Yet now, as they regain speed, he feels the rush of the warm air on his face from the open window, the scent of eucalyptus trees, and there it is once more: the hit, the buzz, the drug. He might as well have rammed a needle in his vein. No, I'm not tired, he thinks, not exhausted, not settling down. And by the way, I'm not finished yet either.

Nearby, an Iraqi shepherd boy wanders aimlessly with his scrawny, filthy sheep. A few of them have broken away from the flock and are running around the road in panic. Like some reporters, it occurs to Danny: terrified of getting separated from the pack.

And then it is only them, on this the loneliest of roads. No more sheep or shepherd boys. The words of his Hostile Environments instructors at Walsingham, where the rolling Norfolk countryside had been transformed into a war-zone training ground, come back to him: 'Just ask yourself, where are all the people? If they've smelt danger, so should you. And if there's no oncoming traffic, you should wonder why.'

The story is sucking him in, though, as it always has. It's just a little further on, down the road and over the bridge. It's *always* just a little further on.

Only about half a mile now. Swallow hard, Danny boy, breathe deep. Relax! Enjoy!

As they come round the bend he sees, a few hundred yards on, the rusting oil drums spread across the narrow road. Clustered around them are the insurgents, six in all, different-coloured kafiyehs wrapped around their faces: orange, red and black. Fat sunglasses cover their eyes. They are armed with a menacing assortment of pistols and AK47s.

Mohammed stamps on the brakes.

'Who are *they*?'

'Don't worry; just a poxy roadblock.' Danny wants to make them both feel better. He's a connoisseur of roadblocks, from Sarajevo to Somalia to Sierra Leone – the well-organised, polite ones; the drunken, chaotic ones; the downright dangerous ones, manned, or rather boyed, by 11-year-old African kids, sky-high on weed, with manic eyes that say killing a white man can be quite fun when you're bored out of your mind.

'Roadblocks, I could write the book on them,' he sighs.

When the first shot is fired, he realises of course that he could not. The bullet blows out a front tyre and one side of the Pajero lurches down on to the road, like a horse gone lame. Danny's desperate hope is that the men in kafiyehs are just trying to scare them.

'Shit. Don't they understand we're only here because their own leader wants to talk to us?'

He sees another of the men raise his Kalashnikov, aiming higher now, straight at them. It's gone wrong so quickly, too quickly, and yet in slow motion too.

'Oh fuck! Reverse, Mohammed. Let's get out of here now. *Now*, I said!'

The driver's corpulent body will not move. Terror has paralysed him and for once he disobeys his master's voice.

'Reverse, Mohammed. Will you do as you're told and fucking well reverse?'

As Danny shouts, a burst of fire hits the windscreen. Instinctively, he ducks as he has done before – all those times when death has, arbitrarily, turned its attentions elsewhere.

He is about to bark more orders when he sees that Mohammed is thrust back against his headrest, blood spreading out evenly in two distinct patches on an otherwise spotless white dishadasha: one around the middle of his sternum and the other a little to the left. The eyes – Saddam's eyes, as everyone used to joke – are wider than Danny has ever seen on any man's face before, peeled back and accusing. The mouth is open, as if it meant to say one last thing.

'Oh shit no, sweet Lord, no! Fuck, no; oh fuck me, no!' Daniel L. Lowenstein, master of reportage, reduced to a rhythm of profanities.

He has slipped from his seat into the footwell, curling up there like a foetus clinging to the womb. Rationally, he knows this is no strategy. Part of the survival lore they'd drummed into him at Walsingham was the fact that bullets can cut through the chassis of a car almost as easily as they penetrate human skin. Between bursts of automatic fire he can hear the insurgents' bloodcurdling cries of 'Allahu Akhbar!'

If only there were some peace and quiet, thinks Danny. If only he had stopped to talk to the occupants of the Toyota rather than launch into an argument. If only he'd never come down this road. If only he'd been warned of what lay ahead. If only he'd listened to his premonition and Mohammed's unspoken fear. If only he'd taken no notice of the worthless assurances of Asmat Mahmoud in Baghdad. If only he'd 'settled down', as he'd been urged to, had children and stayed at home with them – a happy brood of little Daniels and Daniellas. If only he'd never become a war reporter. If only he'd never become any kind of reporter …

The shooting and shouting stop for a while – a minute, maybe only 30 seconds – but to Danny, it's an eternity. He can make no use of it, for now he's as crippled by fear and indecision as Mohammed was. Poor Mohammed. Five children without a father, a wife without a husband, a reporter without a friend. *Nothing can happen to me.* Farrah flies more rings around the lemon tree, Sabeen garnishes the masgouf. Danny cannot bring himself to look at him again.

Instead he stares at the scraped plastic and mud marks on the bottom of the passenger door. Mud from his lucky boots, bought from Silvermans on Mile End Road before the first Gulf War in 1991. He's survived that and every subsequent hellhole he's ever been in, so how could he ever trade them in for another pair, even when they've walked across mass graves, through refugee camps riven with disease, not to mention putrid, Third-World hospitals? God alone knew what dangerous microbes inhabited those worn-out rubber treads, but every time the cab delivered him safely back to his apartment, he would lovingly put the boots back in their box, ready for the next time, certain they had kept him alive. Some worship the cross, Danny worshipped his lucky boots. They'd still be on his feet when his body was discovered – even though, if he were dead, it would surely represent their catastrophic failure. *Not so lucky now*, his friends would chuckle callously, as they stood at the boot-end of his body to identify it.

The car door is opened so that Danny, pressed hard against it, tumbles out. There's a another gratuitous chorus of 'Allahu Akhbar', so familiar from al-Qaeda snuff videos just before they execute the hostage. He cannot bear to look, but finally allows his eyes to meet those of the two gunmen screaming at him loudest. One has unwrapped his kafiyeh, careless now whether he shows himself, and this alone spreads an extra layer of dread over Danny.

The young man's face tells no special story. He is like so many Iraqis Danny has met down the years: bearded, brooding and with fingers welded to his weapon. He is unusually tall, and a scar across his forehead distinguishes him. It is a gruesome burn that makes him look as if he's been branded. He shoves the barrel of his Kalashnikov just below Danny's nostrils, the ring of grey metal hot upon his skin.

'Please, you don't understand – Abu Mukhtar, your leader, Mukhtar – I've come to see him. *Al sahaf*. Interview? Asmat Mahmoud arranged it – you know, big politician, Baghdad?'

Another 'if only'. If only he had learnt better Arabic. He's spent enough years of his life here, but lazily relied on Mohammed, and now his doctor-cum-driver-cum-translator-cum-friend is no good to him, staring manically at the shattered windscreen.

Then – a gift from the heavens. The one with the scar and the muzzle of his gun in Danny's face is muttering something in English.

'You people. So stupid. You come in one car and we shoot. You come in another car and we shoot again.'

'Great! You speak English. Oh, thank you, thank you so much. Now listen, I need to explain. You don't understand …'

'No talk.'

'But you see, I'm a journalist and …'

'We know who you are.'

'Good. That's really good to hear. So I'm a journalist and I'm here to see –'

'No talk!'

Danny decides his best hope is to co-operate. A surge of optimism. They know him. They know English. They must be reasonably intelligent. Shooting Mohammed was a blunder – some trigger-happy idiot who'll have to be disciplined. They won't make the same mistake again, or else there'll be hell to pay with Abu Mukhtar, not to mention Asmat Mahmoud, Danny's gold-plated, copper-bottomed contact.

Anyway, Danny has been this close before and every time it's been the prizes that have come his way rather than the wooden box and the grave that no one can ever quite find the time to visit. Near escapes run through his mind: the mock execution by Serbs on the road to Vukovar; the mob who wanted to set fire to him on a street corner in Kigali, as if he were some heretic to be burnt at the stake. And Chechnya, of course. Always Chechnya.

Now, as then, he is terrified, but it would show disrespect to death not to be: total, all-consuming fear is the price you pay if you want to claim the prize. Inevitably, hours or even days of captivity lie before him, but in due course will come the negotiated release. The mighty Abu Mukhtar, embarrassed by his overzealous foot soldiers, will apologise profusely and beg forgiveness.

The crack of a rifle butt on his head snaps him from these reveries. He mutters again about Abu Mukhtar, but now it's more of a low groan than a statement. Either they don't understand what he's saying or they're not interested.

The leader gestures with his Kalashnikov, jerking it upwards to show he wants the infidel up and away from the car. There is, thinks Danny, something alien about the clarity with which people like him see the world.

As he obeys, he looks again at the small mountain of Mohammed's slumped paunch, the patches of blood on his pristine white gown now merged into one. His progress is not quick enough for his captors; the tall one with the scar and another gunman grab his arms with such force he worries they'll rip them from their sockets. He should yell out in agony as they drag him away, but his fear leaves him silent, a quiet hero. They search the deep pockets of his chinos, and when they find the passport they study it briefly before hurling it aside. It spins through the air and lands at an angle in the sand. It feels as though they have discarded his identity. In that moment, Daniel Leon Lowenstein, born 17th June 1955, has ceased to exist.

A hood is thrown over his head, the dazzling sunlight of the Iraqi day switched off. It is some sort of hessian sack, Danny guesses, rough and scratchy against his skin, and with a musty smell that pollutes his nostrils. It reminds him of a farmyard. The hessian brushes against his lower lip and then his tongue, so that he can taste it too.

His assailants frogmarch him, screaming at him all the while and lashing out with kicks when he fails to respond to their unfathomable commands. Like a drunk in the dark, Danny stumbles, his balance and bearings lost, guided by the shoving and poking of their guns.

The easy flat of the road beneath his feet is becoming more unpredictable, a landscape now of ragged rock. He's being taken further from the car, from the reassurance of everything he's ever known.

The hood has ramped up his fear. He is dizzy, one moment feverishly hot, the next perishingly cold. His chest is compressed, a dead weight pushing down on it, like a cardiac arrest. Lower down, there is only slush and mush, Edwin's curry from the night before. He has lost control of his bowels. Rewinding back to infancy, or spooling onwards to senility, his sphincter widens. He tries to clench his buttocks, but then surrenders. The first trickle of shit starts to ooze into his boxer shorts. He is beyond embarrassment.

Nausea is rising up through him and he needs to vomit, but nothing emerges, merely the foretaste of it in his throat. He remembers the toilets when he's been embedded with the army, the ones marked 'D & V', set apart, as if for lepers, to accommodate troops afflicted with diarrhoea and vomiting.

Just as his body will no longer obey him, neither will his mind. The committed atheist who has spent a lifetime scorning religion is now praying with holy zeal: Please, oh Lord, I promise I will always worship you. I have sinned but am ready to repent. Oh merciful Lord, just get me out of here. Right now, and I mean right fucking now! I'll never set foot in a war zone again, or get on another plane, or write another story, so help me God. Amen.

But he knows that this time there'll be no last-minute reprieve, no scoop, no prize. Instead of the award ceremony, there'll be the funeral. He has pushed his luck one story too far, taken one chance too many, and he wishes more than anything he's ever wished for that he could step back into that refreshing, effervescent hotel shower and start this day again.

Deprived of sight, all Danny can see are his alternative futures. Will it be the one that lasts for just a few more seconds, with a cursory bullet to the back of his hooded, anonymous head; one more death among so many in the catastrophe of Iraq? Or will it drag on for weeks, with the perpetual terror of incarceration in a cage, broken only by video appearances, paraded bowed and broken, begging for his life? And will it end, as it has for so many others, with a screaming madman's knife hacking at his neck, captured in Technicolor? Images flash before him: Nick Berg being slaughtered by al-Zarqawi in person; the four American contractors, shot, burnt, mutilated, and their remains hung from a bridge in Fallujah.

This time he's not reporting the story, he *is* the story. Other journalists will circle over his carcass. He pictures it – cold, blue and flabby – lying on a slab in a mortuary full of flies. The morgue is familiar to him; he's been there countless times in Baghdad, Grozny, Gaza, Mogadishu – all the visits blend into one. He has counted more corpses than any man should have to – hundreds, probably thousands, of them, and now he can add one more. It's wearing the clothes he put on that morning, when he was getting dressed to die, including those lucky, lucky boots.

He sees the funeral too. Who will come? The Junkies, of course; his adopted family, addicted to their work, their drugs and each other. Rachel inconsolable, yet still so fuckable in her sleek black dress. Becky, for once not laughing. Edwin and Kaps, his brothers in arms. Others will be there too – the media glitterati, and some of the Great and the Good who have admired his work: politicians, editors, novelists. There will be generous obituaries, mini hagiographies. Failures and excesses will be discreetly airbrushed out; there'll be no mention of his many sins. All in all, his death will be an ego trip. Too bad he won't be able to enjoy it.

Rough hands force him down on to his knees. A rifle butt smashes his mouth. The shock of it reminds him of his boyhood: Lukas hitting him, Camille watching. He tastes his own blood, sour and sickly. His tongue discovers a couple of uprooted teeth and briefly probes the holes they've left behind.

The final act. One more collective shout of 'Allahu Akhbar!' from his kidnappers, a kind of choral harmony to signal that the time has come. The hood is ripped from his head but he cannot look; his eyes are screwed shut.

The end of a gun is shoved into the nape of his neck. The trickle of faeces becomes a torrent now, running down his legs. Danny is shaking so hard it looks, perversely, as if he's laughing. There are no more memories or predictions, no more thoughts – rational or otherwise. No more hypocritical prayers. His kneeling, hooded body is heaving backwards and forwards with such convulsions that he barely hears the trigger.

2

Jamail, the avuncular hotel manager, had assigned them the 'Presidential Suite'. He said he'd persuaded the owner they could have it for nothing, though it was usually empty in any case. The suite, rather like the country itself, had seen far better days and no self-respecting president would go near it. It sat atop the taller of the Hamra Hotel's two towers with a sweeping view of the city, but the threadbare carpet was blighted by wine and coffee stains, and there were cigarette burns on both the sofas. Rachel and Becky sat on one of them, staring at a dreary painting on the wall – a waterfall surrounded by forest on some other continent. At first they had cried till their throats ached, but now they simply sat in shock. A pair of mosquitoes strafed their ears, taunting them in their grief.

Edwin and Kaps busied themselves at the kitchen table, studying a map of Fallujah, trying to pinpoint where it was that Danny had been ambushed. Edwin, tank commander turned war reporter, was in his element, applying with military precision the various coordinates the US Army had given them. He smoked a Marlboro right down to its butt as fingers, rulers and pencils roamed purposefully around the American map he'd stolen from the Green Zone.

'Look, it must have been here, around this bridge.' Edwin lit another cigarette from the old one, doing it without even looking.

'But why would he have been there?' argued Kaps. 'Where would that road go that would interest anyone, let alone Danny?'

'Oh, stop it!' Rachel shouted. 'What does it matter where the fuck it happened? It's not going to bring him back, is it? He's dead, isn't he? Even if they've kidnapped him, they'll put him in an orange jumpsuit, stick him in a cage and ...'

The others knew she was right. Thoughts of death were consuming all of them; not just Danny's but potentially their own. It could so easily have been one of them and so there was a guilty, furtive exhilaration. *They* were still alive.

Becky had been first to hear the news. She'd just finished lunch when 'Dancing Queen' had rung out on her mobile. It was Adi, the diplomat. Ever since she'd met him at a drinks party in the embassy, he'd pestered her with calls in an effort to 'like ... maybe get to know you better'. She remembered with mild disgust how the folds of fat rolled off him and fumes of halitosis wafted from his mouth. The ring on his chubby finger told her there was a loyal wife – poor, deluded dear – waiting for him back home in the Washington suburbs. However desperate Becky might become, however much she yearned for warm flesh to wake up with, she made herself promise she would never, ever sleep with him. Why couldn't one of his colleagues have propositioned her instead? One of those clean-cut diplomats with perfect partings and bright white teeth, the Paul Bremer clones who looked like the stars of commercials for hair restorer or denture cleanser.

'Hey, Becky – Adi here.' The sound of his voice made her heart sink. She began assembling implausible reasons why she would be busy every night for the next three weeks of her tour of duty.

'Oh, I ... Adi, I was just ...'

'Listen to me carefully. There's been a bad shooting on some road south of Baghdad. Near Iskandariya. I'll get straight to the point: it's Daniel Lowenstein. He's a friend of yours, I believe?'

'Yeah, course he is. Oh my God.'

'Look, I'm really sorry, but his car was ambushed a few hours ago. Shot up pretty bad according to our units up there. His driver's dead and Lowenstein's missing. No sign of his body yet, but it doesn't look good.'

Despite the humidity, Becky began to shiver. The flashback came to her as it always did, unexpectedly, like a mugging in a darkened alleyway: before her yet again, he was dying while she prevaricated. All these years later, she could still hear his pleas for help as the blood emptied out of him and soaked the snow, his ever-weaker voice calling out her name – calling, calling, calling – and her legs running to him, going nowhere. Now, as then, there was only one logical conclusion: that she had killed him.

It took another four or five minutes until she calmed herself enough to ring the others, but her finger still trembled as she dialled their numbers: Rachel first, then Kaps, then Edwin.

Soon they were huddled in the Presidential Suite, its two landlines and their assorted mobiles in frantic, perpetual use till nightfall.

They talked to the *New York Times*. Even though Danny had gone freelance, the assistant managing editor said he would be on the next flight, bringing with him an 'investigator' – a former Special Forces guy. He would work out of the bureau. Danny's older sister was on her way in from Dubai, where she was a big shot at some investment bank. The company was pulling out all the stops to get her to Kuwait and from there she'd pick up a US Air Force C-130.

They talked to Danny's elderly parents in Pittsburgh. Lukas and Eliza Lowenstein were originally from Germany, and the hint of an accent was still there as Eliza repeated, over and over, 'My baby boy.' They realised she would never remember him as they did, but as the infant she'd cradled in her arms.

They talked to Sabeen, Mohammed's widow. What would become of the children, she demanded of Becky in English every bit as fluent as her late husband's; how would she support them? Becky would have liked to assure her, 'Don't worry, you'll be well looked after, you'll want for nothing,' but since Danny no longer worked for any organisation, she could make no promises.

They talked to the Iraqi police, the US military, diplomats and politicians, and – a novel experience for all of them – they talked to the press. The embassy Hostage Crisis Group had recommended a media blackout, so now it was down to the Junkies to persuade their colleagues to hide from the world the news that a fellow journalist had disappeared.

Much of the press corps was staying in the Hamra too; it had become famous for its raucous poolside parties, where reporters, aid workers and diplomats would talk and dance the night away while Danny held court. These gatherings ceased as a mark of respect for him, their missing warrior; the Baghdad party was on hold. No one used the pool at all now. It was as if it had suddenly become contaminated.

The journalists agreed to the blackout – after all, what if it were one of them? Still, they wanted answers for when they finally ran the story. What had he been doing down there? Why hadn't he told anyone he was going? Did his friends think he was dead or kidnapped? And if the latter, how did they rate his chances? For once the Junkies knew what it was to try and fend off these ravenous birds of prey.

'We really can't say much at the moment,' Edwin and Kaps kept repeating. They had decided a party line and were determined to stick to it. 'The embassy and the military have told us it's best not to get into any speculation.' They were stonewalling, and the Danny they knew would have railed against it.

The sun he had cursed that morning was slowly dying, slipping away unmourned behind Baghdad's higher buildings. Shadows of those still on the streets fell long and curfew beckoned. In the morning it would be one day exactly since he had disappeared. His friends wondered if, after that, it would be one week, one month, one year, until all the anniversaries began to flow into an ocean of time where Danny Lowenstein would exist only as a fading memory.

The moment Camille Lowenstein stepped nervously off the Hercules from Kuwait, a phalanx of embassy security guards swarmed around her, weighed down with M16s and 9mm Beretta pistols strapped to their thighs. They wore wraparound sunglasses and tight T-shirts showing off muscles that bulged and tattoos that boasted of lost loves or units. She had never been in the presence of so many big men and big guns. This was her brother's world, she realised, where violence and fear were the norm, peace and tranquillity banished to a distant universe.

She was flanked by Tommy Harper, the lanky executive despatched by the *New York Times*, even though – strictly speaking – Danny was no longer on their payroll. Harper wore little round spectacles and clutched a briefcase. Camille's first impression was that, if she was out of her depth here, so was he. Alongside Harper was Munro, a small, muscular Scot hired by the paper to find out more about what had happened to their distinguished former correspondent. Harper had told her, in reverential tones, that Munro was ex-SAS: 'You know, Brit Special Forces.' So what's he going to do, Camille felt like asking, bring my brother back to life if he's been shot, or rescue him single-handed if he's been kidnapped?

Something about Munro made her feel uncomfortable. His body language implied he didn't see what she could achieve. She didn't even know herself. Baghdad, she supposed, was a dangerous city for those who weren't sure what they were doing; it was a place for certainty, not for doubt.

It was the tremor in her mother's voice that had convinced her to come. 'Please, honey; we need you there for us, for the family,' Eliza Lowenstein had begged. 'He's your brother, after all. Who knows, maybe you can help him.' Help him like you didn't do before, in other words – or was that just how Camille had chosen to interpret it, through the prism of her broken conscience? Besides, there was no excuse. Camille was in Dubai which – if you were looking at a map in Pittsburgh – seemed pretty much next door to Iraq.

Camille had been called out of a meeting to be told the news. She had stood there in the glass palace where she worked, staring out at its panoramic views of nothing. She had supposed she ought to cry, but no tears would flow. Perhaps it was the shock, she thought; perhaps they'd come later. She'd gone home, tossed some clothes into a suitcase and made sure her secretary cancelled everything in her diary, except the dinner date with the man she'd met two weeks earlier: Camille wanted to make that call herself. He hadn't sounded particularly sympathetic nor very bothered that she wouldn't be around. At 52, she couldn't help thinking she was too old for dates anyway. As the bank's limousine eased her past Dubai's lavish skyscrapers, she wondered whether her brother would be dead or alive when she saw him again. Either way, she resolved she wouldn't come back until she knew for sure. That much at least she owed him. She plugged in her iPod headphones and put on some Janis Joplin. It always reminded her of Danny. But she asked herself another question: was it bad taste to listen to music when the corpse of your only sibling could be lying in a ditch somewhere?

At Baghdad International Airport, a lone immigration officer in a slightly tatty uniform waved her through without even opening her passport. He gave her a look that said: Trust me, if you're crazy enough to come to my country, I really have no plans to stop you. Then, as Harper and Munro shepherded her to the waiting motorcade, a plump diplomat in a white shirt and tie stepped forward to greet them.

'Hi, I'm Adi – Adi Duval.' Camille noticed with mild revulsion two dark ovals of sweat around his armpits. 'You need to know we're doing everything, and I mean *everything*, to find your brother.' Adi assured her that army intelligence was on the case, with spy satellites and unmanned reconnaissance planes searching 24/7. They hadn't yet established which group was responsible, but they had a list of suspects. CIA analysts had made it their top priority, and they'd crack it soon, he was sure they would. Danny was a 'distinguished American citizen' who deserved 'our best and fullest resources', he went on, his tone implying that the country's less impressive passport holders might receive a slightly inferior level of service from their government.

He handed her a flak jacket and helmet.

'You'll need to wear these, Miss Lowenstein – just for the ride into town.'

Camille, Harper and Munro were driven at unfeasible speed to the Hamra Hotel, the gleaming white GMC Suburban – bulletproof, of course – swerving and screeching its way through the fiendish chicanes designed to slow traffic. At intermittent checkpoints ordinary mortals were having their papers checked and car boots searched, while Camille's convoy sailed through as though she were the First Lady herself. If only her brother had enjoyed such protection.

An image returned to her – for no reason she could fathom – of Danny aged eight, playing hide-and-seek in the garden of their home in East Allegheny, Pittsburgh – 'Deutschtown' as it was known. Camille, who was three years older, had kept on searching even when she'd seen his foot poking from behind the garden shed. He was enjoying the game so much, she didn't want to spoil it. When she finally pounced and Danny screamed, she thought it was his silly mock surprise at being found at last, but then she saw it, curled up in the grass only a few feet from him: a Copperhead snake, watching him with sullen disapproval. All along, while she'd dragged out her search, poor Danny had been petrified. Head pounding, she'd grabbed a stick and flicked the snake away. As it scuttled off into the trees, Danny had looked at her in admiration, a look that came back to her now. She was his sister, bigger than him and so much braver. He'd been absolutely certain she would never let him down.

So why was it that she had? Not just once, but again and again.

Black curtains across the side windows hid away Baghdad, but the occasional glimpses were enough to make her swallow: so here it was, the place she had watched on countless television bulletins; where Saddam had strutted his stuff; where shock and awe had lit up the sky; where the liberating troops had marched in to such short-lived acclaim. She could never have imagined she would see it for herself.

'At some stage we should be able to get you down to the spot where Danny disappeared.' Adi sat beside her, the smell of his stale sweat wafting into her nostrils. 'First Cavalry are still securing the area, but when they're done, we could have an armed escort take you there. Only if you want to, of course.'

'Absolutely,' said Camille.

'We appreciate what you and your family are going through and we understand you're going to need some closure here.' He chose the word carefully, to imply – very gently, but from the start – that they might well be looking for a body.

'Thank you. I don't intend to leave this country until I have my brother, whether he's dead or alive.'

'He's really an extraordinary journalist. You must be so proud of him.'

'Thank you, I am.'

'I know a few of his friends; they're over at the Hamra, too. Maybe you'd like to meet with them?'

Later, when it was all over, she would think about how different things would have been for her if she'd just said: 'No thanks, Mr Duval.'

'Yes please, that'd be good.'

Soft morning light fell upon the carnage of the night before: a fresh batch of mutilated corpses, dumped around Baghdad like garbage put out for collection. Some lay down alleyways, some amid the bulrushes in the Tigris. Danny's friends knew they would be out there and couldn't help thinking he might be among them.

The Junkies were prone to insomnia at the best of times and now sleep seemed a physical impossibility. Their wakefulness meant there was an eternity of time to fill but work was unthinkable: why head out to cover some new Iraqi tragedy when they had their very own?

'Fried eggs and tomatoes, anyone?' Edwin was buzzing around the suite's kitchenette, pouring olive oil into a scratched old frying pan. 'I'm making breakfast.'

'You're always *doing* something,' said Becky.

He looked confused, so she let it pass.

'Oh, all right then, why not. Two, please, sunny side up.' She had no appetite, and neither had the others, but they would eat because it kept Edwin happy. He had loved to cook for them on the road – the more challenging the circumstances, the better: Bosnia, Africa,

Chechnya, it didn't matter where. It was one of the therapies that worked for him.

When the unnecessary business of breakfast was complete, the long silence began. Everyone slipped into memories of Danny until a knock at the door reverberated around the room and jolted them from their reveries. Becky jumped, as if it was a gunshot.

Adi stood there with three people they'd never seen.

'Guys, I'd like you all to meet Tommy Harper from the *Times*, Jim Munro, who's here as a security adviser, and this is Camille Lowenstein, Danny's sister.'

She was the only one they looked at. She was just like Danny; a little taller and older, but with his presence. For a moment it felt as though he were with them again, back from the dead. The same persuasive eyes peered out at them through Dolce & Gabbana glasses, black and oblong, giving her the stern, studious look of the tutor you admired at university and wouldn't want to cross.

Rachel leapt up from the sofa and hugged her, while the others were more circumspect, shaking her hand one by one and introducing themselves.

'You got here pretty fast,' said Rachel.

'My bank has been fabulous but I'm kind of dazed; one minute sitting in Dubai, the next here in Baghdad – which isn't exactly the sort of place you expect to find yourself at a moment's notice.'

Her educated East Coast cadences rolled easily over them in much the same way Danny's always had.

Kaps led her to the shabby armchair he'd just been sitting in and fixed her a coffee while she took in the faces around her, especially Rachel's and Becky's, with their puffed-up, reddened eyes.

'So how was the flight in?' Rachel, like an uneasy cocktail-party guest, was determined to clutch at small talk. Becky, slumped beside her, said nothing at all.

For half an hour, between more tears and drifting silences, the Junkies told them what they knew of the area where Danny had disappeared, the various insurgent groups who operated there and the extent to which the Americans were or were not in control. At the end of it, Harper and Munro thanked them and said they needed to make some calls.

'I should be going too,' said Camille.

Why, said the look on Rachel's face. What the hell else is there to do?

'Stay if you like. It's nice to talk about Danny.'

When Turner and Munro had gone, Camille asked them again if they knew what he'd been doing in al-Talha.

'That's the beauty of being freelance, and the curse,' said Kaps. 'You don't have to tell anyone your plans, but when it all goes wrong, no one knows what you've been up to. He could be pretty secretive.'

'Really?'

'It's the reason he left the *Times* in the first place – to be a free spirit. Said the bureau had become a fortress, with all the security consultants and armed guards you had to have there. Soldier boys like your friend Munro.'

'He took a lot of risks?'

Kaps chuckled.

'We all take risks. You're taking a risk just by being in this city, in this country. But Danny? Yeah, he took more than most.'

He handed Camille the coffee he'd just made. She grabbed it in the palms of both hands, defying its heat. You're a tough cookie, Kaps thought, and something told him to be a little wary about what he said.

'And what d'you think are his chances?' Camille asked. 'You guys know Iraq so well and I really don't have a clue.'

'Okay then, no bullshit,' said Kaps. 'If this had been down south with the Shia, I'd say good. But we could be talking about al-Qaeda – al-Zarqawi in particular. Not exactly renowned for the quality of his mercy.'

Camille nodded slowly. She was scared they'd think he was Jewish: people often assumed they were because of the family name, when in fact Lowenstein was the town in Germany her parents had originally come from.

'So are you and Danny close?' asked Kaps. He couldn't remember ever hearing Danny talk about his sister.

'Not especially, I'm afraid. Different worlds; me in Dubai, him in all these war zones.'

'When did you last see him?'

'This is going to sound crazy, but I guess it would have been a few years ago.'

She was too embarrassed to admit it was actually twelve: she didn't want to have to answer all the questions it would provoke. As it was, she could sense a frisson of surprise ripple around the room.

It had been 22nd June 1992, to be precise, and she remembered not only the date but his last words before he put the phone down on her: 'I just don't think we have a thing to say to each other any more. I know I'm supposed to love you, but the truth is I don't even like you very much. Maybe it'd be best if you didn't call again.'

For the rest of that week, Camille was busy at the embassy. Adi reported that First Cavalry had pulled in a bunch of local hoods around al-Talha and army intelligence was grilling them, so far without result. The news blackout had been lifted and he wanted her to record an appeal they could put on al-Arabiya television, but no one could agree on what she should say: was she asking for the return of a hostage or a body? And how should she sound? On a conference call with Washington, the FBI advised her to be tough, while the man from the State Department urged a more emollient approach. 'Remember, you may just have his life in your hands,' said the disembodied DC voice.

After the embassy meetings, Harper would go back to the bureau of the *New York Times*, where he was staying, while Munro was happy to hang out with old SAS chums now employed in Baghdad's burgeoning security industry. Camille would have dinner at the Hamra and spend time with Danny's friends. Getting to know them was as good a way as any of getting to know him. She found them fascinating, like rare species in a zoo, so unlike all the expats in her world who had done nothing and seen nothing. These people – she could tell it from their eyes – had seen so much. Too much perhaps.

'He's been in good hands since … well, whenever it was you last met with him,' Rachel told her one evening. 'He was … I mean he *is* … such a good friend to us.'

No one else said anything. Camille was becoming used to these gaping holes in the conversation.

'I do read his stuff from time to time,' she said after a minute or so. 'I mean, I can see what a good writer he is.'

'Unique,' said Rachel. 'And driven like you wouldn't believe.'

'I think I would. Driven is a Lowenstein family trait, and not always an entirely healthy one. But please, go on. It's good to be with the people who were closest to him. What was it that brought you guys together?'

'We were thrown together, I suppose,' said Rachel sadly, but smiling too. 'And I guess we shared a feeling, a spirit.'

'A "spirit"?'

'Well, I'll tell you how Danny once put it. I remember it so well, we were lying on a rooftop in Mogadishu. The al-Sahafi Hotel, starlit and tracer-lit as usual. He said, "We live more in a year than most people live in a lifetime." There was a kind of arrogance about that which I loved, like we were better than mere mortals.'

For a while the only sounds in the Presidential Suite were coughs and sniffles, and the distant din of the Baghdad traffic trying to seep in through the windows.

'And when Danny said that, it made me think about when I was about ten, on holiday with my parents on the west coast of Ireland. We were on a beach, by a loch. Local builders would come along with a big tractor and trailer, and dig up the sand. They wanted it for making concrete and didn't see why they shouldn't just help themselves. I remember going up to them and saying, "But you can't just steal the beach; you can't steal the sand." And they laughed their heads off at this silly girl from America then turned their backs on me. Well, I used to tell Danny we were no better than those guys; we were sandstealers too. I had this vision of an hour-glass – you know, where you pour sand from one bit to another to measure time. The way I saw it, we were stealing sand and stealing time, because every day of our lives was so damned rich, and every year seemed to last so long. Danny loved that, absolutely adored it. From that day on he was always calling us the sandstealers.'

'So when was it you first met up?'

Rachel's eyes twinkled and the tears in them seemed to dry as she was carried back to the day that everything began.

'It was 1994 – in my case, anyway. Another century, another millennium. The truth is, your brother inspired me. I'm really not sure I'd have ever become a journalist without him. I think I was only about 16 when I started reading his stuff. There was nothing on earth I wanted more than to do what he was doing and see what he was seeing, so I went to where I knew he was, simple as that. I just got up one day and went to Bosnia.'

Her friends shifted uncomfortably, wondering if they should stop her reminiscing, but it was too late already.

3

The Balkans, January 1994

Rachel Kelly was a tender 23 when she arrived, via Budapest, in Split. The Croatian port amounted to a backstage holding pen for all those war-zone wannabes who yearned to perform in Sarajevo, the theatre of their dreams, but she couldn't hide from herself a mild sense of disappointment: she'd come to watch a war and so far found only the humdrum routines of peace. In the bustling streets of Split, there were the sounds of bells and buskers, but where were the lightning cracks of gunfire and the thunderclaps of artillery? On a crisp morning, Rachel was breathing in clean, fresh air rather than the cordite of explosives, and it didn't smell good.

The citizens of Split could still scarcely believe their luck. They'd escaped the Balkan inferno, and every day they were glad to be alive. These were beautiful people in a beautiful city, and it gave Rachel an idea of what Sarajevo must once have been – a magnificent painting, now slashed apart by war. Outside her hotel, she watched a young couple canoodling without embarrassment. They kissed in a way that said they appreciated peace and were determined to make the most of it. After all, had they been born just a few miles to the east, they would be fighting now – either killing, maiming and raping, or being killed, maimed and raped. Street-side caresses in winter sunshine seemed endlessly preferable.

By lunchtime, Rachel was happy to be checking in for a UN aid flight into Sarajevo, heaving her bag and rucksack on to the scales.

'These weigh too much,' said the soldier from Norwegian Movement Control – NorMovCon, in UN-speak. Ultra-blond, with slightly feminine cheekbones, he belonged in a gleaming Scandinavian airport with polished floors and expensive shops and bars. 'Twenty kilograms, that's your limit. Sorry, but these are twenty-three.' Rachel decided he was the epitome of precise, European efficiency, no amount of which had been able to save this corner of the continent from sliding into civil war. 'You will have to lose three kilos, please. Thank you.'

She gave him a look to make him melt, as other soldiers would melt in the years of warfare that lay ahead for Rachel Kelly, Arlington's young warrior. Norwegians, she thought: nice, even when they're trying to be nasty.

'All right, just today,' he sighed, thumping one of the many clean pages of her passport with a big blue stamp that said, intriguingly: *Maybe Airlines, Sarajevo*. 'But there is no guarantee you get a seat. P3s are lowest priority.'

'P3s?'

'Journalists. People like you.' He said it with a certain relish, pleased to hint that reporters like her were not fit to wipe the boots of some of the other heroes on board today's flight – peacekeepers, doctors and aid workers. 'We call you if there's room.'

But Rachel *had* to get to Sarajevo. The war had been raging for two years and she was horribly late already. She couldn't afford to miss another day.

She found a broken plastic seat close to a gaggle of photographers who were chatting among themselves. Cameras hung like ripe fruit around their necks, with more around their ankles as if they'd fallen from the tree. They had weather-beaten, battle-hardened faces and the air of people who had seen all there was to see in the world. Rachel, who had seen nothing, was intimidated. The men were tall with stubble on their chins, exotic scarves and an earring here and there, but there was a woman too, which helped Rachel pluck up the courage to approach them.

'Hey there! Look, I'm sorry to bother you, but I just wondered if you guys are heading up to Boz?'

Boz? No one who'd ever been to Bosnia would dream of calling it that, and it sounded even worse in a happy-go-lucky American accent. *Boz*, for Christ's sake! They inspected her for a moment, this new girl, so breathlessly enthusiastic: she was pretty, with conventionally straight, shoulder-length brown hair parted on the left and a flurry of freckles that had fallen on the slopes of a ski-jump nose. No doubt they should have faded years ago, but they'd decided, stubbornly, to stick around.

'Boz?' said the lone female. She wore no make-up and was wearing a black woolly hat and a torn, blue Gore-Tex jacket. It tried to hide a body which was heavier than Rachel's and not flattered by comparison. 'Oh, I see. You mean *Bosnia*?'

Rachel had rather much too much going on in her head to detect the irony.

'Yeah, I'm hoping to get on the flight, only the UN guys said we're low priority.'

''Course we are!' The accent was wild Australian, honed somewhere in the outback. 'We're the parasites, scum of the earth. Then again, not too many people are mad enough to want a plane ride into Sarajevo – that's if the plane ever makes it. They don't call it Maybe Airlines for nothing.'

'That's what they stamped in my passport.'

'Maybe they give you a seat, maybe they don't. Maybe it takes off, maybe it gets shot down ...'

'I'll take my chances,' Rachel said with a cool determination the Australian rather liked. She remembered her own first flight into Sarajevo two years earlier.

'I'm Becky. Becky Cooper. I was just heading over to that shitty little café. Can I get you something? Whatever they put in your cup, they'll add about half a sack of sugar. If that doesn't get you going, you're probably dead already.'

She let out the little laugh which, Rachel would discover, was the culmination of almost everything she said. She used laughter like bad punctuation – randomly, even when she wasn't happy or when what she said wasn't funny. Her face was round and lit up by a big white smile that never seemed to leave her. In time, Rachel would come to see the sadness that lay beneath it.

Becky stepped away from the others, who'd already lost interest in Rachel, or pretended they had, and the two women shook hands firmly, like men do.

'That'd be great, thanks. Rachel Kelly, by the way. So who are you working for?'

'Sigma. They sell my stuff on. Usually *Newsweek* in America, or *Stern* in Germany. Basically anyone who'll pay.'

Rachel was impressed. *Newsweek* had been her weekly bible for years. She'd curled up in bed with it when her friends were reading teenage magazines about pop and puppy love and first-time sex.

Becky handed over a stash of damp, dog-eared notes for two small coffees. As they found a table, she yanked the woolly hat off her head. Balkan sun, fighting its way through grubby airport windows, appeared to backlight her. A tangle of curls tumbled down, flame-red in unexpected contrast to pale white skin. Rachel's immediate thought was Queen Elizabeth the First, the Warrior Queen. A few days later, when she mentioned the comparison, Becky was unusually downcast. *Virgin* Queen more like, she said.

'Anyway, good to meet you, Rachel Kelly. So who are *you* with then?'

'No one, to be honest. It's my first foreign assignment. And when I say assignment, I guess the truth is I've assigned myself.'

'My God, that's brave.'

'It's just something I've wanted to do …' She paused, then mumbled, half hoping Becky wouldn't hear the rest, '… for so long.'

Becky was disarmed. She was warming to this young American. It was what she liked about the war: you could meet someone and be their friend within days, or even hours. Spinoza, one of the other photographers, called it fast-food friendship.

'Well, stick with me and I'll show you the ropes.'

Rachel felt the tension slip away from her. As she sipped the thick, syrupy Turkish coffee, she explained how she'd abandoned her local paper in Arlington ('a tedious little rag') and got a portfolio of strings with some bigger ones, plus an obscure monthly magazine about foreign affairs. It would be just about enough.

'So then, Sarajevo? Quite a place to do your apprenticeship.'

'The truth is I'm lazy. I just can't face crawling up the ladder – all those training courses and job applications and interviews, I'm just not cut out for it. I hate to sound pushy, but why wait ten or twenty years for your guys on *Newsweek* or the *Post* to make me a foreign correspondent when I can appoint myself one – right here, right now.'

'Mmm. And you hate to sound pushy! Well, it all seems deliciously simple.' Becky gave her coffee a sceptical stir but she recognised in Rachel's eyes the same yearning to see Sarajevo that she'd once had. 'As a matter of fact, I *do* think it's pretty simple.' Becky unleashed a gust of can-do Australian enthusiasm. 'You make your own luck in this business. If you've got an ounce of talent, Sarajevo will help you shine. The whole world is watching, after all. Watching that city, but watching it through us.'

Rachel's mouth widened into a grin. For so long people had doubted her. Now here was a pro, and a Bosnia pro at that, who seemed to believe in her. Perhaps her fantasies weren't so crazy.

Becky noticed the wad of photocopied cuttings Rachel had stuffed into a transparent plastic folder. They were tatty from constant reading and re-reading, and when Becky started leafing through them, Rachel felt not only like the new girl but the swot, caught in possession of homework it was most uncool to have.

'You've only got the collected works of Danny Lowenstein in here!'

'I really like his stuff. I find it so … you know … emotional.'

'Yeah, emotional. Fictional, too, sometimes.'

'Really?'

'No, not really. I'm just being a jealous bitch. It can get like that in Sarajevo.'

'D'you know him then – Daniel Lowenstein, I mean?'

'It's *Danny*, not Daniel. And yes, of course I do. All the girls adore him.'

They both steeled themselves for a last sip. *All the girls adore him.* In the long years of pain and pleasure that lay before her, Rachel would find it to be a statement not of opinion but undisputed fact.

When the flight was called, Becky and Rachel were the only journalists allowed on – to the consternation of the other photographers. 'Ladies first,' Becky grinned at them.

Rachel crossed the runway to the plane like an old lady with curvature of the spine; she was bent double beneath her rucksack, which contained not only Danny's epic, 423-page account of the break up of the Balkans but all the clothes she could cram in, including a bulk supply of underwear in case laundry was impossible. There were industrial quantities of soap, deodorant, make-up, perfume and tampons, and – for bribes – cigarettes and chocolate (even if the temptation to eat it herself might well prove overwhelming). There were half a dozen notebooks, a box of pens, her laptop with all its assorted cables, a torch and batteries and a short-wave radio – her lifeline to the world.

Becky put an arm round her as the loadmaster helped them squeeze through the plane's narrow door. The engines were revving louder and louder, and Rachel could no longer make herself heard, but she beamed Becky one of her made-in-Heaven smiles, which said 'thanks' and 'this is going to be fun' at the same time.

'Next stop Sarajevo!' the loadmaster shouted as they taxied for take-off. Next stop your new life, Rachel Kelly. He gave her some squashy yellow earplugs and helped her snap together the complicated, four-pronged seat belt. The Hercules heaved itself off the runway, spectacular in its defiance of the laws of gravity, and Becky quickly fell asleep. The familiar motion of flight drugged her, like a weary commuter on her way to work.

The passengers were crammed together uncomfortably on narrow canvas seats arranged in a long line. Most were aid workers or officials from UNPROFOR, UNHCR and various other acronyms from the UN's bewildering myriad of agencies. Most soon had their eyes shut, but from the moment she first clambered aboard Rachel had never felt more wide awake. She tried to peer through the tiny porthole behind her, but only briefly could she glimpse the Balkan hills and valleys down below, wondering what they had in store for her. As the Hercules reached its cruising altitude, she shivered, coveting Becky's unglamorous woolly hat.

At the end of its journey, the Hercules plunged into a sudden, suicidal nosedive. Rachel's stomach flung itself from her body. She'd always suspected this plane was just too damned big for its own good.

Becky stirred slowly, and bellowed into Rachel's ear.

'Don't worry, it's just in case anyone wants to take a shot at us. Like I told you – Maybe Airlines.'

The plane levelled off at the last minute, and Rachel swung around once more, just in time to see a blur of blackened, roofless houses and the jagged ruins of mutilated tower blocks.

'Hello, war,' she mumbled to herself beneath the engines' roar.

Snow was falling steadily on Sarajevo, trying to hide its horrors from the world.

'Where now?' asked Rachel.

'Oh, I'm getting a ride into town,' said Becky. '*We're* getting a ride.'

There was a tedious, 25 minute wait before finally he strode in.

'And about time too.' Becky gave him a brief embrace. 'This is Rachel, one of your fellow countrymen. You have to be very nice to her, it's her first time – so to speak. Rachel, meet Daniel L. Lowenstein, award-winning reporter and our cabbie for the day.'

Rachel shook his hand, surprised Becky hadn't mentioned he'd be meeting them when they'd discussed him earlier. She couldn't help compare the face in front of her with the immaculately lit, carefully posed picture on the dust jacket. He looked rougher in the flesh, unshaven and uncombed, and the familiar dimple in his chin was largely buried beneath stubble. Now that she could see him in colour, she realised his eyes were a rich chocolate brown. They were good eyes, but they didn't look at her for very long; they didn't seem interested and flitted around elsewhere.

She was in awe of him but quite determined that wouldn't mean developing any kind of crush on him. It would be so adolescent, and above all she needed people to take her seriously. She hoped they'd become friends and close colleagues, though it was quite possible that, as an aristocrat of the press corps, he wouldn't waste his time on an apprentice like her.

'Hi,' he said casually.

From nowhere, a mortar exploded – not far away, though not close either by Sarajevo's stringent standards: perhaps 200 yards. Rachel flinched instinctively. No one else moved a muscle.

'They'll come at you a lot closer than that,' said Danny. 'People say it's the one you don't hear that kills you.'

'Yeah, don't worry,' said Becky. 'Just the Serbs' way of saying hello. Letting you know you're very welcome, Rachel. A few months and you'll be able to bore us with whether it's incoming or outgoing, a shell or a mortar, Russian made or Chinese.'

Rachel nodded. Even if it were only a stray round, here was her first snort on the drug of war and she was hooked already. She climbed eagerly into the passenger seat of Danny's armoured Land Rover.

'This is unbelievable,' she whispered as they eased their way through the butchered buildings of downtown Sarajevo: tower blocks reduced to blackened stumps; happy homes now useless, their walls pockmarked by an acne rash of bullet holes, charred rafters where roofs had been, children's bedroom curtains fluttering like flags of surrender in the snowy breeze. A cosmopolitan city that had once glowed with pride as host of the winter Olympics – demolished, almost at a stroke.

'It gets worse,' Danny promised, as he sat hunched over the wheel, the wipers working frantically to clear the windscreen of snow.

'Worse? It already looks like Berlin in 1945.'

'Half a century on and *plus ça change*.' His voice was husky. It said to her New York, Yale, Democrat. 'It's like all the hatreds way back then went into deep freeze, and now they've thawed out and come back to life.'

As she looked around, she could see what he meant: everything flickered in the black and white of jerky, scratchy newsreel footage. The faces she saw were of the past yet catapulted into the modernity of late 20th-century Europe. What could these people possibly know of mobile phones or U2 or REM? They didn't belong here.

'This is a prison rather than a city,' Danny went on, sounding like one of his articles or a chapter from his book. 'Three hundred thousand inmates with no chance of escape – and who knows when their sentence will end? The best they can hope for is to survive here. Watch them: they're just scavenging around. Existing, really.'

She studied the Sarajevans they drove past. Some were pushing wheelbarrows with the firewood they had collected from chopping down trees by the Miljacka River or smashing up furniture. Others dragged sledges loaded with bottles and plastic containers as they went in search of water. She had read stories of how people were surviving on snails and nettles and fir-tree juice. He was right: *I'm still alive*, they seemed to say to each other with silent shrugs, as if it were an achievement in itself.

'You know the real difference between us and them, Rachel? We can come and go; we've got our UN accreditation and a ride pretty much any time we want on Maybe Airlines, but they can't leave until the war is over.'

Rachel thought it best not to tell him what was running through her head: that she didn't ever *want* to leave.

'And here we are on Snipers' Alley.' Danny was playing the tour guide on the ultimate holiday-from-hell. 'See those blocks of flats? There are Serbs up there who'll shoot at anything that moves, faceless, nameless bastards that they are.'

She saw people walk nervously behind the cover of buildings, then gather in small clusters where they peered across the Miljacka as if they might be able to see the snipers who terrorised them every time they ventured out. Suddenly, they would take their chance and dart across exposed ground until they reached the next block and its temporary sanctuary. She watched an old man willing his weary legs to run as fast as they had when he was young, and a mother trying to zigzag across the open street, dragging her child behind her.

Becky started strapping on her helmet and Rachel wondered whether she should have brought one as well as her flak jacket. Still, Danny wasn't wearing any body armour at all. Later Rachel would learn this was his moral stand: if the ordinary people of Sarajevo had to survive without Kevlar to cover their heads and hearts, then so would he.

'So this is where I turn into the king of drag-racing.'

Like the good, law-abiding citizen that she was, Rachel fastened her seat belt, while Danny stabbed his boot down on to the accelerator and crashed up and down through the gears. Swerving and sometimes skidding, he dodged craters, fallen lampposts, wrecked buses and trams, and the burnt-out, bullet-ridden vehicles of all those racing drivers who hadn't quite made it to the chequered flag. Black ice lay in wait beneath freshly fallen snow, ready to pick them off, just like the Serbs.

'You know what?' he shouted over the groaning gears. 'My greatest fear is to die here stupidly.'

'As opposed to what – heroically?' said Becky from the back.

'Yeah, heroically. A sniper's bullet or a mortar. I want you guys to put up an epitaph for me that says what a brave reporter I've been, not what a goddamned awful driver.'

Rachel was beginning to wish he'd talk less and worry more about the road.

'So, Rachel, why have you come?'

The question took her by surprise. She could have given him so many reasons but wasn't sure where to start. After all, what could she possibly say about Yugoslavia that would be of any interest to someone who'd written 423 pages on the subject? It was easier to say nothing.

'Oh, I … I don't know really.'

'Come on! I'm driving you down the most dangerous road in the fucking world and you don't *know*?'

'What I mean is, I could give you all the usual reasons. But in the end I guess … well, you're gonna think this is really terrible, but I suppose I was just bored.'

Rachel looked at more blackened, roofless homes, but all she kept seeing was the small pink bedroom where she had been hidden for too many of her 23 years. Even as she had packed for Bosnia, she had peered down from their doll's house on Lakeside Drive to the front lawn – manicured to death by her father, who would tiptoe around it with lengths of string, trying to measure the length and width of the hedge so that his shears could trim it with mathematical certainty. A world of meticulous perfection, where she was suffocated by a lonely father's love. A world away from Sarajevo.

'Don't you think that's unbelievable?' said Danny. 'For pretty much the first time this century we're the generation that don't have to fight a First World War or Second World War or Cold War, and yet we race out here in search of, well … war. We've got peace – millions died so we could have it – and all we say is: No thanks, that's a bit tedious. You wouldn't believe the desperadoes who turn up here. Peace is boring, they say, war is fun! I want what you guys had – in 1914, or 1939. I want a slice of the action too. I want to live my dreams living other people's nightmares.'

It was the first of many speeches she would hear from Danny, and she felt chastened. Despite the cold, her face was turning red and hot. Was he calling her a desperado? On one level it was an attack on all the war correspondents in the city – including himself, presumably – but the way he said it sounded like he was accusing her.

The Holiday Inn loomed into view at last, one of the great war hotels. The Commodore in Beirut, the Colony in Jerusalem, the Intercon in Kabul, the al-Rashid in Baghdad – Rachel had read about them all, and now she could say she'd stayed in one.

The ugly yellow box was the one building in Sarajevo most people would have happily seen blasted off the map, an eyesore that belonged not in this ancient Ottoman city but on the dismal outskirts of Anywhere, America. Yet in the space of a couple of years it had achieved mythical status. Journalists flocked to stay in it. Just like them, the Holiday Inn was enjoying a war which was good for business. Hack or hotel, Sarajevo could make your name.

The rooms on the south side, facing the Serb suburb of Grbavica, no longer had windows, or in some cases even walls. Even so, they cost 90 bucks a night, and demand outstripped supply.

The tyres squealed as Danny plunged down a ramp into the hotel's underground car park, a fortified sanctuary where the occasional reporter had been known to hide like a shell-shocked Tommy in the trenches. The car park was crammed with white armoured Land Rovers just like Danny's, tightly packed together.

Becky got out of the car and Rachel noticed her touch a wall three times.

'One of her little rituals,' Danny explained. 'Along with the blue underwear.'

Becky pushed him playfully.

'So? And what about your lucky boots then? He wears the same ones every day, Rachel. Had them for years. They absolutely stink, of course. Anyway, superstition, religion: it's all the same. All about making sure we stick around as long as possible.'

Rachel heaved her rucksack on to her back, picked up her bag, and staggered after the others through the echoing chasm of the car park and up into the hotel lobby. Perhaps Danny had a point: it *was* strange that a generation born in peace should want to come here. And having got here, to kneel at the altar of survival with sacrifices of walls and underwear and smelly boots, just to make sure it didn't die.

The wreckage of her last conversation with her father came back to her; the two of them sitting in the chintzy sitting room, Billy Kelly pleading with his daughter as they waited for the cab that would take her to the airport.

'It's just that there's only you, sweetheart,' he had told her. 'What else do I have in my life? Who else do I have?'

'But I'm not leaving your life, Dad. I'm just going away for a while. Surely you don't want me to stick around here forever?'

His silence had implied he did.

'So when will you be back?' he'd asked. When the war ends, she could have said – that is, unless another one has started up by then. But they both knew there was no certain answer to his question, and so Billy had cried more than at any time since creeping cancer had destroyed his wife a decade earlier, leaving behind a broken husband and a bewildered daughter. It was his fault: he had smothered her with his love, what father wouldn't have? He hated it when she got a boyfriend or a car, or took a plane ride to another city. He wanted to lock her up, his princess in the tower.

Like many Americans, Billy – sales representative, golfer and Sunday Christian that he was – understood very little of Yugoslavia's meltdown. He didn't see what it had to do with him, apart from the fact that the only thing he cared for in his life wanted to run away there. Patiently, like a history teacher, Rachel sat with him and tried to explain how, since the Second World War, the communist dictator Marshal Tito had managed to keep a lid on all its squabbling parts, but his death in 1980 had blown it off. She described the rise of Slobodan Milosevic and Serb nationalism, and how the rival republics had started clamouring for independence, including Bosnia in 1992. She told him how, although Western nations had recognised that independence, the Serbs had not, attempting to crush it by surrounding Sarajevo with their big guns and laying siege to it. When Billy still looked confused, she talked to him with kindergarten simplicity: the Bosnian Muslims were the good guys in white hats, just trying to recreate their homeland in the post Cold War world. The baddies in black were the Serbs, trying to throttle an independent, multi-ethnic, multi-cultural Bosnia at birth. But when Rachel threw in the added complication of the Bosnian Croats, it was just too much for Billy Kelly.

'How in the heck can you have two civil wars going on at once, between *three* sides? This stuff is making my head spin.'

'Dad, it's the story of my generation. It's what I want to do.'

He had grabbed her by the shoulders.

'I promised your mother I'd look after you, I promised her on her deathbed. What if she knew I'd let you go to war? What would she say if you wind up next to her in a grave?'

But as Rachel made her way through the bowels of the Holiday Inn, she was more convinced than ever she'd done the right thing. When Becky opened the doors for her into the hotel foyer, it was as though someone was pulling apart the curtains for the beginning of Act One. Finally, she was stepping on to the mighty stage of Sarajevo.

'My, my, so this is where it begins,' she said, primarily to herself. Danny was walking just ahead, and she wondered what he made of her. Despite his little tirade in the car, did he quite like her fresh-faced, ever-ready enthusiasm, or did he find it irritating? Did he really think she was a desperado? She supposed she shouldn't care.

• • •

It was probably colder inside the hotel than outside, Rachel decided. In the cavernous atrium of the lobby, she could see her breath exhaling in white puffs. She heard the echo of a strange ripping noise and looked up to see another group of reporters pulling apart the Velcro fasteners of their flak jackets. TV crews were coming and going, speaking a multiplicity of languages, heaving silver boxes around, wielding cameras and fluffy microphones. Behind the reception desk sat a couple of greying women in scarves and overcoats. They could have been waiting at a bus-stop.

'Room 331,' said one, handing her the key.

'Thanks, I'm sure it will be lovely.' Rachel wasn't sure of it at all. She pulled out the Maglite torch that would become her saviour, and negotiated her way through the blackness of the hotel stairwell. The hotel lifts looked encouragingly modern, but without electricity they sat lifeless and forlorn – like so much else in Sarajevo, a city slipping back in time. The place reeked of stale cigarette smoke and her feet crunched on broken glass. Even with the Maglite, Rachel stumbled and tripped as she made her way up to 331, where she fumbled the key into the lock.

If the hotel were a fridge, Rachel's room was the icebox. Instead of glass in the window, there was UN polythene sheeting. Instinctively, stupidly, she checked the radiator, praying for a miracle of creeping warmth that never came. No power, no heat, and only sporadic water. A lot of nothing to pay good money for, thought Rachel, I might as well be sleeping in the street.

On the other hand, the room could boast at least some of the trappings of a real hotel. There was a flat yellow phone with a brown receiver. The sheets of her bed were white and clean, and in the bathroom there was even a small, but brand-new, bar of soap, and a toilet sealed with a strip of paper claiming it was sanitised. What was missing, Rachel realised, were the towels. Of course she hadn't brought any and perhaps because of this, or because she felt as though she was getting frostbite, or because Danny had made her feel so inadequate, or because she was alone for the first time since her arrival, she began quite unexpectedly to cry.

It was a raucous voice in the corridor outside that woke her. Rachel was groggily confused: at first she thought she was back in her bedroom on Lakeside Drive, but this was a different place altogether. She was surprised how long it took her to remember – four or five long, perplexing seconds. The voice got louder, until it was followed by a determined knock. Still disorientated, she swung her legs off the bed and staggered over to answer it.

It was Becky, who had just managed to wash her hair.

'There was only a bloody trickle, and so cold I thought it might freeze on my scalp!'

Rachel was unsure if it had been worth the ordeal: Becky hardly looked any different, except that now her curls were damp and limp.

'Just brought you a little present to say hello. You know, welcome to Sarajevo and all that.' She was carrying a bottle of Ballantine's whisky, a Vranac red wine and a Swiss Army knife. From the array of blades, she pulled out a miniature corkscrew: like a good girl guide she was prepared for anything. Rachel made a mental note to buy one next time she was at a duty-free.

Over the Vranac, they talked. Rachel told Becky about her soporific life in America and Becky described hers, on a sheep farm near a place called Piety, three hours from Perth, or as she put it, 'three hours from Earth'.

'Arse-end of the universe. Nothing and no one for a hundred miles, except sheep, of course. I spent months dreaming of going to the nearest town, let alone the nearest city, let alone the nearest country.'

Rachel felt bad for thinking Arlington was boring.

'Dad was an alcoholic and mum was on the way there and, to be honest, I couldn't blame them. I'd have been the same if I'd stayed. Look at me – probably am anyway.'

Piety was where she'd fallen in love with photography. An uncle had given her a camera for her fourteenth birthday.

'I remember the day I took my very first picture. It was just a sunset – the same one I'd seen a million times and never even noticed – and suddenly it was beautiful. And when I got the print, I was hooked forever. I took pictures of anything that moved, which wasn't very much in Piety.'

Becky had left for England as soon as her parents would allow it, but even London hadn't been enough for her. After all those years in Piety, she needed a bigger buzz. She traipsed around a few war zones and then turned up in Bosnia.

'I wasn't bored any more, but lonely as I ever was.'

Becky moved on to the Ballantine's while Rachel, who was drinking almost nothing, started to feel uncomfortable. This woman she barely knew was opening her heart to her. She was an old hand in Sarajevo, brash and domineering, but she seemed to need a friend here. Almost as much as Rachel did.

'Really? But you're beautiful.'

'Not the view of too many men, unfortunately. Reckon the job intimidates them – war-zone headbanger and all that. Maybe they think I'll end up dying on them and they can't be bothered with all the hassle of a funeral.'

They both laughed, but Becky was serious. For too long she had been unloved, unsexed, uncoupled. The only man who was in her life – or who she'd like to be – was here but out of reach.

'Anyway, more mundanely: I forgot to mention there is one other thing you'll be needing …' With that she took off back to her room along the corridor, returning moments later with a Marks &

Spencer carrier bag. 'We call it the water baby. If you're planning on having any hot baths here – or even lukewarm ones – you'll be needing one of these –'

Like a magician, she delved into the bag and produced a large metal contraption that looked like some sort of engine part. It was the element of an immersion heater to warm up bath water, if and when the power came on.

'Usually takes about two hours, but for best results, leave it in all day. Don't get in when you're pissed though, else you'll end up electrocuting yourself. And that, as dear Danny would say, would be a very fucking stupid way to die.'

'Thanks so much.'

'Oh, I'm only lending it to you for tonight. After that you'll have to trade stuff for it – like everyone else does.'

'Trade?'

'You know, medicine, make-up, batteries, coffee – any little goodies you've got stashed away in that great big rucksack of yours.'

'And what happens when there's no water to heat up?'

Becky took a last hefty swig of Ballantine's. 'Horde it. When it's running – which is not too often – you make sure you fill the bath, and the toilet, and any other bowl or bucket you can lay your hands on. Mind you, it's not drinking water here, not unless you're desperate. It's browny yellow, a bit like pee.'

'Yuk. Not cleaning my teeth in that.'

'I've done mine with Coca Cola, even whisky. Oh, and one other thing …'

Rachel was growing weary of her endless list of tips, and feeling slightly patronised. She sensed they would be friends – maybe even good friends – but Becky was trying too hard.

'Next time, bring your own plugs. This is the one hotel where they don't exist. Big one for the bath, small one for the sink. Here you go, I've got a spare.' Becky threw it to her as she left.

'Good night, Rachel – nice to know you.'

Rachel supposed it was nice to know her too: she felt relieved to have met her, but daunted too.

Glad to be alone again, Rachel climbed into bed. She'd slept naked ever since she was a girl, but she quickly realised that in wintertime Sarajevo, nudity was not an option. The pile of discarded clothing was hastily reprieved and she dressed all over again, with the addition of a large woolly sweater. A bedspring dug hard into her back and she knew at once it would be an enemy.

In the narrow glow of her Maglite, Rachel opened up Daniel Lowenstein at page 108. It had been good to meet him, and yet – if she were honest with herself – slightly disappointing, too. He was not as she'd imagined. Like Becky, he seemed jovial enough, but she sensed a darkness in him. He hadn't liked her, she was sure about that now.

She began a chapter about ethnic cleansing in Prijedor in 1992, and for the first time she could hear what he'd written in his voice, as though he were reading it aloud to her.

> When the Chetniks came to the village, they had a wolf's head stuck to the bonnet of one of their cars, and a refrigerated meat truck following on behind. Nermina, who was 12, had seen them coming and she was old enough to understand. She shouted out to her father Kemal, and he understood as well. He was the village doctor. He led Nermina and the rest of his family to the basement: his wife Reima, and their two sons Emir and Senad. Soon they could hear the screams and explosions outside: the Chetniks were tossing hand grenades into houses, machine gunning those who stumbled out of them. Kemal didn't know whether to stay where they were, to come out and surrender, or to try and run. Then they heard men smashing down their front door and, in no

time at all, the basement door as well. Nermina recognised the fat man who was with the Chetniks: he was the village policeman, Milan Krstic, and he lived only a few houses away. He was about 50 with a ruddy face, bad teeth and a big pot belly. She had sometimes caught him looking at her lustfully as she walked home from school.

Krstic had swapped his police uniform for that of the Serb irregulars. He took out a pistol and put it in the mouth of her baby brother Senad, who was only two years old. His little cheek was swollen by the barrel, like having a lollipop inside it. 'Hello, Nermina,' Krstic said. 'Would you like to help your family? Otherwise it will be bad for them.' Then he drew a knife and held it against her cheek and told her to take her clothes off. 'Are you a virgin?' he asked her. He said he liked virgins very much indeed.

Nermina was brave; she could do this thing, she had to do this thing. Once again, she understood. Her mother screamed and begged the policeman to rape her instead, but he ignored her. Krstic yanked down his trousers and the Chetniks cheered him on. Nermina was on the floor and weeping, and he was above her, with his unkempt beard and rotting teeth, and a half-smoked cigarette hanging from his mouth. This was what he had wanted, all those afternoons when he had watched her in her school uniform. But now, for all his desire, he could not make himself erect. The more he tried, the worse it got. His fellow Chetniks laughed and pushed him out of the way so that they could try.

Krstic was angry he had been humiliated. 'Turkish whore!' he screamed at her when the others had all finished. At first he said he was going to kill her, but then he thought of a crueller punishment: he would allow her to survive. One by one, he shot her family. Her baby brother first, then Emir who was eight. After that, and holding Nermina in his gaze, he shot her mother and finally the father she adored.

> Krstic ordered the other Chetniks to leave her there, lying bruised and naked amid the corpses of her family. It was his punishment for her. The Chetniks were confused, but – as usual – Nermina was old enough to understand.

Rachel cried. She felt ridiculous and petty for having doubts about Danny: to unearth atrocities like these and recount them was journalism at its noblest. *She* wanted to meet survivors of ethnic cleansing like Nermina. *She* wanted to tell their stories to the world, so that it could know. Danny Lowenstein had not only been there and gathered this poor girl's harrowing testimony, he had retold it with compassion.

She read a few more pages until the day overwhelmed her. She turned off her torch, put her hands between her thighs for some extra warmth, and drifted off into a half-sleep in which she gave thanks that the Bosnia Danny Lowenstein was describing with such power was no longer an ocean away: it was all around her.

4

Post-Liberation Baghdad, 2004

At the Hamra, a clunk announced the death for the day of the air-conditioning system. Baghdad had devoured its paltry quota of power. There was less electricity than in Saddam's time: for all their billion-dollar programmes, the occupiers couldn't keep the lights on. Soon, the last of the artificially cool air would be gone, chased out of the room by the high fever of an Iraqi summer's day, as overheated as Bosnia's winter had been frozen. The thermometer in the kitchenette said 122 degrees Fahrenheit and the Junkies wiped their fevered brows.

'Drink, anyone?' asked Edwin, his baldness reflecting the sunlight that cascaded through the window. He fetched a couple of large bottles of water from the fridge which, like the air conditioning, was lifeless, as if it had died in sympathy.

'You know what, talking about that Vranac makes me want a glass of wine.' Becky poured some red into a tumbler, even though it was still the middle of the morning. 'Rach, you want some?'

'No thanks. I'm giving it a rest.'

'Ciggy?'

Rachel shook her head again.

'God, that took me back.' Rachel was still smiling fondly. For a while it had seemed they were in Bosnia rather than Baghdad.

'Feels like a lifetime ago.' Becky, having barely said a word, was starting to talk. The wine was helping. 'We were babies really, you especially. I'd forgotten what a baptism of fire it was for you.'

'I'd forgotten quite a lot of things,' said Rachel.

'Oh yeah?'

'Like what a sweetheart you were to me. And what a pig Danny could sometimes be.'

She said it straight, without humour, eyes locked into a steely stare at nothing in particular. Camille recoiled and studied Rachel more carefully. Who was she, this girl who seemed so endearing with all her naive ambition back then in Sarajevo? And a decade on, who had she become?

Munro came in and announced that First Cavalry had secured the area round al-Talha. They were offering to take him to the scene of Danny's disappearance.

'I'd like to come too,' said Camille.

'Not sure you'd find it very useful, and it might be quite upsetting. His car's still there. Bit of a mess, apparently.'

Camille was irritated. Who was Munro to try and stop her? Danny was her brother, not his. She quietly insisted she would go and then, just to antagonise him a little more, she decided to invite Danny's friends as well.

'Maybe you guys want to tag along?'

Becky shivered again, the way she had when she first heard the news.

'I don't think so. Like he says, I'm not sure we would achieve much. Probably just get in the way.'

'Oh, I think we should,' said Kaps. 'There may not be another chance.'

'Look, I just don't *want* to, okay?' Becky snapped.

'Okay, Beck. It's okay.' Rachel stroked her arm. 'No one's going to make you do anything you don't want to.'

First Cavalry were taking no chances. Half a dozen Humvees with Mark-19 grenade launchers and .50-calibre machine guns formed an inner and outer ring around Mohammed's car as if it were the Alamo. The vehicle still sat dead and useless where Abu Mukhtar's boys had killed it.

In the end, all the Junkies had agreed to join Camille, even Becky. It was a question of supporting each other, sticking together. In a huddle they studied the car through their sunglasses. They were surrounded by a plain-clothes security detail from the embassy, requisite M16s on their hips, tight coils of plastic tubing sprouting from their ears and walkie-talkies glued to their mouths. Further away, nervy combat troops squatted on the road or lay face down in the dust and sand, pointing machine guns towards an enemy that could advance from any direction, at any time, in any form: a boy on a bicycle, a farmer pushing a wheelbarrow, a woman with flowers in her hands. The Holy Warriors of Iraq's insurgency came in all shapes and sizes, and often with a belt of death tied around their waist.

Outside in the sun, Becky looked more washed out than ever. She knew she shouldn't have come: her first instincts had been right; this would go badly for her. She'd held Rachel's hand tight throughout the journey, and then cried in her arms when she saw the shattered windscreen and the blood baked dry on Mohammed's seat.

A team of soldiers had started work, examining bullet casings, tyre marks and footprints, taking endless photographs and video footage of the scene. Munro was making his own measurements of the tyre treads on the road, and the distance between the bullet holes. He was in a world of his own, and making no attempt to involve Camille or any of the others.

The Junkies started wandering around, eyes fixed on the dusty ground. They seemed to be searching, too. Kaps, in particular, was preoccupied. He paced up and down imaginary channels, methodically retracing his steps from time to time. Eventually, Camille saw him pick something up; a card, she thought.

'Found anything?'

'Nah. Thought it might belong to Danny, but it's just rubbish.'

She saw him put it in his pocket anyway.

The Junkies stood together again, swaying a little, gently kicking up the sand, lost in thoughts and memories. Kaps wrapped a long, muscular arm round Becky while Edwin let his half-smoked cigarette fall to the ground and pulled Rachel to him, stroking her back with small circular motions of his hand. Not that she could feel it. They were all firmly encased in flak jackets and helmets and wet with sweat.

'What if we never know what happened to him?' asked Rachel. 'You know, sometimes they don't even find a body.'

'We have to stay positive.' Edwin, still holding her, had wrapped his kafiyeh round his head to stop it burning in the sun and slapped some factor-50 over his face. There were white smears of it where he'd failed to rub it in. 'There may not *be* a body. My bet is he's a hostage somewhere, and absolutely fine.'

'Yeah, right,' said Kaps. 'A five-star hotel. The Iskandariya Hilton.'

'But they'll kill him, won't they?' said Rachel, ignoring both of them. 'When was the last time they let a hostage go?'

Camille was a few yards away, the other side of the car, scrutinising the little holes in it. She felt a wind whip up from nowhere; a summer dust storm was stirring. Grit and rubbish and clumps of vegetation started to swirl around in circles, and the palm trees bowed and bent. Camille lifted her head and saw a young shepherd approach. He looked about 16, dressed in grimy rags and disintegrating sandals; he'd been tending a small flock of sheep nearby. There was an untapped intelligence about him. On the assumption that he had come to murder rather than talk, he was being frisked at gunpoint by the soldiers but accepted the indignity. It was just how things were in the free Iraq.

One of the American officers, a major, agreed to hear what he had to say through an army translator. The shepherd boy talked for at least ten minutes, pointing and gesturing, intense, insistent. He spoke calmly but with determination: he had a story to tell. At the end of it, the major pulled out the Washington dollars he kept in a side pocket for rewards. He peeled away a couple of twenties and the boy took them without a smile. It was no more than he deserved.

'What did that kid have to say?' Camille asked the major.

'That shepherd boy? Oh, nothing much.'

'Come on, you were talking to him for ages.'

The major hesitated.

'Okay, I'm not sure if I should be telling you this, but he says he was here when it happened, over on that hill back down the road. Kinda watched it, but only from a distance.'

'And?'

'Look, this may be garbage, but he says there was another car as well as Danny's; two people inside it, he thought, one of them in a blue flak jacket – probably a Westerner. Pretty soon after the kid saw them go by, he heard gunfire from the bridge up here. He guessed they'd been shot up in some sort of ambush, except they managed to get the hell out. Drove back down the road to near where he was. Then he saw one of their tyres had been shot up.'

'You're kidding?'

'That's not all. Seems that it was *after* this that Mr Lowenstein came through on the same bit of road and slowed down to talk to these guys in the first car. But how about this? The kid says they didn't try and stop him, just let him push on straight ahead – into the same damned ambush. How d'you like that? He couldn't believe his eyes.'

'That's extraordinary,' said Camille.

When Munro came over she told him the shepherd's story.

'Mmm. Strange,' he said wrinkling up his face. 'Could be useful. Not sure I'd believe everything he says, though. He's just a peasant.'

'That's what I thought at first,' said the major. 'But he seemed pretty sure. Why would he make it up?'

Munro shrugged.

'To collect some easy bucks? People can tell you a million different things in these villages.'

'Maybe. Maybe not.'

'So does he have descriptions?' Munro asked the major.

'He said he was too far away. He remembers the car was red and white though, some sort of saloon.'

Munro wrote it down as if he had to, but walked away again to finish off his measurements. Camille decided he was surly and unhelpful. When he'd gone, she asked the major quietly, 'Could the boy take us back there, to where he saw the other car?'

It was only a couple of minutes away. The major drove Camille in a Humvee along with the shepherd and the interpreter.

There was nothing to see, but Camille inspected the tarmac and tried to conjure up the picture painted by the shepherd. Down the road the Junkies were still embracing each other, but an orangey-brown cloud had billowed up and was enveloping the landscape. Wearily, because they'd had enough of desert days like this, the troops put on their sand goggles while the Junkies held hankies to their mouths and noses, and half-closed their eyes so the lashes could filter out flying dirt. Soon the wreck of

Mohammed's car was coated in sand. It seemed as though Iraq would like to bury it.

'Okay, let's get out of here now,' the major said. 'We can't see shit and I hate being blind in a place like this.'

5

Sarajevo, 1994

When morning arrived in Sarajevo like an unwelcome visitor, Rachel wondered where to start. She had made it here, but what now? Where to go, what to see, who to talk to? It wasn't as easy as it had seemed back in Arlington. She thought that breakfast might be the best place to begin so she went down to the dining room, a dingy ghost of what it once had been. The waiters were like apparitions too, in their white shirts and black bow ties. Their stoical demeanour insisted that, against all the available evidence, it was business as usual. They could have been restaurant staff on the *Titanic*.

The guests were dressed in fleeces, Puffa jackets and parkas. Rachel sat conspicuously alone, toying with a cold omelette, convinced everyone else was studying her solitude.

From the corner of her eye, she saw Danny approaching and her heart sank. She wondered if he was going to harangue her any more. He was carrying a helmet.

'Good morning. Thought I might find you here.'

'Oh. Hi there,' she pretended she hadn't noticed him coming over.

'A present for you. I never use it. Just let me have it back when you leave.'

'God, that's so …'

'I know, you're pathetically grateful.'

It had a strip of silver gaffer tape across it with *Lowenstein, A Rh+* scrawled in marker pen.

'Obviously you'll want to change the name tag.'

'Obviously,' she laughed, but he wound up the conversation before it had begun.

'Okay then, see you around.'

Rachel played with her omelette for a couple more minutes, and was relieved when Becky arrived. She was heading up to Pale, the Bosnian Serb headquarters. They had an interview with Karadzic – 'the crazy doctor', as she called him – and Rachel was welcome to come along if she felt like it.

''Course she feels like it,' said a deep voice just behind her. 'What else is she going to do here, hit the beach? Hello there, I'm Edwin Garland. *Daily Telegraph*. And you must be the young Rachel Kelly we've all been hearing so much about?'

She was getting used to shaking people's hands.

'Well, if you guys have got room …'

'Sure we've got room,' said Edwin. 'We've got Bessie.'

'Bessie?'

'My armoured car. One of my predecessors christened it Bessie. To be honest, I've never been quite sure why.'

He was English, with a naked scalp that Rachel couldn't take her eyes off. At first she thought it might be from some dreadful childhood alopecia, but then she detected a bluish haze of would-be stubble and decided he must shave it. In which case, how? Did he cover his head in foam every morning and scrape it with a blade, or use an electric razor? The thought of either made her wince, but the more she studied this brutal baldness, the more she realised it quite suited him, accentuating his heavy eyebrows and the dark brooding eyes beneath. It gave him an exotic look – of an eccentric adventurer, perhaps, or, less charitably, a convict.

In the car park, the underbelly of the hotel, Becky touched the same bit of wall she had when they arrived and banged her fist against Bessie's thick armour.

'She makes you feel … well, invulnerable. The only time you're ever really safe in this city is when you're deep inside her womb.'

Rachel struggled to open the passenger door: it was stiff and rusty and a dead weight she had to heave towards her.

'Hope you don't mind me hitching a lift. I feel a bit of a parasite.'

'Well, we're all parasites, I suppose, living off the blood of others. Spilt blood, usually. Anyway, glad to have you with us.'

At the last minute, someone from Reuters joined them too. He was called Kaps, apparently – Rachel was unclear if that was his Christian name or surname – and in stark contrast to Edwin, he had long, sandy brown hair down to his shoulders, gathered and tied up in a ponytail. He sat next to Becky in the back, closer than he needed to since the long bench seats that faced each other offered plenty of space. There was a wedding ring on his finger, but Rachel detected an air of possibility between them. Or impossibility.

They emerged on to Sarajevo streets buried beneath fresh falls of powdery snow.

'He's a bit of a nervous driver, aren't you, Ed?' shouted Becky from the back. He ignored her but she was determined to explain herself to Rachel: 'You wouldn't think he once drove tanks for the British Army. He wrote one of these off last year, you know; managed to skid it into the side wall of a little old lady's home. The poor love thought the bang was a Serbian shell: just closed her eyes and prepared to die. And when she opened them, guess what? A handsome young Englishman stepping out from his Land Rover –

in the middle of her fucking living room. She almost kissed him, she was so relieved.'

Edwin listened patiently but Rachel was embarrassed for him. The story was clearly Becky's party piece, retold frequently and always at his expense.

'Thanks for that recap, I'm sure Rachel's absolutely fascinated.'

'Of course she's *absolutely fascinated*.' Becky performed a caricature of his public school accent – Ampleforth: posh and very Catholic.

'Okay, that's enough. If you don't want me to drive, I'll turn round now.'

Edwin was serious. He'd had enough of being riled and Rachel saw for the first time how sensitive this former soldier could be. His scalp embodied the contradiction: it looked macho enough, but the delicate skin stretched across his skull spoke to her already of a dangerous vulnerability.

As they drove out of Sarajevo and over the hills into Radovan Karadzic's lair, an empty Coke can rolled around irritatingly on Bessie's floor. It was covered with the debris of assorted Junkie road-trips: Mars bar wrappers, half-eaten ration packs, film canisters and pages of ancient newspapers brought out from London long ago, now faded and mud spattered. Edwin rummaged through a stack of cassettes on the dashboard and picked out one labelled *Songs of Sarajevo*. To the sound of Seal performing 'Crazy' – which Rachel would discover was their anthem – she gazed down on the crazy city they'd just left behind. From this height, it looked like easy pickings: a scrawny kid in the playground, smart but pitifully weak, beaten up by the bullies every day. The Serbs of the Yugoslav National Army – the third-biggest military machine in Europe – had their tanks and howitzers up in these hills. In their sights was brave, sophisticated Sarajevo, with its old Ottoman heart still beating, as bold a statement of multi-culturalism as you could find, a living example to the world. Mosques mingled with churches, Orthodox and Catholic. Now it was being blown apart, a foolish dream no one should ever have dared to entertain.

As they climbed higher towards Pale, there was an even thicker shroud of snow.

'You know what's really scary?' Edwin said. 'Just how easily Europe can turn her charms. It's like the Nazis, plotting a holocaust in the forests of Bavaria. It looks so pretty, but behind the picture-postcard scenery, they're busy coming up with clever plans to exterminate a people. There are no devils left in hell, they're all up here in Pale. See these chalets, Rachel?'. Edwin was pointing as he drove. 'It's where the well-heeled of Sarajevo used to have their holiday homes. They'd pop up at weekends for a spot of skiing. And that's the Panorama. Used to be one of the main resort hotels for visitors. Now it's where the Serbs run the war.'

She took in its menace and held her breath. It was only a few miles south of Sarajevo, but it felt like another country.

Inside the Panorama, they shivered for more than 90 minutes. If it were possible, this was a place even more glacial than the Holiday Inn. The cold made their bones ache. Karadzic was in a meeting, they were told. He'd be with them when he could. Around them scurried sullen Chetniks, some with long hair and beards who hadn't washed for days and looked as though they'd just returned from another busy day of ethnic cleansing. One or two glared contemptuously at the visitors, as if to say: Who the fuck let you Muslim-loving, do-gooding Westerners in here? What would you know about us, the proud people of Serbia? What could you possibly understand about the endless centuries of our suffering?

Eventually, the man himself strode in, beaming at them from beneath the shocking mane of his wild grey-white hair.

Rachel had read so many profiles of him, seen him so often on the television, this self-proclaimed poet and psychiatrist, and now he was coming up to her, offering his hand in greeting. She took it and, after the briefest hesitation, shook it. At last she felt part of the war whose every twist and turn she'd followed. Day one, and she was meeting the man who had masterminded the entire conflict, its very architect. Already there was something to tell her children, and for them to tell theirs: that she'd had face time with one of the principal characters of late twentieth-century Europe.

'Hello, sir, Rachel Kelly. From the United States.'

The others introduced themselves, too, but Rachel noticed how they avoided shaking hands, nodding awkwardly instead with thin, noncommittal smiles.

'Shall we go through?' asked Karadzic in his flawless English, so familiar from the television bulletins. 'It's rather cold out here.' He didn't bother to apologise for being late; he didn't even mention it.

For the next half an hour the Führer of Pale explained, over a table laden with French cognac and fine cheese, how the loss of every life was to be regretted, but how the Muslims had made the war inevitable. We wanted to live in peace, he said, but you have to understand, they are trying to launch an Islamic Jihad right here, in the heart of Europe. For the good of Christianity, for the sake of world civilisation, they must be stopped. We *will* defeat them, even if the only friends we have left are God and the Greeks. Remember this, he said as he puffed on a Cuban cigar, soon they will not need to count the dead in Sarajevo, they will need to count the living.

Rachel wrote down every word, her hand soon stiff with cramp.

Towards the end, he offered them some coffee and it was then that Rachel made her cataclysmic error – a 'crime' Danny Lowenstein would call it when he heard. As Karadzic bade them all farewell, he managed to kiss her quickly on both cheeks. She felt his skin on hers, cold and slightly rough. She inhaled the smell of his aftershave and thought it curious he should bother with such vanities in a civil war. It all happened before she realised what he, or she, was doing.

That night it was supper in the dining room. Becky had pushed three tables together and about a dozen of the press corps were sitting round them. Rachel, exhausted but elated after her debut day in Pale, was ravenous. She didn't care what the menu offered, she'd have whatever there was and more.

As she walked in, he was at one end, presiding, the king at his banquet. Taking off her coat, Rachel wondered if she might contrive to sit close to him, but he was already sandwiched in by Edwin, Kaps and Spinoza, one of the photographers she'd seen in Split. The four of them were hunched up together and laughing raucously. Danny was the master raconteur, with an inexhaustible supply of anecdotes, the most trivial incident embellished to make it funnier. Fragments of a story drifted over to her, something about him hiding from the KGB in a hotel room before the fall of communism. Lithuania, she thought she heard him say.

'So I knew they were looking for me, and they were banging on my door going, *"Meester Lowenstein, can vee talk to you?"*' Danny's ridiculous Russian accent provoked more hilarity. 'And I'm butt naked, but I jump out of bed and hide in a cupboard in the bathroom, and my heart's pumping. And I hear them unlock the door and then this big bear of a guy's opening the cupboard and I think I'm toast – and of course it's the fucking room service I forgot I'd ordered, and the waiter's looking at me in all my glory, saying, *"Do you vont some mayonnaise?"*'

Then the stand-up comic turned shrewd political analyst – Rachel noticed how effortlessly he could change gear. He spoke quickly, oozing confidence. Even when he digressed down labyrinthine side alleys, his sentences were so crafted he might have written them beforehand. His voice rose above everyone else's, dazzling, demanding to be heard.

'You see, Milosevic's great trick is to demonise everybody else. The Slovenes? Secessionists. The Croats? Fascists. The Bosnians? Islamic fundamentalists. The Albanians? Terrorists. And d'you know what *he* is?'

'A nationalist, of course,' said Edwin.

'No, not even that. An *opportunist.* He's just ridden to power on the back of this whole notion of a greater Serbia. What was he under Tito? Just another dreary apparatchik, going nowhere fast. What future would he have had in a free, democratic Yugoslavia? Absolutely none.'

Watching him in full flow, Rachel decided his age added to his aura. Most of the others were in their twenties, but he was more than a decade older. He'd been there from day one, living and breathing the battles of Bosnia Herzegovina and, before that, Croatia. UN spokesmen, NATO generals, EU diplomats – they all came and went, but Danny was a constant, rarely taking holidays or retreating into comfort zones. He had written the seminal book on the war even before it was over, and his reports were required reading in the White House and Downing Street. He was everything Rachel admired in a journalist: smart and funny, ethical and angry. She decided to forget his disparaging remark about desperadoes: she must have misinterpreted it.

'It's like all wars,' Danny thundered on, rampaging from one subject to another, 'it's about good and evil, and it's also about religion.'

Rachel would discover later he said things like this to provoke Edwin, knowing this loyal English Catholic resented the idea that his God should be blamed for all the troubles of the world.

Edwin came to His defence as always. 'Oh yeah, it's always God's fault, isn't it, never man's.'

'They're a lethal combination,' shrugged Danny.

'You know what I find strange, though, Danny; you think you're this great atheist – what is it you call yourself, an atheist *fundamentalist*? – but even you need someone watching over you.'

'Meaning?'

'All that superstition, those magic bloody boots. You seriously believe you'll die if you ever take them off. Okay, admittedly I sometimes hang out in churches with incense and relics, but I don't think it's too much weirder.'

Danny appeared to find this territory treacherous so he moved to firmer ground.

'The point is, history is littered with religious wars. Islamist expansion in the seventh century, the Crusades in the eleventh, the Thirty Years' War ... the list goes on and on and on. And what the hell is Israel and the Palestinians, if it's not religious?'

Edwin gave up. There was no point in arguing with Danny when he was at full throttle. He represented not a soul on earth, except his paper and some of his readers, and yet he always had to be right. He'd only end an argument when he'd won it. He pummelled away at people, grinding them down.

As the debate petered out, Danny looked up and caught Rachel's eye. Perhaps she should get up and thank him again for the helmet, or make a joke about how big it was on her and kept slipping off. She tried to give him a half-smile of acknowledgement, yet if he saw it, he didn't reciprocate. In fact, was that a scowl that was spreading slowly across his face, the beginnings of a thunderstorm that destroys a perfect sky? She was probably mistaken; he was just tired and irritable.

At her end of the table, the conversation was less erudite. It ebbed and flowed before settling, for no discernible reason, around

Woody Allen and whether or not he could be called a good director, and Madonna, and whether or not she could be called a good musician. Compare and contrast. Rachel, however, wanted to escape America and her flawed celebrities, not spend all night discussing them. She pretended to listen to the gossipy chatter around her, while filtering it out and concentrating on Danny's words instead.

After a while she slipped away to the toilet and, having peed, took a long look in the mirror and congratulated herself on a first day of achievement. Not bad, Miss Kelly. Not bad at all.

It was only as she was starting to make her way back towards the dining room that she heard Danny's voice rising above the hubbub, as impassioned as it had been when she first walked in. It hit her like a sudden gust of wind.

'But, Jesus, how *could* she? Does she have any idea, any fucking idea, how much pleasure she'll have given him? Even his wife doesn't do that. I mean, hell, she's not exactly a world statesman. She's a hack, and a pretty minor one at that, but he'll have loved it even so. She's an American, after all. He'll milk it, you can bet your life he will.'

A pretty minor one at that. The words were rushing around her head at horrible velocity, a fairground ride spinning out of control.

'Oh, don't be so hard on her,' someone said; a man's voice, she thought. Kaps, the guy from Reuters. Yes, it was definitely that distinctive Afrikaner accent. 'Look, it's her first day, eh? So what if she shook his hand and he gave her a kiss? He was trying it on, the old bull. You can't blame him, he doesn't get to see too many pretty girls up there in his lair. So she made a mistake, didn't get out of his way in time. Well, it's not exactly going to change the war. And anyway, she's a rookie. Wet behind the ears. Give her a break, will you, Dan?'

'And what if she'd kissed Hitler? Or Stalin? Would you still be giving her a break?'

'I doubt she's into necrophilia.'

'It's not funny.'

'Yes it is! Lighten up, you sanctimonious bastard.' It was Becky. Good old Becky, thought Rachel, paralysed in her hiding place. 'Loads of people shake his hand. I saw that guy from the BBC doing it the other day.'

'We don't,' said Danny, categorically. We, the Something Must Be Done Brigade, who despise the Serbs and demand that the world should act against them. We, the gang that Rachel wanted to be part of. Not now, though. Club rules broken. Membership denied. 'And we certainly don't kiss him.'

'Now *you* kissing Karadzic!' Kaps shouted out. 'What a pretty picture!'

It was another valiant attempt to puncture Danny's righteous indignation. Rachel heard the whole table laugh. She silently thanked Kaps for defending her, she thanked him from the bottom of her aching heart.

Still, she had made a mistake. Everyone conceded that much, her defenders as well as her detractors. Fuck, Rachel said, almost aloud. I've only just got here and already I've screwed up. Not an inaccurately reported fact, not a missed scoop, but an error of judgement that would offend and alienate those she most wanted to be close to. She should return to her meal, but all she wanted to do was to scurry back to the sanctuary of the toilet and lock the door. She did neither, staring at a curled-up, dried-out piece of wallpaper that seemed to resemble her career.

A pretty minor one at that.

Maybe that's all she would ever, could ever, be. Maybe Billy Kelly was right and she should have stayed with him, where she belonged. Maybe Maybe Airlines would have to fly her straight back to Arlington and that box bedroom she never should have left. Thoughts of home made her want to go upstairs, curl into a foetal ball and fall asleep, but somehow she had to carry on: it had been almost five minutes and she had to go back in. Later, she would think it took more guts to walk back to the table than on to any battlefield.

By the time she got there, the conversation had moved on. Only Becky saw the dewy glint of tears she was trying to hold back.

In her room that night, Rachel read more of Danny's book. She didn't much feel like it, but she needed to have her faith in him restored. It was towards the end of the chapter on Sarajevo.

> The only reason I paid any attention at all to Ljubica was because she was a little girl with no front teeth and her hair in pigtails. I guessed she was six or seven, and when I walked past her, near the Unis towers, she was skipping in the snow and laughing hard. In Sarajevo, laughter had become something out of the ordinary, enough to get you noticed. I smiled at her and she smiled back.
>
> I had just turned the corner when I heard the mortar's impact, and part of me knew who its victim had to be. I ran back the way I had come and she was already in the arms of a heavily bearded man – her father, I assumed, though I dared not ask. He was screaming at the sky, accusing it of this atrocity. He shook a fist at whatever gods up there he thought had done this. Ljubica's little body had been torn apart, her pigtails were wet with blood. Somewhere in her dying face, I thought I could see a trace of that same smile she had given me, that laughter that got her noticed.

It was the Lowenstein technique again. She doubted she'd ever have the confidence to write about laughter being 'enough to get you noticed', but whereas the day before, she'd have admired its audacity, now she thought it might just be corny. She asked herself if it was all entirely true. Had Ljubica really smiled at him, or was that just poetic licence? Had he embellished his story, as he embellished his well-worn anecdotes at the table? What was it Becky had called his writing? *Fictional.* For a moment she wondered whether Ljubica even existed, or Nermina either, for that matter.

Becky knocked on Rachel's door again, with more Vranac.

'I brought something to cheer you up.'

'But I'm absolutely ...'

'I know you heard. That man's just so far up himself sometimes.'

Rachel gulped down the dry red wine and soon it was working its wicked magic. Becky drank in sympathy. Rachel was grateful for her company. She might have been suspicious why this perpetually cheerful stranger had latched on to her quite so fast, but on a night like tonight Rachel realised that if Becky needed a friend in Sarajevo, then so did she. Becky had stood up to Danny for her, and she couldn't ask for more than that.

'You need to learn to ignore him. And anyway, it was our fault. We should have held you back from snogging the crazy doctor.'

'It was a peck not a snog,' protested Rachel.

'Well anyway, I find him quite attractive in an older-man kind of way. Don't tell Danny.'

The drink helped turn Rachel's shame to anger. How dare Daniel Lowenstein – or Danny or whatever the fuck he called himself – who barely knew her, by the way – judge and condemn her, and on the very first story of her on-the-road career? Well, fuck him, the wine said; fuck him and his sanctimonious bullshit.

'He was my hero, you know.' Rachel might as well have been confessing to a sordid fantasy.

'Who, Karadzic or Lowenstein?'

'Lowenstein, you idiot.'

'We noticed. Listen, he still can be. He's a great guy and a fabulous journo. We love him to death. We go back a long way.'

Becky started talking about how they had all met three years earlier during the Serbs' other war, against the Croats. Edwin had just left the army in 1991, knowing plenty about war but nothing about journalism. Kaps was the opposite, an experienced wire reporter but new to the battlefield. Danny had taken both of them under his wing. Becky had been there at the same time, with another photographer called Frederique.

'Freddie, we called her. She was only 20, and way more talented than me. We were all driving in a convoy to Vukovar one day, the five of us. The Serbs had flattened it, as only they know how. We were in soft-skins and a round came through the window. Took off half of her face, that lovely, lovely face. The worst thing was her eyes, though. Her agency in Paris paid for the best eye surgeon in the world. She couldn't lose the gift of sight, the gift of taking pictures. She couldn't; but she did. The operation failed.'

'I'm so sorry. What happened to her?'

'Freddie? Oh she's alive and kicking, but her world's a darkroom otherwise she'd be out here with us now.'

Rachel wondered if she'd been lined up as a replacement and it sent a shiver through her, but Becky was moving on, so fast it was hard to keep up.

'Just take it as a warning. Anyway, d'you want to know how to really piss him off – Danny, I mean? When we were up there – in Pale – this really seedy guy offered me a kind of facility, to go and see some Serbs in action. I told him I didn't want just any soldier, I wanted a sniper. I want to know what it's like to be on the other end of that high-powered rifle. I want that picture of him looking down on his victims, to see his finger on the trigger, his eye gazing through the telescopic sights. Picture of the bloody year. Well guess what? The guy agreed.'

'You're kidding?'

'Nope. Said they're going to line up Sarajevo's kingpin sniper for us.'

'*Us?*'

'Of course. I do the pics, you do the words.'

Becky explained how they would cross over the front line into Grbavica. It was only a stone's throw from the Holiday Inn, but they would have to go the long way round, across the airport and back into the city from the Serb side, stopping off at Lukavica barracks for Republika Srpska paperwork and a minder.

'In peacetime, we'd be there in five minutes, but it could take us three hours. Still, I guarantee it'll be a story. They say he kills half a dozen Muslims every day. Most of them babies in their prams, probably.'

'So why would he want to talk about it to us?'

'Because he's a cocky little shit, I expect. Pleased as punch he's top of the league and wants the whole world to read all about it. It's the whole Serb propaganda thing.'

'And we're playing along with it? I'm not so sure I want to be part of that.'

'Oooh, so we've decided we're not covering the Serb side of this war, have we? Fresh into town, and we've already worked out who's in white and who's in black?'

'Ain't exactly rocket science.'

'Ain't exactly objective, either. I think you've been listening to Mr Lowenstein after all. Look, the point is, we crucify this sniper prick. Let him hang himself. Whatever he says, your readers end up hating him.'

The prospect of a good old-fashioned exclusive – her first in Sarajevo – started to appeal to her. She didn't want to let Becky down, not after she'd shown such solidarity, and if she lost more of Danny's respect – well, he didn't seem to have too much for her in the first place. Before she knew it, she could feel the moral high ground collapsing beneath her feet as if there'd been a landslide.

'Okay, deal.'

They performed a drunken high-five in which their hands very nearly missed each other and set about planning their day out on the Serb side of town, a day that would haunt them both for the rest of their lives.

They find him on the fifteenth floor of a boarded-up apartment block, hiding out in a child's bedroom. A doll's house lies broken on the carpet, its roof smashed in. Little plastic people are scattered around it, dead or horribly wounded. Schoolbooks are littered everywhere, an empty satchel nearby. It is as if the child has had a tantrum, hurling her belongings from the shelves, but she has gone: it is the Serbs who have ransacked her room, of course, looking to loot money or jewellery, but finding only dolls and toys and fairy stories. And in place of the pretty schoolgirl who used to live here, the room has a new occupant: a man with a bandana round his head and a tattoo on his left forearm depicting the symbol of Greater Serbian unity – four Cs back to back, 'their version of the swastika', as Danny called it. By his side there is a bottle of slivovitz – homemade brandy. It is full. Perhaps he does not drink until he has something to celebrate.

His name is Dragan and he lurks between the girl's Disney curtains that show not emblems of Serbian nationhood but scenes from *Snow White and the Seven Dwarves*. He is gazing out across the Miljacka River, looking for a kill. He is a god, dispensing life and death as he sees fit.

'*Zdravo*,' mutters the sniper when they come in: hello. He turns round briefly to check them out before hauling his eyes back to the streets below, the eagle in search of prey. He only has four hits that day, two of them kills for sure. So far the pickings have been slim.

His masters in Pale will be disappointed. Productivity must be increased. The dream of Greater Serbia must come true.

'*Zdravo*,' say Becky and Rachel in reply. They have come with Alija, Edwin's translator who is not long out of college but already, with his small spectacles and an impeccably groomed beard, bears the permanently quizzical look of a university professor. He's half Serb – on his father's side – and when he's in this bit of town, he changes his name to Bosko. He enjoys his alter ego as though he's creating one of the characters in the books he reads.

But what are they doing here, exchanging pleasantries with a man who is gratuitous Serbian cruelty personified? It seemed such a good idea when they were knocking back the Vranac, basking in their defiance of Danny Lowenstein, but now they have entered the sniper's lair, they can scarcely believe they are in his presence: it's a journalistic scoop but an ethical abomination. Kissing Karadzic – even having sex with him – could hardly compare. Rachel dares not even imagine what Danny would say if he could see them now.

A face at last for the anonymous marksman who is terrorising this part of Sarajevo. He turns to them briefly. He is young, probably no more than 25. Green eyes, electric green. Becky supposes he works with them in the same way she does: looking through the sights of a gun, looking through the lens of a camera – the sniper and the snapper are perhaps not so very different. Both have their victims.

Most of the time, he stays hunched over his gun and with his back to them. He is reluctant to leave his work, even for a minute. He has a stilted conversation with Alija, two such different products of the same crumbling country: trained killer and trained intellectual. A redness is spreading across Alija's erudite face. His eyes are watering.

'What is it? What did he say to you?' asks Becky.

'Nothing, just chit-chat.'

'Come on – what? You look upset.'

'No, really, I …'

'You're here to translate for us, not choose the bits we're allowed to hear.'

'All right, all right. I told him I'm half Serb and he asked me which half. I said from my father's side. He said in that case, he'd like to fuck the cunt of my mother and after he'd finished, to slice it open with his sharpest hunting knife, and carry on cutting up through her body until he reached her throat, and then he'd put his cock in there as well. Satisfied?'

'Shit, I'm sorry.'

The sniper talks some more and this time Alija translates simultaneously, lest anyone accuse him of holding back.

'His name is Dragan. Don't be afraid, he says. Come up and join him here. He says it's his window on the world.'

Becky and Rachel creep forward nervously, worried a rival sniper from the Bosnian government might pick them off, and already trying to think through their potential complicity in the assassin's work. Still, it is why they have come, isn't it? To get Sarajevo's other story. And to get the picture. Picture of the bloody year.

They stand either side of him, peering down into the streets on the Muslim side of town, their side of town. Only a few hundred yards away is the nauseating yellow of the Holiday Inn itself. They can't help watching the city as the sniper does, scanning it, scouring it for signs of life, for potential targets. Every now and then matchstick figures dash from their cover, waiting for the crack and the whistle and – if their luck is out this chilly morning – the sudden, catastrophic explosion of pain.

The matchsticks need to make life-and-death decisions every minute of every day. Which route to take, whether to walk or run, whether to bear a fatalistic straight course down a street or to zigzag, duck and dive, in and out of alleyways. Anyone can be a target any time. The more vulnerable the victim, the keener the sniper is to select them for the kill, for it serves as proof to Bosnians that they can never expect even the most meagre drop of mercy from the Serbs, only ceaseless cruelty. An elderly pensioner here, queuing up for food, a mother and her baby there. Death has its eye on them, and death is a handsome young man called Dragan.

'He says conditions are perfect. A cold clear day is the best. It means people wrap up with lots of clothes.'

'Why's that good, then?' Rachel isn't sure she even wants to know the answer.

'He says because it makes them bigger targets. And if there's no fog or mist or rain to obscure his vision … well, so much the better.'

'Does he … enjoy it?' she asks.

A pause. The sniper squinting hard into his sights, dozens of tiny facial muscles stretched hard in concentration. Eyeing up a kill, or just thinking about an answer?

'He says it's a job, like any soldier's job. He's good at it, he says, so there's a certain satisfaction. But it's not so different from an artillery gunner or an infantryman. In this war, he says, every Serb must play his part. Unity is strength.'

The answers sound like he's been drilled in Serb propaganda slogans, taught them by rote just so they can be recited to Rachel and Becky.

'So how many kills?' Becky decides it's time to cut to the chase.

'He says today or altogether?'

'Both.'

'Two today, and maybe a couple of hundred altogether. He says he doesn't keep count. Anyway, he doesn't always go for the kill, he says. Sometimes you hit them in the knees, just to bring them down. It ties up enemy resources and manpower to look after a casualty, whereas if someone's dead, they just have to be buried. Nice and quick, he says. Too quick.'

Rachel writes it all down in her notebook, scribbling furiously, cursing the fact that she's never bothered to learn shorthand. While she scrawls away it is Becky who is thinking up the next question, reporting now rather than taking pictures. Her conviction is that to photograph people properly, you need to understand them.

'But sometimes he goes straight for the kill, right?'

'Yes.'

'So how does he decide – you know, when to maim and when to kill?'

The question is translated and when Dragan hears it, he puts down the long, ungainly rifle. His voice falls to a hush and Alija has to ask him to repeat what he has said.

'He says when the mood suits him.'

'And what sort of mood is he in today?'

A long pause before he answers.

'He says stick around and you'll find out.'

'Is he okay if I take his picture?'

'Sure, but he wants to wear something over his face. And you mustn't use his name. Not even just his first name.'

Why so jumpy, they wonder, when he's so high up here, so invulnerable, doling out mercy or cruelty upon a whim, allowing life to carry on as normal or snatching it away in a fraction of a second?

Dragan pulls a purple handkerchief from his back pocket and ties it over his mouth and nose, cowboy style. He is hiding his face, just as he is hiding his body behind these Snow White curtains. As Rachel and Becky study him, it occurs to them this is a very personal style of soldiering: the crew who fire their shell or their mortar bomb have no idea who it is they kill, and neither does the humble infantryman who sprays machine-gun fire from the hip. The sniper, on the other hand, selects his victims with the coldest calculation. He knows what they cannot know, that they have been hand-picked for the kill, that they are about to die.

Bow down before the God of Sarajevo.

With the bandana round his head and the handkerchief covering the lower half of his face, there is little left to see now except the predator's piercing green eyes. Becky, who's been in a trance for a moment or two, starts to work at last. The long zoom hanging on her shoulder is unused; instead she selects the short zoom round her neck, for this is to be a close-up study of a killer. At first there is too much daylight streaming in, and his face ends up a silhouette. Then she gets it right: the perfect portrait. She's even come up with a caption: 'Eyes of a Sniper'. It will make cover for *Newsweek*, no question. She is so absorbed in her shot that she doesn't realise he's preparing for his.

An enormous crack, the window shaking.

The shutter clicks, again and again.

Another crack and then another in quick succession. A pure, clean sound, echoing slightly amid the boarded-up apartment blocks.

Before she knows it, Becky has burnt off a roll of Fujicolor film, and grabs another from the pouch around her waist.

Sniper and snapper at work together, in tandem.

She looks down on to the street. It's empty. No one dead, no one dying, much to her relief. Must have been a few rounds for practise. Or was it just for show? Becky has had men all over the former Yugoslavia posing for her with their guns. Wankers. Silly little boys with toys. Probably got small pricks, she thinks. This is where people like him belong, in a kid's bedroom, skulking around between Disney curtains.

Dragan points over to a darkened alleyway on the far right-hand corner of the street. He is matter-of-fact about it, not boasting. The expert's finger helpfully pointing something out; not something, someone. Becky can see now, wondering quite how she has missed her. A middle-aged woman sprawled on the pavement in a pool of blood. From this distance it looks the colour of red wine. A bag of onions she was carrying has spilt out all over the pavement. Red wine and onions, red wine and …

Becky's hands and fingers work quickly, instinctively, abandoning the short zoom for the long, focusing in on a distant shot of the victim down below: someone's mother, wife, daughter. Another motionless statistic.

And then the wave of revulsion. And guilt. And panic. The killing of an innocent woman, and she has connived in it. No, not the 'killing', Becky corrects herself: that suggests a legitimate act of war. The cold-blooded murder.

There is no room for Rachel at the window. Just as well. She has been spared Becky's trauma, but all the same she has heard the shots. And as they have rung around the city, all of Sarajevo has heard them too, everyone asking the same, stark question: who? For the sniper's bullet is unlike any other in a war zone. It has one single name lovingly engraved upon it, nobody else's will do. The simple sound of its crack and whistle haunts because of all that it implies: a bullet meant for just one human being, selected by another.

'What's happened, Beck? He hasn't actually –'

'Yes, he fucking has. He's gone and killed a …'

'Who?' Like Sarajevo, she needs to know the answer.

'A woman. Shit, I don't believe it. Bag of onions in her hand. Poor bitch. Poor fucking bitch.'

Rachel thinks she can hear the sound of crying in Becky's broken voice, but she isn't sure.

Wisely perhaps, Alija translates none of this for the sniper.

There is a pause. Twenty seconds, maybe more. Becky cannot bear to look out of the window again, but she wants to know what's happening – she needs to know. Is the woman really dead? Or maybe just badly hurt, with others already rescuing her, racing her up to Kosevo hospital and a miracle cure? She pops her head up again to take another look, convinced the woman will have a happy ending, just like Snow White and her dwarves. But the woman and the onions and the wine are still there. Alone. No one dares approach. They know too well the sniper's game.

It is precisely what he wants, and Becky watches him now, finger at one with the trigger, in loving harmony. He is waiting for some hero or heroine to creep out – against their better judgement – to try and save a fellow Sarajevan.

This can't be real, Becky is telling herself. She has broken out in a hot flush. Well what did she expect? That this pretty-boy sadist would put his killing on pause for a while, so he could pose for her? That he'd just let her walk out the door afterwards, morals intact, conscience all clean and tidy?

Rachel is pushing her way up into the window. Like a child who feels excluded, she wants to see what everyone else can.

'You okay, Becky?'

'Never fucking better.'

'Mind if I take a look down there?'

'Be my guest.'

Now Dragan has a new co-pilot in his cockpit, and he smiles at Rachel – a smile that disturbs her even before she spots the fruits of his labour in the alleyway below.

She knows she needs to elicit more quotes from him, or there will be no story to go with Becky's pictures. Where is he from? What drives him to do it? Does he have a family, does he have a mother like the woman he's just killed? Does he sleep well at night or is he tormented by bad dreams? But Rachel cannot bring herself to talk to him at all and, for a man who has just snuffed out a life, every question she half-frames in her mind sounds far too antiseptic. Instead it is Dragan who decides to interrogate her.

'He wants to know why you hate the Serbs,' Alija translates.

'We don't,' says Rachel.

'He says you're liars. He wants to know why you've come here today.'

'To hear his side of the story, his side of the war.'

'Bullshit, he says. You could get that from any Serb soldier – any one of thousands. He says you're voyeurs, both of you. Says you're fascinated by someone like him, someone who kills like this. That you think he'll make a ...' Alija hesitates.

'Go on,' says Rachel. 'We think he'll make a what?'

'He says you think he'll make a sexy story.'

Tell him he's right, she wants to say, but he already knows it. They all do. And now Dragan is planning a way to make it even sexier.

'He's asking if you want to have a look through his rifle. To see Sarajevo the way he sees it.'

'Um ... no. No thanks very much.' Rachel is tempted all the same.

'He insists. He absolutely insists.'

It is more than bad taste, she knows that: it is morally reprehensible. Danny would have them expelled from the country, boycotted by the international press corps, cast out as lepers for the rest of their careers. But who is going to tell? Not her, and not Becky either, since they are both in this together, for better or for much, much worse. In any case, Dragan doesn't look like he's giving her a choice. He stands aside from the gun and motions for her to put an eye to its sights. She obeys and, to her relief, it is at first a hazy, out-of-focus blur. Rachel moves away.

'*Hvala*.' Thank you.

'No, he wants you to look some more, he says. Until you see someone else.'

'Well, thank him again, but tell him I've seen enough. Really.'

'No, you don't understand. I'm afraid there is no option to refuse.'

Another shiver, and the dawning realisation that Dragan is playing a game with them. Bosnia mind-fuck for beginners. She returns reluctantly to the telescopic sights, and is horrified to discover that now she can see through them. A mother and her little daughter cowering behind a bus-stop, paralysed by indecision, wondering whether or not they might be spotted.

Hide and seek. Can he see us? Of course he can see you, idiots! Now move! Move while it's me looking down the barrel of this goddamned gun and not him! Please, in the name of whatever god you want to worship, just move away from that fucking bus-stop!

But they don't. The woman lies near them, red wine and onions proof enough of the dangers of venturing away from cover. No, they will stay put, convincing themselves they are safe even though they're sitting ducks.

'He's asking if you've seen anyone.'

'No.' But Rachel's throat is so dry she can hardly speak. 'No one at all.'

'He says not even that mum and kid behind the bus-stop? Surely you can see them, he says.'

Alija's voice is trembling too. He has a sense of foreboding about the direction of this conversation, and he would give anything in the world for it to stop. Why did they ever bring him here, these silly girls who understand so little about the Serbs?

Rachel does not answer, but her silence is enough. The sniper can smell her fear, just as he can smell it from the people down in the street, hundreds of feet away. The scent wafts up to him. Unmistakable. Irresistible.

Then he is saying something else, pulling down the handkerchief from his mouth to make himself more clearly understood.

Lest there be any doubt. Alija does not translate though: he will not, he cannot.

'What's he saying? Please tell me.'

She doesn't really want to hear it though, and neither does Becky, who is busying herself in the black pouches of her Domke camera belt, fiddling with her mini-flash, checking her supply of film, creating work, trying to lose herself in it the way she has done all her life.

'I … I don't think I know how to translate what …'

'*Tell her!*' Dragan is suddenly speaking English, surprising them all. It is a command, not a request, and Alija obeys.

'I'm afraid he says he wants you to choose. Which one he should kill. Of the two people behind the bus-stop. He says he will kill one and let one live, but he wants you … to decide.'

Rachel stares at Alija, but dares not even look at Dragan. Waves of panic engulf her. What should she do? Why didn't she just stay at home in Arlington, in her little girl's bedroom – not so very different from this one.

'Tell him to fuck right off.' Becky is out of her camera bag again, out of her reverie.

'I'm not sure I can. You see he says if Rachel doesn't pick one – the mother or the child – he will simply kill them both. It's up to her. He says she should look at it positively. He says she has the power to save a life today.'

'Oh no.' Rachel wants to weep.

'Ignore him, Rach,' says Becky, back on her feet, aware of her responsibilities, stronger, wiser, more experienced – handing out tips on everything from water heaters to ethical dilemmas. 'We're getting out of here right now. The guy is a freak. You can tell him we'll be complaining to the people in Pale, the people we arranged this through. He's going to find himself in deep shit. We have a hotline to Karadzic himself.'

Alija translates laboriously and they wait with pounding heartbeats.

'Fuck the people in Pale, he says, and fuck Karadzic. They're all cunts; spineless, low-life cunts. You don't leave this room until you make the choice.'

In slow motion, they watch him pull a pistol from his belt. He waves it around vaguely in their direction. He is smirking with the timeless grin of a Serb who wants to prove a point, who feels a victim of history. Becky has seen it before, in countless leery Chetniks, but this one is different: he is handsome when he smiles. Again he addresses them in English:

'Now!'

He gestures for Rachel to get back to the window and look through his sights once more. To select her victim. Roll up, roll up, come and play God for a day! To her despair, they are still there, trembling by the bus-stop. Why the fuck didn't they run for it when they could, when she was keeping Dragan talking? Why didn't they take their chance to sprint across the street, or back to where they came from?

'Well?' Dragan is relentless.

'Tell him … I just can't … he knows I can't possibly …'

The sniper screams, and Alija struggles to keep up with the litany of derision.

'He says you're pathetic, just like all the Western governments who can't decide what to do and who to help. Just like all the bleeding hearts who come to a place where they don't belong. He says you should … well, fuck off back to America and leave Serbia to the Serbs. He says you're both dirty little whores, you deserve to be – I really don't want to translate this – gang raped up the arse by Arkan and his boys before they cut your tits off and stuff them in your mouths.'

Rachel's hands are shaking violently, volts of fear electrocuting her body.

'*Novinari!*' shouts Becky. 'We're fucking *novinari!*'

Journalists. As if that one word is an excuse and a reason and an alibi all wrapped up in one.

Dragan pushes Rachel aside, so hard she tumbles from the window and sprawls on to the floor. There is a shot, just like before. Five seconds later, another one.

Silence. No screams, just the hush of three people in shock and one who thinks he has proved a point.

'Oh my God,' says Alija eventually.

'I think we should leave now.' Becky is carefully closing up her pouches.

The sniper looks round at them again: another smile, this time of total contempt.

'He says he wants you to come back up here and take one last picture. For posterity, he says. For history.'

'I …'

'Becky, please. It really is an order.'

What have we done, she asks herself. What has Rachel done? Why didn't she just choose? It was not nice, it was not fair, but why couldn't she have saved a life, the deal Dragan had offered? Becky braces herself to see a dead mother and child by the bus-stop and a black cloud of irrational anger overcomes her.

'Oh, Rachel, for pity's sake. Why couldn't …'

But as she looks out, there is only empty pavement around the bus-stop. No bodies. No dead hand reaching out tragically from parent to child. No more red wine.

Dragan is laughing, a raucous bellyache of a laugh. Bosnia mind-fuck. You disgust me, his laughter says, you and everyone else in the self-satisfied, Serb-hating world you come from.

And of course he disgusts *them*, except what troubles Becky is that his is a face that, in another time, another place, she could quite easily have fallen in love with. The devil's face. She catches a whiff of his slivovitz and yearns to take a slug of it.

As they prepare to leave, Rachel can barely feel her legs. She curses herself, she curses Becky and she curses Dragan. But most of all she curses Danny Lowenstein, without whose cruel jibes she never would have been here.

6

Post-Liberation Baghdad, August 2004

When the convoy delivered them back to the walled sanctuary of the Hamra, Rachel, Edwin and Kaps agreed they should write about what they'd seen amid the dust and sand at al-Talha: the bullet-ridden car, the bloodstains, the nervy troops who'd only just managed to secure the area. It was the hardest story they'd ever had to file. Should they make it a heart-wrenching account of what had happened to their lost friend Danny, or a conventional report on the missing American citizen Daniel L. Lowenstein, couched as if they'd never met him? They had no doubt which Danny would have chosen: he'd have milked it dry.

They went to their offices and tapped away at battered laptops. Words that usually rolled off their fingertips were suddenly elusive. Even so, it felt good to be reporting again. Only Becky couldn't bring herself to return to work. She hadn't been able to take a single photograph in al-Talha – she hadn't even taken her cameras – and now she sat in the Presidential Suite, waiting for the phone to ring. For the first time she was alone there and she poured some whisky into a teacup. It was rough, like bad petrol, and it scalded her throat, but she drained it quickly.

She used to think somebody could just come along and mend her – a shrink, a counsellor, a lover – but now she doubted that anyone could help. She heard a voice she barely recognised emerge from deep inside her, cracked and hoarse:

'Oh sweet Jesus, how did it come to this?'

Tommy Harper and Munro had announced they were meeting some Sunni tribal 'contacts'; when Camille asked if she could join them, Munro said that in his experience the presence of a Western woman might make things harder. He was sure she'd understand. Camille was irritated: perhaps she was being oversensitive, but he seemed to regard her as unnecessary baggage to be dumped at the hotel.

She stood on the terrace where, she'd been told, Danny and the Junkies used to have their poolside parties. She could almost see him amid the creepers and the trellises, his languid body stretched out on a cheap patio chair, reflected in the rippling water. His spirit seemed to stalk the place. She wondered what she would do, what she would say, if she came face to face with him after so many years. For a guilty moment, she felt relieved he wasn't standing there in front of her.

She could recall the moment it began, or at least the moment she first noticed. He was 14, she was 17 and their school report cards had both arrived. Hers was average, his was scintillating: top of everything, star pupil of the year, head and shoulders above the rest. When Danny thrust it into his father's hands, full of expectation, Lukas Lowenstein gave it a glance before tossing it on to the kitchen table. 'Not bad,' he said. With Camille's, Lukas took twice as long, and pulled her to his chest. 'Well, this is fantastic, honey. I'm so proud of you.' She looked across the kitchen and Danny's face had crumpled, with a glistening in his eyes and a chin that quivered. As Danny's big sister, she was supposed to watch over him, but here she was, if not inflicting pain on him, then colluding in it. She told herself her father was just trying, in his own cack-handed way, to make her feel a little better, but over the years she came to see it as the start of Danny's punishment.

It was precocious intelligence that had been his downfall, Camille was sure of that. If only he hadn't been so damned smart. It was his own fault, in other words – not hers.

At first, she assumed he'd be their father's favourite: he was, after all, son and heir to Lowenstein Steel, the small but thriving family firm in Pittsburgh. The more he read and thought about the world, however, the more he challenged Lukas Lowenstein's politics (conservative Republican), his lifestyle (corporate America) and his religion (Lutheran Church). Danny was too interested for his own good in subversive literature: books that challenged capitalism and tore apart the Bible. He asked too many questions, had too many doubts. She wondered why he couldn't just read detective stories like all his friends.

Camille, on the other hand, did everything her father asked of her – she went to church, read her Bible, sang in the choir – while Danny wanted to go to Washington to protest about Vietnam.

Slowly, inexorably, a wedge was being hammered between the siblings. Lukas spent less and less time with Danny: he couldn't find anything they had in common. It was Camille, he felt, who really needed his attention.

As usual, the lift had a sign in English saying 'out of action', because the power was out of action, because the country was out of action. Camille was about to take the stairs back up to her room when she caught sight of Jamail, the kindly hotel manager who'd been so helpful to her. He was grey-haired and stout, with a flattened nose that had big pores in it, and a slightly crooked back. From the day she arrived, he'd made sure she had everything she needed – phones, faxes and speedy room service. He was the only Iraqi she'd ever talked to properly – albeit in his broken English – and her heart had warmed to him: when there was so much to disorientate her, she found his presence reassuring. He told her Jamail meant 'charming', and she decided the name suited him. From what she had heard about her brother's murdered driver, Jamail and Mohammed were very much the same, both gentle and generous men. True Iraqis.

He was going through some paperwork at the reception desk when she saw him, occasionally handing out or collecting a room key.

'Ah, Miss Camille, hello!' He gave her his usual lifting smile. 'Anything we can do for you?'

'I'm fine, thanks.'

She could tell he had something on his mind. He was looking around to see who else was in the lobby; no one was, but he lowered his voice anyway.

'I want to say to you, I have friend – Saddoun.'

'Uh-huh?'

'We fight in war together, against Iran. The long, long war. Too long. You hear of Fao Peninsula?'

'Yes, sure.'

'We fight in trench there. Many friends die. Me and Saddoun we okay, thanks be to Allah.'

Camille wondered how any of this might be relevant to her, but he deserved her patience.

'I get work for him here in hotel. With journalists. Yesterday, his son call me to say Saddoun gone. Disappeared. He hide, afraid for his life.'

'Right.' There were plenty of frightened people in Iraq, Camille was tempted to say; in fact, very few who were not.

'"Why?" I ask him. "Why disappear?" Because he drive journalist, say his son. He drive one of Mr Daniel's friends, he say, very best friends. One day only, big money. They shot at, but Saddoun good driver, like racing driver, like Michael Schumacher! He get away. He – how you call it? – he make them feel small. In Iraq that very bad thing, you understand? So he frightened, too much frightened. They know his face, they know car.'

Camille was transfixed.

'That's incredibly interesting. So who was this journalist he was driving?'

'Saddoun's son not say.'

'Well, all right then, where is this son so I can talk to him?'

'That is it, that is problem. Now he gone too.'

That evening, when they had filed their stories on Danny and al-Talha, Edwin cooked them up a green curry. There might not be electricity but at least there was some gas and he'd persuaded one of the hotel staff to buy most of the ingredients he needed from the souk. His wiry hands wielded a small knife, and with the controlled frenzy of a professional chef he chopped the components of his paste – green chillies, garlic and lemongrass – before throwing in some cumin, coriander and fish sauce and slicing up the cold, pink chicken into finger-sized strips. He felt the pain ease. The kitchen was his best friend, the church where he found his peace. No one else was allowed near him while he worked. He fried and stirred, boiled and drained, washing up as he went along, switching pans between stove and sink with bewildering speed and a manic zeal, until finally he dropped one with a clatter and Becky jumped.

'A curry was Danny's last meal here, the night before he went,' said Kaps.

'Yeah, that really spicy lamb madras,' said Edwin. 'He told me it could have done with more coriander though. Fussy bugger.'

Rachel looked up from her usual place on the sofa.

'Do you remember those curries you used to cook in Sarajevo?

Then it was any old meat you could find. I reckon you used to throw in bits of cat and dog without telling us.'

For the first time since they'd heard about Danny, they all laughed, including Edwin. Camille was reminded she was the outsider, a stowaway on wistful journeys to another decade. She made a move to leave.

'Not before you've had supper,' said Edwin. 'It's my new recipe, especially for you. Exclusive!'

He drained the rice and dolloped the curry on to the chipped crockery of the Presidential Suite: five plates, all of them slightly too small for the amount he had cooked, so there was a constant threat the whole soggy brown stodge would spill over the edges.

'To be honest, I'm not all that hungry,' said Becky.

'Oh, come on, girl, I've spent hours on this. Besides, you need to keep your strength up. For Danny. We all do.'

Camille, like Becky, felt revolted by the prospect of a steaming curry at the end of a steaming day, but steeled herself to eat it.

'Hey now, that's the best green curry I've ever tasted,' she said, surprising herself with the extravagance of her lie. 'I can't believe you just knocked it up.' Then, casually, and through a mouth half-full, she threw it in: 'By the way, I did have one question for you guys. I was wondering what all of you were doing when Danny went out there? It's just that I'm still trying to figure out why he'd go off on an assignment like that all alone.'

Edwin managed to find some chutney hidden in a corner cupboard behind the crockery. He passed it round, the consummate waiter as well as chef.

'Like we told you before, he could be secretive,' said Edwin. 'We assume he was on to some sort of story, or had an arrangement, because al-Talha's not the sort of place you go on a fishing expedition.'

'And did he like to "fish" alone?'

'Yes and no,' said Kaps. 'It's complicated. You can be part of a team but sometimes you want to do your own thing too, get your own scoop. Danny especially. I'm sure it's the same in the world of banking, isn't it? You have your pals, but you still want to …'

'Screw them?'

They looked startled.

'Well, not quite,' said Kaps. 'Compete, I was going to say.'

'I get it, compete. So when he was up there in the badlands – fishing, *competing* – what is it you guys were doing?' Camille noticed she needed to repeat her question.

'Oh just getting bored stiff in the Green Zone, as usual.' Edwin tucked into his meal greedily, leading by example. 'Danny would have really hated it. It was just one of those bullshit briefings the army give about how it's all going terribly well, and no one's dying really, and that we should go out to report the good news for a change, the reconstruction programme and that crap. Dull as ditchwater, but now and then you have to show willing. Danny would have nothing to do with it, of course. He used to say, "Who do they think we are, Pravda? Show me the good news in this hell-hole and I'll show you a liar or a neocon, or possibly both. And as for those people back home who whinge about how we only ever cover the bad stuff, well, they're sitting on their fat asses in Manhattan or DC, and we're out here getting shot at, so let me guess which one of us might be right." That was your brother, Camille. Never one to hold back.'

They ate in silence for a while, all except Becky who watched them. When the meal was finished, Edwin cleared the plates and washed them up. The others didn't offer to help; there seemed to be an unspoken understanding that he needed to do these things and the low, white-tiled walls of the kitchenette were his preserve.

By just after seven thirty, they all realised that a long hot evening of nothing stretched out before them, an evening as long as the sand-strewn road they had travelled on that morning. They could have gone to their own rooms but no one felt the least bit tired nor did any of them want to be alone, so they sat together, sometimes talking, sometimes quiet, and drifted back to their past. Or it drifted back to them.

7

Sarajevo, January 1994

Sarajevo was being slowly strangled as the Serbs laid their medieval siege, but in a basement discotheque they were preparing to party. Soon the deep thud of drums would pound out of it, like a heartbeat of the city. We're not dead yet, it would say and the young dancers inside would hope the Serbs who surrounded them could hear it.

The party was in the name of CBS, the American TV network. It wasn't only the press who'd be there, but UN staff and aid workers and any young Sarajevans who knew them: soldiers taking a break from the frontline, who'd swapped their uniforms for leather jackets, and girls who made themselves up with black market cosmetics – eyeliner, mascara and lipstick painted on to the faces of a desperate people.

Becky had been looking forward to the CBS night out, perhaps too much. She'd worked as hard on her face as anyone, washing and brushing her curls, colouring her alabaster skin, trying to plump up her skinny lips. The Gore-Tex and woolly hat had been dumped on the floor of her room in favour of her only dress. Rachel barely recognised her.

'Wow. You look incredible.'

'You too,' said Becky kindly, though Rachel – unsure of the party etiquette in a war zone – had applied only the lightest powdering to her face, just enough to dampen down the freckles.

Edwin was in the lobby, as arranged, on the dot of seven thirty. Danny turned up a couple of minutes late, and Rachel was careful not to catch his eye. Of Kaps though, there was no sign at all and Becky was despondent.

'Why can't he be on time, just once in his life?'

On her chunky, digital watch she monitored the minutes jumping by. At quarter to eight, disappointment began to crush her. She had constructed too many hopes upon the fragile edifice of this evening. It had happened before. Their something-and-nothing relationship usually ended up as nothing.

'I'm going to look for him.'

Kaps was in his room, wondering who to let down – Becky again, or his twin sons, whose fifth birthday it was, and whom he'd promised to call. The aerial on his satellite phone had a loose connection and by the time he got it working, he found the line to his home permanently, frustratingly engaged. He imagined the scene of domestic heaven: new toys all over the bedroom floor and the drifting smoke of blown-out candles in a kitchen festooned with bunting, balloons and birthday cards. Only one thing was wrong: Daddy wasn't there. Daddy was never there. Daddy preferred to hang out for month-long stints with insane people in insanely dangerous places. The boys didn't mind so much now, but he knew it couldn't be many years before they would come to resent him and his self-indulgent absences. Daddy hadn't even called. How many more birthdays did he have to miss – and sports days and school plays and the rest – before they decided that he wasn't much of a daddy after all and that they could do without him?

As he redialled for the twentieth time at least, the handset read *too frequent call attempt*, and Kaps flung it on to his bed, telling it to fuck itself.

Shortly afterwards, impatient knuckles were rapping on his door.

'Hey, Kaps! You coming to the ball or not?'

He opened it to find Becky standing there with an expectant grin.

'Oh, hi. Listen, sorry, but I've got to file. See you there later, eh?'

She knew it meant he wouldn't.

'Oh, spoilsport. What are you working on so late? It's been a news-free day.' She made herself even jollier than usual. 'You have to come, it's compulsory.'

'Try telling my editor. Some of us have deadlines.'

The deceit slipped out easily and he wondered why he was taking the trouble to lie to her.

'Oh.' For the first time Becky sounded as deflated as she felt.

'Look, I really will try and get there. When it's nice and sweaty.'

She trudged back down the corridor. How could he make her feel so blissfully good about herself, and other times so shit? She wondered whether to abandon the night right now, return to her room, and sink some more Ballantine's or Vranac, or anything else she had left.

Kaps closed the door and thought guiltily of Judith at home in Brighton, overwhelmed by domestic drudgery. He finally got through. A twin answered, but since they sounded as identical as they looked, he had no idea which one. Charlie or Tom, Tom or Charlie?

'Hey, big boy! Happy birthday, darling!'

'Thanks, Daddy. What are you doing today?'

What was he doing? Going to a disco with a woman he had just lied to; and so now the only thing to do was lie to his five-year-old son as well.

'Not so much, sweetie. Just working.'

'Are they still shooting at you?'

'No, love, they're not.' Another lie, but one Kaps found easier to justify. 'No one shoots at me, so you mustn't ever worry about that, you hear?'

'But I've seen it on TV. All the soldiers shooting.'

'Hey now, how about you tell me what presents you got?'

And as Charlie (he thought), then Tom, listed all their gifts, Kaps barely listened, wondering instead how they would fare without a father if he ever got divorced or killed or both.

Judith came on the line, her voice curt and strained.

'You might have called earlier.'

'I couldn't get the satphone working properly.'

'And you couldn't borrow someone else's?'

'Look, I don't want to argue. It's been a hard day.'

'Oh, and mine hasn't, I suppose? You try running a party for 16 five-year-olds, and listening to two little boys who never stop asking when their daddy's going to call.'

'I said I'm sorry.'

'No, actually. You didn't.'

'Well, I am, and I'll be home again next week.'

'Yeah, for a few days until you get bored of us. Then you'll be itching to be back out there.'

'Judith, can we not do this now, please?'

'What?'

'You know very well. Fight.'

'Why? What else have you got to do?'

Jump into Bessie and head off to the CBS party for the night, he could have said. Be with a loud-mouthed Australian called Becky Cooper, who's got a big arse and an ordinary face but who warms me with that smile until I glow.

Instead another lie slithered out.

'I have eight hundred words to file in the next hour.'

'Well then, you'd better get on with it, hadn't you? Wouldn't want to waste your precious time.' She cut the line he had spent so long trying to establish.

He held his head in his hands, remembering words Danny had spoken to him soon after the twins were born: 'You can be a good husband and a good dad, or you can be a good reporter, but trust me, you'll never be both; so my advice is don't even try. Kids will fuck up your career, and your career will fuck up kids. Everyone winds up the loser.' What would Danny know about it, he'd thought at the time; the permanent bachelor who had never come close to marriage or fatherhood, and quite possibly never would; the man who would always have something missing from his life. Now though, he wondered if Danny might have been right after all, as he always had to be about everything.

There was so much to envy about Danny: his looks, his talent, his soaring reputation. But what Kaps sometimes envied the most – an envy he despised – was Danny's freedom: to hit any story that took his fancy, to stay with it as long as he liked, to take as many risks as he dared. It was a freedom Judith had stolen from him.

He'd met her outside the South African embassy in Trafalgar Square: the two exiles chanted slogans, carried placards denouncing the monstrosities in their homeland, and then went to a coffee shop to talk about it. They had tumbled into heady, idealistic love and anything seemed possible; she the LSE student, he the draft-dodger who had fled to England in the nick of time. They married too young, too soon, and Charlie and Tom were conceived too quickly. In the years that followed, they could agree on the evils of white rule but very little else. Now apartheid was dying and so was their relationship, though neither would admit it, if only for the sake of the twins.

Perhaps, thought Kaps, I should give it all up, run back to Brighton and rebuild the scorched ruins of my family. Yes, but when? He could almost hear Judith's exasperated voice asking him the question. Soon, was the most he would promise himself and her. Just as soon as I've filed that ultimate story, the one that makes me a name as big as Danny Lowenstein and defines me, the one that makes everything worthwhile. In the meantime, all I have to do is stay safe, and away from Becky Cooper. Then I'll be just fine.

Bessie was their carriage to the ball and Edwin, once again, their chauffeur. This time his *Songs of Sarajevo* cassette played Cat Stevens, and they all sang along to 'Wild World'. Rachel thought it could have been written for her.

As Bessie rumbled through the cobbled streets of Sarajevo old town, passers by looked on quizzically at this strange white beast. Inside, the would-be revellers were squashed in so tight they could barely move, limbs and torsos squeezed against each other like cruelly transported livestock. In a tiny pool of torchlight was Alija, deep inside *The Canterbury Tales*. He had been quiet since the trauma of their day with Dragan.

'Alija, is there a place on the planet you won't read?' shouted Becky above the music.

'I can't think of any, my dear, not off the top of my head, at least.' His accent was an odd Balkan attempt at English upper class.

'You sure you really understand that stuff?' She was genuinely perplexed. 'I mean, I did Chaucer at school, in the peace and quiet and with all the lights on, and I didn't get a word of it. And shit, English is my first language. It's gobbledegook, isn't it?'

'Each to his own, Becky; each to his own. The world would be a duller place, would it not, if we were all the same?'

Alija was not interested in trying to justify his favourite literature to the philistines he spent his days with. He was impatient to get back to the fictional, medieval lives that were such a distraction from the real ones he saw around him. He had discovered that the more a book demanded of him, the further he could run from Sarajevo. He didn't need films or television, he only needed words.

Bessie trundled on, Chaucer for Alija, 1970s pop for the rest of them.

'You wouldn't believe English is his third language,' Becky bellowed to Rachel.

'Fourth, actually,' Alija corrected her. 'Serbo-Croat, Russian, French, and then of course Shakespeare's beloved tongue.'

He kept reading with his exhausted torch, whose imported batteries had just another hour or two of life, while Rachel took the chance to snatch a look at Edwin's silhouetted profile. Aside from the dramatic baldness, there was a certain Roman nobility in his nose. He reminded her of the better-looking emperors she'd seen in history books. Edwin caught her stare.

'You know, I didn't really expect to be partying in Sarajevo,' she gabbled, scrambling for something to say.

'Well, you seem to have settled in all right. And I'm glad to see Becky's been leading you astray already.'

Leading her astray? Oh, not really, unless you count the minor transgression of almost helping a sniper select his victims. Becky's picture of Dragan had made the cover of *Newsweek* just as she'd predicted, while Rachel's story had only made the *Baltimore Sun*, but at least they'd had the grace to splash it. She had agonised about whether to include the personal trauma of her dilemma. Was it too subjective too soon, or the most powerful mechanism with which to convey the enormity of Dragan and his work? After lengthy consultations with Becky, she had opted for the 'I'. The piece sang, she knew it did. But what would Danny say when he found out? Kisses for a war criminal were one thing, collusion with a killing machine quite another.

'That sniper piece really was a cracker,' said Edwin.

'Really?'

It was the first time anyone had praised her journalism and she wanted to hug him. Even as she was writing it, she had begun to sense – without conceit – that reporting might be her gift as well as her ambition. She had found a voice too: although this piece was more personal than she felt entirely comfortable with, her style was less passionate and polemical than Danny's. Stark and simple, she would let her facts tell the story.

'Yes, really. I have a sneaking feeling even Danny boy liked it. Not that he'd have written it that way in a hundred Sundays. In fact, come to think of it, not that he'd have written it at all.'

'I wouldn't know. He's not talking to me. Even more than he wasn't talking to me already.'

'Well, that really is not talking to you! Give him some more time, Rachel. He will.'

She wondered how Edwin could be so certain, and whether she even cared any more what Danny Lowenstein thought of her.

The CBS party was as packed as Bessie, and just about as dark. The music was throbbing too, but infinitely louder, and naturally Seal had usurped Cat Stevens. Having dismounted from their armoured vehicle, the troops filed in and prepared to party.

'Drink?' Becky shouted in her ear as they pushed their way through the throng, a closeted, cosmopolitan mix of Bosnians and foreigners. Rachel watched some of them dancing on a parquet platform that had become sticky with spilt Sarajevsko Pivo, a local beer made with a wartime recipe of rice among other dubious ingredients. She had often thought the ritual of waving arms and legs around to music to be palpably absurd, but here, in the midst of civil war, it was more surreal than ever.

'Yeah, thanks. Whatever they've got.'

Soon Becky returned with a clutch of white plastic cups, warm white wine lapping over the tops.

'Right,' she said, after they had gulped a little down. 'Let's get out there and bop.'

Fuck Kaps if he didn't want to come. She was damned if she'd mope around all night pining for a married man. She began to dance frenetically, trying to unburden herself of him, not to mention Sarajevo's abominations. She needed to shed them on the dance floor like a pile of dirty clothes.

Soon she was perspiring heavily, no mean achievement in a sub-zero Sarajevo where the elderly had been known to freeze to death. The lights began to spin and blur. There was a smell that managed to combine new sweat, old perfume and bad alcohol.

While Becky hurled herself around, Rachel did her best to keep up. She felt more inhibited, unsure if she had even earned the right to be here.

It was half an hour before they agreed to take a break. Rachel, sodden with perspiration, found her way to the ladies' toilet, which had no paper, a broken seat and a noxious trail of urine on the floor. Pretty obviously, men had been using it too. She peed even so, but after three attempts to flush, gave up. Edwin walked in.

'Hello, Rachel,' he said nonchalantly.

'Oh, hi there. Um, did you know this is the ladies'?'

'Sure. Both are using both, if you know what I mean. It's a unisex sort of thing.'

He was more interested in inspecting the contents of a small plastic bag he'd just extracted from his waistcoat.

'Need some dope?' He sounded matter of fact, as if offering her a cigarette. Automatically, she shook her head. Edwin grabbed some and shoved it in his mouth, munching greedily. She had flirted with cannabis a few times but certainly never eaten it.

'It's good stuff, I promise you.' Clearly no one had taught him not to talk with his mouth full.

'I'll bet it is. Possibly a little later on.'

She pushed past him to re-join Becky, but was disappointed to find her dance partner had vanished. Suddenly Rachel found herself adrift in a sea of strangers. She couldn't let people see her standing there alone – they might feel sorry for her – so she squeezed past them purposefully.

When she finally spotted Becky, she was huddled on a leather couch in an alcove. It was the perfect hiding place. Something about her had changed: the laughing, happy-go-lucky Becky had been replaced by an altogether darker, sadder woman. Rachel didn't dare intrude.

Sitting next to her was Alija, his head still buried in *The Canterbury Tales*, as oblivious to the pulsating music around him as he was to the sounds of war. His weary Maglite, ever faithful but now in its death throes, struggled to shed light on the words of six centuries earlier. Rachel found herself looking back and forth between the two of them, Becky and Alija; one pained by her solitude while the other seemed to revel in it.

A little later, through a swirl of cigarette smoke, Rachel glimpsed the distant face of Kaps. He had come after all. She wondered if Becky had noticed or whether she should go and tell her. He towered above everybody else, unmistakable amid the close-cropped heads. He and Danny were, as so often, in earnest conversation.

Even Danny boy liked it, Edwin had assured her. But still Danny boy won't speak to me, will he? Did he sometimes watch her, as she was watching him? If so, no doubt he would have already castigated her preposterous dancing.

She wandered over to the bar and bought herself another drink.

'Wine?' asked the barman.

'Yeah.'

'Red? White?'

'Whatever it comes in.'

Soon cup after cup was flowing too easily down Rachel's throat. She thought she already had friends in Sarajevo, but now saw how premature she'd been. She couldn't go anywhere near Kaps and Danny, Becky was morose and Edwin was intent on getting quietly stoned. She had little choice but to drink, then drink some more. She noticed no particular effect until she sat down on a stool and almost missed it.

'Oops,' she said with an apologetic giggle to the barman, who towered above her. She guessed that, in another life, he might have played basketball for Yugoslavia.

'What's your name, by the way?'

'Budo.'

'Hey, I'm Rachel. All the way from America. I love it here. I love your country, I love your city.'

'Thank you.'

She was curious why he wasn't in a trench somewhere. Surely there could be no conscientious objectors here? This was hardly Vietnam, after all; not a war of choice but a struggle for survival. He had something though – a pretty Balkan face, a goatee beard and a stud in the lobe of his left ear which served only to confirm her suspicions of pacifism.

'Say, Budo, shouldn't you be out there fighting?'

'Is that any of your business?'

'No, it really isn't, but then again I'm a reporter, see. Another one of those nosey, snoopy reporter people.'

'Well, if you want to know, I am fighting, but I'm also trying to earn some money on my days off, to help my family. My father has been killed and so has my brother. That leaves only me, my mother and my sister.'

'I'm really sorry, I didn't mean to ...'

But he had already turned his back on her to serve another customer. That was it, she decided once and for all. It was time to grow up.

The music started hammering into her brain. She needed to get back to the hotel. All she craved was her bed, even a bed in an icebox, but there was no chance of leaving the party till the Bessie love bus made its return journey through the snow, and who knew when that was scheduled?

As her head entered a tailspin, she felt a tap on her left shoulder and hoped it was Becky. Shit, it was Danny.

'Oh, hi,' she said, smiling feebly.

'Hi. About that sniper piece, I just wanted to tell you I thought it was very nicely written.' So Edwin had been right, Danny boy *had* liked it. 'But you know what? The story itself absolutely stank. I mean, what in the name of God possessed you to go and talk to a murderer like that?'

Please no, she thought. She couldn't face an argument with him, not in this state. He thundered on regardless, sounding more than a little cut himself.

'It's just the sort of propaganda they love in Pale – a Serb hero like his forefathers, a defender of the faith, all that crap.'

'Actually, I called him "a calculating killer".'

'But don't you see? It's the picture of him looking out over Sarajevo like he has it at his mercy. It's all the quotes from him about the power he feels – the Serbs will adore all that. It sends a message to the world that they're still strong. Did it ever occur to you that's why they laid it on? What, you think out of the goodness of their hearts they wanted to help you with a cute story for your first few days in Bosnia to set you on your way?'

She felt woozy, like a boxer who's up against the ropes and taking too many blows. Normally she could have fought back, or at least tried to, but no arguments would come to her, let alone any words. Now he was preparing one last jab, the knockout punch.

'You know what, Rachel, I wouldn't put it past them to have spotted you when you went up and kissed old Karadzic. They saw a puppet who had just showed up in town and thought they'd pull your strings.'

Later he would remember this as the moment he had gone much too far and feel a certain shame. At the time he meant it, though. Who was this pretty neophyte, so wet behind the ears, to walk into Sarajevo and give succour to the Serbs? And as for Becky, she should have known better.

Rachel looked hard into those eyes she had thought were good when she first met him. They didn't dance around like they had done that day, they stayed on her, and now she saw how little there was in them, nothing kind or soft.

She stirred herself to stagger off the ropes and offer some resistance.

'You really are quite insufferable, aren't you?'

He was shocked, as if a blow from nowhere had caught him on the chin. He stood there for a few seconds and then, contemptuously, he walked away.

After Becky had watched him disappear into the crowd, she came over and put a hand on Rachel's.

'What's he been saying now? Has he been a prick again?'

'I just don't get it.' Rachel was absolutely determined she wouldn't cry, or that, if she did, he wouldn't see her. 'Why does he hate me so much? He doesn't even know me.'

Becky wasn't sure herself. The only reason she could think of was Danny's insecurity. She told Rachel he was paranoid that one day someone better than him would show up in Sarajevo, a new king of the jungle. He wasn't too worried about people like Kaps and Edwin – he knew they'd never be anywhere near as good as him, they didn't have his drive or his flair. In Rachel though perhaps he saw a rival who had the same passion, the same obsession, the same powerful way with words.

'Probably thinks it's best to strangle you at birth, which is what the Serbs say about the Muslims.'

Five songs later, the dance floor was even stickier, but Becky got Kaps on to it anyway, walking up to him and grabbing him by the wrist. She had abandoned her introspection and he his caution. At last they could simply dance, unhindered by war, unfettered by doubt. Each time a song ended, they both worried it would break the spell. Neither wanted a conversation, it would be too beset with hazards. Dancing was so much simpler.

At first they tended to avoid one another's gaze, looking instead at other dancers, or the DJ or the bar, but then, from time to time, they would allow their eyes to meet, and as the night wore on, to linger.

Becky ached for him to hold her. She had wasted endless hours of endless days just thinking of him, until sometimes she felt that he inhabited her. She would go to sleep longing for him, and dream of him so intensely it was a sadness to wake up. There was always the possibility it was mere infatuation, a carnal desire for on-the-road, down-the-corridor sex, but she hoped and feared it was something more profound. All she knew was that this one night she didn't care if he was married, she had to take him.

Kaps' body, so muscular and strong, was weak with the same desire, except that occasionally he saw other faces in the strobing disco lights: Judith's and sometimes Charlie's and Tom's as well. All the lyrics of all the songs they danced to seemed to dwell on infidelity. Even so, when Becky held out a hand, slippery with sweat, he reached to grasp it without hesitation, hungry for her. Ravenous.

• • •

By the time Bessie delivered them home at last, it was very nearly five in the morning. It had snowed heavily again while they were dancing, and Bessie slid and skidded her way back to the Holiday Inn, as drunk as the rest of them. Edwin, stoned, struggled to control her. As usual, without electricity, night-time Sarajevo was an unrelenting blackness. He only flicked on his headlights for a few seconds at a time – any longer might bring hostile fire from the hills – so he could hardly see a thing. After one wrong turn he almost headed for the frontline until Alija, stone-cold sober, corrected him with a sigh.

When Rachel finally staggered into room 331 it came as a huge relief to collapse on to her bed, however uncomfortable.

Barely three hours later, a barbaric knock jerked her from the deepest, most necessary of sleeps. Once again she was disorientated. Was it day or night, Bosnia or America? My, it was never normally this cold in Arlington! She curled her body back into a ball and waited for the world to go away.

The knock came again, even louder. Ignoring it was not an option.

'It's me – Becky. You've got to get up, there's a big story on, fucking big. Didn't you hear the bang?'

Rachel realised she was still fully dressed and even had her coat on. She was lying on top of her narrow hotel bed rather than in it. As she swung protesting legs on to the floor, the preliminary symptoms of a hangover were only just beginning to kick in.

'Oh crap.' Not her first big story now, please. She stumbled to the door just as Becky was about to hammer on it one last time before leaving her for dead.

'Hi, Becky. Um … what time is it?' she asked through lips that barely bothered to part.

'Just gone eight. Look, I know we only got to bed a few hours ago, but they've just mortared some sort of queue. Big fuck-off explosion which sleeping beauty slept right through, of course. Loads of dead, apparently. Shedloads. I'm going down there now with the others. You coming? You really ought to.'

'Right. Thanks. Okay then.' Waves of nausea washed over her, and the first darting pains in the frontal lobe of a dehydrated brain. Water. She needed lots of it. Fuck, there was none. Nothing running from the taps, and no bottles either. How could Becky, on as much alcohol and as little sleep, be so unfeasibly fresh? And how could she know anything at all of events in the world outside their hotel?

'We're going now, Rachel. You coming or not?'

'Um, can you just give me a couple of minutes?'

'Nope, I can't. It's now or never, as in today. Look at you, you're fully dressed. Even got your coat on, you pisshead.'

'But I ...'

'I know. You've got a stonking hangover. So have I. So has the entire Sarajevo press corps. And the last thing any of us needs is a massacre on too much booze and too little sleep. But the Serbs don't do their killing to suit our body clocks, or our drinking habits.'

She fumbled for a pen and notepad in the few seconds she had before Becky grabbed her hand and dragged her along the corridor like a recalcitrant prisoner. Down in the foyer, a cleaner mopped the floor while camera crews and photographers ran past her excitedly. Kaps, Edwin and Alija were waiting by the reception desk. They looked like they'd been there all night, knowing all along sleep would be a pointless project.

'Anyone seen Danny?' Becky asked.

'He's up there already,' said Edwin.

Rachel would find that was often how it was with Danny: he'd make his own way to a story, preferably well ahead of the others. He was with them but against them.

They headed, at a brisk walk, down to the car park, where the lumbering herd of white armoured cars was starting to move out in a mass migration.

'Any idea how many dead?' Becky asked Alija.

As always, it was a loaded question, pregnant with grim expectation. It could make the difference between a piece tucked deep inside the paper's foreign section, and a lavish front-page splash. If it bleeds, it leads.

'Who knows; minimum ten, maximum forty.'

'Holy cow.' Rachel cursed the inconvenience of a major story – perhaps a mega story – on the one day she was physically incapable of reporting it.

Bessie trundled towards the scene, only to stall halfway there. Her battery had died and Edwin couldn't resuscitate her, at least not immediately.

'Fuck it, let's walk the rest. It's only round the corner.'

Except they didn't walk, they ran, of course, darting left and right erratically in case of snipers on the morning shift. Rachel wondered if Dragan would be on duty, or whether he too had had a heavy night. She'd make a pitifully easy target. With alcohol curdling in her bloodstream, she was still drunk and disorderly in a war zone and certain she'd have to vomit fairly soon. A combination of pride and shame kept it down, but her lungs were ready to explode and a stitch was ripping through her waist. The sprint brought back high school track events where the only consolation was that last place couldn't get you killed.

The mortar had landed on a bread queue only a few minutes from the Holiday Inn. Often, the corpses had been cleared away by the time the press pack arrived, but not today. Rachel, Becky, Edwin and Kaps thought they'd got there late, but actually they were early, too early, and all around them was news in its rawest form – bleeding, screaming, dying news.

Rachel spun round in a 360-degree turn, and the bodies were everywhere – north, south, east and west of her. Her pounding head was filled with new songs of Sarajevo: wailing ambulances, screaming survivors, the anguished cries of loved ones and the moans of a nearby mosque. Noise; louder, more incessant than she had ever imagined it. Why couldn't they all be *quiet* for a while, just until she could get herself together? It was too much, too soon.

She stood stiffly like an actress who had frozen on her first night. Sarajevo: the biggest stage of them all, and she couldn't even remember her lines. The notebook she'd hastily stuffed into her back pocket stayed there. The rookie reporter had turned into nothing more than a mawkish voyeur, the worst kind of gawping rubbernecker.

She watched, transfixed, as passers-by piled casualties into the backs of cars, vans, lorries, noticing the clinical efficiency with which they did this, as though they were all part-time paramedics. She guessed that in Sarajevo you had to be. The improvisation was ingenious. Strips of corrugated iron, even a door, turned into makeshift stretchers. Scarves, stockings, socks became bandages. Yet often the victims who got helped first were simply those who screamed the most hysterically while those who were dying lay sprawled on the road in noble silence, the lifeblood trickling out of them, draining away along the gutter.

One young man was draped over the pavement railings, a neat round hole blown through the middle of his body so that Rachel could see out to the other side, like a conjuror's trick. Nearby she realised a couple of corpses had been decapitated. A missing head was in front of her, perched on an overturned stall and staring out as if ready to welcome back the customers.

The living ran around her, checking themselves to make sure they were really still alive, while the wounded tried to work out which bits of their bodies had disappeared – arms, legs, hands, feet, ears and eyes. Even if these people survived the day and went on to survive the war, they would have to cope with decades of disability. Might they even come to think it would have been better if they'd been killed outright on that snowbound winter's day when they ventured out for nothing more significant than a loaf of bread?

She caught a glimpse of Danny. He had already got all the quotes he needed and was about to leave. Her car crash of a conversation with him a few hours earlier was coming back to her. Had he really called her a puppet? Had she really called him insufferable?

She looked at Becky, busily hoovering the horror into her cameras. She would pick up the short zoom, snatch some wide shots, then let it fall again as she grabbed the long zoom for her close-ups. She stood, squatted and even lay on the blood-soaked road to achieve the various angles of death she required, ploughing through roll after roll of film, alternating between camera bodies so she could shoot both colour slide and black-and-white in order to maximise her sales. Her face was rigid with concentration: there was no longer any make-up, a lurid aberration wiped away as though it had never happened – like the disco itself, and the silly notion that anyone could ever just have fun in Sarajevo.

From the corner of one eye, Rachel glimpsed a young woman running in her direction, her mouth stretched so wide with pain that it looked oddly like a smile. She was holding aloft an arm, partially severed just below the elbow; it appeared that someone – perhaps even the victim herself – had shoved a piece of dirty cloth around it to hold back the spurting blood. The woman's skin was eerily translucent: Rachel wondered if it was the cold or the shock or the blood loss, or all of them combined. To her dismay, this grotesque casualty was approaching her, jabbering manically in Serbo-Croat. Rachel willed her to go to someone else, then looked around to see if Alija was available to help with a translation. He was only a few yards away, but sticking puppy-dog close to his master, Edwin, who wanted precise details – what time the attack had happened, where exactly the mortar had landed, how many people were queuing, how long had they been there, why they were queuing when they knew it was dangerous, would they queue again – so many questions, Edwin and Alija could have been there all day.

Rachel held up both her hands in a gesture that said: Look, I don't speak your language and I'm not a doctor.

Then what are you doing here? was the woman's silent accusation.

What am I doing? I'm doing nothing. I'm not even taking notes while you all die.

The woman wouldn't give up. She wanted to live, and like a drowning swimmer who'll grab hold of anyone in the water, she had seized on Rachel. She accepted now there was no point speaking to this useless foreigner, so instead she begged her with her eyes: For the love of God, do something, girl. Look, we are the same age, give or take a year or two. In another life, I could have been you and you could have been me, standing here, slowly bleeding to death in minus whatever-it-is-today degrees. I want to live like you are living. I want to drink and dance at discos like you do, and then have storming hangovers just like yours. Surely it can't be my time to die already?

But I've just arrived, I don't know the city, Rachel replied in their wordless dialogue of beseecher and beseeched. I haven't even got a bandage, let alone a car. I'm here to report on your plight, not to change it.

Well, so far you haven't even got your pen out.

In the end, both of them were saved by Edwin, who had finally stopped asking questions.

'Looks like this lady could do with a little help,' he said to Rachel gently.

'Yes, but …'

She was preparing to repeat her defence, this time aloud.

'Let's just bind this up a bit better.' He grabbed the exotic fawn Pashmina that was round his neck, a bargain buy from Peshawar on his way up through the Khyber Pass and into the wilds of Afghanistan. He tore it apart like a worthless rag and wound one half around the gory mess of her lower arm while the other became an impressive tourniquet below the shoulder. It was hard to believe that he'd been in the ladies' just a few hours earlier, chomping like a rabbit on his grass.

'Now, young woman, you hold it aloft above the heart – like so.' And with Alija effortlessly translating, he showed her how to keep the arm high, at an angle of 45 degrees, to staunch the blood loss. 'And then you also push down here.' He demonstrated how she should put pressure, with the fingers of her good hand, on the brachial artery.

'Okay,' said Edwin. 'The next thing is to get her to hospital, very fast indeed.' He looked around; the only vehicle he could see was a lorry laden with dead bodies. Its driver was running around shouting, but otherwise, like Rachel, contributing little of value. Edwin shepherded the woman up into the cab of the truck. Globules of her blood were dripping out through the Pashmina, her arm like a pipe whose lagging could staunch the leak but not quite stop it altogether.

'*Bolnica!*' he commanded the driver, in the voice with which he used to give orders to his troops. Rachel realised she wanted someone to boss her around as well.

'You coming too, Rachel?'

She looked up in vain for Becky. In the time it had taken to play out the drama of the bleeding woman, her new sister-in-arms had disappeared again. Lesson one of war reporting, she would think later: you might have friends, but when it comes to the crunch they'll look after themselves. Lesson two: they might even fuck you over.

Rachel didn't much want to go with Edwin, Alija and the bleeding woman. To board a lorry-load of corpses could only make her more likely to throw up very soon indeed. Still, she needed to find a way into this story and perhaps the best angles now were the survivors and the hospital where they were being taken.

'Great. Thanks.'

She almost had to sit on Edwin's lap. This was what working in a war zone was like, she guessed: spur-of-the-moment decisions that could take you anywhere, or nowhere. At least she had a purpose now. She felt more composed, though the colour refused to return to her face and, strangely, she was whiter than the woman beside them, who must have lost at least a pint of blood.

'You okay? You really look like crap, you know,' said Edwin, slowly getting his breath back as the truck lurched into first gear.

'Thanks again.'

'I mean, it's all right. All right to be … shocked.'

'It's more the hangover from last night, if you must know.'

'Oh yeah, of course,' said Edwin. 'We're all a bit the worse for wear. But I've been in this town all the way through and that … stuff back there; that was as bad as anything I've seen here.'

Stuff! Oh how the English had mastered the art of the euphemism, she thought. Except that, with Edwin, rage bubbled beneath the tranquil surface of his words.

'They really did it this time, didn't they,' he added abruptly.

'Who? The Serbs.'

Edwin laughed.

'Yes, the Serbs; of course, the bloody Serbs – and I hope they burn in the hottest part of hell. But not just them, Rachel: the world that scratches its spotty arse while a nation bleeds to death. Clinton, Major, Mitterand, Boutros-Ghali and the rest of them.

Non-intervention? You ask the people on the back of this truck what they think of non-fucking-intervention.'

She supposed he had a point. This was the lesson according to the Prophet Daniel, and after all, Edwin was one of his disciples. The mighty Daniel who had been and gone so quickly – serene, walking on water, walking on bodies. The messiah, knowing that he'd been right all along, that he'd told the world, and the world had ignored him, and that she – that hack, a minor one at that – had kissed the devil whose handiwork this was and allowed the puppeteers of Pale to tug her strings.

The woman started groaning and, with her good arm, rubbing her stomach.

'What's she saying?' Rachel wanted to focus on anything other than the puke pushing its way up through her throat.

'Oh, just that she happens to be pregnant as well as dying, that's all.'

Edwin stared at the cobbled road in front of them, unaware that it was one that would lead to bliss and utter ruin, and that at the end of it he'd never be able to forgive Danny Lowenstein.

8

Post-Liberation Baghdad, August 2004

Eight days after Danny's disappearance, the embassy and the various players in Washington – White House, State Department, Pentagon, FBI, CIA – agreed it was time for a televised appeal. The FBI experts said it should be filmed in Camille's room at the Hamra with a crew from al-Arabiya TV. Camille wore a hijab and no make-up and read from a carefully prepared text, written and re-written so many times it could have been a UN resolution. She was horribly nervous: her mouth dried out as she read it and she kept swallowing halfway through so that entire words vanished. It took three attempts to finish the recording.

'Just over a week ago, my brother Daniel Lowenstein disappeared in the village of al-Talha. I, his loving sister, am pleading now for anyone who has information about this disappearance to contact the Iraqi police or military. Please, please, please let us know if Danny is alive. He has always reported on this country fairly and objectively. He loves this country. And we love him. We miss him very much and we want him home. Please help us.'

She wondered if Danny would ever see it, and if he did what he'd make of her calling herself 'his loving sister'.

It was agreed that after the appeal she'd do a press conference for the other networks based on the same text. The TV crews set up in a semicircle on the steps of the hotel: ABC, NBC, CNN, CBS, BBC. There was an unseemly squabble between two of the cameramen about who should put which tripod where. Camille watched them jostle each other and briefly she feared there might even be a fight: perhaps it was just the way these people always were. By contrast, Rachel, Kaps and Edwin stood quietly amid the reporters. Becky was nowhere to be seen.

The cameramen insisted they needed the sun behind them, which meant Camille had it in her eyes. She had to squint to see anything much at all. Then the tapes were rolling and the questions coming at her quick-fire. Was she beginning to lose hope? Did she accept he was probably dead? If he were alive, who was holding him and why had there been no demands? Were the American Army and Iraqi interim government doing enough to find him? Camille, with Adi at her side, brushed aside most of the questions with the formula he'd suggested: 'I'm so sorry, but it's really too early for me to comment on that.' She was courteous and helpful, she felt, but noncommittal.

The last two questions were harder. What was Danny *like,* a Canadian radio reporter wondered. Don't ask me, she felt like saying, I only knew him in another life. Then a pretty girl at the back who introduced herself as Anne-Marie Lacroix from *Le Figaro* spoke up in a syrupy Parisian accent.

'I would like to ask if you have heard a rumour. There's a story there were some other people in a second car that got shot at by the gunmen but managed to escape?'

Camille froze. Then, without thinking, she looked over at the Junkies and searched their wrecked faces for a response.

The journey across the Tigris was only a short one but every driver of every car seemed to be a threat, every young man on every street corner a potential killer, lying in wait with an ambush or a suicide bomb. Camille was on her way to the embassy for a meeting with the ambassador, and as she was driven through Baghdad, her mind made a movie of Danny's disappearance: sinister gunmen, blood-curdling cries, unspeakable fear; her brother running for his life, masked maniacs chasing him until he stumbled and they could move in for the kill.

What if it had been her? What if a couple of the Lowenstein genes had been differently dispersed, and *she* had become the family rebel who eschewed a life of money and ran away to war? She looked either side of her in the car at the two heavily armed bodyguards with their steely, trained-killer demeanours. Munro, the inscrutable Scot, sat in the front, a pistol nestling on his lap. Harper was following on behind in another GMC with another bunch of tough guys. They weaved their way through traffic till they reached the Green Zone, once Saddam's sanctuary from the real Iraq and now America's.

The Green Zone was developing an ever thicker skin to protect itself, layer upon layer of concrete. Camille lost count of the check-points on her way in: manned, at different stages, by Peruvian security contractors, Iraqi police and American soldiers in M1 Abrams tanks, Bradley fighting vehicles and Humvees. This cocoon, 'the Bubble' as it was known, was protected by the original walls Saddam had built around it, now reinforced by an endless obstacle course of blast barriers, earth berms, coils of razor wire and tyre spikes. Even when they had penetrated all of this and shown their passes several times, Camille's entourage still had to fight their way through metal detectors, body scanners and sniffer dogs, a Russian doll of searches upon more searches, leading to a sign that read DO NOT ENTER WITHOUT PERMISSION OR YOU WILL BE SHOT.

When they were finally in, it was like landing on another planet, a calm oasis of palm-lined boulevards and lush lawns stretching out for several square miles.

Saddam's fortress was home to the new kings of Iraq. Around the Republican Palace, soldiers and contractors jogged, played volleyball, fooled around in the pool and sang karaoke over a few beers.

Inside, computers and cables, printers and photocopiers had been transported into the Palace's neo-Babylonian kitsch. Diplomats worked amid the grandiose colonnades, marble floors, gilded doors and chandeliers. Camille walked past the cafeteria, catching the smells from the kitchen that had once prepared food for Saddam and glancing at that day's menu: a choice of sirloin steak and baked potatoes, pizza margherita, cheeseburger and freedom fries (of course) or a healthier option of prawn salad. Much of the food was flown at vast expense all the way from America; the joke was each steak had its own seat on the plane. The US Army in Iraq might have lacked moral and political support, but a shortage of food would never be its problem.

When they finally saw the ambassador, it was – as Munro had gloomily predicted – a waste of time. He was pleasant enough, and offered them coffee, muffins and brownies, but while he oozed concern for Danny, it was clear he knew no more than they did.

On the way out, Adi took Camille aside.

'Sorry he hasn't been able to meet with you till now. He's been on a visit to Basra. The Brits have let it go to rat shit down there. Which doesn't mean to say we haven't let it go to rat shit up here as well, but it's nice to blame someone else once in a while.'

From the embassy, they drove a short distance to CPIC, the Coalition Press Information Center. The ambassador had suggested Camille should think about a second news conference later in the week, only this time for the entire press corps. She was daunted at the prospect and, in the hope of putting her more at ease, Adi had agreed to show her the hall where she'd have to speak.

CPIC was in the convention centre, a bland, low-rise modern building surrounded by swaying palm trees. Camille strolled around its sunlit atrium, glancing up at its dreary Ba'athist architecture and reading the notices on the walls. Americans – some uniformed, some not – were striding around, busily making the world a better place. She saw one talking to what looked like a couple of reporters, and she tried to picture Danny here, seeking information from contacts or perhaps haranguing them.

Adi introduced her to the CPIC desk man and got him to take her on a tour of the briefing room while he disappeared to find a colleague. She stood at the podium, looking at the rows of empty chairs and realised this was where the others must have been on the day of Danny's disappearance. If he'd gone with them he'd be safe and well, and she'd still be locked up in her own glass cage.

'Real sorry to hear about your brother, ma'am.' The sergeant looking after her had read her thoughts. He was swarthy and Latino, with 'Ramirez' imprinted on his uniform. She wondered if he'd ever even seen the Iraq outside this fortress and if he had to serve out there, whether he'd survive. 'I sure hope he's okay.'

'Thank you. Actually, we've been trying to piece together all the things that happened that day. There was some sort of press briefing here, right?'

'Quite probably. I'd have to check.'

He led her back to his office.

'What day would it have been again?' he asked, pulling out a file.

'The second.'

'Yeah, sure. General Peters.'

'Any chance you have an attendance list – you know, something that shows which reporters were there to hear him?'

'Media? No problem, ma'am.' Ramirez didn't question why she might need it. He dealt in freedom of information, the right to know, and had no interest in suppressing it. Besides, everyone understood that if the poor Lowenstein guy hadn't been killed already, he was a dead man walking. Ramirez sometimes thought about how his family would feel if it were him: he had a wife, a two-year-old kid and another on the way. Occasionally he got itchy to see some action, but most of the time he was content to have a desk job.

'Let's take a look.' He launched a search of the small office, brimming with the can-do spirit of America. 'Thing is, sometimes we take names and sometimes we don't. Kind of depends on if the boss guys ask for it.'

'Right!' Camille chuckled to imply she understood the way of these things, the capricious whims of management the world over.

'I wasn't on duty at the time, so I'm not quite ...'

He was rummaging through various heaps of paperwork and a couple of box files. It looked chaotic: soldiers trying to be secretaries and failing miserably.

'Listen, forget it. Don't worry, really. It's no big deal. I'll leave you my cell and maybe you could call if you find anything.'

Ramirez's rummaging continued.

'Hold your horses there! I think this may be it. Yup, this *is* most definitely it!'

He held it up triumphantly, a small victory in this particular theatre of war. Even from a distance, she could see that it was not so much a list as a jumble of names. The entries had been written in an anarchic series of scrawls across the page. The reporters clearly resented such petty bureaucracy and could barely be bothered to make the effort.

She grabbed it greedily from Ramirez and scanned through the biro-scribbled names, organisations and nationalities. One by one, she checked off the Junkies' names as Ramirez watched.

'Is there any way I could get a photocopy of this?'

'See no good reason why not, ma'am. Ain't exactly classified. Is there something specific there you're looking for?' He was vaguely curious but also keen to offer further assistance.

She lifted her eyes from the sheet of paper, peering at him over her spectacles like a judge.

'You know what, Sergeant, I'm not really sure.'

Before they left the Green Zone, they drove past Saddam's parade ground and underneath the spectacular vulgarity of the crossed sword arches, the so-called Hands of Victory. The enormous swords were said to have been made from melted-down tanks and guns from the Iran–Iraq War, and the fists holding them were replicas of Saddam's: they'd even put a plaster cast on his arm to make sure they got it right. As if to prove the old regime was truly dead, the driver – some old SAS buddy of Munro's – spun the wheel so that the GMC performed a neat figure of eight on the tarmac where once the dictator had inspected his troops.

''Course, if we'd gone for a ride like this in Saddam's day, he'd have had us up against a wall and shot.'

Camille was exhilarated. She remembered the television footage of him here, so proud and presidential, a trilby on his head, hunting rifle aloft, and for a few seconds she got it: she understood the rush her brother must have felt stepping into history in places like this. Danny would have hated her life of staring at computer screens, but she was beginning to envy his. Her mind galloped back again through the decades, back to Pittsburgh, and the choices they had made.

It had started as a normal Sunday. The church bells were ringing, insisting on the presence of the Lowensteins. Lukas was nervous; he was reading the lesson – Matthew, Chapter 26. He had read before, but it always gave him butterflies. All those people looking up at him from their pews, and that echo that bounced around the stone walls, so that if you made any sort of slip-up, you heard it coming back to you, again and again. Lukas hated fluffing his lines. He was in the new suit, delivered that week by Egleton's, the tailors. It was a little tight under the arms, but he felt good in it and, more importantly, he looked good. He was, officially, a pillar of the community.

They were at the front door waiting for Danny, who was always the last one out of the house; it was his petty protest and everyone had learnt to live with it. Today though, as the big clock in the hall ticked on, they sensed it was going to be different. Eliza called up, then Camille, then Eliza again. When no reply came back down to them, they were filled with foreboding and a grim certainty about what would happen next. Lukas, inevitably, lost his patience and strode off to get him, leaping up the stairs with giant strides so that he was hot and panting when he got to Danny's room.

Danny was sitting on his bed, reading. He had no intention of going anywhere.

'God is waiting for you, Daniel.'

'He's not my God.'

'Well, He's waiting for you anyhow.'

'I said, He's not my fucking God.'

The second slap followed straight after the first, one on either cheek. They were the slaps a woman might give a lover: not hard, not particularly painful, just enough to sting the skin and redden it slightly. Even so, Danny knew that in this moment everything had changed. He had thrown down the challenge, and now his father had accepted it and battle could commence. They had been dancing around his rebellion for too long. It was time, in Danny's eyes, for his family to takes sides, and, in particular, his sister. When he looked past his father, whose eyes bulged with fury, he could see her in the doorway. She was a beautiful young woman now, about to go to Princeton and with too much to lose. She stood there and watched them both, saying absolutely nothing.

After a slow drive back through the checkpoints and snarled-up traffic, they returned to the Hamra. As they weaved through its security chicane, Camille's mobile came alive.

'Hey, ma'am, Ramirez here again. From Public Affairs.'

She was surprised to hear from him, and assumed it was a question about the plans for her news conference at the convention centre.

'Oh yes, hi there, Sergeant. Listen, thanks so much again for all your help.'

'Sure, no problem. I was just calling about that briefing you were interested in. I managed to find out who was on duty.'

'Oh. Okay.' She didn't really see that it made a difference or why he'd bothered to ring, but Ramirez was trying hard to be helpful.

'Yeah, it was Sergeant Moore. Anyhow, I just found him and mentioned about you and that list. He said something kinda strange. Said some reporter fellow came by just before the curfew and asked if he could add a name to it; he'd forgotten to put it down at the time. Well, Moore remembers because he thought that was weird, like, why would you bother an' all? Especially media; I mean, they don't care much for our lists at the best of times. Just thought I ought to mention it, that's all.'

Camille was hanging on every syllable.

'I'm grateful, Sergeant. Who was it? Can you give me the name?'

'Moore says he didn't watch this guy write it down.'

'Oh, well, anyway that's …'

'But he does remember he was English, with an accent like the Queen. Oh, and bald. Bald as a baby's butt.'

9

Sarajevo, 1994

When the truck – part hearse, part ambulance, part press vehicle – rolled up at Kosevo hospital, Edwin jumped out and swept up the wounded woman, carrying her like a haemorrhaging bride. Edwin had once read an entire treatise by a Professor of Media Studies at Harvard entitled 'The Modern Reporter's Dilemma on Intervention'. It was about when and where it might be permissible for the journalist to 'cross the line', to participate in events rather than just to observe them. The danger, it was argued, was that journalists could distort the reality they report, as a time traveller who interferes with history might change the future.

These were not doubts that troubled Edwin. He was an ex-soldier, after all, and no stranger to 'reality distortion' as the Professor called it – the slaughter of young Iraqi conscripts in Kuwait, for example. This Sarajevo morning, Edwin had a notion he could somehow redress the balance of lives taken with lives saved, so if there were any lines to be crossed, he was happy to walk straight over them. Perhaps the good Professor from Harvard had never found himself standing in the middle of a massacre.

It looked more like a butcher's shop than a hospital. Blood was smeared over walls and floors, the raw red meat of open wounds waiting patiently to be closed and covered up – if one of the few hard-pressed doctors or nurses happened to be free. The stench was a noxious blend of blood, gangrene and disinfectant. Edwin took only shallow breaths.

There was none of the frenzied screaming of the marketplace. Instead a low collective moan filled up the wards and corridors of Kosevo, as though the patients were too polite to make more noise than was strictly necessary. The cries of agony came only when an operation would begin, either with the bare minimum of anaesthetics, or none at all. Electricity at Kosevo hospital was sporadic: it depended on generators, which in turn depended on fuel. Today the medical teams had to work in a murky half-light with torches, lamps and even candles. They stepped over their patients and tried, amid the gloom, to work out who was worth trying to save and who would only squander scarce resources before they died. Every so often, the men from the mortuary would come in to take away the dead, in order to make a little more space for the living. Even so, the hospital's corridors and hallways were crammed with beds, and some of its patients could only find room on the floor. They shivered as they waited to be treated. It was minus seven and the cold seemed crueller than anywhere else in Sarajevo.

'It couldn't get much worse here,' Edwin told Rachel. 'But I suspect the Serbs will make sure it does.'

The shattered windows, broken glass and familiar pox of bullet holes showed that, in Bosnia Herzegovina, hospitals were deemed to be legitimate military targets. After all, they represented life and hope, and Bosnian Serb command was determined to crush both.

Edwin made sure the woman got attention. He found a doctor who didn't look much older than a student. She wore not a white coat and stethoscope but a shabby denim jacket over a *Dark Side of the Moon* T-shirt that might have been older than she was, faded jeans and worn-out trainers. She was pulling hard on a cigarette.

On closer inspection, assorted specks and smears of blood were spattered all over her clothes, giving her the appearance an over-excited young artist who'd sprayed herself with paint.

'Excuse me, are you a doctor?' said Edwin. 'English? You speak English?'

'Yes, and yes again.' She clearly spoke it well, and with a transatlantic twang that suggested she'd spent some time abroad.

'Right. Great. Look, we've brought this woman in. She's pregnant. Needs help.'

The young doctor looked at Edwin as though he were a fool. Why else would anyone come to this disaster of a hospital? Without a word, she set to work on the woman's arm, unwrapping the drenched Pashmina and replacing it with proper dressings. Edwin watched so intently, he might have been a relative.

'How's she doing?'

'I don't know. It's too early.' There was no time for pointless speculation.

'She'll pull through though? And the baby?'

'I said, I don't know.'

Edwin persevered, attempting to kick-start a conversation.

'It's a nightmare down there.'

'Of course it's a nightmare.' She worked on without looking at him. 'Not for you, though.'

'Excuse me?'

Dr Amra Ismic, who thought reporters were vultures, had asked the other doctors to ban them from the hospital. They refused, saying the world had to know of Sarajevo's pain. Nonsense, she had argued, reporters are no use to us; they can't fight and they can't save lives so they should just go home. She despised them.

She left the pregnant woman in the care of a couple of nurses and moved on to other patients, a one-woman whirlwind, spinning around the blood-soaked wards and corridors. Something about her zeal compelled Edwin to follow her, wanted or unwanted. He had been thinking of a close-up piece about the woman he'd helped to save, but now he'd stumbled on another heroine. Of course! This photogenic doctor, a chain smoker just like him, with the weight of a violent world heavy on her shoulders, her face collapsing with exhaustion: she was the one his breakfast readers would fall in love with as they buttered their toast and slurped down soggy cornflakes before rushing off to catch the bus or take the kids to school.

Edwin let Rachel wander off to do her own thing. He'd become impatient with her wan expression, and couldn't help contrasting the two young women: one wrecked by too much work, the other by too much wine. Anyway, if Rachel was so desperate to be a reporter, she should get on with it. He'd tried babysitting her and he was bored of it. Sink or swim: it was the one thing the army had taught him that he didn't disagree with.

He held back for a while, watching from a distance the doctor's frenetic work rate. She could have been the last one on earth, tending to all its patients. Her hands were a blur – unfurling, cutting, wrapping bandages; taking pulses, holding a stethoscope to feeble hearts; filling syringes and injecting them into groaning, writhing people. It was when she shone a torch into the eyes of an unconscious schoolgirl, a rucksack full of textbooks still beside her, that Edwin decided to move closer and attempt an interview.

'So when did you start working here?'

'Not you again.'

She gently returned the girl's hand to where it had lain and moved on to an elderly man who appeared to have lost an eye. Edwin peered into a large, blood-filled socket, and could see no trace of one.

'Must be tiring work. What sort of hours do you put in?'

'What do you think? Strictly nine o'clock to five? Look,

I'm trying to save some lives. Now I don't know what you are trying to do, sir, but perhaps you could go and bother someone else.'

It came out with more vitriol than she'd intended. Edwin made sure he looked hurt.

'Look, I'm sorry. I don't want to be rude. I've had bad experiences with the press.'

'No, *I'm* sorry. You're right, I shouldn't be wasting your time. My name's Edwin, incidentally. The *Daily Telegraph* of London.'

'Amra, Amra Ismic.'

She said her name reluctantly and because universal standards of civility demanded it, even in Bosnia. Then she turned her back on him again and strode off to the operating theatre – what was, in effect, just another room, except with larger pools of blood puddled on the white-tile floor. He gave her five minutes before sneaking up to its double doors and easing them apart.

There were no surgical masks or gowns, no nursing assistants to hand her swabs and scalpels. This was do-it-yourself surgery, Sarajevo style. A couple of flak jackets lay in the corner, in case the shelling started. Amra had stopped smoking at last: even she couldn't delve into the chasms of another human being with a cigarette still in her hand.

This time her patient was a little boy, eight or nine, perhaps. A piece of jagged shrapnel was protruding from his intestines, waiting to be removed. Edwin could see Amra hunched over him and watched the ridges of her shoulder blades.

She used scissors to cut away the thick winter clothing that was stuck to the wound. With an implement that looked little more sophisticated than a pair of pliers, she tugged at the metal, yanking it out of him. When it came free, she almost fell backwards with the momentum, and then rushed to stem the spurting blood. Finally, having cleaned the wound as best she could, she pulled together folds of bloody flesh and stitched them up with a needle and thread. She looked like a tailor who'd wandered into an abattoir by mistake.

It was only now, as Amra turned towards the door, that she saw him skulking in the shadows.

'Get *out*! Get out of here right now!'

'But –'

'I told you before, we don't need you people here. Now get out or I throw you out.'

She would have screamed at him, but she couldn't upset the patients.

'Okay, okay. I'm sorry if I've intruded. Maybe we could just … when you've finished, we could just talk for two minutes. Literally.'

It wasn't quite the truth. To get enough for a full-page spread, he would need half an hour at least. How many patients could she treat in that time, how many lives could she save? It didn't stop him asking.

'I will think about it.' She said it to get rid of him. She wouldn't stop till dusk, and he'd be long gone.

Ten hours later, darkness had long since closed the eyes of this deathly day. Dr Amra Ismic was conceding that if she stayed at work much longer she'd fall asleep on her feet, quite possibly with a surgeon's knife in her hand. She pulled on a scruffy blue anorak and was walking out through the hospital entrance when she saw him sitting, almost asleep himself, shivering in the cold.

'You don't give up, do you?' Amra lit another cigarette with the barely surviving end of an old one. From death, new life.

'Two minutes, I told you.'

'Yeah, or two hours. I know you people. You're not the first reporter I've come across, Mr …'

'Edwin, just call me Edwin. I did introduce myself before.'

'You did. I apologise. And I'm sorry I shouted. It's just that …'

'I got in your way and I had no right. You're doing an amazing job here, and I just want the outside world …'

'Oh please don't say that. Anything but that.' She sat next to him on a row of six plastic seats bolted uncomfortably together. 'You want to know my training? A couple of years, that's only half the course. Before this war, I never operated on anyone for real. Now look at me. I cut people up all the time, and I stitch them back together. God knows how.'

'You're still performing miracles in there.' Edwin needed her to continue. From saying nothing, she was talking in soundbites. His readers would lap this up. At first he wrote nothing down, for fear of scaring her away. He would have to remember what she had said and fill in – with a little journalistic licence – the bits that he forgot.

'Hah! Miracles! If only I believed in them. You want something to write in your paper? Every day I have to decide who to try and save, and who—'

'To let go?'

It was another Edwin euphemism.

'To let die, yes. A day like today? Not enough of us in the hospital. So I – a medical student, remember – I have the power of life and death. I'm like the Serbs: I decide who should live and who should die. God knows what it does to me. When all of this is over, I …'

Edwin dared to slip out his tiny pocket notepad, about the size of a policeman's. As unobtrusively as possible, he started filling it with shorthand squiggles, struggling to keep up with her.

'But, Amra, you couldn't work any harder than you do. Look at the time now, and you've been here since …'

'Since six this morning. You know why? I have this crazy idea that if people are dying because we don't have enough time to treat them, then I'll just make more time. The more hours I work, the more lives I can save.'

'You'll burn yourself out.'

'Look into my eyes. Am I not burnt out already?'

He could see she was right.

'Cigarette?' He offered her one of his Marlboros, so much better than the cheap Drinas that had her hooked. She inhaled deeply, trying for a hit.

'I know, I smoke too much. It stops me getting hungry. Even if I had time to eat, there's no food here.'

Edwin offered to buy her a meal at the Holiday Inn.

'No, no. Not there. I don't go near that place any more, not with those reporters.'

He couldn't help wondering what the press corps had done to scar her so badly.

'Then let me drive you home. It's the least I can do after keeping you here so late.'

'I always walk. It clears my head.'

'If a sniper doesn't shoot it off.'

They both knew it wasn't especially funny, yet she laughed for the first time that day, and infectiously, so that Edwin started laughing with her.

He dropped her home anyway.

It was up a winding, narrow street near the Lion Cemetery and more like a bomb shelter than a house. Amra's parents lived in fear of a Serbian shell ripping into them from a cloudless Sarajevo sky, and they had sandbagged up the windows. No wonder the city was so quiet when the shelling stopped: most of its population were barricaded into their homes or living in cellars. Edwin thought this was what it might have been like to endure the Blitz, living with the daily possibility of sudden, violent death in your own living room or kitchen, or even as you bathed or slept, or sat on the toilet and pondered the world's insanity. At least with a cemetery round the corner, they wouldn't have to take you far to bury you.

'They want you to stay and eat,' said Amra helplessly, after a brief, whispered conversation with her parents on the doorstep. 'For some reason, they are grateful you brought me home. They say you are an English gentleman. I tried to tell them you're a reporter.'

They were, he guessed, only in their late forties, yet the daily trauma of their lives had turned them into premature pensioners, their hair greying by the week, their faces shrivelled up and wrinkled. There was an absence in their eyes, as if their minds were elsewhere, as if in fact – like so many in Sarajevo – they had already died.

'Oh no,' said Edwin. 'Please tell them I couldn't possibly.'

'I did already, and I meant it, but they don't take no for an answer. Bosnian hospitality, it's so stupid.'

Despite Amra's energetic protestations and his half-hearted ones, he took off his snow-clogged hiking boots and walked in his thermal socks through the dark, narrow hallway and into the tiny sitting room. A wood stove burnt weakly in the corner: they had almost no fuel for it and just a few embers glowed, the only source of heat in a house where the temperature was, he guessed, much as it had been at the hospital: well below zero. Nearby there were empty shelves: Amra's parents had no doubt long since burnt their books for a few degrees of extra warmth.

The room was a shrine to Amra, the only child, the entire reason for their continued existence. Edwin toured the pictures that seemed to fill every inch of wall space, all of them of Amra: baby, infant, schoolgirl, cocky teenage rebel, brilliant medical student and now Bosnia's surgeon-general.

They talked for a while, Amra the interpreter on top of everything else, facilitating polite conversation between the visitor and her parents. After a while they scurried off to prepare some cevapcici. Edwin and Amra were left alone.

'Listen, Amra: I really do want to write about you for the paper. You're an inspiration.'

He might as well have told her a joke. The locked jaw of her sadness broke into a flicker of a smile, which in turn became a grin, and then that belly laugh again, like the one she'd made at the hospital. He wondered how often this house, this city, had heard Amra Ismic laugh. He looked through to the doorway of the tiny kitchen, cloaked in orange Formica. Amra's mother was standing there and he could have sworn he saw her smile as well. What was she thinking? That this young man from England had brought some joy back into her daughter's life – or could do, at any rate?

'And that's exactly why you're not going to write about me, because you'll come out with things like that. Sentimental bullshit.' She was right, of course, he would. Then again, he was certain it was true.

Amra turned to the window, and he saw a shudder from the shoulder blades he'd admired in the operating theatre.

'I'm sorry. I didn't mean to make you cry.'

'Please don't say anything nice about me. I'm not an inspiration, I'm a failure. Go and put that in your paper.'

'Amra, that's ridiculous. You're the most –'

'Shut up. If you want to write, you have to listen. Failure – you don't even understand the word. No one dies because of you. When *you* fail, it's a bad story. Perhaps they don't put it in the paper or the readers don't want to read it. Big deal. When *I* fail … what happens? A life ends. Could be a young woman like me, gone just because I fuck it up. Because I didn't read all the books, because I didn't have the time, because I was a lazy student. The beautiful baby, the brave soldier, the sweet old lady: they're all my failures.'

She started crying, softly, for she could not let her parents hear her. Even in her own home, she worked to spare others from pain.

Edwin was no longer pretending to himself he was here as a journalist. He would write the article, but what he really wanted was to hold and comfort her, to wrap his arms round her unfed body. For the moment he dared go no closer, but sought another way.

'Actually, I *have* failed, if that makes you feel better.'

'I doubt that.'

'No, really. I was a soldier. In the British Army. Three years ago, we were kicking the Iraqis out of Kuwait. Desert Storm, remember?'

'Of course.'

'The night we invaded, we killed dozens of them, mostly conscripts. I was commanding a tank. We had thermal imaging – basically we could see people at night, little specs of blurry green like space invaders. I only saw them for real when I got out of my tank the next morning. They were young men just like me. Their bodies, Amra: they were just black skeletons, with bits of skin and uniform hanging off them.'

Edwin paused as the vision returned to him, the charred skulls with clenched teeth and then the worst sight of them all, the one he knew would be with him till he died himself. He had found him curled up at the bottom of a trench, an Iraqi teenager in a man's uniform, most of his head and body burnt, his stomach open and death on its way to fetch him.

'He was just a boy, for fuck's sake, and in the most unimaginable pain. He was whispering something to me. I knelt down to listen. You know what he was saying? "Kill now. Please kill now."'

Edwin remembered looking at his men, who in turn had looked at him. He had touched the pistol on his hip. Could he just put down this kid, 'destroy' him like a vet destroys a dog? What would it be – a kind of battlefield euthanasia, or a war crime? His corporal had come up to him: 'Put him out of his misery, sir?'

'So what did you do?'

'Just held the poor bugger's hand – the coward's way out. I cried and cried, right there in front of my men, in front of a dying enemy soldier.'

'And that's why you left the army?'

'How could I stay? My first sight of war revolted me, and that's not what they call an acceptable reaction. The army was what my father did, and his father before him, but the Garland family trade was not for me. Anyway, I always hated authority. It's why I shave my head. The army were always nagging me to have shorter hair. This was my way of resisting them – if I couldn't grow it any longer, I'd get rid of it completely.'

'So that's when you became a journalist?' She gave him a coquettish tilt of the head he hadn't seen before.

'Told my colonel I wanted to be a writer not a fighter. Pretentious, huh? But I wasn't exactly a subversive. I mean, the *Daily Telegraph* – I couldn't have found a more Establishment paper if I'd tried. And of course they sent me straight back to war. I just swapped one battlefield for another. I sometimes wonder what's more immoral: being paid to watch death or take part in it.'

He looked up at an old clock above the fireplace.

'Oh shit,' he said.

'I beg your pardon.'

'Sorry, it's just that I've missed my first deadline. I got carried away.'

He had not filed a single word on the biggest story in Sarajevo for weeks. Amra was right: it was a failure, a catastrophic one by the unblemished standards of his career to date, but compared to letting someone's life slip from you, it meant nothing. He got what she was saying. By understanding how light was his burden, he began to appreciate the excruciating weight of hers.

'Thank you,' she said and, to his surprise, kissed him on the cheek. As she brought her face to his, too briefly, he could smell a sweet scent, not of perfume but some fragrance innate to her skin and all of her own. It was intoxicating.

When he got back to the Holiday Inn that night, Edwin filed for the second deadline and was castigated for missing the first. He told the night editor something had happened which would make a separate story; the night editor said it had better be a fucking good one.

He wandered along the pitch-black corridor to find the Junkies and felt a pressing need to talk about her. He was so different from her, and yet so much alike. When he tried to clarify for himself what it was they had in common, he realised – a little to his surprise – that it was death that preoccupied them both. It was a strange reason to fall in love.

From the noise spilling out of Becky's room – just five doors away – he could tell the others were coming down from the big story high. He let himself in without knocking. The only light flickered from half a dozen candles dotted around the room, wax dripping down, white puddles forming on the grim, dark wood of the Eastern European furniture. On the walls were maps and lists of phone numbers in marker pen, and prints of Becky's more memorable pictures. In the midst of them, her Australian sunset, the first photograph she'd ever taken.

Kaps was with her, perched beside her on the bed. Danny was on the grey sofa that had a long tear in its Draylon cover, exposing the cheap foam beneath. Rachel had insisted on taking the floor, as if she knew her place in the pecking order of Sarajevo's press corps. Spinoza was there as well, and a couple of Australian cameramen – *all* Sarajevo's cameramen seemed to be Australian – called Shark and Hacker. They still wore the various thermals, fleeces, coats and Puffa jackets they'd had on all day, and they were passing around the latest in a long line of joints. The remains of its predecessor lay on a side plate commandeered into service as an ashtray. A permanent cloud swirled around the room. Even Rachel, in search of relief, had decided to smoke as much as came her way. She smiled at Edwin dreamily and he felt guilty about abandoning her.

'Hey, Rachel. How d'you get on?'

'Great, thanks. Some really nice quotes up at the hospital.'

Nice? Nice quotes from dying people? He wondered what Amra would have made of that.

'Glad it worked out. Sorry we got kind of … split up.'

He told them about Amra, and what he planned to write about her. Even as he described her to them, the warmth returned.

'You sound a bit smitten.' Becky never liked to take him seriously, especially when that was how he took himself.

'She's an amazing character, that's all. Doesn't mean I have to …'

'Fuck her?'

'Fancy her, I was going to say. Do you always have to be so bloody basic? Anyway, somehow I managed to miss the first edition. London said they lived with the wire copy. Probably yours, Kaps; probably preferred it anyway.'

Becky jumped up, obviously stoned.

'Ooh, that's a good idea. Let's see, Kaps, what was your intro?'

He looked embarrassed, certain they'd find it uninspired.

'Oh, I can't remember really …'

'Come on!'

'Just something bland like "Eleven people were killed in Sarajevo when a mortar crashed into a bread queue."'

'Edwin?'

'I don't know; something similar, I think. "Sarajevo witnessed another bloody massacre yesterday when 11 ..." blah, blah, blah.'

Rachel was relieved she wasn't even asked for hers. Becky had already turned to Danny.

'And now, the master.'

He shook his head. 'This is a crap game.'

'You know you want to!'

'Just fucking tell us, and let's move on,' said Shark, who didn't understand these print people at all.

'Oh, all right,' said Danny. 'I think it was: "Ejup Nezigovic didn't need any bread, he was saving a place in the queue for a friend." There. Satisfied?'

'You see?' said Becky. 'Genius. Hook 'em with the individual.'

Edwin clapped his hands together.

'And that's exactly why I want to write about this doctor. Something different for a change, *someone* different.'

'Get you!' sneered Becky.

'Don't you ever stop to think: what does another massacre really mean to our readers? Why not try and tell them what this place is really like for once, through someone who goes to the limit every day? This is a story – well, it's about the nobility of the human spirit.'

'I take it we're talking about your new girlfriend here?' Becky collapsed into a fit of giggles.

'Oh, piss off and roll another fucking joint, will you.'

'Best idea you've had all day,' said Kaps. For all of them though, there was only one drug that really gave the buzz, the rush, the hit that they all craved: the story drug, and that day's news had certainly done the trick. The dope itself didn't give them a high so much as help them come down from the one they were already on.

When friends would ask them what it was like in Sarajevo, and they attempted to explain, they'd be met with looks of disbelief. A 'buzz'? How could the slaughter of human beings possibly give you a 'buzz'? Which was why the Junkies preferred not to begin the conversation in the first place, because they knew exactly where it would end.

Edwin dragged deep on the last of the old joint, soggy with the saliva of all their mouths.

'What the fuck are we all doing here, anyway? I blame my parents. It's all because my fucked-up father wanted me to be a soldier.'

'My fucked-up father wanted me to work for his fucked-up company,' said Danny.

'My fucked-up father wanted me to stay at home,' said Rachel.

'My fucked-up father didn't care what I did, he was too busy getting drunk and throwing saucepans at my fucked-up mother,' said Becky, not to be outdone.

They all looked at Kaps.

'Actually, I love my father. And my mother. And I'm pretty sure they love each other.'

'Oh dear Lord, that's *disgusting*,' said Becky. 'You're normal!'

'So why are you here then, Kaps?' asked Danny, who had slipped down from his chair and was stretched out on the floor, not far from Rachel. It was strange for her to see him stoned and it didn't endear him to her any more. 'I mean, okay, so you have the perfect parents and the perfect family at home, wife and two little cherubs, all nuclear and lovely. Domestic fucking bliss.'

Rachel thought back to the way Danny had interrogated her on Snipers' Alley. Why did he keep asking people what they were doing in Sarajevo? Was it only him who had an unquestioned right to be there? Even the cannabis couldn't soften him.

Kaps inhaled deeper and longer than he meant to. It sent him reeling, and he had only a few moments of lucidity left before he disappeared.

'Domestic bliss? Let me tell you, there's nothing more tedious on the planet.' He slipped the joint on to Becky who was almost comatose beside him. It passed slowly between their fingers which, for a moment, intertwined.

No one said anything for a while, but Becky was clear she wanted to keep talking about something. Anything.

'So then, what else?'

Kaps adored her for the way she asked it. He thought about those suburban dinner parties in Brighton where a black hole in the conversation was greeted with horror, and panic-stricken guests would grab hold of the nearest life jackets – those safe, familiar topics of crime, education and property that could always be relied upon to save them. Here in the Holiday Inn though, no one worried what to talk about. They just said 'what else?' because the important thing was to be together.

They rambled on for an hour before being overwhelmed by the sleep that had been so cruelly interrupted earlier that day. It could have been a week ago.

'Bastard, bastard Serbs,' Becky drawled as the dope brought flashbacks. The severed limbs and dying children had not disturbed her at the time because, as usual, the lens had been her saviour, protecting her better than dear old Bessie. Now though she saw dying people whose faces she had shoved her camera into, assaulting them with the whirring motordrive. The drugs swept her into a dream about how it would be if they had turned the tables, treating her as the victim to be pitied, not them. 'Poor love, what a tragedy,' they were saying. 'She can't get a proper man, you know, though she'd be happy to make do with a married one. She'll never get married herself, of course – well, only to her pictures.' And with skin peeling from their faces, and arms and legs dropping off their bodies, they were snap-snap-snapping away at her, grabbing that cover photograph of this most horrendous of Sarajevo casualties.

Rachel dreamt too, except that she was a sniper, picking up her high-velocity rifle and poking it out of the window of her box bedroom back in Arlington. Across the road, a pregnant woman walked, carrying a bag of shopping, admiring the carefully manicured lawns on either side of her. It was the woman from the massacre, Rachel realised, the blood still dripping from her. Her bloated belly filled the telescopic sight, and within the crosshairs Rachel could now see a foetus, as if it were part of a scan. She softly squeezed the trigger, surprised at how little pressure was required, absorbing the shock of the recoil with her shoulder. She watched the foetus explode into fragments of pink flesh.

The paper ran all 3,000 words of Edwin's feature on Amra. 'Sarajevo's Dr Miracle', it called her, much to his disgust. It was crass and clichéd, the handiwork of some glib sub he imagined commuting from Carshalton. Still, apparently the piece had grabbed everyone from his readers to his editors. They all wanted to get to know Amra Ismic a little better and so, if he were honest, did he.

Edwin sat in his room at the Holiday Inn, paralysed with cold. He had wrapped himself in thermals, two shirts, two sweaters and a coat, so many layers in fact he could barely move. He had lost his woolly hat, and what body heat he had was fast disappearing from his head. He opened a tin of Spam to cheer himself up.

On a bad satphone connection, he spoke to his deputy foreign editor, an endlessly cheery Yorkshireman called Jake who was close to retirement and always whispered conspiratorially as if someone were eavesdropping.

'Really good story. You won't believe the reaction! We're getting calls and letters all the time; people want to give money, send medicine, take in patients. You've really hit a nerve, or she has.'

'Glad you liked it.'

'We bloody loved it. Special praise from the editor himself, by the way. Said his wife was sobbing. Singled you out for despatches at the morning conference. So the thing is, we'd like a follow-up, even a whole series on her. You know – One Woman's War, that kind of thing. Yes, One Woman's War – come to think of it, I rather like that.'

Edwin could only imagine Amra's reaction.

'I'm really not sure she'll play ball.'

'Listen ...' Jake's voice became even softer. He could have been passing on state secrets. 'What you need to remember is that Bosnia is boring people rigid, myself included, if you must know – and I'm on the bloody foreign desk! It's supposed to be my bread and butter! Bosnians, Serbs, Croats, Bosnian Croats – too many sides, fighting in too many places with unpronounceable, unspellable names. And for far too fucking long.'

'Well, I'm very sorry; I'll go out there and tell them to stop right now.'

'You know what I mean. People like your little Florence Nightingale bring it home, make it live.'

'She's not a Florence Nightingale. For a start, she's a surgeon, not a nurse.'

'Anyway, go and see her again, would you? Another couple of thousand words for tomorrow, please. And do ask her about the series, eh?'

He switched off the satphone. The Spam had failed to fill him up so he cut himself a slice of Edam cheese with the longest blade of his Swiss Army knife. Then he started shaving his scalp in cold, brownish water that trickled from his tap. He found it curiously therapeutic. It was like cooking and praying, the other activities that helped him cope. And falling unexpectedly in love.

See her again. It was all Edwin had thought about, and now someone had asked him – no, *ordered* him – to, there was every reason to go back to her, this woman who was starting to consume him.

Until now, he had looked at his life as the pieces of a broken kaleidoscope which never formed a pattern however much he played around with it. What had he been doing, snatching away young lives in the desert? Who had given him the *right*? And if he was so appalled by what he'd seen, why had he come straight here – to Sarajevo – to see some more? There were times when it disgusted him, this adopted trade of his: at least Bosnia's fighters had something they believed in, whereas he had nothing except the possibility of a front-page splash. He couldn't have discussed any of this with Kaps or Becky, and certainly not with Danny, but Amra had listened and understood, because she was the same.

Once he might not have given a second glance to her sickly, sallow face if he had passed it in the street. Now though, he cherished hers as a beauty higher than that of any model. He wanted to do so much for her, with her, to her. He needed to be back with her now, this minute, in the hospital or her home, anywhere would do.

The razor slid gracefully across him, clearing a path through the shaving foam like a plough through snow. It eased its way down the gentle slopes of his scalp until, eventually, they were satisfyingly smooth. He dabbed the skin dry with a small towel.

Who cares for the carers, he asked himself; who heals the healers?

At first he could not find her anywhere. Edwin searched the wards and overcrowded corridors until he heard a scream. Of course. She was back in the 'operating theatre'.

The nurse outside spoke little English but signalled it was an amputation with a crude sawing gesture beside her leg. Edwin flinched.

'Who?'

'Girl, little girl. Not anaesthetic.'

Another scream, far worse than the first. It drilled right through him. Forty minutes later, the door swung open and Amra emerged, yanking off the green surgical cap so that her hair could spill loose, then pulling away the mask. She saw Edwin and started talking to him at once, her words babbling out.

'She was in so much pain. Too much pain.'

'You did your best.'

'I felt like I … like I was torturing her in there.'

'You were saving her …'

'She's five years old. She doesn't know what this war's about, she doesn't have a clue. All she knows is that there's this mad woman who cuts away at her.'

Edwin could see now this wasn't false modesty; this might be someone on the verge of a nervous breakdown. In any other hospital in the world, they'd have tactfully suggested she take a break at home or arranged some counselling, but not at Kosevo. Here it was all hands on deck, always. It didn't matter how screwed up you were, or even if you were going very slightly mad. If you could wield a knife and hold it steady, they were never going to let you rest.

They found a corner of the corridor with two half-broken chairs side by side and took the risk of sitting on them.

'"First do no harm." That's what the Hippocratic Oath says, you know.'

'Well, you're not doing any harm, of course you're not.'

'Sometimes I think I am though.'

'You think they'd rather die? Wouldn't you want someone like you, if the only other choice was death?'

'Maybe, but that girl in there, she reminded me of myself at her age. I could see myself in her eyes, but even so I thought maybe for once it would be kinder to let her die. I wanted so much to make her pain go away, I'd have done anything to stop those screams, even if it meant …'

'Killing her?'

'Wasn't that what you told me you thought about, in the desert? Anyway, you've come back to write some more about me, I suppose. Let me guess, Sarajevo's Florence Nightingale.'

'Something like that,' he said sheepishly.

No, I've just come to get to know you better. He was too English and embarrassed to say it, even if she'd just sawn the leg off a five-year-old girl without enough anaesthetic and they both knew there were worse things in the world than embarrassment. Sarajevo couldn't afford the niceties of 'dating' or 'playing cool' or 'hard to get'. There were no cinemas or theatres to ask a girl out to and no time in any case; those were the luxuries of peace. In this city, prospective lovers might be dead by dusk.

Amra looked at him from sunken eyes. He wondered if any surgeon would ever be able to remove the sadness from them.

'Listen, I'm still working. Come back later when I've finished work.'

'You *never* finish.'

'I will tonight. Promise. Cross my heart and hope to die.'

And at last he allowed a little of the passion to spill from him.

'Oh, don't say that, Amra, don't ever say that.'

When he walked her from the hospital to Bessie, moonlight fell upon them, and Sarajevo's power blackout lit up the stars. She was shivering and he insisted she wear his Gore-Tex. He laughed when it swallowed her up.

'Thank you.'

'For the coat?'

'No, for talking to me. Even if you *are* a journalist.'

'Why is it you hate us so much?'

'Them, not you,' she said. 'I hate them because they use us. Because to them we're just a story, however much they say they care.'

'But there's something else?'

'Okay, and also because they can leave.'

'So could you. I could get you out.'

He imagined himself smuggling her across Mount Igman, a stowaway inside Bessie, hoodwinking the Serbs who would have gladly raped and butchered her had they known. She smiled at him, and wrapped her hand over his as it clutched the gear stick.

'I would rather die here than leave my city.'

'You won't die. You'll get through this and when there's peace, you'll have babies, and one day they'll be proud of everything you did.'

Her street was an ice run and he slowed Bessie by crunching down through the gears, and only dabbing the brakes now and then.

'I suppose you want your jacket back?'

'Keep it. I've got another one.'

'You're so kind. You know, you give me hope.'

They held each other in their eyes, unashamedly. Neither of them could think of any more to say that didn't sound too little or too much. He smelt that scent again – of her, not some cheap perfume – and it overwhelmed him. He could wait no longer, he had already waited long enough. He moved his face to hers and then his lips. Amra's were closed at first – not pursed, just closed – and he let his rest upon them. It would have been enough for Edwin, but then, after several seconds, her mouth opened up, gently, magically.

'You give me hope, too,' he said when they finally stopped kissing.

• • •

The next couple of weeks were the happiest of Edwin's life. When he wasn't filing, he would pick her up from the hospital at night and drive or walk her home. Sometimes they would talk into the early hours, holding, cuddling, kissing, each night more extraordinary than the last.

Amra liked Edwin so much. He was different from the others, kind and troubled and able to speak directly to her soul. And yet she couldn't afford to give herself away again, not with all her work at the hospital: it would be too much of a distraction. Her last lover had overwhelmed her, and almost destroyed her. And now he had decided to come back to her, just as she was on her feet again, just as she had found this new English friend. It wasn't fair, in fact it was cruel. Poor Edwin; she knew she ought to tell him, but where to even start?

Edwin, meanwhile, wanted only to nosedive into love with her and he didn't care how fast was the descent.

It was around ten each morning that the madness usually began. Even so they still called them the Five O'clock Follies, in honour of the daily press briefings in Vietnam where hapless American spokesmen would try and make out that, despite appearances, black was white, death was life and humiliating defeat was actually inspiring victory. In Sarajevo, Danny always said it was not the United States this time but the United Nations who were the great dissemblers.

'UNPROFOR are delivering food to all who need it,' he would say mockingly. 'The safe havens are safe, Dr Pangloss has just become UN Secretary General and everything is for the best in the best of all possible worlds.'

Later in that week of the massacre, Danny led the Sarajevo press corps past the sandbagged defences of the UN headquarters and into the bunker of its briefing room. Outside, snow-white armoured personnel carriers were parked in a row, as useless to

Sarajevo as exhibits at a war museum. Inside, a suave and olive-skinned Italian with a goatee beard called Alessandro Mendini was fielding questions. 'Alessandro Mendacious' Danny called him.

'Well, it's hard to be precise about the source of the detonation,' Mendini explained as the briefing began. The reporters were sitting in a five-deep semicircle of chairs. Danny always chose one in the third row, off to the side. The spokesmen – and the UN got through plenty of them in Sarajevo – came to know where danger lurked and would dread the Lowenstein ambush from Row Three. He didn't so much ask questions as hurl them in like hand grenades. As the self-styled commander of the Something Must Be Done Brigade, he was a guerrilla leader, ready to blow up all half-truths and platitudes. If he could shoot down the oleaginous UN spokesman too, so much the better.

'Excuse me, but by "detonation" d'you mean the mortar that just took 11 lives?'

'I mean detonation.'

'And you can't say it was the Serbs who fired it?'

'Our crater analysis is inconclusive.'

'I see,' said Danny, the tip of a forefinger filling the perfect dimple on his stubbled chin. 'So could you speculate as to who else might have fired it – if it wasn't the Serbs, that is.'

'There are other parties to this war.'

'You think the *Bosnians* might have done this? What, to themselves?'

'There would be … benefits, shall we say.'

'Mmm. Benefits. Could you just run us through what those might be? A husband watching his wife dismembered before his eyes? A kid seeing her mother get decapitated?'

'I really don't think it helps to get over-emotional about …'

'Oh no, absolutely not. I forgot. The UN doesn't do emotion, does it?'

Rachel was the busiest reporter in the room, assiduously scrawling down every word that anybody said, a courtroom stenographer. She was too new to this particular piece of Sarajevo theatre to separate the significant from the rhetorical rubbish, so she wrote it all down anyway, just in case. When she looked at Danny, she saw he was barely writing anything at all.

'Do you have a question for me anywhere, Mr Lowenstein? I mean, to ascertain a fact?'

'Okay then, Signor Mendini, specifically what benefits to the Bosnians do you mean then?'

'Propaganda benefits. They're trying to have the arms embargo lifted, after all.'

'And why shouldn't they? This siege is making Sarajevo the worst place in the world right now.'

'Again, this is not factually correct. According to UN statistics, there are probably at least ten worse places, in terms of malnutrition rates, life expectancy ...'

'Oh sure, we're in paradise, aren't we? We're only number eleven, after all.'

'Can we move on, Mr Lowenstein?'

'Just one last thing – and don't worry, it's definitely to ascertain a fact. Is there any truth to the report that part of the UN mission here is being renamed the United Nations Strategic and High-Intensity Team, Sarajevo?'

Mendini looked baffled but relieved that for once such a matter of dry, bureaucratic detail should fall from the impassioned lips of Danny Lowenstein.

'No, not that I'm aware of, Mr Lowenstein, and it doesn't sound too likely. But I can certainly check that out with New York.'

'Yes, please. Much appreciated.' At which point half the room – the half that was in the know – tittered like naughty children playing a prank on the headmaster. Rachel only learnt later that

Danny had done this before when he was fed up with a particular UN spokesman: tossed them a self-igniting acronym. In months gone by, it had been UN COWARDS and even UN WANKERS. In this case, it was simply UN SHITS.

'Bloody brilliant!' Edwin congratulated Danny as they left the UN bunker, the Junkies in a huddle crunching through the snow back to Bessie.

Rachel watched them patting Danny on the back, courtiers around the king. A few days earlier and she'd have wanted nothing more than to join them. Now she kept her distance and listened with a certain detachment as they piped up with suggested headlines.

'UN says Bosnians may have massacred themselves.'

'Bosnians may "benefit" from massacre, claims UN.'

'Don't get emotional over massacre, UN warns Bosnians.'

'He deserves it,' said Danny coldly, as if he'd just taken out an enemy.

A dank, dawn mist covered Sarajevo, a sheet of tissue stretched across its hills and trees. Bosnian soldiers, like the men of the Somme, were mustering for a fresh offensive, doomed once more to failure.

Soon they were racing up the hill, and as the mist dispersed, burnt away by an emerging sun, Becky began to find them in her lens. She had forced herself from her bed in the middle of the night, and here was her reward: one of the great shots of the war, she knew it as soon as her finger hit the shutter. It would make centre spread in *Stern* and the *New York Times* magazine, and maybe even turn up in the history books of the future. This was the moment she lived for, when briefly she became one of her heroes, a Capa, a Rodger, a McCullin. Her elation was tempered when she thought about the men in her epic composition who were about to die: indeed they were required to if her picture were to be truly poignant.

Edwin was studying the advance through his binoculars.

'It's a bit like us.'

'What is?' Rachel asked.

'Those poor fuckers up there. Plenty of them are going to get it – wouldn't be a war if not – but they have to hope it's someone else who buys the bullet.'

'So why's that like us?'

'Because we know the statistics are some hacks won't make it through this war either, but just like those guys, we convince ourselves we'll be lucky, that we're some sort of protected species. But what if we're not? What if it's all just Russian roulette?'

Rachel wished he'd stop talking about death so much. She loved his vulnerability – such a contrast with Danny – but something about him scared her too. He had such a morbid fascination with Fate. She supposed it was the Catholic in him.

As the troops advanced, a reverential quiet fell across the city. It was as if there had been a terrible mistake: there was no war, no noise, no gunfire. Perhaps the Serbs had all gone home. Soon enough though a thunderstorm ripped apart the sky. Rockets, shells and shrapnel lashed down like driving rain. Rachel took shelter beside Becky and Edwin. Kaps and Danny were nearby with Shark the cameraman, poking their heads out from behind a butcher's that had long since stopped selling meat.

'Look at us,' said Edwin. 'We're bloody lemmings, sticking together, following each other around.'

They watched the battle as if they were an audience at the movies, enthralled, chewing on their popcorn. Distant flashes and puffs of smoke peppered the faraway horizon, matchstick men running here and there. Then the shells were getting louder, coming closer, until the first one landed among them, tearing through the big-screen canvas and into the front row. They had become actors in the film, or extras at the very least.

The screeching whistle told them to fling themselves to the ground. Rachel reacted even quicker than she had on her first day at the airport, landing badly in a culvert, mouth open so she could taste the dirt. She thought she might have bruised a rib and possibly sprained an ankle.

Then came the blast waves of the explosion, hammering on her eardrums, filling her lungs with smoke and choking dust.

She looked around to see someone else was alongside her, sharing the modest cover offered by the culvert. It was Danny. For the first time since the CBS party, he spoke to her.

'You all right, Rachel?'

'Uh? Uh … yeah. I'm fine. Thanks.' She brushed herself down, irritated that it was his helmet perched comically askew on her head. Becky came running towards them.

'Now *that* was close! Everyone okay?'

The smoke cleared. A quick look round confirmed no one had been hurt. No one could be, after all: they were invincible, immortal. Becky was up and away again, snapping a helpless old woman who'd borne the brunt of the blast and lay spreadeagled on the ground, her legs asunder. Blood was trickling from her forehead, filling up the crevices of her crinkled skin, a face ravaged by the years of yesterday, then cut to shreds by the madness of today. She had lived in this street her entire life, long before the Serbs who did this to her were even born.

Becky zoomed in and locked on to her. Dead or dying? At first she could not tell. Then weary eyes flickered open, and her mouth.

'*Tsigareta?*' she said softly.

Becky lit her one and inserted it between the woman's trembling lips. A great shot had just got even better, two in one morning. Shark joined her for the kill.

'More war porn for the viewers back home,' said Edwin.

Shark moved on but Becky stayed. She was absorbed: checking light readings, adjusting the aperture, switching camera bodies to make sure she did plenty of black-and-white: this was how her heroes in the legendary Magnum photographic agency took their pictures.

'Becky, come in from the open, will you!' Edwin screamed, the trained officer taking charge, England's finest. 'Get some fucking cover now.' His Sandhurst brain was thinking the way the Serb gunners were thinking: first find your range, then have another go.

'In a moment,' she said, though mainly to herself. Becky had always taken risks, but now more than ever. She sometimes wondered whether it was because she had so little to lose. No children, no husband, just a potential lover who everyone knew was a potential disaster.

It engulfed her like a monster wave, not crashing somewhere near this time, but swallowing her up into its epicentre, knocking her down, before picking her up and tossing her around, shredding her leg with its fragments of shitty, dirty, twisted metal, blinding her with a flash that burnt so bright upon her retinas she wondered if she'd ever see again. Her first thought, even now, was for her Eos cameras: they were already battered and dented from their long years at war, but would they survive?

Then, the most searing pain she had ever known, a dentist's drill in her thigh, followed by a slow fade to unconsciousness which promised to make it disappear.

For a few seconds she lay there, sprawled in the street, prone and lacerated like the little old lady. It took a while for the others to open their eyes, adjust their focus and spot her. Rachel was the first to scream out her name, before scrambling over and cradling her dusty, bloody head.

'Oh, Becky. Talk to me. Please talk to me.'

Other photographers and cameramen who had been nearby ran to be by Becky's side too, but also – surreptitiously – to sneak a picture of her. An injured Australian was worth a hundred Bosnians. Rachel wanted to scream at them to get their lenses out of her friend's mangled face, but she held her tongue: after all, what had Becky been doing before she joined the fallen?

When Kaps came over, he had no such qualms.

'Fuck off out of here! Just fuck off, the lot of you!'

They hauled her back to Bessie. Edwin drove. He already had a plan. He would get Amra to give her special treatment because Becky was … what? A Westerner? A journalist? A buddy? He prayed she wouldn't ask for reasons.

'Please, you've got to help.'

Edwin had found her fetching water from the back of the hospital in a couple of plastic buckets. One had a hole in it so that it was leaking even as she filled it. The old, irritable Amra might have argued that all her casualties were equal, but she saw in his face the fear she'd seen in so many of those who sought her out – that a loved one was about to be lost.

Unusually, it was a quiet morning at Kosevo. There was an improbable calm about the place, no screams, no pools of blood. Doctors and nurses walked rather than ran, talked rather than shouted. Patients stared from their beds instead of screaming. Even Amra looked different: she had slept well for once and the rest had wiped some of the troubles from her face. Soon enough everything would be back to normal: they'd be bringing in casualties by the lorry load from the latest failed offensive. For now though, Becky's privileged position was to be one of the first patients of the day.

As Amra examined her, Edwin, Kaps, Danny and Rachel crowded round. Their hopes and fears rested in the doctor's tender hands. Edwin made a sign of the cross over his flak jacket and put his palms together.

'Relax. She's going to be fine,' said Amra. 'A bit of blast concussion, some small shrapnel to her face and leg. There's a lot of blood, but it's not as bad as it seems.'

Edwin felt a surge of pride as they hung on every word of her diagnosis. Like him, they admired the speed and dexterity with which she worked, the calm professionalism of one so young. Now perhaps they would understand.

Only Danny seemed ill at ease. He shuffled from foot to foot and studied the hospital floor rather than the doctor tending to his friend.

'You okay there, Danny?' said Edwin. 'You're looking a bit pasty.'

'Yeah fine. Just the smell of hospitals, I guess. Always gets to me, the antiseptic and blood and stuff.'

Edwin nodded as if he understood, though he'd never noticed before that Danny had any aversion to hanging out in hospitals.

Amra cleaned and re-dressed the wounds, and as she doused Becky's face in warm water, the patient opened one eye, then two, and finally her mouth.

'My cameras. Where the fuck are my fucking cameras?'

They all laughed, even Amra and in the end Becky too.

'Look, they're right here!' Rachel had dumped them on the end of her bed, dented and chipped but otherwise remarkably unscathed. Like their owner, they were lucky to be alive.

'And this is the amazing Dr Ismic,' said Edwin. 'She says you're going to be okay. A few cuts and bruises. Silly girl, just got too close to the sun. Bit like Icarus.'

They all beamed Amra warm smiles of gratitude. Danny glanced up from the floor at last and briefly met her eye. With too much haste, both of them looked awkwardly away again. Edwin caught the moment and tried to fathom it.

'Well thank you, Dr Ismic.' Becky was euphoric at having cheated death but, like bad dope bought at a rip-off price, the hit was nowhere near as good as it could or should have been. 'Then again, I'm not sure anyone would really miss me.'

Rachel rolled her eyes.

'Oh, don't be so bloody maudlin. I would, for a start. A hell of a lot, in fact.'

Becky, though, was talking about someone else entirely who dared not say a word, let alone hold her hard against him the way she needed.

That afternoon Kaps came back to visit, alone. Her face was lacerated and puffed up with bruises, as though she'd been beaten to a pulp. She seemed to him more vulnerable than at any time since he had known her, but her crazy courage, her relentless quest for *that* picture, had never been more attractive. He knew she wasn't perfect: you could criticise the nervous way she laughed at everything, whether it was funny or not. You could say she was too big. You could argue that no one part of her was genuinely beautiful. And yet the combined effect of Becky Cooper was enough to blow him off his feet, just as she had been that morning. She was better and braver than any man in the most manly world of war photography. He didn't just respect her, he bowed down before her; not that she could be allowed to know it.

'You could have died out there, you bloody fool.'

She smiled and propped herself up against a bloodstained pillow.

'So you *do* care!'

It had been a mistake to come; she would read too much into it. After all, he was only here as a worried friend.

'I care about all of us, I don't want any of us getting killed doing this stupid damned fool job. Out there – you took too many chances, Becky. Staying in the open, and staying there far too long. No story is worth a life. A couple of years and everyone will have forgotten about Bosnia, why the hell would you want to die for it?'

'I'm the best, or so everyone keeps telling me, and you don't get the best pictures sitting in the hotel. Apart from that, I suppose I just don't have too much to lose.'

'You have us to lose. You have –'

Kaps hesitated. To cross the Rubicon, or stay well away from its treacherous waters, knowing they could devour him and even his family? The seconds dragged like minutes while they both watched each other and waited. The sentence had formed in his head but sat there unspoken, awaiting further instructions. It was only when he saw the first tear crawling down her cheek that he delivered it.

'Well, you have me to lose.'

Quickly, before procrastination could paralyse him again, he laid his large, strong hand on hers. She had it back for the first time since the basement disco, and she wasn't going to let it go again.

Fingers stroked tentatively at first, then rubbed, then squeezed. Body temperatures rose. Confused minds throbbed with the wrongness and the utter rightness of it all.

As she lay there amid the musty, unwashed linen, she was careless of who else in the overcrowded ward might see them. Finally, gloriously, she pulled him down on top of her for what would be, she knew for certain, the sweetest kiss of her whole life.

In the Holiday Inn's dining room that night, they sat around with other journalists: familiar faces like Shark and Spinoza, and strangers like Luis, a dashing Spaniard from *La Stampa* who'd just arrived and whose first priority was a decent drink. Edwin had bought six bottles of Bordeaux from some French Legionnaires, and they toasted their survival, minus Becky who'd been told by Amra she'd have to stay in hospital for a few more days and might need a wheelchair for a while. The Australian government wanted her airlifted out and everyone agreed to make it happen – Amra, the Bosnians and even Maybe Airlines. Only Becky said no, I'll take my chances like Sarajevans have to. There wasn't a soul who dared to argue with her.

'Here's to us – and Becky – and staying alive!' Edwin shouted. They would remember his face that night: handsome, carefree, vibrant.

'To us and Becky!' they echoed, as if it were a prayer ritual.

Edwin found Danny and topped him up.

'You okay? You looked a bit shitty back there at the hospital.'

'I'm fine. Sorry.'

'Sorry for what?'

'No. Nothing.'

'Come on, man, sorry for what?'

'Oh, it's just that … hospitals bring out the worst in me. Sorry I wasn't much use.'

Danny went quiet again and sipped his wine.

'Can I ask you something else?' said Edwin. 'You and Amra. I thought I saw you … looking at each other. Have you met before?'

He was remembering some of the first words Amra ever said to him, about the Holiday Inn. *I don't go near that place any more, not with those reporters.*

'I think … I mean …' Danny, for once, was tongue-tied.

Long after it was over, Edwin would curse his curiosity. Time and again he'd tell himself how much better it would have been if he had never known, but instead he had to have his answers, even if the only place they'd take him would be a distant, darker shore.

10

Post-Liberation Baghdad, August 2004

Camille's daily routine had been a hundred lengths at her health club in Dubai. It helped tone her ageing muscles. Now, in the claustrophobic confines of the Hamra, she eyed the hotel's abandoned pool with disappointment. Against the white-washed walls, its water was a dancing turquoise blue and it was the only thing she'd seen in Baghdad that looked remotely tempting. She was sure other guests wanted to use it too, but they stayed away out of respect for Danny and, ironically, for her as well.

She dived in with an iconoclastic splash and did alternate lengths of backstroke and breaststroke and then front crawl, ploughing through the bath-warm water. It seemed to wash everything away from her. Quickly, too quickly, she approached her hundredth length and was dimly aware of a shadow in the water. Someone was watching her, a disapproving journalist perhaps, concerned her grief had come up short.

When she climbed the steps and rubbed her face dry with a towel she saw it was Munro.

'Oh, hello there.'

Camille was embarrassed to be standing in front of him in her swimsuit and irritated he should intrude on her.

'Sorry. It's just that we've been thinking.' We, as in me and Harper, because we know best. 'We wondered if you – as next of kin – might consider giving us permission to go into Danny's room. We thought it could help us understand what he was doing out there.'

Next of kin. It made her sound like she was being informed of his death. Maybe she soon would be.

'Well, I'm not entirely …' Until now it had never occurred to her to enter his room. Would he want strangers – and this stranger of a sister – rummaging around his things, trying to get to know him? It would amount to breaking and entering.

'Only if I can go with you.'

It was on the seventh floor, at the end of the corridor. Camille wondered if this had been a deliberate choice, to be as far away as possible from the others. It seemed to be how he liked it: with them, but separate; together, but alone. As Munro unlocked the door and slowly pushed it open, as if to maximise the moment, she breathed in deeply, trying to absorb her brother's smell. There was only a vague whiff of aftershave, and the mustiness that pervaded everything about the Hamra. The room was small, neat and ordered. She imagined Edwin's would be the opposite: a scruffy, student tip with clothes dumped all over the floor and cigarette butts littered everywhere.

In the wardrobe, she found an array of linen shirts, mostly pink or blue. A couple of pairs of chinos were hanging there too, ready for action, their hems stained and frayed from trailing around too many war zones. She thought of Danny as a little boy in the shorts that always seemed too big for him.

In his bathroom, there was his toothbrush, toothpaste and some dental floss, a razor and shaving foam, a half-empty bottle of Marc Jacobs aftershave and three cans of deodorant – all carefully set out beside the sink.

She came back out and saw a photograph tucked into the mirror frame above the double bed. It was Danny in some war zone a few years earlier, with Edwin, Becky, Kaps and Rachel. They all had their arms wrapped around each other's shoulders. Danny's chin was grubbily unshaven and his hair tousled, small tufts of it sticking up. He was grinning, and his teeth shone white. Soft sunlight fell upon him and he looked handsome and contented.

Camille felt a pang of jealousy. The bedside photo should have been of Danny with his *real* family, not these surrogates. She, his only sibling, was nothing in his life. Then again, she had only herself to blame.

On his bedside table was an enormous hardback, *The History of the Mesopotamian Kings*, with a bookmark about three-quarters of the way through. She opened it up and, with a strange feeling of being him, read the words that he'd been reading last. She swallowed hard.

On the other side of the room Munro was snooping around the desk where Danny obviously wrote and filed his stories. A satellite phone was set up, a laptop was plugged in and the charger for his mobile phone snaked across the carpet. There were piles of notes on Iraq, reports from people like the UNHCR and International Crisis Group. His return plane ticket to Washington via London lay on top of them.

'I think this is his diary,' said Munro.

'He always kept one as a boy. It was when he really started writing.'

'I wouldn't feel entirely comfortable reading it, but I'm sure you could. Being family and everything.'

Hypocrite, thought Camille. You don't mind poking around his things, but when it comes to reading his diary, you want someone else to do your dirty work.

She remembered finding his first one, when he must have been only about seven. It was just a couple of pages of an exercise book, and on the front he'd written: *privat – kepe out.* She'd smiled and thought how cute it was. Even then, he'd wanted so much to be an adult. When he was 16, she'd made the mistake of finding another of his diaries, tucked at the bottom of his wardrobe. This time it was full of adolescent vitriol and denunciations of her treachery. *My bitch sister*, he called her, and then: *if she even* is *my sister.* Camille had cried for days.

Three decades on, she was opening his diary again. She did so carefully, as if it might be booby-trapped. On the first page, a few words stood alone, written in the extravagant handwriting of a 19th-century novelist, all swirls and loops, the product of some exquisite fountain pen:

Daniel L. Lowenstein: the Memoirs, Volume Four

Despite the grandiose title, it turned out to be little more than a collection of random daily thoughts, waiting to be processed into autobiography. The pages were plain and unlined, yet Danny had managed to write his sentences in horizontal perfection. None sloped or veered away. They were packed together, so tight and dense that almost no white space was left around them. It was like reading the typeface of a book with scarcely any crossings out: he wrote as he spoke, without hesitation or mistake.

Camille scanned the pages, half-hoping, half-fearing she might see her name amid them somewhere. The thought was absurd though: he'd obliterated her from his life long ago. Then she searched for any reference to his friends, digging through the silt for the smallest nugget. She was disappointed to find only turgid notes on trips to Ramadi, Kirkuk, Basra and an account of a largely uneventful embed with the military near Tikrit.

Having started at the day before the ambush, 1st August, she worked her way backwards through the pages. It was just as she was beginning to tire of his daily ramblings that she found the entry for the 14th July:

> Baghdad AGAIN! Dreadful flight with Brits from Kuwait via Basra. Can't believe am back here quite so soon. Last time for a while maybe? Inshallah! Heat unbelievable. Unbearable. Gave M his presents; invited me to BBQ at house. Masgouf. Gorgeous kids. Real Iraq. Others at dear old Hamra, R, B, K and E. Good to see them all, but food as shit as ever. Poor E even more wasted than usual. SO fucked up and still hates me. Still can't get over me and Amra.

'Anything useful?' asked Munro.

11

London, 1994

The London rain was a poor substitute for Sarajevo's snow – dreary rather than dramatic, a drizzling inconvenience. Bessie had been replaced for the night by two black cabs that swept them along Park Lane instead of Snipers' Alley.

Outside the Hilton, a doorman in top hat and tails welcomed them. Guests were already surging in, the men in their dinner jackets and bow ties, a colony of penguins shuffling behind each other, the women in their flowing gowns. Precariously high heels trod on red carpet as soft as crushed velvet, and then a polished – and endlessly re-polished – marble floor. It could almost have been the Oscars, but for a big sign in golden letters that announced, more modestly: *Welcome to the International Press Awards, 1994.* Still, the Junkies had come to collect their prizes, and what was rightfully theirs. They glanced at themselves in gleaming, full-length mirrors as they made their entrance to the ballroom, and basked in their reflected glory.

A week in a wheelchair had been enough for Becky. To anyone who knew her, what was incongruous was not that this doyenne of war photographers should now be walking with a stick, but that she was wearing a white silk dress. Her blood-red curls cascaded around its neckline. There wasn't a more dramatic human being in the room.

'Best of luck,' said Rachel. 'I just know you're going to win!'

'Shouldn't care, but I do. I suppose it's the Aussie competitive spirit – starts off with the annual swimming gala at school and ends with these stupid press awards.'

They found their name cards at the same table as Danny, Kaps and Edwin, one of 30 squeezed into the ballroom for the ceremony. Danny leant over to them.

'Hate to admit it, but that sniper shot will clinch it for you. Morally dubious, of course, but it still has to be picture of the year.'

Becky smiled at him graciously. With his bow tie and tuxedo, he'd acquired a matinee-idol look.

'Well, that's sweet of you, but you know full well you're the only person in here who's a sure-fire winner. You only have to enter.'

Kaps pushed them apart playfully.

'Oh, please! What is this, some Mutual Admiration Society?'

There was a serrated edge to what he said. He was a wire reporter, which usually meant disappointing anonymity. Even when his stories made the papers, heartless sub-editors would drop his byline in favour of 'from our foreign staff'. Danny usually won the prizes, but this was the year Kaps thought the crown of Journalist of the Year might finally be his. His walk into the Maglaj pocket, a besieged Muslim enclave, had been a world exclusive.

'Well, for what it's worth, my money's on you, Kaps,' Danny told him. 'And Rachel, of course. Reckon you're a shoo-in for Young Journalist.'

She was taken aback: the man who had dismissed her and all her dreams was praising her. She thanked him, but with caution and suspicion. Rachel had found it hard to believe she was even a nominee for Young Journalist of the Year, let alone a finalist, let alone Danny's tip. Her good fortune was that, by some anomalous quirk, stories from the first week of January could be entered. Becky told her to submit her account of their day with Dragan, and throw in her controversial Karadzic profile for good measure. Initially Rachel had laughed at the idea: 'But that would be just so *arrogant*. I mean, to put in my very first stories for an award …' Becky had told her not to be so silly: in this business, no one ever gave you a prize unless you asked for it, and as for arrogance – well, the entire press corps was suffering from it, so why should Rachel be immune?

Edwin was the only one of them without a nomination. The judging panel had deemed his 'One Woman's War' series too sentimental.

An army of waiters and waitresses threaded their way through the narrow gaps in between the tables, bearing mass-produced vegetable tartlets to start, followed by medallions of lamb with sautéed potatoes and broccoli. Edwin monitored the champagne supply, ensuring everyone's glasses were permanently full. By halfway through the main course, they had already drained four bottles between five of them.

'More of your best bubbly, please, waiter!' Edwin called out.

The compère rose to speak, a glamorous television anchorwoman who had never set foot in a war zone but was on a hefty fee to read an autocue as portentously as possible.

'Yet again, journalists around the world have shown tenacity and courage in the reporting of its wars, large and small. Tonight, some get their richly deserved rewards, but first we want to remember those who have, tragically, paid the ultimate price.'

The lights dimmed and on a big screen, the names of 'media workers killed in international conflict' came and went, a roll call of the dead from Africa, Asia and South America, as well as the Balkans. There was a silence, broken only by the sound of the staff offering up more tartlets and champagne.

'Thank you,' said the anchorwoman when the lights came back up, relieved to have got this macabre bit of business out of the way.

'And so now to tonight's awards.' Kaps clenched his knuckles beneath the table and felt the muscles in his stomach tighten. It might be the only chance of a big prize in his whole career. He knew it was absurd to get so worked up about it, given that most people in the street had never even heard of the International Press Awards. At that moment though, they meant everything to him: recognition from his peers that, for a while at least, he wasn't only good, he was the very best.

'The war in Bosnia has dominated news coverage this year,' the anchorwoman continued. 'While several distinguished reporters have shown enormous courage in bringing us news from the frontline, the judges felt that they wanted to recognise someone who has gone to the most extraordinary lengths to find the truth …'

Kaps was sure it must be him. The walk into Maglaj had taken him two long days and nights. What lengths could possibly be more extraordinary than those? People had warned him it wasn't only dangerous, it was suicidal, but he had been determined to prove something to himself, that even if he were a family man, he could gamble with his life just like Danny did. The trouble was, it wasn't only his life to throw away any more: it belonged to Judith and Charlie and Tom, and there were times he wanted to scream at them, 'Get off me! It's my life and if I want to risk it for a poxy statuette and a certificate, well, why shouldn't I?'

The autocutie paused, for what she felt was dramatic effect.

'… and who has also, once again, got behind the shooting and the shellfire to tell the stories of real Bosnians, and to prick the conscience of the world; a man who's not only been brave in what he's done, but in what he's written.'

As soon as Kaps heard 'once again' he felt he had been winded, as though the glitzy woman from the television had wandered over and punched him in the stomach.

'The award for International Journalist of the Year goes to ... Daniel L. Lowenstein of the *New York Times*!'

The ballroom erupted into thunderous applause. As Danny pushed back his chair with feigned reluctance, Becky kissed him on both cheeks, Edwin patted him on the back and even Rachel briefly touched his arm. Kaps shook his hand and forced a beaming smile. He was sure the whole room was watching to see if he could accept defeat with good grace and sportingly acknowledge that the better man had won. Sometimes Kaps didn't think Danny *was* the better man: his journalism could be lachrymose, too full of unnecessary emoting – too full of shit, in fact. Most of the time, though, he had to admit the fucker was in a class of his own. Besides, the fucker was also supposed to be his friend.

Danny began to weave a weary path through the other tables until he reached the stage. He didn't need a script or an autocue.

'Thank you, and thank you from all of us who work in Bosnia,' he said as the last ripples of applause echoed around the room. 'I'd like to see this as an award that's not just for me but for every journalist who's trying to open the eyes of the world to the tragedy in the Balkans, in particular my friends and colleagues here tonight. Ladies and gentlemen, I'm sorry if this puts you off your dinner, but, as we sit amid this splendour, it's hard to conceive that only a few hundred miles from here, unborn babies are being cut from their mothers' wombs, and fathers are being told at gunpoint to try to rape their own daughters, and men are being nailed alive to the doors of their local mosques. Only the other day I interviewed a survivor of Omarska camp and he told me how the Serbs forced him to bite the testicles off his fellow prisoners and then dig a shallow grave for them. If he'd refused, he'd have been shot. My message to you tonight is that if Auschwitz was evil, so is Omarska. If Hitler was evil, so are Karadzic and Mladic. If they had a set of gas chambers, don't tell me they wouldn't use them. Ladies and gentlemen, can this really be happening again, at the end of the twentieth century? It can and it is. Can our generation stand idly by as this happens on our continent? It can and it is. Let me leave you with one thought: of the many atrocities I have witnessed in the past year or so, there's been none greater than the inaction of the world, its ceaseless, *spineless* ability to look the other way. Where's our conscience? If we don't find it soon, my belief is that we're not just witnesses, we're accomplices.'

'Trouble is,' whispered Becky at the table, 'it's not his bloody continent, and it's not mine either!'

'Nor mine,' said Rachel.

'Or mine,' said Kaps.

Their sniggers drew an admonishing glance from the next table, where Danny's homily had been treated throughout with solemn respect. It was the least he deserved, and when he had finished they rose to their feet as one to give him a standing ovation, and even admiring whistles. By making his audience feel so bad about themselves, Danny had managed to make them feel surprisingly good. It was what he did to his readers every day. He left the stage clutching the statuette presented to him by the TV anchorwoman, and occasionally holding it aloft.

Long after the backs had all been slapped, Danny and his friends sat together drinking yet more champagne. It was a scene much like any evening at the Holiday Inn, except that, for one night only, they had exchanged its gloomy chill for the brash glitz of the Hilton. In the bar on the 28th floor they surveyed the sprawling splendour of London's lights and felt they really were on top of the world, the only place that they belonged. Rachel was finding it difficult to believe that, like Danny and Becky, her fingers were tracing the outline of a golden statuette. It was the most precious thing she'd ever held. The judges had commended the 'stunning impact of her prose' and 'the bursting originality of her coverage'. They singled out the sniper story for her ability to 'reach into the darkest corner of the Serbian mind with a stark, almost brutal simplicity of style.'

Danny perched beside her for a moment on the velvet couch.

'Hey, superstar, well done.'

On a night she already found hard to believe, this moment was the most surreal.

'Thanks. Well done to you, too.'

'The thing is, what I really wanted to say was sorry. For judging you when I shouldn't have. You know, that whole Karadzic thing. And whatever I said when I was pissed – to be honest, I don't even remember but I'm pretty sure it wasn't very nice. I get too angry, it's my worst fault; but that doesn't give me the right to ...'

He trailed off, perhaps expecting her to gush forth with forgiveness. There was a time when she would have done, but this evening she had come of age. She didn't owe Danny Lowenstein anything. She was stunning and original. She was the best young reporter on earth, for one year at least, and she'd only just begun. The world might be at Danny's feet, but now it was at hers as well.

'Thanks, Danny, apology accepted. Would you excuse me, I really need the bathroom?'

The Hilton's finest champagne flowed and so, naturally, did the war stories. Then there came the Margaritas, Pina Coladas, Rum Punches and something quite devastating called the Oscar Wilde. They all slipped into a familiar state of warming drunkenness, with no prospect of an early-morning massacre to stop them sleeping off the hangover. It was well past two o'clock when Edwin, his dinner jacket long abandoned and black tie hanging loose around his neck, took Danny aside from the others. His words ran together in such a slur it was hard to pick them apart.

'Danny, can I ask you something? You know we talked before, that day at the hospital, about you and Amra?'

Danny was even drunker. He'd been more nervous before his speech than any of them would have guessed, and had sought to calm himself with fast champagne. Afterwards, the relief meant he just carried on. Six hours' worth of alcohol was sloshing around inside him, inhibitions tossed into the cityscape below.

'Oh yeah, Amra. The lovely Amra. She's doing a great job there, great job.'

'So you do know her?'

'Well, you've written all about her, haven't you? And you're always talking about her. Always talking, talking. Think you've made damned sure we all know her.'

'But had you actually met her before? That's what I'm getting at.'

Danny closed his eyes, drowsy but gently aroused. She was in his room at the Holiday Inn, her bare back arched above him in helpless, abandoned pleasure, a squeaking from the bed in rhythm with her moans.

He smirked into his glass.

'Well, we've been fucking, if that's what you mean.'

Edwin decided later this sentence was like a drunk being hit by a bus. He was aware of the calamity that had, in an instant, destroyed his world, and yet for a while the shock and alcohol anaesthetised his pain. He tried telling himself it was a joke, that Danny was just fooling around as he often did. But he knew what he had heard.

No one else celebrating that night at the pinnacle of the Park Lane Hilton, at the pinnacle of their young careers, caught what Danny said to Edwin. No one else realised that their friendship could never be the same again.

PART TWO

12

Post-Liberation Iraq, August 2004

Danny's cell is the size of an average garden shed. If he lies down on the concrete floor, he calculates only four other people could stretch out beside him before every square inch of it would be filled. The light is murky, but there is just enough for him to see the walls. Someone, a long time ago, has taken the trouble to paint them blue, but now the paint is cracked and blistered and in large areas it has disappeared. These naked patches of grey remind him of land masses amid the seas and oceans of the world.

At the top of one wall, near the ceiling, there is a hole about two inches in diameter. It allows a single shaft of sunlight to creep in apologetically and Danny has come to rely on it. The hole lets him follow all the heartbeats of the day – dawn, noon, dusk, night. It creates a pool of light on the concrete, a perfect circle. Since there is nothing in his cell, this light becomes a piece of furniture, and in it he has stored all the reasons he should hold himself together: his career, his future, his friends – anything he can think of to give him hope. In the darkest corner of the cell he has stacked up the reasons he should fall apart: his terror, his loneliness, his remorse.

They bring him only one meal a day, usually at dawn. It's always a plate of cold rice, stale bread and a hunk of meat (on one occasion it was coagulated mutton stew, which made him sick). There's also a large beaker of water to last the day. Each morning he carefully sips a quarter of it, and keeps the rest for later.

There's a thin, stained mattress on the floor, though he can never sleep for long because the chains around his wrists and ankles are bound so tight that they cut into his skin every time he moves. His only comfort is a single blanket. It's surprisingly soft, and sometimes he clutches on to it.

He is in the same clothes he was captured in, the linen shirt and chinos he put on that morning after his shower at the hotel. They are almost black with grime and sweat, and badly torn. His lucky boots have been removed from him. His feet are bare.

The toilet is about 15 yards down the corridor, but if he needs to go he must shout for a guard to escort him there. It's the traditional Arab concept of a porcelain hole in the ground with two resting places either side for the feet. The difficult trick is to squat above it. The toilet is partially blocked, and the white-tiled floor around it has become a shallow lake of urine with small chunks of faeces floating around on it, a stinking flotsam that makes him gag. When the stale piss laps up over the lacerations on his ankles, he worries his wounds will become infected.

Outside he occasionally hears dogs barking, and even children playing. There are wails from a local mosque and sporadic volleys of gunfire.

Whenever he's covered other people's kidnaps – in Lebanon and South America – he's always wondered how they have coped with such an expanse of time, but Danny discovers he is never bored: boredom would be a luxury he could wallow in. Instead he lives in perpetual terror, always waiting for the cell door to open and the announcement of his execution. When lovers used to ask him what he was thinking about, he would laugh to himself because he could boil down everything in his mind to two broad subjects: sex and stories, stories and sex. Now it is as though these have been cut out of his brain like a pair of cancerous tumours, to be replaced by a new one: fear. Sometimes it produces a dull ache in him, sometimes a shooting pain, but it dominates every moment of his being.

It is day nine, by his calculation. They have been long days of nothing, but, for his own sanity, Danny has taken care to count them, determined time will not trickle away from him unrecorded.

A guard unlocks the door and flicks a switch in the corridor outside. Harsh artificial light floods in. When Danny adjusts his eyes, he can see a guard bearing the day's paltry rations of bread and rice and a chicken leg. This one he calls Scar because of the disfigurement on his forehead, a pink strip of skin, raised and slightly rippled. It was Scar who pulled him from the car; tall and broad shouldered, he is an immense physical presence in the little cell and needs to stoop slightly. He sets down the food carefully, like a waiter. In a voice that is measured and reasonable, he resumes the interrogation that first began on what Danny remembers clearly as day four.

'You spy for who, please? For CIA?'

'No, no one. Don't be ridiculous. I told you before, I told you lots of times, I'm a journalist.'

'We found maps in your car. Three maps. American maps.'

Danny remembers the US Army map in the glove compartment. It was a mistake to have it. *Beware your maps*, they had told him once at Walsingham.

'Well, you have to get around,' Danny blusters. 'It's not like you can just go and buy a map in Iraq these days. Doesn't make me a spy.'

Danny hasn't heard his own voice for days. It's good to be talking again, even if the only conversation he ever gets is interrogation. *Talk to them*, the instructors at Walsingham had said: *talk about whatever comes into your head – even pretend you've got a wife and kids – anything that makes it harder for them to kill you.*

'Or Mossad?'

'Excuse me?'

'CIA or Mossad? You are Jewish, yes? Zionist? *Lowenstein*.'

Scar still sounds calm, which gives Danny a certain confidence.

'No! Certainly not. I'm German American, but not Jewish. It's the town my parents came from in Germany. Near Stuttgart – look it up. Listen, I support the Palestinian people. Read some of my articles from Gaza and the West—'

'You want anything?'

'Yes. I want to be released. I've been here more than a week already.'

Scar laughs as if weeks in the tortured history of his country were only seconds.

'Okay, if not, some proper food and water. Clothes, books, a radio. I want … I want a cigarette.'

Scar holds out a packet of a cheap Iraqi brand. Danny takes one hungrily and stuffs it between his chapped lips, waiting for a flame from the lighter Scar produces. This is good, he can hear them say at Walsingham. Small beginnings, Danny; small beginnings.

'Want, want, want!' Scar screams suddenly. 'You know what *we* want? We want Americans to go home. We want our country back. Death to USA, death to spies, that's what we want.'

Danny feels the boot crush his testicles. The pain is delayed at first and then unleashed across him, nauseating in its intensity. In the half-light of the cell, more blows follow, hard and heavy. Fists and feet from nowhere, anywhere, everywhere. He can no longer bear to look, but with eyes scrunched shut, he hears: Scar's grunts and heavy panting sound like a man engrossed in frantic sex.

After a few minutes, Danny starts to imagine it's Mohammed who is punching and kicking him. How *could* you let me die? How *could* you leave my wife without a husband, my lovely children without a father? Sabeen takes over for a while, and little Farrah, her blows the weakest, but also the most painful.

'*Now* you have cigarette,' Scar says eventually, holding out the packet once again, getting his breath back.

Danny is a heap of battered flesh. Still they speak to him from Walsingham: it's not too late, it's never too late. *Establish the bond, however hard it seems.* He reaches out an aching arm for a second cigarette and as he takes it, Scar grabs his hand and flicks on the lighter underneath it. The prisoner lets out a primeval yell as a licking flame melts the skin around his knuckles. Scar moves it carefully from left to right so that it becomes a blowtorch. Perhaps he's trying to recreate his own disfigurement. He flings Danny back on to the floor where he writhes around clutching his hand.

The interrogation proceeds as if nothing has happened.

'So, who were the people in the other car?'

'I don't know …'

Danny is kicked again, this time from behind and on his coccyx.

'More "journalists"? More spies?'

'Please, for the love of God, I have no idea.'

'You think, you remember. Later I come back and talk to you some more.'

Scar slams the door, leaving Danny doubled up and coughing blood. He tries to keep his eyes open, fearing what they'll see when they are closed. His mind is in constant rewind, back to the minutes before he was captured in al-Talha, back through his years on the road, back all the way to East Allegheny, Pittsburgh.

For the Lowensteins, Sunday became not a day of rest but a day of family crisis. All week would be a nervous countdown to it.

Once Danny would have sat in his big sister's room, talking about school and friends, reading books, listening to the records she'd just bought: Janis Joplin, Dylan, the Rolling Stones. Then, as things changed, Camille was always there alone, trying not to listen to the new sounds down the corridor. Her album collection was stacked up on the floor against a wall and obsessively she'd arrange and rearrange it – by artist, then alphabetically, then chronologically – while her father and her brother did battle yet again.

Sometimes Lukas would only shout at him: 'I don't even *know* you any more.'

Sometimes he would slap him. 'You're making me do this.'

Sometimes he would try to pull him from his room, twisting the skin on Danny's wrist. 'I'll drag you there if I have to.'

'And what sort of church is it that has to drag in its worshippers?' Danny would reply, pleased with his point, taunting Lukas, watching his eyes widen. Now he could see them again, they seemed interchangeable with Scar's.

As Danny passed from boyhood into manhood, he could have fought back. At 15, there was the first flowering of stubble on his chin and he was already two inches taller than his father. The reason he never defended himself was that he believed he had won the moral victory, and also because he knew that, in time, he could hurt his father much more effectively. He could walk out of the life Lukas Lowenstein had planned for him.

Danny's rebellion over church was only ever going to be a springboard. Next he began to question all that America was doing in the world, especially in Vietnam. He read and watched everything about the war and felt ashamed. He learnt to despise his country as well as his father.

Soon he mastered other forms of disobedience so that it was not just Sundays when he made a stand: he stayed out late and partied, he dated girls and fucked them, he did drugs when could find the money. He stole it from his parents, or went on shoplifting sprees. It was part of his crusade against capitalism.

He started calling his father Lukas instead of Dad and pushed him further away. He ignored the voice that told him all he really wanted was to be closer, like he had been once, like Camille was. Danny told himself there was no room in his soul for self-pity: he needed to be strong, and with a hardened outer shell to protect him from the pain.

'Why can't you be more like your sister?' demanded Lukas one Sunday.

'What, and then you'd love me more?'

'Give me a *reason* to love you, Daniel. You never have.'

At times like this Camille would sit in her room and put another record on, usually Janis Joplin. Danny suspected his sister only liked her because she was loud and drowned out all the noise.

13

Bosnia, 1994

After his return from the Hilton, Edwin had been only too happy to trade its superficial delights for hardships he felt more at home with: the cold and hunger of life on the frontline. As the soldiers of the Bosnian Army, the BiH, sang songs about their homeland around a campfire, he snuggled into his sleeping bag. The ground beneath him was rocky and uneven, and sleep was fitful. He would lie there for many hours, thinking endless thoughts of her.

The unit he had adopted was trying to smuggle arms and ammunition into Srebrenica, one of the designated 'safe areas' for besieged Muslims: so safe that almost eight thousand unarmed men and boys would be massacred there the following year, some shot as they tried to escape, others forced to dig mass graves before being buried alive in them. The soldiers with him this night were brave and he did not begrudge their singing. Soon many of them would be dead as well. As they belted out their anthems, he reached once more for the Pink Floyd T-shirt he kept in the side pocket of his rucksack. It was his holy relic. Occasionally, at times such as this, he would take a drag from it, sniffing its cheap, synthetic material as hard and deep as his nostrils would allow, inhaling Amra's odour. Naturally he took drugs too – plenty of cocaine now, as well as cannabis – but this was the best of them, the one he depended on the most.

One night in her tiny bedroom, she had pulled it off and handed it to him. 'Keep it,' she'd said. 'Remember me by it while you're away.' She had stood there in her black bra, more of a woman and less of a doctor. He had moved forward to touch her flesh, and she let him trace his fingers along the lines of her undernourished body: the vertebrae on her back, her shoulder blades, her breastbone. In pleasure, she had rolled her head from one side to the other. He sensed she was too fragile for sex, and was determined he would not rush her into making love. He would wait till she was ready, till she demanded it; the anticipation would make it all the more remarkable. Time abounded because their love was special, different, pure. Sarajevo love.

It wasn't how he saw it now. Dysfunctional, more like. Hypocritical. We've been kissing, but with Danny … well, we've been *fucking*, haven't we, Amra?

At daybreak, he woke in the middle of another Amra dream. She was entwined with him in his sleeping bag, laughing and kissing him. She was a different Amra, an idealised version, in love with only him, unsullied. He tried to get back to sleep, but the birds were too noisy and the light too bright. His cocaine was the next best escape: after the Hilton, he had bought a shitload. It was 'full fat', according to his dealer, far better than the usual 'semi-skimmed'. Now, inside his sleeping bag so that the troops wouldn't see, he cut a couple of lines on the front cover of his notepad and snorted them through one of the pink party straws he carried everywhere. Soon, sensuality overwhelmed him and he was wrapped around her once again, writhing against her skinny body, both of them naked and ready to make love at last. Then he was inside her, and after a while he came where Danny had.

He felt the sticky goo on the lining of his sleeping bag and cried.

Clouds hung over the valley as Edwin and the soldiers around him prepared for the day ahead. As they cooked themselves some breakfast on their campfires, he shaved his scalp and massaged it with moisturising cream: without it, the skin would dry and shrink. The process caused daily mirth among the troops he travelled with, but he liked them to laugh even if it was at his expense. Who knew when they would laugh again?

When he was done, he stood above the river that cascaded through the woods, holding Amra's T-shirt. Suddenly he raised it above his freshly razored head, as if to hurl it at the rushing torrent. It would be her punishment, even though she would be as ignorant of it as of her supposed crime. Only he would lose.

Edwin collapsed to his knees on the jagged rocks that had refused to let him sleep for more than a few minutes at a time, careless of the dagger pain they caused him now. He wept again, inconsolably this time, hunched up and shuddering. The men around him paid little attention. In this war, everyone had their shit to deal with.

Just as the Serbs were trying to wipe away the Muslims with their ethnic cleansing – steadily, methodically – so Edwin needed to obliterate Amra from his mind. When his life was most in peril, he almost succeeded. More often though he failed, and he would end up sniffing her shirt, then sniffing some more of his full-fat coke.

He knew that to blame her was unfair, and it wasn't that he didn't want to be near her again: just that physically he could not, even if that were to be the tragedy of his life and maybe hers as well.

Neither could he be near Danny. They hadn't spoken since that night in London and Edwin had no idea whether Danny would even remember his intoxicated confession, let alone regret it. Edwin tormented himself with the supplementary questions he longed to ask. How and when did it begin? Was she in love with you? Was she very good? Why didn't she tell me? Why didn't you?

Edwin could not face returning to Sarajevo, even though it was the place where, indisputably, his heart belonged. His paper started to get jumpy that he wasn't there and when the satphone rang out in the loneliest room in the Hotel Tuzla, Edwin knew it was the order to go back home. Jake's gently familiar whisper wafted down the line from London.

'We were wondering about Sarajevo again, dear boy.'

'Oh? You know what, I'm really pretty well placed out here. Trust me, Srebrenica will be the story of this war.'

Jake tried to be tactful.

'Some other time. We just feel we've been ignoring the old place a bit. I mean, it's on the bloody telly every night and all the competition are there. Agency stuff is fine for a while, but – well, you know how it's never quite the same. Anyway, what is it with you? First we couldn't get you out of there, now we can't get you back in.'

Reluctantly, sulkily, Edwin accepted defeat. Like the commander of a beaten army, he planned his retreat to Sarajevo.

The girls were playing Travel Scrabble in the dining room when he walked in, the prodigal son returned. The dried yoke of half-eaten fried eggs lay congealed on their breakfast plates, a film of grease hardening on them. On the tablecloth, hunks of stale bread had been nibbled and then abandoned, while only vaguely wanted coffee was now too cold to drink. It didn't matter though: at the Holiday Inn, breakfast was more of a meeting place than a meal.

'Ah, my lovely witches.'

'Edwin!' Becky and Rachel shrieked in unison.

'Where've you been?' demanded Becky. 'We've missed you.' She jumped up and hugged him to show how much she meant it, and for the first time he regretted his absence. He had missed them too.

He noticed how, even in the few weeks since he'd last seen them in London, they had changed, none more so than Rachel. The war zone debutante looked as though she'd been here all her life. She'd acquired the full Sarajevo uniform: a woolly hat, a hulking Gore-Tex jacket just like Becky's, and a pair of Timberland boots. Her bright eyes seemed more wary; she had begun to shed the cloak of her naivety like a caterpillar sheds its skin.

'You do realise that we haven't seen you since the Hilton,' said Becky reproachfully. 'My God, that was debauched!'

'Anyway, it's not like you've missed much. You know – same old, same old,' said Rachel reassuringly. Sarajevo's worst massacre – when dozens would die in the city's marketplace – was still some days away. The slaughter of the bread queue had merely been a dress rehearsal.

'It's good to see you, Edwin. So damned, damned good.' Becky hugged him again, and this time, to her surprise, he held her so tight that when she went to pull away, he wouldn't let her go.

14

Post-Liberation Iraq, August 2004

Danny nurses his melted hand, and through the pain he thinks of the people he has hurt in so many different ways, deliberately or inadvertently. He forces himself to dwell on all his victims. They're like his skin, blistered and full of pus, the wound he'd rather not even look at but feels he should.

Poor Amra. He can still remember when she fell for him. He had gone to Kosevo's mortuary on the first of his gruesome body counts. They were the earliest months of the war in 1992 and she'd just started operating; she was in shock and vulnerable. Danny had offered her whisky and maybe a little dope back at the Holiday Inn – 'trust me, you need to relax.'

At first the cannabis – procured, ironically, from Edwin – had only made her giggle. They sat together on his bed in room 339 and laughed, and then they lay on it and eventually, just after midnight, they made love on it. For Amra it was an escape from all the pain around her, a glimpse of another world where pleasure for its own sake still existed.

He fucked her while she was stoned and woozy. Over the next few weeks he fucked her a few more times as well. And then he dumped her. At the Holiday Inn reception, they got used to the pretty young doctor: she would come by every other day and leave him messages saying she was hopelessly in love with him. The little scraps of paper piled up. *Please* could they meet, if only for some rich, thick Turkish coffee and burek. *Please* could she just talk to him? He ignored them all. The ladies on reception shook their heads with the sadness of it.

So why couldn't he ignore her again when she started seeing Edwin two years later, why couldn't he be happy for them both? What perverse instinct was it that made him want her all over again, as though she were a different woman, suddenly more desirable? Edwin; kind, sweet Edwin. Why did Danny have to compete with him for Amra like rivals on a story? And what had he got out of it in the end, except the most hollow satisfaction – not even another Hilton gong, just another screw.

15

Sarajevo, 1994

Edwin studiously avoided Kosevo hospital just as he had avoided the city itself. It was harder to ignore Danny, but he managed to keep contact with him to a minimum, murmuring the occasional 'hi' and 'hello', or offering a reluctant nod as they passed each other in the hotel corridors or restaurant. The others never understood why Edwin was so cold to him.

Sarajevo changed too. The next massacre, which killed 68 people in the marketplace, was a turning point: NATO would finally do what Danny had been demanding and threaten airstrikes, and the Serbs would grudgingly pull back their heavy weapons. First though, they couldn't resist one more onslaught.

On the day it happened, the sky was ravishingly blue and the air was mountain clear. The journalists arrived for the Five O'clock Follies clad in their armour, looking like a platoon of soldiers as they rushed into the sandbagged, razor-wired entrance to the UN compound, hurling themselves inside for its protection. Even the suave Alessandro Mendini seemed shaken as he tried to brief them on the latest diplomatic developments, his reports of steady progress punctuated by sceptical booms.

It was an hour later, as they were emerging from the press conference, that Kaps overheard a couple of UN blue helmets talking about the Kosevo hospital: word was coming through that a shell had hit it. Kaps passed it on to Becky, who told Rachel, who spread the news to everybody else. Edwin was the last to hear. He had stayed behind to talk to Mendini off the record.

'Ed, did you hear? They've hit the Kosevo,' Becky said when he emerged from the briefing room. 'We should get up there. That's bad for the Serbs, if it's true.'

Edwin was already pushing past the others, past Danny Lowenstein especially, as he jumped into Bessie and drove to the hospital faster than he'd ever driven anywhere in Sarajevo.

He knew from several streets away, as soon as he saw the smoke. As he got closer, a tableau of madness unfolded in front of him. Dazed survivors staggered around, while those who had to help slipped too easily into the familiar roles of stretcher bearers and ambulance drivers, except where do you drive the casualties when it's the hospital itself that's been blown up, and where do you find the doctors and nurses who could treat them?

As he stumbled through heaps of rubble that still smouldered, he had a growing sense of dread: that somewhere in these ruins lay his saint.

Not my Amra, surely.

Not before I've explained why I went away and didn't come back.

Not before I've kissed her one more time.

Not before I've made love to her. Like Danny did.

A woman – a nurse, perhaps, or the mother of a patient – was wailing and beating her chest. Edwin felt like doing the same, but the British army officer in him seized control and he joined a dozen Bosnian men who were clawing their way through fallen masonry to reach a basement. The search for survivors endowed Edwin, like them, with almost supernatural energy. He watched himself tearing at whole slabs of broken wall with his fingers. He watched them bleed. 'Amra? Amra Ismic?' he asked one of the volunteers toiling alongside him, a bearded man as obsessive in his work as Edwin, his face and hands white with brick dust, as if someone had tipped a sack of flour all over him. The man shrugged. 'A life is a life, no matter what the name,' he seemed to say.

It was 25 minutes before they broke through into the stretch of corridor cut off by the rubble. By now the men were spluttering from the smoke and dust they had inhaled, but nothing could hold back Edwin's desperate cries:

'Amra! Amra!'

He followed the other rescue workers through into the darkness and found a clutch of people who had been trapped – patients and medical staff alike, some remarkably unscathed, others with appalling injuries.

'Amra!'

There was no sign of her. Perhaps she'd been having a day off. No, fool! Amra didn't have days off!

'*Am-ra!*' This time it was not the call of the rescuer seeking response, but a wail.

It took another quarter of an hour for him to find her. Stumbling in the murk like a blind man, he had missed her entirely. She had been carried from the wreckage of her beloved hospital and was lying, barely conscious, on a stretcher at the back of the building, close to where she used to fetch the water. The only visible injury was some blood dripping from her ears. He gave thanks to his God and praised Him, but two minutes later he was cursing Him. The wounds were internal, of course they were: trust Amra to hide them from the world.

He stood over her, repeating her name again and again like an incantation.

'What took you so long?' she whispered when she understood who it was towering above her, his face smeared with grime. He knelt down and held her hand, so delicate and skinny, squeezing hard enough to break it.

'Oh, my Amra, I'm so sorry.'

'Sorry? For what?' Her eyes were blinking from the dust.

He could not begin to answer but screamed instead for doctors to come to her. There could be no other casualty more important.

'Forget it. I've already told them I'm low priority. Look at me, I have no injuries.'

'But, Amra, you …'

She shook her head. There was no point arguing with her. As so often at Kosevo hospital, she had taken command of the triage and selected who should live and who should die. It was a simpler choice than usual, for this time she was the unlucky loser and not some poor, bewildered child. At least there would be no heart-breaking explanations to relatives, no nausea of guilt. It was almost a relief.

'Amra, let me get you away from here. I can get you to the UN. They have some really good doctors there.'

'We have really good doctors here,' she said with a worn-out smile. 'Only the very best.'

He smiled back at her, and cradled her head in his arms, stroking her hair obsessively in the hope that alone might somehow cure her. And even amid the choking dust, he caught her scent, the drug he'd lived on for so long.

He kept watch on her eyes lest they close, all notions of crime and punishment banished now, no longer embarrassed to bare his love for her. He should have done it long ago. Had he not told himself to seize the day? Had he not warned himself that in this accursed place there was no time for the cat and mouse of courtship?

Amra returned his gaze, not pretending either. Strange, she thought; once upon a time she wouldn't have minded leaving it all behind, the chaos and carnage, but now she had stumbled on this Englishman, so bald and yet so handsome and so kind, she wanted to stick around. She had found him and, gradually, fallen for him. They understood each other: both were preoccupied with death, and yearned to escape the hold it had on them. They were its creatures and it helped when they could talk about it.

With Danny she had been infatuated, but this was different – less obsessive, a gentle, slowburn sort of love. But then he had disappeared, without a word of explanation. He hadn't even left a note for her. It was her fault, of course; it was always her fault.

She had missed him beyond measure, and realised how she had needed him to talk to at the end of each day's nightmare. He had calmed her, enabled her to carry on. He had gone, but now he had come back to her at last, and she would have liked … would have liked …

In the Muslim way of things, Amra's funeral was that night. In the Lion Cemetery, near her home, the place she had always assumed she would be buried, the Junkies gathered round the grave. They came because they remembered what Dr Amra had done for Becky and, more urgently, because they were supporting Edwin, who was in no state to be left alone. They had mourned for friends before, but never had they seen one of their own so snapped in two by grief.

Women were not allowed at a Muslim funeral, but no one stopped Becky and Rachel standing either side of him; they were outsiders, after all, and they didn't seem to count. Their arms interlocked with Edwin's; they were worried that otherwise he might collapse into the grave itself. Above the distant rumble of occasional artillery, the imam chanted out his prayers. Edwin thought about offering up his own, except that suddenly he hated God as much as Danny always had. All his belief had died with Amra.

Once the Lion Cemetery had been a park containing just a few graves, but now it had been pressed into war-time service. Like the young men of the city, its country needed it. Its soil was forever being dug up, until soon it resembled a ploughed field. The problem was that this graveyard, with its burgeoning crop of hexagonal wooden markers for the Muslim dead, lay on exposed ground. Mourners often had to dive for cover behind a freshly shovelled mound of earth or even jump into an open grave. For Amra's funeral, the Junkies had worn their helmets and flak jackets: it was a sacred place but also potentially lethal. Even here, Amra Ismic could not be safe from the Serbs. It was no place to rest in peace.

The piece of wood by which she'd be remembered lay on the ground, waiting to be hammered into her grave. *Amra Ismic, 1972–1994* was all it said, scribbled out in pen. She was shrouded in a white sheet and soon spadefuls of soggy soil were being tossed upon her, each clump landing with a thud. The mourners had their hands cupped in prayer. Edwin glanced up at Danny, who was standing awkwardly behind them, not sure where to cast his guilty eyes, not sure whether he should have come at all. He was shuffling from foot to foot, as he had been that day at the hospital.

Amra's father and friends were clustered around Edwin as if he, who had barely known her, were the bereaved husband in need of consolation. For their sake he tried to remain composed. But when the last of the soil had fallen on her, and they had placed their flowers across it, finally it was time to hammer in her name. Each bang of the mallet rolled around the hills like a crack of sniperfire and Edwin was overcome. He sank to his knees, pushing two knuckles into his mouth and biting on them to gag himself. Even this could not stop his scream and when it came, it was a terrible, high-pitched howl that rang around the whole cemetery and far beyond.

For a while it seemed to be the only sound in Sarajevo, one that put the war on hold while everybody listened to its pain.

16

Post-Liberation Iraq, August 2004

Scar enters the cell with a bag slung over his shoulder. Danny is wondering if it holds some medieval instruments of torture, but instead Scar pulls out an orange jumpsuit.

He has two other gunmen with him, one of whom bounds around energetically while the other is more lugubrious, with a glazed look about him. Danny thinks their names are Abu Hamid and Abu Ibrahim, but for convenience, and in the strange world his mind has become, he calls them Quick and Slow. Together with Scar, Quick and Slow bundle him into the jumpsuit, stuffing in his arms and legs. Danny squeals as the zip catches the mushy tissue of his burn. The huge canopy of its blister has burst. It is yellow now, and septic.

'Shut *up*, American!' Scar shouts, and his acolytes pick up the theme. 'Death to Amer-ee-can, death to Amer-ee-can.' They take turns to spit into his eyes, then shroud him in the same stinking hood he wore when they brought him in. Finally they frogmarch him out of the cell, along a corridor. He stumbles like a blind man, off balance and disoriented.

When the hood is ripped off again, he is in another room, bigger and brighter than his cell. He notices the video camera perched on a black tripod, on what is clearly the set for whatever movie Scar and his friends are about to make. There is a lilac sheet draped on the wall with Arabic writing on it, presumably some slogan. Beside it are four other gunmen, clenching their fists and waving Kalashnikovs excitedly. They wear ski masks and balaclavas and stand beside a single chair, where Danny assumes he will be told to sit.

He scours the room for any sign of a sword or a knife, the blade he dreads. Perhaps Scar will produce it with a flourish at the crucial moment, for surely he will be the designated executioner. No one else will get a look in.

Part of Danny feels he's lived his death already, at the roadblock. *You cannot kill me, for I have died before. I am a corpse already.* His hands are shaking violently. He hopes he might have exhausted his supply of fear by now, but he's wrong – there's more. He supposes that there's always more.

Scar pushes him down on to the chair and still he waits for the first glint of steel to catch the light.

'You talk to camera,' Scar demands. 'You tell we treat you well. You say Americans must leave Iraq, Bush must save your life. No tricks, no codes. No secret messages to CIA and Israel. Okay?'

'Okay, okay, whatever you want.' Relief courses through Danny. They don't mean to kill him after all, not yet, at least. His death may still be inevitable, but it has been postponed and it strikes him what small triumphs men will sometimes celebrate.

Danny complies enthusiastically with every instruction. He even tries to smile at Scar, but only a scowl comes back. One of the sidekicks turns on the small, silver Sony camera, surprisingly state-of-the-art. Danny has time to wonder, pointlessly, where they've bought it from and how much it cost.

He goes through the motions of denouncing his country, his voice filtered through the tunnel of his missing teeth and blood-encrusted lips. Still, he delivers his lines with as much conviction as he can muster, as if they really could save his life and the President really might pull all his troops out of Iraq – just because this particular hostage has told him to.

Danny imagines his parents watching him on the nightly network news shows. What will his father think? Will he feel sorry for him at last? And what about Camille, will she regret their years apart?

He imagines the rest of the press corps watching in Baghdad, wondering if one day it might be them. Rachel, Becky, Kaps: will they mourn him for a while, and then forget him with indecent haste? And Edwin, with such good grounds to hate him; will he smile to himself with silent satisfaction?

He imagines Sabeen and her brood of children: at least he's still alive, she will probably be telling them. Not like my poor Mohammed, your poor father.

And when Danny has said all they want him to, he's unsure, even now, if the gunmen might descend on him and make their bloody sacrifice to Allah. Instead, they turn off the camera, bundle him into his hood again and return him to his hovel. His legs have almost gone from under him and the guards drag him along the final few yards to his cell.

By the time he gets back there, he knows the day is over: the little pool of light has disappeared.

'Dancing Queen' burst out across the Presidential Suite, horribly cheerful. In the screen of Becky's phone, Adi's name flashed up.

'Hey, Becky! How are you guys?'

Becky had just come back from the bathroom where she'd swallowed another handful of her pills. She'd never felt less like small talk.

'Getting by, thanks. Any news?'

'Yeah, and I think it's positive.'

She sat bolt upright. Why couldn't he just say it up front? She could almost smell his bad breath and body odour down the line and she was thankful at least that he'd called rather than come straight round. God, he was repulsive.

'Honey, we have some indications Danny may be alive,' he said after a theatrical pause. 'The CIA think some sort of video has been handed to Al Jazeera. They're saying it shows Danny begging for his life.'

Honey? What right did he have to call her 'honey'? She despised the way he was using – abusing – the power of his information to slip in these surreptitious advances. She would say nothing for now, she decided, but when it was all over she'd tell him straight to his face what a fucking jerk he'd been.

'Listen up, everyone,' Becky announced. 'It looks like he could be alive!'

They leapt up and embraced, hugging each other hard. Danny was back from the dead. The reprieve might be temporary: his kidnappers could turn him into one of their snuff videos any time they liked, but for now there was a chance, however slim.

'He could escape,' suggested Rachel, who jumped on to the coffee table and heard its smoked glass crack beneath her weight. 'Or we send in Delta Force and rescue him. Or we buy him out; Jesus, we've already spent a trillion dollars on this fiasco, a few more won't hurt.'

For a few giddy minutes, anything seemed possible. After so much despair, it seemed only reasonable that they should be allowed to hope.

Reception on the Presidential Suite's TV screen was abysmal and they watched it in blurry double vision. Danny emerged, surrounded by gunmen in sinister masks, two of them pointing their weapons at his head gratuitously. Behind them was a banner which they were later told said 'Swords of Allah', the name the gang had chosen for themselves, as if they were a rock band. Danny looked smaller than they remembered, with the beginnings of a beard. There was a gaping absence where several front teeth had disappeared. What shocked them most was the orange jumpsuit. In any other setting, it would have been almost comic, transforming Danny into an unlikely road sweeper or a car mechanic. Here though, in its angry reference to Guantanamo, it marked him out for death. The Junkies realised their celebrations had been premature because, for Danny, the end had only been delayed. No one would admit it though; how could they?

'Oh, our lovely Danny,' said Rachel, fresh tears falling.

'Wait … shush!' said Edwin. 'He's going to say something.'

And there it was, that assured East Coast voice, though it lisped a little now.

It occurred to them that some of the anti-Western propaganda he had been ordered to regurgitate was not so different from what he actually believed: a denunciation of the American and British occupation, a list of their crimes in Iraq and a call for their troops to leave immediately. There were some specific demands, including the release of all '500 political prisoners' from Iraqi jails, and then something far more chilling.

'This is the tenth day of my captivity. I would like to confess to being a spy. I am working for the governments of Israel and America. My kidnappers tell me that if their demands are not met by the end of this month – that is August 31st – they will execute me.'

'Oh no!' shouted Rachel. 'Please God, no!'

'Hang on, there's more,' said Edwin.

Danny closed with words that at last seemed to be unscripted, his voice cracking open.

'I'm tired but I'm being well treated. I'm okay. To my family, if I never see them again: goodbye. To my friends, I'm sorry for all the times I've let you down. Truly sorry. To the President of my country: please listen to what I have said. Please do what these people ask and get me out of here. Please, Mr President, please. You have 21 days.'

One of the goons standing alongside him snatched the microphone away like a drunken singer on karaoke night, and bellowed into it 'Allahu Akhbar', before his comrades in arms, not to be outdone, joined in. Danny's time was up, and the screen erupted into a blizzard of snow before Al Jazeera cut back to their anchor, who looked concerned but rapidly moved on to other news.

'Oh my God, they're really going to do it, aren't they?' Rachel slumped back into the sofa's sagging springs. Becky, Edwin and Kaps all held each other's hands. That deranged cry from the kidnappers had told them there could be no miracle of negotiated release or rescue. These were killers who would see it as a gift to God to carve open Danny's windpipe.

Everything had changed, and nothing. He had three weeks to live, but what could they do? There was so little time, and yet they felt it stretching out before them.

Camille stared at the screen, even though her brother's face was long gone.

To my friends ... I'm sorry for all the times I've let you down.

The 'Free Danny' campaign was officially launched across America. The *New York Times* helped organise a rally in New York, and a 25-foot poster of Danny was unfurled outside its offices with an electronic counter to show how many days he'd been missing. There were candlelit vigils at his high school and at Yale. People wore badges, put up Danny's picture in front windows and tied yellow ribbons to anything they could find: every tree in

Pittsburgh seemed to have one wrapped around it. A woman in Arizona volunteered to travel to Iraq and offer herself as a hostage in Danny's place: she said she'd always admired his journalism and that he was more use to the world than she could ever be.

Danny's parents were deluged with cards, letters, calls from everyone up to the President, who phoned to let them know he was thinking of them. The FBI suggested they should make a video, calling for Danny to be released. One expert said it ought to be Eliza Lowenstein who made a plaintive, tearful appeal for her boy's life. Others insisted it was Lukas who should talk, as tough as he wanted to, *demanding* Danny's freedom rather than meekly asking for it. It was always better to show strength than weakness.

A daily conference call was set up for noon EST, eight o'clock at night Baghdad time, so the FBI and CIA could compare notes with the embassy's Hostage Crisis Group in Iraq, US Army intelligence, Adi, Turner and Munro – and, of course, Camille. She would join the call from the Presidential Suite with the Junkies gathered round her. Outsiders had already started referring to them as Team Danny.

17

London, July 1994

Heathrow Airport, where every adventure seemed to begin and end.

Becky and Rachel felt like impostors as they joined the queue of chattering tourists who were checking in for Nairobi. The other passengers, in their premature straw hats, T-shirts and sunglasses, were already thinking of the white-sand beaches and the exotic wildlife that awaited them on their once-in-a-lifetime holidays. The Junkies were thinking of genocide.

'But are you sure this is our sort of story?' Rachel asked Becky, as they inched their trolley forward.

Leave behind the safe truths of Sarajevo? Embark on a voyage to Africa instead, a continent to which none of them, bar Kaps, had ever been? Of course she wasn't sure.

'Sure I'm sure.' Becky was still dragging her bad leg. Like a war veteran, her wound gave her a certain aura: everyone could see she'd go one step further in search of the story. 'I know we talk about genocide in Bosnia, or at least Danny does, but it isn't really, is it? I mean, that's just his hyperbolic bullshit. It's the odd mass grave, a concentration camp if you're lucky. But this … this is the dictionary bloody definition. Quite literally the murder of a people. Close on a million people, Rach, our generation's holocaust. We *need* to be there.'

But the truth was they'd already missed it, which probably upset them as much as the killing.

When it began that April, the global village abandoned all interest in Bosnia and switched its fickle gaze to Rwanda instead. The Junkies had been left stranded in Sarajevo, unwanted and unread. They huddled around their radios as the World Service hissed and crackled with sensational news from Kigali – that the President's plane had been shot down and that some people called the Hutus were embarking on their very own Final Solution. Their victims, it was carefully explained, were the Tutsis – Rwanda's minority, often fatally distinguishable by their taller bodies, thinner noses and lighter skin. The Tutsis' mistake, it transpired, was once to have been embraced by the country's Belgian colonists as the natural aristocracy. Breathtaking bulletins described industrial killing, where sometimes tens of thousands of people would be put to death in a single day by former friends and neighbours. Machetes were being used, maces, clubs, knives – even screwdrivers.

'Sounds like Bosnia on speed,' Edwin had suggested.

Almost overnight, the Sarajevo story became as undesirable as an embarrassing ex-lover. Most of the press corps were happy to abandon it for the easy spoils of an African slaughter. The lobby of the Holiday Inn was busy with people preparing to leave: Shark was heaving around his silver boxes, Spinoza dragging a trunk across the floor.

Edwin was keen to join the exodus – after Amra's death, he had to get out. Everything in Sarajevo reminded him of her, especially Danny. He tried to distract himself with more drugs, but they were never enough. The others were tempted too: Kaps because it was his continent and Becky because she was infatuated with him and wanted to be wherever he was, genocide or not. Even Rachel, starting to hit her stride, wondered whether to set out on a new adventure. Only Danny had argued they should resist the temptations of journalistic promiscuity and stay faithful to their Sarajevo. 'It's just trophy hunting, don't you see?' he told them one April evening as they lounged around Becky's room. 'Everyone else parachutes in and out of places. TV's glamour boys and girls, you know the type: the ones who fly in with a flak jacket on Monday, fix their make-up on Tuesday, do their turn on Wednesday, then pack up and head for home on Thursday. Just in time for the Friday drinks party where they can tell their pals tall tales from the frontline. We're different, we don't *pretend* we're across the story when we're not. I've never even been to Africa, let alone Rwanda. We should stick with what we know, and what we know is Bosnia – because we live it, because it's our war.'

'No, Danny, it's *their* war, actually.' Edwin was fed up with Danny's homilies. 'I for one am bored of living here and sticking with a story no one gives a flying fuck about. We deal with news, Danny, and news – in case you didn't realise – is whatever's new, wherever it happens. Bosnia is old hat, Rwanda is a whole new horror show.'

'And what happens to the people in this one? We just forget about them? Let the world ignore their plight, even more than it does already? All because we're "bored", because the kids want new toys to play with? "Bosnia fatigue" – God, that phrase is so pathetic. D'you think anyone ever had World War Two fatigue?'

Edwin got up and left, but Rachel had been chastened by Danny's words, and moved. He may have humiliated her, he may have been the most supercilious, opinionated man she'd ever met, but no one could deny how much he cared for Bosnia. It had eaten deep into his soul. Having admired him, then detested him, she was going to settle for something in between. In any case, she had decided to stay: she'd spent so long waiting to get to Bosnia that she couldn't pull out of it just yet. Becky and Kaps though were still prevaricating. By the time they finally called in to offer their services, their editors had already despatched other, more decisive volunteers.

In the days that followed, each bulletin they heard from Rwanda compounded their misery and they could hardly bare to listen any more. As the story got exponentially bigger, so – they realised – did their mistake. They turned into the forgotten outposts of their respective organisations. Phone calls to news desks were unreturned, ideas ignored, pictures unused, stories ignominiously spiked. They began to think there was no point in even filing. Their confidence, once impregnable, collapsed like a child's sandcastle in the evening tide. They had missed the story of the year or even of the decade and now they moped around, uncertain how to fill their days.

'Nothing worse than being in the wrong place at the wrong time,' Kaps complained to Becky as they lay in her bed one evening. He was caressing her thigh and then her buttocks but he did it absently, for once distracted from her flesh. 'And nothing worse than risking your life when no one cares if you're here or not in the first place.' He wouldn't be able to hang around much longer. It was getting harder to explain to Judith why he should stay, when the only plausible reason was that he'd fallen in love with another woman.

Becky the ruthless professional wanted to be in Africa too, but Becky the woman and the lover was happy to stay wrapped up in Kaps' arms on a quiet spring evening when the snipers had given it a rest. For the first time in her life she was not lonely and sex was a delicious routine. Stories would come and go, like the sounds of war in Sarajevo, but this love affair she had stumbled upon – so surprising, so delectably intense – would never be repeated. She wasn't going anywhere without him.

• • •

It hadn't been until deeper into that blood-soaked year that the Junkies glimpsed a second chance. In a final twist, the Tutsi rebel Army, the RPF, took control of Rwanda and the Hutus, fearing reprisals, fled from their homeland. They went to the wastes of the Rwandan–Zairean border, where they died by the tens of thousands. This time it wasn't man but cholera that was the killer. God's justice, said some. It was officially another mega-story.

'Oh well, better late than never,' said Rachel, shuffling along the check-in queue for the night flight to Nairobi.

Becky trailed behind and scanned the passengers one last time to see if Kaps was coming. She was willing him to join them, not sure she could bear to witness Africa's suffering alone. In the rituals of her superstition, she touched objects everywhere she went – railings, suitcases, airline notices – drawing puzzled glances from passers-by.

Initially he'd been keen to come: it was the only reason she'd booked herself on to the flight with Rachel in the first place. Then he said his editor at Reuters wasn't sure. Was it really his boss, she asked herself, or was it Judith? Communication with him had been impossible while he was 'at home', that other universe of which she knew so little.

'Oh look, there he is!' Rachel shouted, and immediately wished she hadn't. Far too late, she saw that he was bidding dutiful farewells to his family. 'Oh crap. Sorry, Beck.'

'That's okay. I do realise they exist.'

But she had never *seen* them, which they both knew was the point.

The scene was a touching one. Kaps, unaware he was being watched, held a twin in each arm. He looked different from how he was on the road: his hair was scraped back so hard into the constraints of its ponytail, it could have almost passed for a short back and sides if you only saw it from the front. He had shaved closely too. He gave Judith a lingering kiss and Becky stepped back in shock. She tried to look away but her head jerked up again like a rubbernecker driving past a car crash. The twins were as beautiful as he was: no wonder he adored them. Then it was Judith who sucked her in. Surprisingly pretty, Becky was generous enough to concede. Slimmer than her, too, with better legs and definitely a better arse. Short cropped hair and wearing some sort of functional, zip-up fleece and a pair of baggy jeans. She looked tired. Were the twins keeping her up at night? Or her husband? Was she having rows with him or sex with him? Becky thought about his penis inside Judith and felt sick.

'Come on, let's keep moving.' Rachel tugged at her sleeve.

'No. I want …' She was transfixed by Judith's face. There was absolutely nothing she knew about this woman, she realised, apart from her name and – now – what she looked like. Kaps never spoke of her, the subject was taboo.

Did she work? If not, what did she do all day? What were her passions? How had she met him, this mesmerising man? Did she still fuck him, and if so, how often, in what positions and which rooms? How far would she sink if he left her? It occurred to Becky she could walk across the terminal there and then, through the bustle of the crowd, and explode the fraud of his double life with a mere handful of words:

Hello, Judith, good to meet you. I'm not sure if anyone told you this, but I'm shagging your husband. In fact, not only am I shagging him, but I'm totally in love with him and he's in love with me. And tonight, just as soon as you've said your fond farewells, we're flying off together into the African sunset.

'Beck, this isn't going to do you any good.' Rachel coaxed her forward.

'I may be lame, but I'm not a total cripple, thank you very much.'

Rachel remembered the first time she flew to Bosnia, when Becky had been her compass. Now she was guiding Becky, another Junkie blown off course.

While Kaps was still trying to tear himself away from his family, Edwin arrived to join them in the queue for his second trip to Africa. Becky and Rachel both threw their arms around him and were shocked by how wasted he'd become: a skimpy waistcoat and tight jeans stretched over bones that jutted out in all directions, and his eyes were darkened hollows. After Amra's death he had sought solace in cocaine, ever-multiplying lines of it. His nose was running from the damage to the membrane in his nostrils and he kept sneezing.

'He's shitfaced,' Becky whispered to Rachel. 'He really needs some help, you know.'

Edwin was embarrassingly, irritatingly high. He'd been snorting in the terminal toilets.

'Any baggage?' said the nice lady at check-in, wearing a bright uniform and company smile.

'Only the people I've let down in my life – a young soldier in the desert and a wonderful lover who didn't deserve to die. Is that too much for you? *Excess?* Shall I leave some of it behind?'

Becky rolled her eyes while the check-in lady gave him a patient, patronising smile. She'd heard it all a million times before. With a queue stretching back to the terminal doors, a wise-cracking smart-arse was the last thing she needed, but Edwin was certain everyone was keen to hear from him.

Rachel and Becky handed over their new frequent-flyer cards. The lady asked Edwin if he had one too, and braced herself.

'If you really want to know madam, I detest your petty hierarchy of blue cards, then silver and then gold, and then – but only if you're really, really good – platinum. And that means – oh, joy! –

you can go to the lounge which has a shower in it, except that of course you can't have a shower because you're never there for more than ten minutes by the time you've worked out where the lounge is in the first place, and found the boarding pass you need to get in with. And anyway, your towel is all packed up in the suitcase you've just checked in.'

'Actually, we do provide towels.' The check-in lady said it quietly, to prove a point, but Edwin was on a roll, angry not only with the world and all its wars, but with its trivia too. He loved the new-found freedom with which he could talk: all of a sudden the words flowed from his mouth as easily as Danny's.

'It's like those reward cards you get in the supermarket,' he continued, 'where you spend your entire life collecting a billion points, anally obsessing about how many more you get if you buy ketchup instead of vinegar, only to find out on your deathbed that all the ones you've saved up translate into the glorious total of three pounds sixty, and it's too late to spend it anyway.'

'Window seat, sir?'

Rachel and Becky looked at him, a fading shadow of the man they'd known, and cursed the day he'd ever met Dr Amra Ismic.

An hour later they shuffled along the aisle of the plane, holding in their stomachs to squeeze past plump tourists stuffing their bags into the overhead compartments. Becky was still thinking about the Kaps family farewell.

'You okay, Beck?' Rachel took her seat and shoved into the pouch in front of her the water she had bought, the new book, the newspapers and magazines. They had both got the latest editions of *Hello!* and *OK!* magazines – celebrity tittle-tattle for when Africa's cataclysm got them down.

'Yeah, fine. She looked nice, didn't she? They ... looked nice.'

'I'm not getting into that shit. I'm really not.'

'Do you think he saw me?'

'No, I'm sure he didn't.'

'Is he on the plane?'

'Of course he's on the fucking plane. The whole damned press corps is on the plane. The small portion of it that isn't already out there. This story's a runaway bestseller.'

'So why didn't he tell me he was coming? Why didn't he get in touch?'

Rachel was losing patience with her. She loved Becky, but at times like this she could be self-obsessed.

'And why is he screwing you when he has a happy family? And why are you screwing him?'

Becky was surprised, but it was true: the questions, once you started asking them, would never stop, like blood from a wound that just won't scab.

'I'm not sure I can bear it any more.'

'Then end it. No one's forcing you to be with him. It's not making you happy and it's not making him happy either.'

'I feel like I'm sharing him, like I have half a man.'

'Perhaps you should be grateful. Perhaps half is better than none.'

Becky looked at her – the girl she'd only met six months earlier, the friend she knew so well yet not at all – and considered the possibility that Rachel was lonely too. She felt ashamed it hadn't occurred to her before, probably because Rachel was prettier and more petite, but for a moment it made her feel a little better.

Kaps' seat was about 20 rows behind them at the back of the plane, but he swapped it with an elderly lady who was stranded between Edwin and Becky, and had got fed up with them talking across her. In any case, she didn't like the look of Edwin. Kaps slipped gratefully into the old lady's seat, and back into his other life. Now the four of them were packed in tight together: Kaps and Becky in the middle, holding brazen hands as if Judith and the twins had been a figment of all their imaginations; Edwin and Rachel, flanking them, pretending not to notice, silent accessories to adultery.

It was almost one in the morning when the food came, preposterously late because of a delay in take-off. The menu claimed it was beef lasagne.

'Mass starvation when we land,' said Edwin, 'but for the moment only gluttony.'

He bought eight miniatures of Moët Chandon, two for each of them, and started singing:

'Eight green bottles, sitting on the wall …'

Rachel was happy to drink. Once she would have swotted up on her cuttings, but now she only glanced at them. She put on her headphones, drifted into plastic pop and let the lovers talk.

'Can't tell you how good it feels to be back together,' Kaps told Becky tentatively.

'I don't understand. Why didn't you tell me you were coming?'

'I didn't hear for sure until this afternoon. Ridiculously late call from the foreign desk.' Becky had no idea whether or not to believe him. Judith didn't get the truth, so why should she?

She didn't want to tell him about what she'd seen – she knew it would sound petty and undignified – but it spilt out of her anyhow.

'I saw you, you know. Saying goodbye to your family.'

He flinched and looked away, his face ablaze.

'Oh. Did you? I'm sorry. If I'd known …'

'What? You wouldn't have let them come to the airport? Or you'd have worn a disguise?'

'Okay, let's not do this, please, Becky.' He was worried her voice was getting louder with the Moët Chandon and that the passengers nearby might hear. Absurdly, he was more concerned with what they thought, these strangers he would never see again, than what she did, the woman that he loved.

'Let's not do what?'

'Torture ourselves.'

'Torture *me*, you mean, because it's me who's getting hurt here. Not your family, because they don't have a clue, and not you, because you've got the best of both worlds, haven't you? Nice wife and kids when you get home, nice bit on the side when you're away.'

'It's nothing like that, you know it isn't.'

'Do I? Then leave her.'

She had never said these words to him before, never even hinted at their possibility. He didn't reply, terrified his tongue might misspeak and deliver rash promises to which – like some politician – he'd one day be held accountable. He opted for the right to silence.

'Well, say something.'

'You haven't suggested that …'

'We're in love, aren't we? I sort of thought it might follow that we should be together.'

'We are together.'

'Yeah, together watching people die. I wouldn't mind something a little more normal, that's all. A bit more fucking mundane. How about watching a movie together, or a concert or a play? How about a nice old-fashioned dinner in a restaurant once in a while, or is that too much to ask?'

The other passengers had tuned into them. He lowered his voice till it was barely audible, in the hope she might follow suit.

'Becky, can we please not have this conversation on a jumbo jet full of people?'

She turned away from him, her tears falling like late October leaves, in soft abundance. Kaps tried to put an arm around her, but with half a heart, expecting it to be flung back in his face. Instead she grabbed it as though it were a lifeline and sobbed into the sleeve of his linen shirt. It darkened with the wet.

Soon she was asleep and Kaps dozed fitfully, recalling the last few days at home. They had dragged too slowly. All he had wanted was to return to the road, to rest his face on the white slopes of Becky's breasts, to hear that wicked laugh and see those smiling eyes.

The dinner party had been his nadir. Even before it began, Judith was nagging him.

You don't want to go, do you?

I'm tired, just tired, that's all.

Funny how you're always tired at home, but never when you're on the road.

That's just not true.

You don't think our friends here are as exciting as your friends out there, in Sarajevo.

I didn't say that.

You didn't have to. You think they're boring, don't you, just because they don't get off on being shot at.

Judith, that's crazy.

I'll tell you what's crazy. Going off each month to a place you might be killed, so that your kids grow up without a father and I become a widow. Not just crazy but perverse.

The cabin had turned unnecessarily chilly. Kaps pulled the thin airline blanket from its plastic wrapper and spread it over himself and Becky. So that was him, a war-zone pervert.

The dinner itself had been even more disastrous. An Edwardian house in Brighton about which he despised everything: the gas-guzzling Range Rover in the pebbled driveway, the snobbish plaque that said 'no hawkers', the net curtains and chandeliers, and the dreary Scottish landscapes on every wall. The hosts were parents of a kid at Charlie and Tom's nursery, but he barely knew them: a corporate lawyer of some variety (he couldn't be bothered to find out which) and his wife called Angela or Andrea or something, who sat herself next to him at dinner. When they had picked away at the scrawny bones of suburban conversation – *the estate agent came round to value our house the other day; apparently poor Susan's car was broken into; they say the grounds are very good at that new school that's opened* – Angela/Andrea finally posed the question he always dreaded: 'So what do *you* do?' He yearned to say he was 'a banker' or 'a builder' so that she would rapidly lose interest and turn to someone else, but Kaps decided there were enough lies in his life already. When he told her, her narrow eyes opened up and sparkled.

That's so interesting. Tell me, how do you cope, seeing all those ghastly things?

(Frankly I want to see more of them, because they make great stories and, who knows, one of them might even win me an award.)

I mean, it must really affect you? I suppose you have bad dreams?

(Only about missing deadlines. Or getting scooped. Or losing out to Danny on all the prizes.)

So, what's it really like out there, in Bosnia?

(Oh you know, a little like Brighton, what with all the burglars and shoplifters.)

He had yearned to crawl under the table and away from her, for here was another perversity: in his copy he'd happily answer such questions for his readers – people he'd never even met – but he wouldn't do it for someone sitting next to him whose name he couldn't even be bothered to remember, a living, breathing reader too, keen to hear anecdotes from this other world. Why couldn't he just be the raconteur she wanted so she could recycle his war stories and flog them off like second-hand clothes at her next dinner party?

18

Africa, July 1994

Africa at last, but Jomo Kenyatta Airport sat in a chilly drizzle to match that of the Heathrow they had left behind. Small pools of warm rainwater lingered on the runway. Their assumption of a sun, big and perfect in the sky, was misplaced: confusingly there was only a murky grey to greet them.

They were surrounded by half a dozen would-be porters, squabbling as they offered up their rival services. The pungent smell of stale sweat assaulted them. Edwin, though he'd made the same journey earlier that year, was out of it, while Rachel and Becky had hangovers. It was Kaps who took charge. At six foot two, he stood head and shoulders above the fray.

Rachel watched him, her head still woozy from the champagne. They were so different, the South African and the Australian – his naturally sunkissed skin against her chalky white, his slim, muscular body against her fleshy one – so different and yet so much the same. It wasn't hard to see why Becky was in love with him, but he needed her as much: they belonged together, and Rachel was surprised how, away from England, everyone conveniently forgot he was married with a family. They were all living the lie, conniving accomplices, and to help with the deceit he'd taken down his ponytail so that the hair that had been swept back with such severity in

London now hung loose and wild again. A simple night flight to Nairobi had transformed him into a bachelor.

Rachel couldn't help but admire his efficiency as he took command, picking out two porters and shooing away the rest, changing money, negotiating customs and finally hailing a couple of Kenya's black Hackney cabs, another reminder of the London they had left behind. Kaps personified what Rachel would come to love about the travelling circus of international journalism: the ability to drop easily in and out of continents.

She realised she was in awe of him, the way she had been of Danny the first time she saw him in Sarajevo. These were places both men bestrode. She wondered if anyone would ever look at her and think that this was *her* story, *her* country even.

They dozed as they drove to Wilson, Nairobi's junior airport, and when she woke up again, there was the little charter plane that would take them on, deeper into Africa.

'It's tiny. Like a little car that's sprouted wings.'

'What d'you expect?' said Kaps. 'No airline in its right mind is going to fly you to a civil war.'

'Suppose that's what's so nice, though,' said Rachel. 'Flying into places everyone else is flying out of. Makes me feel … I don't know … different.'

Kaps smiled at her.

'Trust me, in a world of six billion people, different is a pretty good feeling to have.'

Next to the higgledy-piggledy heap of their luggage, they stood on Wilson's runway waiting for a pilot to turn up. When he eventually emerged, he was a wiry Yemeni in a dazzling, freshly pressed white shirt with impressive epaulettes, yellow stripes on black, and sunglasses so mirrored that all they could see in them were their own wrecked faces.

'Hi there, I'm Amen – your skipper for the day. I'll be flying you into Goma.'

Goma. He said it so cheerfully, it might have been Ibiza or Corfu, but it had already become synonymous with death, like Korem or Baidoa before it.

'Amen, was it?' asked Becky.

'That's it. As in the prayer, except you won't be needing any today. The bad weather has cleared, so if you guys want to load your stuff, I'll just fuel up and we can get you on your way.'

They formed a human chain. Reporters turned baggage handlers, they busily passed rucksacks, satellite phones, laptops, cameras and boxes of food and water along the line before stuffing it all into a hold which didn't look much bigger than a cupboard.

'I suppose it's … safe?' asked Rachel.

'Oh yes.' Kaps sounded sassy and confident. 'I've flown in these lots in South Africa. Only thing is, when there's turbulence you get blown around like a feather. Still, I'm sure it's got a great engine.'

'*A* great engine? You mean there's only one?'

She was suddenly nostalgic for her trips down Snipers' Alley, and just to make her feel worse, the others were whispering advertising slogans.

'Air Amen,' suggested Edwin, 'the World's Least Favourite Airline.'

'No, no,' said Becky. 'Air Amen: the Answer to Your Prayers.'

The pilot chuckled.

'Don't worry, guys, I flew for five years in the Yemeni Air Force. Only shot down once.'

'Really? What happened?' asked Becky.

'Jumped. With a parachute, of course.'

'Right,' said Becky. 'Next time we'll remember. Let's see now: cameras, film, laptop, mosquito spray … parachute.'

Amen laughed again and collected up their cash, 500 dollars each. He started counting the bills as he completed a cursory check of the cockpit instruments.

'We're all going to die,' Rachel whispered into Becky's ear, 'but at least he's got the right money.'

Amen crammed the wad into his money belt, switched on the engine and turned round to his passengers with his own, unique version of a safety drill.

'Okay, you're all big boys and girls now. Up to you if you want to put on seatbelts or not. Frankly I don't really give a damn, but obviously no cigarettes or we all go up in your smoke. Now, someone close up, will you, so I can get this thing into the sky?'

As if it were a car door, Kaps slammed it shut.

It wasn't long before they were gazing down at the giraffes and zebras on rolling plains which yielded eventually to Lake Victoria. Amen had settled into a gentle cruise. With one hand on the steering shaft, he held a thick Tom Clancy novel in the other, glancing up once in a while, 'presumably to check there isn't a 747 heading in our direction,' Becky muttered.

The flight was smooth enough and they drifted in and out of sleep until it hit the turbulence Kaps had warned of. There had been no gravelly voiced message from the captain to alert the passengers to what was coming, no 'ladies and gentlemen, things might get a bit bumpy for a while.' Instead the plane lurched abruptly, then just dropped, leaving their stomachs on the ceiling. It reminded Rachel of her first flight into Sarajevo, but this time they were plunging through a rain cloud that was exploding into thunder. It was serious enough for Amen to put down the unputdownable, for a while at least. Angry rain lashed against the windscreen, torrents of water hurling themselves on to the glass.

They glanced nervously at the green blur of Amen's radar screen and prayed it was accurate. Visibility was close to zero.

'Everyone okay back there?' Amen shouted.

'Course,' said Kaps. 'Whoever heard of a war correspondent afraid to fly?'

By the time they had fought their way through to the other side of the cloud, everything had changed: the weather, the landscape, the country. The sky's temper tantrum was over. It was calm and clear again, like an argument that had never happened. Below, the lake had given way to the rolling hills of Rwanda, greener and more luscious than anything they'd ever seen. So these were the famous 'Mille Collines', the thousand hills that had borne witness to a million murders.

'Check out the killing fields,' said Amen.

They pressed their faces against the scratched plastic of the portholes. It was easy enough to make out the roads, which were coloured in the bloody red of Rwanda's soil and sliced through the vegetation like wild slashes on naked skin. They imagined the Interahamwe at work down there, Rwanda's very own SS, killing with the same methodical madness, though with machetes rather than gas chambers. Ordinary Hutus had joined the frenzy too, mothers, even grandmothers – the quest for racial purity urged on by radio appeals to go out and 'kill the cockroaches' and 'bring in the harvest'. From the air, the Junkies saw tiny, toytown huts, churches, schools and prisons, and wondered how many bodies still lay in them, unclaimed and rotting.

The weather had transformed itself by the time they reached Lake Kivu on Rwanda's border with Zaire. As Amen eased the plane down to Goma, it was finally what they had assumed an African day to be: a bloated, equatorial sun in a cloudless sky. Now there was a different problem. About 200 children were on the runway, barefoot but dressed in a rainbow of vibrant colours. They were scavenging for scraps of aid, the odd sack of grain or rice accidentally discarded. Undaunted, Amen prepared to land, both hands on the joystick at last, straightening her up before nudging her down. It was a test of nerve to see who blinked first. The children did, leaving it to the last moment to sprint away.

Amid all the eager little black faces on the runway there was one white one. Danny was walking to the plane, anxious to be reunited with his tribe. Rachel wasn't sure she could face him again. It had been a relief not to be around him for a while.

One by one, they staggered down the wobbly steps, blinking into the glare, fumbling for their sunglasses. Edwin took the black-and-white kafiyeh that was round his neck and covered up his head before it burnt. Like the others, he was wearing a T-shirt, shorts and sandals. Banished was the winter wear of Bosnia.

A marvellous wall of heat hit them hard. They felt like explorers in the dizzy wonderland of Central Africa, entranced by its exotic smells and sounds.

Hutu kids surrounded them, hungry and thirsty but almost delirious with excitement, shouting an insistent welcome: '*Jambo, jambo!*' The children had no idea who or what the Junkies were, but it was enough that they had descended on this magical machine from the sky: they were Westerners, VIPs, royalty, White Gods all rolled into one.

'You see, they love you already,' grinned Danny, with a flash of his brilliant white teeth that caught the sunlight.

The others could see he had been energised by the people around him, even if half of them were dying. The Junkies felt it too, the thrilling rush of newness: new place, new people, new story, new news. It would become the way they lived, this promiscuous quest for fresh adventures. Never again would they restrict themselves to the monogamy of Bosnia.

'Welcome to Goma. I've managed to get you the last four rooms in town, plus some wheels.'

'First you tell us not to come,' said Kaps, 'then, hey presto, here you are ahead of us.' It was as if the captain, facing mutiny, had decided to jump ship and take command of a new one. Kaps was irritated that this was his continent, and yet still Danny had managed to beat him to it. Kaps' only comfort was that, unlike Yugoslavia, Danny didn't know any more about the story than he did and if there were prizes to be won, for once it would be a level playing field.

The two drivers Danny had hired, Innocent and Boniface, loaded up the luggage. On the brief journey to the Hotel des Grands Lacs, Rachel was flustered to find that the only place left for Danny was next to her on the back seat. She was tightly pressed against him, hemmed in by rucksacks and boxes of water. Both of them were in shorts, and Rachel could feel the perspiring flesh of her right thigh welded to his left, like Siamese twins joined at the hip. In Sarajevo, after the disastrous start to their relationship, they had never managed to get beyond cool civility. Despite his apology, the Karadzic and sniper sagas still hung over them, rain clouds that refused to catch the breeze and drift away. For both of them – in different ways – they remained a source of shame. Rachel tried to wriggle her leg free.

Becky was in the front seat so she could take pictures as they drove. Nothing in Bosnia or beyond had prepared them for what they saw from their leather-upholstered hire cars. Rolled-up pieces of matting lay all along the roadside, hundreds of them, as far as the eye could see. It was as though a carpet seller had neatly laid out his wares.

'The latest crop of corpses,' Danny explained. 'They go to sleep on those straw mats, and if they don't wake up, their bodies just get wrapped in them. The TV crews love it, they get to show dead bodies without upsetting viewers.'

He told them that of the one million refugees who had settled here, the cholera was killing up to eight thousand a day. Their curse was to have settled on the black, igneous moonscape of volcanic rock Goma was built on. The refugees couldn't dig themselves latrines, or graves.

'Welcome to Camp Cholera, and it's getting worse by the hour.'

Becky and Rachel shook their heads, but both felt a distasteful surge of relief. The last thing they wanted to hear was that the crisis was abating just as they arrived. Danny read their thoughts.

'Still, I guess for us bad is good and worse is better.'

'But some of them are so tiny.'

Among all the carpeted corpses, Becky had noticed a row of short ones, no more than two or three feet long. Then, under a tree, she saw a mother and child coiled into each other, perfectly still.

'So why aren't those ones in mats then?'

'Probably not quite dead yet.'

'Can we stop for a sec? I'll just grab a shot.'

'They're not going anywhere, Becky, apart from over to the other side. Let's get you checked in first, then come back and feast your lens.'

Becky ignored him. Once she saw a picture, nothing and no one could ever stop her. She might as well have been in a trance.

'Driver, can you pull up here for a moment? This light is extraordinary.' The car was still slowing down when she opened the door and jumped out, running to stop herself from falling. Danny sighed.

'She's like some old gunslinger from the Wild West, just shoots first and asks questions later.'

Becky clicked away and both mother and baby son half-opened their dying eyes to cast a weary glance into her fat, black Canon.

'Thank you very much,' Becky said to them politely, as if they'd had any choice in whether their last moments on earth should be recorded.

A few hundred yards from the dying, the Grands Lacs was set back behind high, whitewashed walls. They kept out undesirables and the smell of death. In its car park sat an array of plump, plush Land Rovers, the aid agency fleet all bright and white, a forest of radio antennae rising from them. Black iron gates led through to a path bordered by lemon trees and bougainvillea. The lawns were so manicured they reminded Rachel of her doll's house garden in Arlington, except that here the flowers were tropical with extravagant colours and exotic scents. Eventually the path led up to the dining area, where lunch al fresco was being served. A small coterie of NGO staff was dining off red-and-white chequered tablecloths, with immaculately polished cutlery. A few were having prawns but most had chosen steak and chips, washed down by red wine or big bottles of Primus beer, followed by cappuccinos with whipped cream on top.

'Uncomfortably comfortable,' Danny said as they threaded their way through the tables. Becky disappeared to the toilet, so that he and Rachel were left standing together in the Grands Lacs reception where they scrawled lazy signatures on check-in forms and waited to collect their room keys. A wooden fan whirled away above them on the ceiling. It felt like a long time since they'd been alone together.

Danny saw her in a way he hadn't seen before. She was a woman now, no longer the silly girl of Sarajevo. He found himself taking the chance to study her every time she looked away.

'Still, an improvement on the Holiday Inn?' he asked her.

'I guess so, if there's power, hot water and a bar.'

'So, is it good to get away from Bosnia?' For Rachel, it was a surprise to hear Danny asking her one question, let alone two. She wondered whether to make an excuse and slip away, at least till Becky came back.

'Yeah, definitely. I mean, I miss it, but I was ready to try something else.'

'I agree. You know I didn't want to come – I argued against it – but now I'm here, I feel kind of liberated.'

'But God, this is such a terrible story.'

She knew as soon as she said it that it was a banal statement of the obvious, the sort of thing he'd pick up on and pillory, but he was preoccupied. He wasn't even listening to her.

'Rachel, there's something I've been meaning to say to you.' She looked around the foyer at anyone but him, pretending she hadn't heard. 'You know at the Hilton, when I apologised about the Karadzic thing and what I said at that party? I want you to know, I meant it.'

His eyes were fixed on her with an intensity she hadn't seen before. She looked away from them again.

'Really, you don't need to keep apologising. It was months ago and I've completely forgotten about it.'

'Well, whether you have or you haven't, I was wondering if we could just start over?'

'Sure, of course we can, but honestly, it was never a big deal.'

'Good, I'm glad that's settled then. Friends?'

'Friends.'

Becky came back from the ladies' and wondered why on earth they were shaking hands.

19

Post-Liberation Iraq, August 2004

It's the 14th day of his captivity, 16 more until his death. In the corner of his cell another rat appears, or perhaps it is the same one as before. It scurries busily around his feet, sniffing at his filthy toes. Danny is oblivious because he's thinking about Rachel.

She was so young then, so determined … so like him. He sees her the first time they met, when he drove her down Snipers' Alley and her sense of wonder was beautiful to behold; at least, it should have been, but he had allowed himself to sneer at it. He'd thought he was a better person.

His mind spools back and forth, and memories mutate into dreams and suddenly Rachel is in the Toyota with her pretty nose squashed up against the windscreen. His other friends are crammed in next to her – Becky, Edwin and Kaps – and they take it in turns to pop up behind the glass. Except that they're not his 'friends' – why does he persist with this stupid fiction? Kaps jealous, Edwin betrayed, Becky angry and Rachel … well, surely she at least had loved him?

When he asks if it's safe to go on, the four of them nod together: just slight movements at first, then much more vigorously, until their heads are rocking back and forth and their mouths are gaping open. They had looked sad but now they laugh as they wave him to his death, giggling and guffawing. Keep going, Danny, don't be afraid! After all, you're braver than us, aren't you? You're a better person!

When he wakes, he is panting and sweating. The nightmares rampage through his sleep so he wishes he could stay awake forever. What has woken him is the demented barking from the wild dogs outside his cell, and persistent gunfire. The sounds are familiar: this is how he used to spend his nights in the Holiday Inn, listening to gunfire in the Jewish cemetery.

The guards are shouting at each other, an edge of panic in their voices. He pictures poor Slow: confused no doubt and awaiting orders.

And is that the distant throb of helicopters? He's been on so many of them in Iraq: Apaches, Cobras, Chinooks. There would be an indulgent, small-boy thrill every time he sat by their open doors, balmy air blowing out his cheeks as the pilots swooped low and fast over the rooftops of Baghdad, Fallujah and Ramadi, making sure no insurgent could line up a shot against them. They were rides that evoked the heady days of Vietnam – not his war, but the one he longed to have been a part of.

Now they're getting closer, almost directly overhead, the clatter of their rotor-blades so loud they could be landing on the roof. Can it be another dream? He touches the septic mess of his burn to make sure, and winces. His pulse quickens. Briefly, he lets himself slip into the fantasy of a comic-book rescue in which good guys storm in and greet him with a handshake and a jokey 'Mr Lowenstein, I presume?'

But then the helicopters fade slowly into silence and the crackles of gunfire are no more.

20

Goma, 1994

The Grands Lacs was the base from which they commuted to catastrophe, with Mugunga their most regular destination. Its lunar expanse lay about nine miles to the north. Tens of thousands of refugees had set down their weary bodies here after weeks of walking. The Hutus thought Mugunga was a sanctuary from the invading Tutsi Army, but instead it would become their 'Valley of Death' as the newspapers came to call it.

A permanent haze hung over Mugunga, drifting up from campfires before mingling with ash and dust from the brooding Nyiragongo Volcano nearby. Extended families crammed into makeshift hovels, flimsily assembled from strips of UN plastic sheeting and branches that had been hacked down with machetes. The trees had long since been reduced to stumps.

Cholera ripped through them so fast they didn't even have time to wrap up the bodies in mats or sheets. As if asleep, the dead lay beside the living – beside men chopping wood, women cooking beans and children crapping in the open. The half-dead were there as well, writhing in the final, delirious throes of their cholera. The smell was a noxious cocktail of decaying flesh, sweat, campfire smoke and the faeces that lay unapologetically on top of the pockmarked lava rock. Mugunga, it seemed to the Junkies, was the most godforsaken place on the planet. They couldn't keep away from it.

'What gets me is the way they all just sit here waiting.' Rachel was stumbling through the dead and dying for the fourth straight day. 'I mean, waiting for what?'

'For help, or for the end,' said Danny matter-of-factly. He walked with her while Becky was working the other end of the camp, by a banana grove. 'Perhaps they think it's Divine Retribution. Natural justice, to punish them for what they did to the Tutsis.'

'But look at these little kids – you can't tell me they're guilty of a crime. They don't even know the difference between a Hutu and a Tutsi.'

'I wouldn't bet on it. They learn it from birth. Like Muslims and Serbs in Bosnia. Or Protestants and Catholics in Belfast. Still, thank God for ethnic hatred: we'd be out of work without it.'

She wasn't sure what to make of his cheap cynicism. It was so different from the moral passion of his writing. Sometimes she thought there were two entirely separate Lowensteins, the Danny and the Daniel. Why did he feel the need to sound so callous? Was it a shield, she wondered, or was this what he really thought when he forgot to be impassioned?

At the same time, she was enjoying his company. If she were honest with herself, she might have begun to seek it out, even if it meant stepping over corpses together in Mugunga. It was how she had originally imagined things would be, except that she had moved on from his fawning groupie to something more like his wary equal. After her award, he had come to treat her with the respect she believed she was entitled to. Her most recent pieces from Sarajevo, and a couple from Goma too, had been syndicated across the States. Three had made the *Los Angeles Times*, two the *Washington Post* and one – to her incredulity – the *New York Times* itself.

She decided that perhaps Africa had changed Danny, reinvigorated him. She looked at him now as he listened intently to a young doctor from Médicins Sans Frontières, and noticed how tanned he had become. In the Balkans he was pallid and pasty, but here he radiated a glow and the darkening skin around his eyes enhanced them.

Becky had teamed up with some of the other photographers who wanted to hit Mugunga hard: Lacroix from AFP, Spinoza from AP, Dirk from Gamma and Jason Krontz from *Time Magazine*, the gang Rachel had first seen her with in Split. She limped along after them, a wounded animal trying to keep up with the herd. Becky cursed the fine volcanic dust that kept getting into her cameras, but she drooled again over the soft early-morning light of Africa. It reminded of her of Australian dawns and dusks when she had learnt her craft.

Frame up: a six-year-old was carrying his baby sister on his back, his bare feet bleeding from the razor-sharp edges of the rock. Click.

Frame up again: this time closer in on the little sister's face, and those eyes, so glassy, rolling around in their sockets. Click click. Her brother was probably carrying her off somewhere to die. In silence, so no one would be bothered with her passing. Click, click, click.

Becky wiped the sweat off her forehead with her sleeve but she wasn't satisfied. 'It's almost too much. Too grim, too epic.' Ever since arriving in Goma, she'd been in search of one image to define the catastrophe, but still she couldn't find it. The baby sister on her brother's back was good, but not enough. 'Too … I don't know, too samey.'

'That's what death is,' said Krontz philosophically. 'In the end, it's the same for all of us. It's just fucking samey.'

They had almost given up hope when Spinoza spotted something in a rare and precious shadow beneath an awning. An aid worker – Austrian he thought, and from the Red Cross – sat on a patch of dried-out grass with a sickly baby in her arms. She was smartly dressed in a crisp linen shirt. She had undone three of its buttons and pulled out her left breast, its startling, creamy flesh exposed to all of Mugunga. The baby fed from it, his fragile rib cage rising and falling, black skin pressed hungrily on white. Flies congregated around his streaming nose and eyes sticky with disease. On a boulder not far away sat his own mother, her drooping breasts exposed as well, but shrivelled up and useless. Shame hung heavy over her.

Becky shrunk back.

'Guys, we can't. It's too … God, it would be so intrusive.'

But Dirk and Krontz had already followed Spinoza in whipping up their cameras, and then Lacroix joined in as well. If any of them had heard her they weren't listening; photographers didn't have time for dilemmas – use the shot or lose it. After a few moments of uncharacteristic indecision, Becky started snapping too. Even as it filled her lens, she knew it was the killer picture: a skeletal African head nuzzled into a European breast so generous, so ample, it looked like it might suffocate him. None of them dared ask the aid worker for permission to photograph her, for it carried the risk she might say no, or – worse – simply turn her back on them. That she didn't, they took as tacit acceptance that they could carry on. Front pages and magazine covers beckoned.

'Amazing,' said Krontz when they had finished. He couldn't believe their luck. 'Trumps a mass grave any time.'

When Becky caught up with Danny and Rachel, she filled them in so they could write about it. They too needed a defining image but in words not pictures, and they could tell the aid worker scene was, as Krontz put it, '24-carat gold'. Danny started scribbling notes for his opening paragraph before he'd even seen her: in his notebook, he put *milk of human kindness.*

By the time Becky retraced her steps and led them to the spot, the embarrassed Austrian had – quite sensibly – disappeared.

'Fuck,' said Danny and Rachel, almost at the same time.

'Oh well,' said Becky, not displeased. 'Easy come, easy go.'

Disconsolately they decided to head back to Goma, Nyiragongo looming above them with the quiet menace of a bully, muttering threats that one day this place would have more than just cholera to contend with.

The road from Mugunga became steep and winding and they closed in on a truck ahead, struggling up the hill. It took a few seconds for them to realise the nature of the cargo that weighed it down: the latest delivery of dead from Mugunga. The bodies were in a pile that narrowed to a peak, and there one of them – a young girl in a pretty pink dress – was perched precariously. As the lorry bounced over bumps and holes in the road, she would leap a few inches into the air, as if given new life, before landing back down again among the other dead.

The Junkies were just a few yards behind now, trying to overtake. The first whiff of decomposing flesh came floating in through an open window, and Rachel gagged instinctively. The smell – sickly sweet – was unlike any other she had come across, the worst smell in the world. She clutched at the handkerchief she was wearing over her nose and mouth, but it didn't seem to help. Her eyes fell upon an advertising slogan painted on the back of the lorry: *Guinness is Good for You.*

The lorry hit a pothole, and the dead leapt into the air as one, bouncing together on a trampoline. The girl in pink leapt the highest and this time when she landed she slid down the steep gradient of corpses and right out of the back of the lorry, tumbling like a broken doll on to the road in front of them. Innocent, their driver, slammed hard on the brakes and spun the wheel to avoid her.

Rachel closed her eyes.

The lorry trundled on, leaving the girl in the road.

'What do we do now, pick her up and follow him?' asked Danny.

'Don't be ridiculous,' said Becky. 'She's riddled with disease.'

They drove around her, comforting themselves that a resting place in the middle of the road might be better than a mass grave.

'I want to follow the truck, though,' Danny announced. 'It'll make good colour.'

The others could see which way his mind was working: it was a classic example of the Lowenstein technique. He would nose off his story on the girl in pink. If he couldn't have the breastfeeding aid worker, she'd have to do instead. Doomed innocence, he could never get enough of it. He'd turn on the prose until the readers thought they knew her, but to get the full, emotive punch, he'd need to see where she had been buried. It was why, 20 minutes later, they arrived at Trench Nine.

As they opened the car doors, the stench was overwhelming. Rachel thought about the micro-particles that must be inside her nostrils and retched, a mouthful of saliva and a small amount of vomit projecting from her mouth. In Bosnia, Danny might have rolled his eyes, but now he put an arm round her briefly and asked if she would like to stay inside the vehicle.

'I'll be fine. Sorry.'

'Don't be. It's the natural reaction.'

Rachel thought back to her first massacre in Sarajevo. Six months on she had come a long way – she'd won an award, for God's sake – but she hadn't yet developed Becky's and Danny's immunity to horror.

He held out a tub of Vicks chest rub.

'Stick some of this around your nostrils and it'll mask the smell.'

'Thanks.'

'A trick of the trade.'

They turned together to watch the corpses being raised by the lorry's noisy hydraulics, then dropped into the freshly dug trench, arms and legs flailing around as they slipped out from the bed of the truck – the first few reluctantly, one by one, then the rest, en masse, a great coagulated lump of human flesh and bones. Men in masks and yellow rubber gloves oversaw the process, as detached and bored as workers at a meat factory. A bulldozer moved in to spread the anonymous corpses around, making sure none took up too much room, pushing them back and forth so that not a square inch of space was wasted. After all, there were more bodies on the way. It wouldn't be fair on the others.

Rachel noticed a woman's head that had got caught up in the elbow of bulldozer's arm. It was being slowly crushed, until a spurt of bloody brain shot out, like the juice from an over-ripe tomato. The girl in pink was lucky, after all, Rachel decided. This at least she had been spared.

Beside her, Danny took notes – details, descriptions, times, numbers. Worse is better. Rachel started scribbling a few lines as well and Becky was just in front of them, working the dead with her cameras. After a few minutes, Rachel became impatient.

'Okay, guys, that's got to be enough. Can we get out of here now?'

'Sure. I'm sorry,' said Becky. 'Just one more sec. Takes a while when you're trying to make a mountain of dead people look nice. I have to frame it so it doesn't offend Middle America – in the unlikely event that Middle America will ever get to see it.'

She finished off a couple of minutes later, and they walked back to the car.

'Doesn't shit like that ever get to you?' Rachel asked her.

Becky didn't mention how she had hesitated to intrude on the aid worker and the baby. She had a reputation to maintain: ruthless, and ridiculously brave.

'I've got my lovely lens to protect me, a nice thick glass wall that stops me getting hurt. Not bullet-proof, but pain-proof definitely.'

Even as she said it, Becky was considering the other ways that pain could reach her.

That evening, they met for dinner as usual on the terrace at about eight. After filing their stories, each had showered, washed their hair, dug the dirt from their nails and scrubbed hard at skin they assumed to be contaminated.

The waiters of the Grands Lacs were polite, but the hotel was filling up fast and they were overworked, mopping their brows and upper lips as they scurried around the burgeoning clientele. More of the world's media had descended on the Grands Lacs in search of a new hit story. The latecomers were forced to camp out at the airport, a tented city bristling with TV satellite dishes, cameras and cables. Others were in Goma's handful of hotels, but the Grands Lacs was *the* press hotel, the place to be, and reporters had stuffed themselves into it, sometimes three or four to a room. It was taking longer and longer to order, let alone get any food.

Danny and Rachel found themselves side by side at the dinner table. Only a few weeks earlier, she had concentrated hard on making sure their paths didn't cross like this. Ignoring him had become an obsession. Now, whether by accident or design, they kept sitting next to each other. She was irritated with herself that she would glance up at him, liking the small things about him: the little fallibilities of his stupid boots and the leaking fountain pen he always wrote with, and the tear in his chinos he had no way of mending. Rachel didn't want to have to like him. She had changed her mind about him once already and it seemed too complicated to do so once again.

'Good to see the global village has finally woken up to what's happening here,' said Danny. He'd downed two bottles of Primus in quick succession, while Rachel was sipping a large South African white wine. It was warm and sickly, but she needed it. Her guilt was wearing off: the harder they worked and the worse the sights they saw, the less they cared if their evening meal was just down the road from the dying.

'I hate the way they all arrive en masse, like a package tour,' he said. 'Take a look over there. They're all the big American network boys. That's Todd Diamond from CBS. I mean, *Todd Diamond* – what kind of name is that? I bet it's not even really his, just like that mop on his head.'

She saw a man in his late fifties holding court in much the same way that Danny liked to do. He was a big network star. The little hair he had was thin and wiry, like a well-worn scouring pad, and he combed it hard across a bald patch.

'That has to be the worst cover-up since Watergate,' said Rachel. Danny fell about. It was the first time she'd ever made him laugh.

'Absolute asshole,' said Danny. 'I actually saw him putting hair-spray on it the other day, like he even needs it. But can you believe that? The wind carried a cloud of it right into the refugees behind him. How *about* that? You survive the cholera, but choke on Todd Diamond's fucking hairspray!'

'Didn't he get shot once?'

'Yeah, briefly.'

'Vietnam, wasn't it?'

'And my God, will he let us forget it? Always banging on about Nam this, Nam that. Really, who gives a fuck?'

'But you'd love to have been there, wouldn't you? You'd have had a field day.' Rachel was confident enough now to rile him. 'And anyway, when you're his age you'll be banging on about Bosnia, won't you. Boz this, Boz that. And some guy twenty years younger than you will be saying, "but who cares any more?"'

Danny laughed again, to her surprise. He didn't seem to mind if she cut him down to size; in fact, he quite enjoyed it.

They were so tightly squeezed around the flimsy plastic table that his right leg brushed against her left. It was like the car ride from the airport, except this time Rachel didn't feel so flustered. He wriggled it away as soon as there was contact and murmured an apology, but the second time it happened, he left it there a fraction of a second longer, not a statement but a hint.

After dinner, Rachel and Becky took a stroll through the hotel gardens, and tried not to think of those surrendering to death outside. Occasionally she thought she caught a whiff of dead flesh floating in on the evening breeze, but she decided it was her imagination, or some bit of her body she hadn't scrubbed clean enough. They set themselves down on a strip of well-kept lawn which was thick and spongy, almost artificial. Sprinklers soaked it every few hours, while the refugees had to walk for miles to fetch their water. Lying on their backs, they looked up at a star-spattered sky, heads together and legs outstretched in different directions, the four points of the compass. Cicadas, hidden all around, were giving out a shrill, incessant warble.

'Oh, Africa,' sighed Rachel. 'I think I may just have fallen in love with it.'

'Well, we all know someone who's fallen in love with you, young lady.'

'I don't have a clue what you're talking about.' But her heart pumped harder.

'He's going crazy for you, you know he is.'

'Don't be so ridiculous.'

'And don't you be so coy. Everyone can see it. I just can't believe it after those bastard things he said about you in Sarajevo. Men, I'll swear they have hypocrisy written in their DNA.'

'First of all, he most certainly is *not* in love with me. And secondly, I've forgiven him for all that stuff. I quite like him now. I think.'

'Just remember what I told you the first time we met. All the girls adore him. Sometimes he has this power over women and I don't think it's always healthy.'

Rachel looked confused.

'What the hell does that mean?'

Becky was still unsure whether she should tell her: it could tip the balance of their friendship. Becky rolled over on the grass so her face was buried in its wide blades of vivid green.

'Me and Danny, we …'

'Oh shit.'

'I mean it was ages ago – back in '92 when Bosnia was just beginning. It only lasted a few weeks. But Danny, he picks women up and well … I just don't want him to hurt you.'

'Are you warning me off?'

'No, just warning you. They have a phrase for it where I come from: hump and dump. Danny loves women, but I'm not sure how much he likes them.'

Rachel thought about it. It was a curious thing to say, but she had a bad feeling there might be some truth to it. Still, she wasn't sure it would stop her.

Becky rolled back over. She had said her piece and now she could face Rachel once again.

'We mustn't ever let him come between us.'

''Course not,' said Rachel. 'Why would we?'

For a few minutes, they lay on their backs and marvelled at the dazzling universe above them.

'Are you over him?' asked Rachel.

'God, yes.'

'Of course, now you have your prince, your *married* prince.'

'Is that Saturn, that big bright one?'

'Don't you dare change the subject.'

'We're getting on well, if you must know. Really well.'

'I can hear that every night.'

'I'm sorry.'

'My fault for getting the room next door. Look, I don't want to see you hurt either, and I worry that he's using you.'

'How?'

'Fun on the road, happy families when he goes back home.'

'That's not fair on him. Anyway, if I can survive a war zone, I can survive a bloody love affair. Survived Danny, didn't I?'

I don't know, Rachel wanted to say: *did* you?

'But how does it end, Beck? With him leaving Judith and the kids? Or you … well, humped and dumped?'

'All I know is I love him and he loves me. It's enough. For now, it's enough. Maybe he's just out on loan.'

'Strange kind of loan. Inappropriate, even.'

'Look, I know it's a bad thing to do. All right, *inappropriate.* I grew up watching my parents tear each other into little pieces and I don't want to put his kids through all of that. But I also know I've never been this much in love before. Who knows, I may never be again. If you want the truth, I ache for him. I've been roaming round the world for five years now, from one battlefield to the next: Desert Storm, Georgia, Nagorno-Karabakh, Croatia, Bosnia – you name it, I've got the frigging T-shirts spilling out of the wardrobe. And you know what? In every one of them I've been lonely. I'm not cute like you. I've got this weird red hair and a big arse and you, Rachel – you don't even have to try.'

'That's just not …'

'No arguments, please. Apart from the fact you've got no tits whatsoever, you're a catwalk model by comparison. It's a matter of objective fact, men like Danny want you, they just do.'

'He wanted you too.'

'Not for long and only because there was no one else in town. Besides, now I've got a fucking limp. Bloody hopalong Becky. So here I am in Goma, still taking pictures of the babies I ought to be having by now. Anyway, the point is that men have always passed me by. Till Kaps. By some bizarre miracle, he finds me beautiful. He makes me feel like I belong to him, even when I don't. Lord knows what he sees in me, but he may well turn out to be the one guy on the planet who truly wants and loves me and the bugger of it all is that I don't think I can ever make him mine.'

'I'm so sorry.'

'The truth is, I envy you. A bit of me might even hate you, because you'll get him in the end.'

'Who? Danny?'

'Whoever you want.'

Rachel put her arms round her and squeezed hard.

'Oh, I know how much worse life can get,' said Becky. 'I could probably find someone who'll die right in front of me tonight and cheer me up.'

'You do what you want, Beck. What makes you happy. No more sermons, no morality tales.'

'Except you think it's "inappropriate".'

'You know what? I'm not sure love is ever inappropriate.'

If I *am* prettier, Rachel thought, if men *do* notice me more, then how come I've never fallen in love like her? And as for sex, why haven't I had it since the fumbled, awkward one-night stand with that college tutor in Virginia. So inappropriate.

'When do you think we'll stop all this?' she asked Becky.

'This what?'

'This wandering round the world. Seeing shit. Telling people about it.'

'Jeez, you've only just begun. Till we're old and grey, I guess.

Martha Gellhorn was in her eighties when she finally packed it in. Which gives us at least another half a century on the road. That'll be me, a dried-up prune with a bunch of cameras round my scrawny neck, still happy-snapping round the shitholes of the world and only you lot for my family.'

Rachel wanted to ask her why, if she was so worried, she didn't go back to Australia, meet a man and settle down. Becky, it seemed to her, was hooked on this life but wanted another one as well. Rachel wondered if soon she would be the same.

They floated back into the stars and all the black holes next to them, and there were no more words, just thoughts of who they were and what they needed to complete themselves.

When Becky crept back into her room she found Kaps already there, naked in her bed and fast asleep, his hair sprayed wildly around the pillow. The mosquito net he had tried to hang from the ceiling had collapsed on top of him, so that the mesh now covered his long brown back and whiter buttocks.

'Make yourself at home, why don't you?'

He was waking up slowly and fumbling for his watch.

'It's two in the morning!'

'I've been talking with Rachel.'

He reached across for her as she got undressed. She unfastened her bra and her large breasts fell out, and he watched her, more awake now and aroused. It only ever took the briefest glimpse of Becky's flesh. What was this power she had over him? It was wrong to succumb to it, but he comforted himself with the belief that he had no choice.

'Actually, I don't think we should have sex in here any more,' she announced, turning from him primly. 'Rachel can hear everything next door.'

'Don't scream so loud then.'

'Ha bloody ha. The bed, not me.'

'There's something else.'

'We got talking. Rachel was giving me advice.'

'Don't tell me; I'm a bad apple, all rotten and rancid. Time to chuck me out the barrel.'

He pulled her on to the bed, and took a breast in each hand. It was where he wanted to be, all the time: between them, and between her legs. It was lust, but also more than that: he knew with absolute certainty that her body was a place where he belonged.

Becky looked wearily disinterested.

'She said you're using me. Said you like the double life – happy family at home, happy shagging on the road. Well, I'm fed up with being the mistress. I don't want the role any more. I hate the script, I hate the part.'

He didn't want this conversation now. Why couldn't they have it later … next week, next month, next year?

'I told you, I love you. I absolutely love you.'

'It's not enough any more, you have to do something with that love. You have to prove it.'

'How, abandon my family?'

'Make a choice. You can't put it off forever. I want you in a house, not just a hotel. And I don't want to be Martha bloody Gellhorn.'

'What?'

'Still doing wars when I'm 80, with a scraggy neck.'

'It's a gorgeous neck,' said Kaps, who started to kissing it, hoping to re-ignite her desire and burn away the doubts, for another night at least. He couldn't not be with her, but neither could he give up his boys: these were the two truths that clamped him like a vice. He wondered if there were some way to grade his love, so that he could choose just as she'd demanded. But his love for Becky and for his sons never seemed mutually exclusive – it was only Judith that didn't fit. Sometimes he had a fantasy, so grotesque he was ashamed to even think about it. It was that just as one day the dark cloud of Danny Lowenstein would disappear from his life – a car crash, a stray bullet or mortar round, even a heart attack – so would Judith.

'If you don't go fishing ...' Danny was telling them at breakfast.

'We know,' said Edwin, who hadn't had much sleep. 'You don't catch fish. Spare us the sermons, it's too early in the morning.'

In fact, it wasn't. It was almost quarter past ten, and the Junkies were enjoying late boiled eggs and coffees. The same waiters who'd been serving them till midnight the night before were back on duty, feeding and watering the Goma press corps. The morning news conference – held, for the convenience of that press corps, along the terrace – had just finished. Spokesmen and women from the rival aid agencies had sparred with each other over disputed malnutrition rates, while a torpor had set in among the journalists. Ten days into the crisis, they'd had enough of watching, hearing, smelling people die. At first they'd been hungry for catastrophe, but now their stomachs were swollen with it and the agreement was unspoken but collective: it was time for a day off.

'Write up the briefing quotes,' suggested Edwin. 'Throw in the latest death toll, add some unused colour from the day before and – hey presto – there's your easy-story recipe.'

'Lazy bastard.' Becky munched a cold slice of plain toast. The butter dish contained only yellow liquid.

'Look, they ran 200 words of what I sent them yesterday, that's precisely ten per cent. D'you know what some spotty sub told me? Said he wasn't sure the readers could take much more. Tosser.'

'He has a point. We're not so much slipping down the agenda as plummeting.'

'Then let's push it back up!' shouted Danny, with all the zeal of a convert. 'I'm going for a cruise round town.'

'Mate, let me guess! Please don't tell me!' said Becky. 'Mugunga, just for a change. Oh, what joy! I mean, really, just pure delight.'

'No such thing as a tired story. Just tired eyes.'

'And this morning my eyes are very fucking tired indeed,' said Edwin. 'I'm going back to bed.'

'Suit yourself. Anyone coming with me?'

No one moved.

'Well, screw the lot of you,' he said cheerfully, setting off for his room to collect his bag. He was just as happy to work alone.

'Hang on, Danny, I'll come!' Kaps yelled. That morning, despite the strange unslept beauty he saw in Becky and his unfulfilled longing for her, he had chosen the abomination of Mugunga instead. He needed a break from her ultimatums, and in any case he wanted to keep an eye on Danny. Kaps was wary of his old friend's energy, which never waned whether it was day one of the story or day ten. How was it that even in a continent he'd never reported from, Danny already knew so much more than everyone else? Why were his angles always fresher, his quotes more powerful, his analysis more profound? Kaps watched him walk across the terrace, bidding a jovial *bonjour* to an old acquaintance from *Le Monde*, and he couldn't help admiring him for the way he had when they'd first met in Vukovar in 1991.

Within 24 hours he would despise him.

21

Post-Liberation Baghdad, August 2004

Footsteps clattered down the corridor. The door flew open and Melissa, an efficient young producer from NBC, burst into the Presidential Suite.

'Just heard from our people in DC: the White House are making a statement about Danny.'

Kaps turned on the suite's dusty, decrepit television set just in time for them to catch the President's spokesman.

'The President would like to appeal again to the kidnappers of our citizen Daniel Lowenstein: do the right thing, release him now, today. As we have said before, we have been shocked by his abduction and the conditions in which he's being held. The demands we have been given and the deadline we've been set are abhorrent. We want to make it clear that the United States does not, has not and will not deal with terrorists. There will be no talks, no bargains, no pay-offs. To the kidnappers, we say again: Daniel Lowenstein is one of this nation's very finest journalists, a reporter who represents everything that is good about our free press: enquiring, challenging, compassionate. No one cares about Iraq more deeply than he. He is a supreme humanitarian and a great American, and we want him home.'

The TV cut to recycled pictures of Danny in his jumpsuit. They flicked through the channels and saw his battered image everywhere. His torment had been processed into a news commodity, tumbling off the production line with all the other stories of the day – a cut in federal interest rates, another hurricane in Florida, the Olympics in Athens. Danny might be a few days away from the most excruciating death imaginable, but he still had to wait his turn on the global running order.

'"A great American!"' said Rachel. 'Danny would so love that. Never mind that he hated everything America ever did in the world, and especially this administration. He'll have that framed in gold, if he gets out of this.'

If he gets out of this. It dragged them back to the cheap, red clock that hung at a slight angle on the wall above the kitchenette. Its plastic hands, so relentless, were the countdown to a world without Danny.

'Easy for that smart-arse at the White House to be all high and mighty.' Edwin mimicked the spokesman's glib certainty in a namby-pamby drawl: '"No talks, no bargains, no pay-offs" – I wonder if he'd be talking that tough if it was his pretty-boy neck on the block. Anyway, what's so wrong with doing deals? The Italians do it every time.'

'And the French. And the Germans,' said Rachel. 'Whereas we just tell him he's a "great American" and hang him out to dry.'

The day after the helicopters came is his worst since he was burnt.

Dawn is rising when Scar stomps into the cell with a shout of 'Allahu Akhbar', Quick and Slow in close attendance. Danny's stomach lurches. They unlock his chains but tape up his arms and legs and tie a blindfold so that his already darkened world is black again. Danny is taken outside, and stuffed into some sort of wooden crate. He can smell its timber. Maybe it's his coffin.

When the lid is slammed shut, he is seized by a raging claustrophobia. There's only a limited supply of oxygen, he thinks; soon he'll have used it all. In panic, his mouth and nostrils gasp for stuffy air. His body squirms, as if somehow he might wriggle himself free from the tape that confines him. With each futile movement, he is hotter and more breathless. This, he is sure, is what it's like to be buried alive. He longs to be back in his cell. At last he can appreciate its luxuries: air, space and his little pool of light. Even the rat was company of sorts.

The crate is lifted by guards. He can hear them curse its weight, then drop it down on to what sounds like metal. An engine starts with a growling rumble – he is in a vehicle, a truck or van. It sets off on a journey in which every bump in the road smashes his head against the wood. The pain is, at least, a distraction from his claustrophobia.

He convinces himself they are travelling along the same road that led him to the ambush. The potholes feel the same. And there is the dog they killed and the shepherd on the hill. And there is the red Toyota with his friend inside. One friend, though he knows it could have been any of those who've been starring in his dreams, laughing at him and wishing he were dead.

After half an hour, the engine dies. Danny hears the lid of his crate being levered open and he is hauled from it again. His blindfold slips a little and sunlight seeps through. He can smell fresh air for the first time since he was captured, the hint of a coming wind – warm and aromatic – and the scent of a eucalyptus tree.

'Where am I?' he asks quietly, but no one answers.

With less than a fortnight till Danny's scheduled execution, the Junkies had never felt less like work, but they couldn't just do nothing: the days would have dragged too slowly and besides, there were stories to be filed, pages to be filled. In August, when news could be sparse, editors relied on places like Baghdad where it never stopped, thank God, not even for the summer holidays.

They did their job like sleepwalkers. Rachel worked on a feature about the power supply, or lack of it, in the slums of Sadr City; Kaps ventured outside Baghdad on a 48-hour embed with First Cavalry; *Paris Match* asked Becky to photograph an Iraqi policeman who was staying in the job even though his wife had been murdered because of it. Edwin was commissioned to work up a two-page profile of Moqtadr al-Sadr, the shi'ite cleric the world had started to worry about.

Camille was left by herself in the Presidential Suite, waiting for the nightly conference call. Though Jamail had thoughtfully given her a key, she'd never been alone there. The four of them had always filled it, slumped in a sprawl of sadness on its chairs and sofas, pacing around its floor, standing on its balcony, filling its space with cooking, eating, drinking, smoking, talking. Now it was like a home whose family had moved out – silent, empty, dreary. She sat in the sofa that Becky and Rachel had made their own, and thought how strange it was she missed them.

'Hello there?'

She had left the door ajar, hoping they'd wander in, but instead it was a pleasant-looking young Englishman who put his head inside. His name was Jonathan, he said, from the *Independent*, and he was after Edwin. He had a package for him, a large brown envelope that was bulging out of his pocket like a fat present that sticks out of a Christmas stocking.

'He's not in his room, but they said I might find him here.'

Camille told him he could wait if he wanted, Edwin might swing by. Alternatively, Jonathan could leave the package with her. The suggestion had him in two minds.

'Thing is, I would, but it's cash. Quite a lot of it, as a matter of fact. His office in London asked me to bring it out for him. Besides, I'm sure you've got enough to worry about.'

He had recognised her immediately as Danny Lowenstein's sister and already felt bad that he'd intruded.

'No really, I'll make sure he gets it. I'm sure I'll be seeing him tonight, or if not, in the morning.'

Jonathan smiled gratefully and handed it to her, relieved to have passed it on.

'They told me there was twenty grand in there, but I haven't counted it. Tell him to get in touch if there's a problem. Oh, and by the way, I really do hope there's some good news soon.'

Camille supposed that journalists were always pigeoning out large sums of cash: after all, in Baghdad, you could hardly pop into a high street bank. At the time, it didn't strike her as the least bit strange.

She was still dozing when the angry fist hammered on her door the next morning. It was one of the rare days that she'd managed to sleep in, and to be dragged from her bed was infuriating. She opened the door in her dressing gown, puffy-eyed without her spectacles, and saw that it was Edwin, in a dark, thunderous mood. For a moment she thought he must have news of Danny.

'I gather you've got my money. I really wish you'd given it to me last night.'

Camille was confused.

'Oh, I'm sorry, I had no idea it was urgent. You were supposed to be coming up to the suite, I thought I'd see you then.'

Edwin said he'd had other things on his mind and Camille felt like telling him that she did too: a brother who was about to die, for one thing. She let it pass, the way she always let things pass.

'Well, if I can just take it *now*,' said Edwin brusquely, and when she handed it to him, he barely even thanked her before disappearing down the corridor, his walk breaking into a trot.

The idea of following him was absurd. It was one of those decisions she'd been taking recently that surprised her – like coming to Baghdad in the first place – and yet it felt right, and inevitable. She supposed she might have just gone back to bed if Edwin hadn't been so uncharacteristically bad tempered, or if Ramirez had never made his call, or if something about Danny's friends just didn't add up. As it was, it only took her a split second to make up her mind.

She threw on the previous day's clothes, which lay in a convenient heap on the floor, and made it down to the lobby just in time to see the four of them walking away from the hotel with a strong and purposeful stride: Edwin, Becky, Kaps and Rachel. The glare of sunlight assaulted her as she stepped outside; she hadn't had time to find her sunglasses.

Within a couple of minutes they had reached the tea house down the road, where Jamail was waiting for them. They hardly seemed to say hello before they slipped inside.

Having come this far, Camille hadn't a clue what she should do next. On another day, she might have told herself to snap out of it and then gone in to join them for some welcome morning tea. Instead she made another of her strangely irrational choices: she looked through the grimy window and studied them.

She doubted the glass had been cleaned since the invasion, but inside she could see that a television was on while about 40 men sat around, ignoring it. They were mostly middle-aged or elderly and wearing open-necked shirts. They slouched in little groups on cushioned benches, leaning back and gossiping, sipping sweet tea, smoking from hubble-bubble pipes and playing games of backgammon. Behind them, the walls were cluttered with pictures of old Baghdad, clocks, copper pots and jugs.

Tucked away in a corner, Camille could see that Becky and Rachel had just sat down on one of the benches: they looked incongruous, like women who had walked into an old-fashioned gentleman's club where the rules said they weren't allowed. Kaps was standing next to them, tall and strong, jabbing a finger at the smaller figure of Jamail. She couldn't hear a word, but it was obvious they were shouting at each other, characters in a silent movie. Then Edwin intervened, pushing them apart with a palm of each hand on their chests.

What happened next astonished her: Edwin pulled out of his pocket an envelope – unless she was mistaken, the same one she'd just given him – and with an angry flourish, handed it over to Jamail.

Danny is sitting cross-legged on a green carpet. It is cheap and garish no doubt, but to him it has an inner beauty: it has replaced the concrete floor of his cell. He likes to run his fingers up and down its velvety softness. This new room he's in is also dark, but only because its curtains are permanently drawn. On a sofa near him, a woman and her daughter are watching cartoons on the TV: *Tom and Jerry* and *Scooby-Doo* and other classics from his Pittsburgh boyhood.

Danny has tried hard to smile, but they ignore him. He's expected to sit with them and not to talk or move. The bargain is unspoken: he gets the luxury of a thick-pile carpet so long as he causes them no trouble. He's like a dog, brought in from the kennel to the living room, but only if he behaves.

He reckons the girl is about six years old and he's heard her called Aisha. Her father, who has a long, Mujahadeen beard, seems to have taken charge of him. The man spends most of his time talking not to his wife and daughter but to a clutch of other men who call him Abu Omar. They are always walking around the house with guns and wires and, on one occasion, they wear jackets round their bodies that look horribly like suicide vests: a family home has become a bomb factory. Danny wonders what poor Aisha and her mother make of it.

Mostly he keeps his eyes to the floor, on the assumption that it is safer not to see their faces, but they don't seem to care. If they look at him it's with quiet disdain, but never the threat of violence. It's as if he isn't even there. Danny likes it that way. Invisible.

He has no idea why he's been passed on to new captors. He could have been sold, he supposes, or it's just their turn to keep him for a while. Maybe he's like the relative who no one wants much, but everyone must have to stay. All he knows is that Scar and Quick and Slow have vanished from his life, and that, compared to his old cell, this is a little piece of paradise. Perhaps, with time and good behaviour, he'll get more privileges; perhaps one day they'll even let him sit on the sofa with Aisha and then eventually, after enough long months of tedium, they'll tell him that he's going home. There'll be a certain sense of anti-climax, a crushing sense of time wasted, but nothing worse. He'll watch one last *Tom and Jerry* and be gone forever.

On a morning that Aisha and her mother aren't there, Abu Omar rams a cassette into the video machine and instructs Danny to watch. For once the screen shows not cartoons, but a series of exploding American army vehicles set to jaunty music with shots of dancing insurgents. Abu Omar jabs a finger at the TV and laughs before slotting in another cassette. This tape is slightly damaged and the images are torn and wobbly, but they are of Danny in his jumpsuit, begging for his life: he's probably the only person in the world who hasn't seen them until now. Abu Omar laughs again and points childishly, first at the screen and then at Danny. He fast forwards until the elderly couple appear, side by side, in the Pittsburgh mansion. It is Eliza Lowenstein who does all the talking. An Arabic voice speaks over her, nagging and loud, but in between the translation he can hear snatches of her, pleading for her son's release. His father stands next to her; he says nothing, just as he's been saying nothing to Danny all his life. He is so much greyer than Danny remembers, smaller too, more hunched and wizened. Somehow more pathetic, as though he too is getting ready to die.

Afterwards Danny tries hard not to return there, but in the barren plains of his solitude there is nothing to distract him.

It is the day he told his parents about Sophie Heller, his pretty high school date: 15 and feisty, just like him. Her father was one of Lukas' friends in corporate Pittsburgh and in the East Allegheny Rotary Club, so it might even have been a match Lukas could approve of, until Danny came home and, over dinner, announced that she was pregnant with his child.

Danny felt nauseous with shame, but managed to convince himself it was an effective protest against everything his parents stood for. The more he thought about it, the more he realised this was so much more dramatic than refusing to go to church, or joining a march against Vietnam. This was a real rebellion against the *ancien régime*.

'We're keeping it.'

'Don't be ridiculous.' Lukas Lowenstein knew that everything he'd worked for in this town was in jeopardy: his company, his friends, his reputation, his standing in the church. How could they ever ask him again to read the lesson? His son's depravity – so deliberate and wanton – disgusted him.

'What exactly was it I did to you?'

'Nothing. That's *exactly* what you did.'

But Lukas only shook his head. If it were true that somehow he'd chosen Camille over Daniel, then surely this was proof that choice was justified. How could you *not* choose a delightful, hard-working, God-fearing daughter over this … well, this scumbag of a son? How could you pretend there was some equality between them?

Danny left the table and retreated to his room, the way he did so often. Camille and her parents finished their meal in silence. The only sound was the tinkling of cutlery on crockery, a grating, discordant sound that echoed through the house.

Lukas was already planning what to do. He would arrange a round of golf with Sophie Heller's father and very quickly they'd come to an agreement. After all, if they left it much longer, people in East Allegheny would start to talk and that would be bad for both of them. Sophie would be sent to the clinic straight away, within hours perhaps. Danny wouldn't even know about it till after the event.

22

Goma, July 1994

Innocent drove Kaps and Danny around but it was aimless and they were just hoping to stumble on a story. Even Danny had to agree the coughing, spewing, dying wasteland of Mugunga was losing its appeal, so instead they tried their luck at Kibumba camp a few miles away.

At first all they saw were the familiar lines of refugees with the yellow canisters on their heads, walking for miles in search of water. Then it was as if the Gods of News had decided to reward persistence. A group of refugees started punching and kicking each other, 50 or 60 of them brawling on the ground.

'They're fighting for food!' Danny sensed the fresh angle he'd been looking for all day and scribbled down some notes.

Clouds of dust. Tearing clothes. Tearing skin.

Younger children trampled underfoot. By older ones.

Kaps shook his head in disbelief.

'Natural selection. The Darwinian theory of evolution right before our eyes.'

Danny nodded and made another note.

Survival of the fittest.

They could both see the story taking shape, though ideally they'd have a picture to go with it. Where was Becky Cooper when you needed her? It was then that Kaps noticed the crew from Italian TV.

'I don't believe it, she's throwing them *sweets*. That stupid bitch is actually throwing sweets to the kids.'

The reporter was glamorous and chic. From the Billingham bag around her shoulder, there emerged – as if by magic – boiled sweets of assorted flavours and colours. As each fistful exploded above the refugees like a starburst, the children fought for what they could get, no matter if some got nothing. One woman – one intruder from Italy – had managed to reduce the dignified misery of Kibumba to anarchy, and naturally her cameraman was there to film it.

'I think I might have to be sick,' said Kaps.

'So will those kids. Can you imagine what that'll do to their stomachs in the state they're in?'

Danny and Kaps shouted at the woman to stop, but the look she gave them said, Who the hell are you, and what could possibly give you the right to tell me what to do?

'Oh, let's just get out of here,' said Danny, disgusted.

On his way back to the car, he went up to the Italians' vehicle, a plush four-wheel drive much like their own. Its driver had left it for a second to watch the spectacle. Danny put his hand in through the open window, grabbed the keys from the ignition and hurled them 20 yards away on to the barren, dusty ground.

'Christ, Danny,' said Kaps, who saw something demented in him. 'That's a bit extreme.'

'I just hate people who say they care when really they don't give a fuck.'

Innocent drove them back to Goma and they toured the town again, reluctant to return to the hotel empty-handed. In the fore-court of a boarded-up petrol station, Kaps caught sight of a mother and two little boys. They must have been about three or four years old, and they were squatting in the dirt with no shelter from the sun. It looked as though they were about to give themselves up to their cholera, quietly, without a fuss.

He couldn't help thinking of Judith, Charlie and Tom, and Becky's demand that he should leave them. Three sets of eyes were looking up at him from the ground, helpless. 'How could you?' they said, as the journalists drove on by.

By mid afternoon, they had secured interviews with some impassioned Irish aid workers. 'If there's a worse place on earth, I've yet to see it,' one told them in a lilting Dublin brogue. 'No human being should have to die like this.' Kaps and Danny were quietly satisfied: the quotes fattened up a story that had been perilously thin.

They passed the petrol station again.

Kaps realised that the mother and her sons had collapsed. They were sprawled amid the fine volcanic dust, gazing up and down the road in search of help, knowing it was more likely to be death that came along to sweep them up.

The reporters drove on for a couple of hundred yards, until Kaps spoke, his voice soft but certain.

'I want to go back and help those kids at the petrol station. We need to turn around.'

'What kids?' Danny hadn't even noticed them and he was always suspicious when a journalist mentioned the word 'help'.

'We've passed them twice now. They're getting worse.'

'They all are, in case you didn't realise. I think we should keep going. We don't have enough yet.'

'Look, give me five minutes, will you? I just can't keep driving past them.'

Danny raised his eyebrows. Kaps was as misguided as the Italian woman. These people just didn't get it.

'Come on, we're not aid workers. We start picking people up, we'd never get a story filed.'

Kaps could feel the anger rising up in him, hot blood pumping through his brain. Why did Danny have to argue about everything? Why did he always insist on being right?

'Okay, but we are human beings, aren't we? Five minutes, that's all I'm asking.'

'You do know there are about a million refugees here? How many more are you planning to help today?'

Kaps wasn't going to be dissuaded. It was a point of principle now; he couldn't let Danny boss him around, and he couldn't let him win all the prizes. It had been a mistake to come out with him, but there was no going back.

'What about when Edwin helped that woman in Sarajevo? For once in his fucked-up life, he did the right thing.'

Danny sighed loudly and ordered Innocent to swing the car around. By the time they were back at the petrol station and Kaps had walked up to them, the mother was unconscious and the flickering eyes of her sons were closing for longer than they opened. They rolled languidly around, beseeching him.

Kaps tried to turn the mother on her side. He had a notion he should make sure her tongue was free in case she choked. Putting the patient into the recovery position was one of the first things they'd been taught at Walsingham. She lay in two puddles of watery puke and shit, however, which made him heave.

'For God's sake, man, she's got *cholera*!' Danny hadn't even left the car but was shouting from the wound-down window. 'There's nothing we can do for her.'

Kaps felt another surge of anger. Shut up for once in your life, he wanted to shout.

He looked into her vacant stare and realised the life had drained from her, along with all the bodily fluids. It had probably happened in the last hour or so, while they'd been driving round looking for more news. Her boys wouldn't be far behind.

'Maybe not her, but we can still save the kids.'

Save. To Danny, it was another word like 'help': never to be used by journalists in the context of themselves. They observed, they wrote, they even campaigned and agitated – but they didn't help or save. That could only be about the ego of the reporter, gesture journalism. Knowing Kaps, it might also be about his guilt that he was screwing refugees for stories. Or screwing Becky.

Kaps carried the two boys to the car, one after the other. They weighed nothing, their gangly, spindly arms and legs drooping low, scraping the road, so brittle he thought they might snap like twigs as he laid them on the back seat. Two faces looked up at him, confused but full of beauty, tight black curls knitted upon their scalps, teeth and eyes the brightest white and flat, squashed noses that marked them out as Hutu.

'Great,' said Danny. 'I really can't believe you've just done that. So what happens now, we check them into a double room at the Grands Lacs?'

'Don't be a cunt, Danny. I'm taking them to the French military hospital by the airport.'

The two soldiers at the gate wear berets that are immaculately tilted. Proud French tricolours decorate their shoulders.

'*Ce n'est pas possible*,' says one.

'*Nous sommes désolés*,' adds the other, not sounding as though he means it. There are systems and procedures for bringing patients to their field hospital, and rather like Danny, these troops see the scruffy, unkempt South African who stands in front of them as an interfering busybody who should stick to his day job. Kaps dredges up his lousy schoolboy French to plead with them.

'*Mais ils vont mourir!*'

The soldiers shake their heads and wave their hands, gesturing upwards. Kaps gets it in the end: they want him to make the boys stand up, a test to see if they're really as sick as he claims they are.

'Incredible, just incredible,' he says, but since he has no choice he drags them out and holds them up beneath their arms, one by one. And one by one they collapse, like newborn foals that try to walk and can't quite manage it.

The soldiers shrug. It will take more than this to convince them.

Exasperated, Kaps rummages around in his various pockets and notebooks and finds, inside his passport, the scrunched-up card of one of the doctors he has interviewed here, a Jean-Michel Maillard. Upon such trivia, he reflects, hang the slender threads of human life.

The boys are admitted within minutes and instantly declared priority cases. In the arms of nurses, they are rushed to the high-dependency tent, their mouths, noses and arms immediately stuffed with a bewildering array of tubes and drips, doctors frantically busy around them. From a state of weary disinterest, there is now nothing the French nation will not do for these two little Hutus.

It is touch and go, a nurse explains to Kaps gravely. '*Peut-être oui, peut-être non.*' She seems as affected by their fate as he is, and close to tears. Even Danny is drawn in, no longer castigating Kaps or itching to return to Mugunga. Like an anxious father, Kaps decides to stay at the boys' bedsides until they pull through or slip away. They are Charlie and Tom. Their eyes, when they can open, implore him for protection from the apocalypse of genocide, disease and divorce. Help us, they say. Give us clean water, medicine and a loving father.

Dr Maillard consults some charts. He speaks good English but quickly and in such a heavy accent, they have to strain to understand him.

'They have both suffered the failure of the kidneys. They're also very badly dehydrated and in shock. It happens when the cholera is too severe.'

'So you think they'll die?' asks Kaps.

'I hope not of course, but it could be, yes. We give them the intravenous rehydration drips and we put in them antibiotics for the diarrhoea. It's supposed to be Erythromycin for the children, but we only have Tetracycline. Normally it is for the adults, but it will have to do. New supplies are coming on a plane tomorrow, but we have no time to wait.'

For more than an hour, they sit on two stools in a corner of the tent, which is full of dust and noise. It's been erected next to Goma airport's only runway, where the thunderous engines of aid planes announce the world is waking up to another African catastrophe, but late, so late.

Kaps and Danny watch the boys writhe around, curling up their skinny bodies like contortionists, their stomachs and thighs seized by excruciating cramps. Kaps leans over them and puts the back of his hand on each of their foreheads in turn. He is shocked that in a tent of such stultifying heat, they could be so icy cold.

'Look at their skin,' he says in Danny's direction. 'It's this clammy grey instead of black. And their faces, they're like death masks.'

A couple of nurses check their IV drips and try to clean away the diarrhoea and vomit, but both flow continually. It's hard to understand where any more liquid can come from, so shrivelled are their bodies.

Kaps, as staunch an atheist as Danny, says a silent prayer. It is a time for faith not scepticism, but a few minutes later he wonders what he's even doing here, begging for a miracle. Perhaps Danny was right and this is all absurd and even self-indulgent. Perhaps it isn't about the two boys at all, but him. And yet he can't leave now, he can't abandon them, and he's grateful at least that Danny does not suggest it.

For a moment Kaps is convinced it's over and that they have died, but they've just fallen asleep, exhausted by the struggle to stay alive. He monitors their chests, in case the weak, barely perceptible undulations should cease. He thinks of the times he's read Charlie and Tom a bed-time story and watched them slip sweetly into sleep. Then he thinks about all the time he has been away from them and starts to add it up: it's probably two of the five years they've been alive. And now Becky's proposal is that he deserts them altogether, that they grow up in a one-parent family, where the most important lesson they'll be taught is to despise their father.

A quarter of an hour later, one of the boys – marginally thinner and weaker than the other – wakes with a coughing fit. The coughs are as fragile as he is, high-pitched like a newborn baby's. They became louder and more incessant, rasping, until Kaps thinks they must be ripping out his little throat. Blood trickles from his mouth and Kaps leaps up to run for help.

'He's choking to death,' he shouts at the nurse nearby. He puts a hand to his own throat in case she doesn't understand.

She manages to calm the boy and turn him on his side, and gradually his hacking cough becomes a gentler splutter, but she gives Kaps a sad look that says there is little to be done and he should probably prepare for the worst.

Kaps sits back down to keep watch once more. Danny jots the occasional word in his notebook but the two reporters make no attempt at conversation. Kaps is not in the mood for idle chit-chat or the usual Junkie gallows humour; not in the mood, in fact, to talk to Danny at all.

The silent vigil only ends when Dr Maillard returns to carry out more tests. He holds his stethoscope to their brittle ribcages and delivers his verdict, journalists and nurses alike hanging on his words.

'Je crois qu'ils vont vivre.'

Kaps throws his arms around him. He feels like falling to his knees and giving thanks to the God he has believed in for a day.

The next morning Danny arrived late for breakfast, missing the daily news conference.

'Wow, this is a seriously powerful piece.' Michel from the UNHCR was waving around a rolled-up fax. 'My guys in New York sent it over. They were getting pretty choked up about it.'

Danny half-smiled in acknowledgement but concentrated on sprinkling some salt on the boiled egg he had just decapitated.

'What piece is that?' asked Rachel.

'Oh, just a little feature thing I did last night.'

'I have it here, if you want to look at it,' said Michel helpfully. Danny seemed uncomfortable.

She started reading the two thin, shiny pages of fax paper, the ink on them slightly smudged. Becky, Edwin and Kaps, with nothing better to do, crowded round behind her.

HOPE AND LOVE IN THE TIME OF CHOLERA

by Daniel L. Lowenstein, Goma

Their coal-black skin had become a clammy grey, their faces were like death masks. French army doctors never knew their names but christened them Hope and Love, two Hutu boys we found on the roadside in Goma. Three thousand refugees died in the town yesterday, but these two young lives at least were spared and doctors said it was a sign that international aid could begin to bring down the savage death toll here.

We came across the boys at a petrol station where their mother had just died, sprawled in her own vomit – yet another victim of the cholera and dysentery that have scythed through the refugees

> here for the past fortnight, killing an estimated 35,000 of them so far. Already the boys were orphans and, like so many here, soon they would be corpses. After driving them to the French Army medical unit I watched and waited as they struggled for life …

Kaps had heard enough.

'"I watched and waited"?' I'm sorry Danny, but where precisely do you get the "I"?'

Danny was conveniently engrossed in conversation with Michel and pretended not to hear him, so Kaps yelled at him, surprising himself.

'Hey, Daniel L. fucking Lowenstein – I'm talking to you!' The jealousy that had grown in him had found a voice at last. It felt marvellously iconoclastic to insert a 'fucking' into Danny's pretentious byline, like throwing a brick through a stained-glass window. Breakfast at the Grands Lacs was jolted to a standstill. '*You* didn't want anything to do with them. We're not aid workers, you said. *You* were quite happy to let those kids die with their mother by the roadside.'

'Calm down, will you; it's no big deal.'

Kaps' whole body quivered. The others watched him with alarm; they'd never seen him like this.

'Oh, it most certainly is. You really are a fucking hypocrite. I mean, where do you get off, stealing other peoples' stories?'

'Don't be so goddamned sanctimonious. You could have written it up too, no one was stopping you. Sure, it was your idea to take them to the hospital, and that's why I said "we".'

'You said "I" as well. And look at this: "Their coal-black skin had become a clammy grey, their faces were like death masks." Wow, that's poetic, what a grabby intro, but I'm just wondering why it somehow sounds familiar. Jesus, I could probably sue you for plagiarism.'

Danny knew that plagiarism was one word for it and theft was another, but it was an insult too far. He didn't see why he should take this shit from Kaps, who had, in his eyes, always been his junior, a sort of protégé. Danny had helped him in Croatia back in '91 when Kaps was a novice at war reporting who knew no one and nothing. Now Danny had caught sight of Rachel – that other novice – and saw confusion creep across her pretty face. She was trying to make up her mind who was wrong and who was right, and it pained him. Danny needed to defend himself.

'Listen, Kaps; you say I was happy to let those kids die. Well, *you're* quite happy to let a hundred others die every day we go through the camps. Why don't you set up a shuttle service to take them all to the hospital? In fact, why aren't you out there now instead of eating breakfast? Come on, why just help those two boys and no one else?'

Because they were my sons, Kaps could have answered. Instead he squared up to Danny, as though he were going to throw a punch at him.

'Okay then, here's a question for you. Why write about them at all, if it's so invidious to pick out individuals? Why single out Hope and – what was it? – oh yeah, Hope and Love. Such cute names, how could I forget? Funny though, I don't remember anyone mentioning them at the time. Silly me, I must have missed the christening ceremony. Or is that something you just made up as well? Love, yeah. Fits really nicely with "in the time of cholera". A bit like the book, eh? Tailor made for a clever headline. Anyone would have thought they'd planned it. Or that you had.'

Rachel was horrified at the thought they might start a brawl. How undignified could you get: two of journalism's elite rolling around in the midst of an African catastrophe, squabbling like spoilt kids while people died just down the road from them. Pre-emptively she put an arm around Kaps.

'Come on, guys, let's both cool it, shall we? I think there's been some sort of misunderstanding.'

'Yeah,' said Kaps. 'A misunderstanding of what the truth is.'

He was burning up with righteous anger and embarrassment and the day's young heat. Kaps didn't want to argue any more. He knew Danny was clever enough to turn the tables on him, so instead he stormed off towards his room, theatrically hurling the fax to the floor and stamping on it until the top page was embossed with his sandal print.

Michel retrieved it, brushed off the dirt and re-read the piece that had caused such consternation, first in New York and now at the Hotel des Grands Lacs. Whatever the morality behind it – or immorality – the copy was compelling.

After a few yards, Kaps decided to risk one last attack. He couldn't resist it. He stopped and turned back to Danny.

'You know what, you *exploit* people.'

'We all do, in case you hadn't noticed. Every story we ever touch.'

'Well, maybe we do, but let me tell you something, Danny boy: when it comes to using people you're in a whole fucking league of your own. I'll never trust you again, not as far as I can throw you.'

Danny shrugged. The Junkies were his friends, the people he hung out with on the road and occasionally screwed over: he had never spent too much time worrying about whether they actually liked him. What was most important to him was to be respected. Kaps would get over it. He always did.

'Just chill out, will you?'

'Shall I tell you what I hate most, Danny? People who say they care, when really they don't give a fuck.'

In the crowded bar that evening, there was no formal decision to ignore Danny, but they didn't feel much like speaking to him either. At one end of the room, Kaps sat at a table with Edwin, Becky, Spinoza and Krontz. They drank gin and tonics, and studiously avoided looking in Danny's direction. He was at the other end of the bar, engrossed with some people from Dutch TV he wouldn't normally have bothered talking to.

Kaps had waited all day for his anger to subside. Part of it, he accepted, was anger with himself. Danny was right, he *could* have done the story. He was the master at letting opportunities slip away from him, leaving places too early or reaching them too late, always telling himself there'd be a next time. Danny was sharper, more instinctive, more tenacious: it was no fluke he always got the prizes.

The only times Kaps came out top were in his fantasies – *story* fantasies, he called them. He'd create his own war or crisis in a mythical land where somehow he would be the only journalist, and the world would hang on every word he wrote. When he came home, he'd be adulated as a hero by his colleagues and readers alike; they'd queue up to offer him book deals, shower him with awards. Kaps would even rehearse his acceptance speech. Sometimes, in the shower or the bath, he'd catch himself delivering it, and smile. The very best thing about these story fantasies was the absence in them: Danny didn't even exist.

Kaps sat there in a trance, his fingers tearing up Edwin's empty cigarette packet into pieces, arranging them neurotically into patterns on the table – triangles, squares, crosses – and then rearranging them all over again. His hair hung either side of a face locked in furrowed concentration as he thought about how he had loved and hated Danny Lowenstein. Danny had revealed himself as a charlatan and a cheat, and Kaps had allowed this 'friend' to use him. Perhaps it was why Danny had made sure they became so close in the first place: so he could steal stories from him.

Rachel came down from her room, having filed and called home to her father. She noticed that Danny cut a shunned and lonely figure at the bar. She couldn't have ever imagined feeling sorry for him, but at least a part of her did. Her triumph at the Hilton had given her new confidence in her own judgements and she had decided to opt out of the collective punishment. She didn't see it mattered much whose idea it was to save the two boys' lives. The breakfast squabble had been unseemly, and the wider issue was that Danny's prose might – yet again – wake the world from its complacency. It had been a searing article and she would give praise if praise were due, though never again for the sake of it. Reputation no longer intrigued or intimidated her. She went straight towards him, and Danny lost interest in the people from Dutch TV. He had no use for them now.

'I really don't give a damn what Kaps says,' she told him. 'It was good stuff.'

'That's generous, but I don't think so. He has a point. I suppose, all things considered, I took advantage.'

'He's just sore because he didn't think of it. Anyhow, if anyone's a fraud it's him, lying to his family.'

Immediately she wished she hadn't said it. She had no right to moralise, let alone betray a friend.

'I suppose we're all frauds in a way,' said Danny. 'You know, sipping our G and Ts, while for people out there the world is ending.'

Tonight she saw him differently. In Sarajevo, she couldn't separate his good looks from his arrogance. They were *too* good. Now, in his isolation – a sort of solitary confinement – he was vulnerable, and some of the beauty was restored.

'Drink?' he said.

'Sure.'

On a humid night, it would go down well. They chatted easily, and in defiance of the lingering hostility nearby. As the alcohol released her, she felt a pressing need to explore him: she had known and not known Danny for too long.

'So you see, Danny Lowenstein, Daniel L. Lowenstein, I've been wondering who you are. The crazy thing is, I used to read so much of your stuff, I thought you were like a friend of mine before I even met you. Then when I did, it was like you were another person.'

'I already apologised for that Karadzic –'

'And I appreciated the mea culpa. Like I said before, it's a long time ago. Prehistory. But I want to know what drives you to be so sure about things.'

He looked into his drink, stirring it uncomfortably. He supposed he'd always been sure about things, right from his teenage years. Too sure.

'You're not big on self-analysis, are you?' she asked, taunting him a little.

'I'd rather analyse the world; it's what I'm paid for.'

'You're different, you know, when you get off that high horse of yours.'

'Yeah, but it's such a long climb down.'

It was a surprise to see him poking fun at himself, and she laughed loudly.

'I'm interested in that passion you have. "The journalism of commitment" – isn't that what you call it in your book? You always want to take sides, good against evil.'

'You think I should be in *favour* of evil?'

'Sometimes the readers can figure it out. Take the mass graves here: they sort of speak for themselves.'

'Maybe. But "on the one hand this", "on the other hand that" – it's all so bland. If you're supposed to be the readers' eyes, you should tell them what you see, not pretend you're blind.'

'Sure, what you see – but not always what you think. Don't get me wrong, I love your stuff. And your drive. Yesterday, for example, you just wouldn't take some downtime.'

'And look where it got me.'

'But where does it come from? You're so … relentless.'

'I'm from the pushiest family in America, and as you know, that's a nation of pushy families. My dad was Mr Corporate America and my sister couldn't wait to get there too. An entire family with their snouts in the trough, imagine that. They were horrified when I became a journalist. It wasn't about making money and they just couldn't see the point.'

'But it must give them pleasure – what you've achieved.'

'I wouldn't know, I never talk to them.'

She wanted to ask him more but could see she'd just exposed a gaping wound.

'Sorry, I don't mean to pry.'

'And what about you, Rachel Kelly? Do I get to ask some stuff about you as well?'

She liked the way he used her surname as she had his: it hinted at a new intimacy between them. She fiddled with a bracelet and stirred her gin and tonic.

'My family don't think so much of me being a reporter either. That is to say my father; he's all I really have. He hated the whole idea of me being on the road, on any road except the one we live in.'

'You've changed, you know. From when you first arrived in Sarajevo.'

'I irritated you, didn't I?'

Danny remembered his contempt for her naivety. He supposed he had seen in it all the failures of the West – how they, and her, were happy to be hoodwinked by the Serbs, by Karadzic with his kiss, by the sniper of Grbavica. At that moment Rachel had represented to him NATO and the UN and all the weak-kneed politicians of the world.

'I was too wrapped up in it. I thought it was my story and no one else's, let alone—'

'Let alone some Rachel-come-Lately who couldn't possibly know what she was talking about?'

'Something like that.'

'I bet you didn't know what you were talking about when you arrived.'

'Probably not. But, Rachel, you've flown in these six months. I don't want to patronise you, but my God you're just about the most naturally gifted writer I've ever read in a newspaper. You were born to write.'

Rachel almost spat out her drink. She didn't know if it was flattery for a purpose, but she could feel her face burning up the way it always had when people said nice things about her.

'And by the way,' he continued, 'I don't make a habit of paying compliments to my rivals.'

When Danny tried to explain to himself quite where and when his infatuation had begun, he came up with the day in Sarajevo when Becky had been hit. As soon as he saw Rachel dive into the culvert, his helmet all askew on her, he realised to his surprise that he wanted to protect her. After that, he had tried to reach out to her, but she'd ignored him – understandably, he had to admit. In Goma, he had waited for the Junkies, hoping she would be among them, and when she was – Hallelujah! – he had contrived to sit beside her on the car ride from the airport, and at every meal. There was something ludicrous about it – he was nearly 40, she was in her early twenties – but something marvellous too. He had lost control of his emotions and he liked the way it made him giddy.

'So I'm a rival, am I?' said Rachel.

'Of course. But a friend as well, I hope.'

Soon they were discussing her favourite topic of conversation, the Kelly career plan, he in the role of wise adviser and she the willing pupil. Danny was wrapped up in her entirely now, oblivious of everything else in the bar, everything in Africa. For Rachel, there was a feeling of relief: this was how it should have been from the start. It was as though she'd just met a new person, a new Danny, the one she'd always imagined. A rival and a friend.

On the other side of the bar, Edwin had disappeared to do some coke with Spinoza and Krontz. Becky and Kaps weren't in the mood for it and were left awkwardly alone.

'Those kids really got to you, didn't they?' she said.

'They just – oh, it doesn't matter.'

'Go on. I think it does.'

He knew it would sound hopelessly irrational. How do you even start to explain that two Africans you've never met before have made you decide to love your children more?

'Look, they reminded me of Charlie and Tom, if you want to know. They were so vulnerable out there on the road, especially when I knew their mother hadn't made it.'

'That's understandable. And commendable.'

'No, not really. It was freaky, like they really were my kids and I had to help them. I have no idea why.' Kaps looked down the fat brown neck of his Primus beer bottle, as if the answer might be somewhere inside it. His head was spinning with Danny and Becky, Becky and Danny. He needed them both to go away for a while. He needed to be with his boys instead.

'And?' Becky said.

'And what?'

'I get the feeling you want to tell me something else.'

Kaps had no idea how to begin or end, so he just blurted it out. It was like killing something: it was best to do it quickly.

'It made me realise I can't ever leave them, I can't abandon them. It helped me see how much I've taken them for granted. I think I have to sacrifice something for them.'

'Which is?' Becky's voice broke as she asked it because she already knew the answer. Kaps stared at his feet, dangling from the bar stool. He knew he'd never have the guts to look at her when he said it.

'My happiness. Our happiness.'

She stared at his avoiding eyes, disgusted by their cowardice. How could he do this to her? A whole life she had so foolishly, so prematurely, fantasised about: a future that swept them into the remote mists of old age – all of it disintegrated in that second, and she watched it die.

'Bullshit.'

'I wish it was.'

'What the fuck was it, some holy revelation by the roadside? Some message from the gods that you shouldn't screw around?'

'I'm so sorry, Becky.'

'So who gets to rescue me from the roadside? Or am I just one of the thousands that get passed by?'

He put a hand on hers, and she threw it off.

'Don't you dare.' She pushed back her stool and ran out of the bar before Kaps could see her streaming tears. No one else would ever want her the way he had. And even though they'd spent so little time together, she knew no one else would care for her like Kaps. They were meant to be, and meant not to be, and that was the curse of both their lives.

Becky hated everyone at that moment: Kaps, his wife, his sons and the two Hutu boys he had saved. She hated Hope and she certainly hated Love.

As she barged her way through the noisy crowd of customers, she saw Danny and Rachel looking at each other and she hated them as well.

• • •

It was almost one o'clock when Rachel said she was tired and needed to get some sleep. Me too, said Danny. They walked together from the bar, without looking up to say goodnight to the stragglers. The route back to their rooms led them along a narrow, winding path bordered by exotic flowers. It snaked across the lawn where Rachel had lain with Becky, searching the stars for what lay ahead. She felt a pinprick of guilt, but the gin ensured it was no more than that.

They had talked easily at the bar, but now, as they approached their rooms and the imminent choice they had to make, Rachel fumbled for something to say.

'Amazing sky.'

'Yeah, extraordinary.'

Soon, a little too soon, they reached the ground-floor corridor where her room was. His was two floors above.

'So good night then, Rachel Kelly.'

She could feel the tension between them rise, and a dizzy lightness in her head.

'Good night, Danny Lowenstein.'

They both stood in silent indecision, knowing there were a couple more seconds before decorum would dictate that one or other should turn away with a chirpy 'Sleep well, see you in the morning.' Random thoughts occurred to her: her startling hypocrisy, her overpowering need to be held by him no matter what he'd done, Becky's warning in the same garden under the same sky, and the fact that she had been with him.

The face before her was not necessarily kind, Rachel decided, and not as caring as it should be, but there was nothing bad or wrong in it either, and nothing cruel. She thought she even saw a helplessness in it. Danny looked as though for once his powers had deserted him and it only made her want him more.

She would never be sure what made her take that single step towards him: the gin, or the hot African night, or just that she wanted to be the one who began it all, not him.

When their lips met, and then their tongues melted into one, she considered the absurdity of it all: that this was Danny Lowenstein she was kissing. But she was too tired now to go back over all their troubled history. Too tired and too excited.

'Are you coming in?'

As they tumbled through the door, she was embarrassed by the clothes and underwear that lay scattered all around, on chairs, on the bed, on the floor: to Rachel the joy of a hotel room had always been that no one was ever going to tell you to keep it tidy. Not even a new lover.

'Do we need more fish fingers?'

Kaps heard his question echoing down the aisle and it sounded ridiculous to him. They already had a freezer full of food, and riches beyond their dreams.

Barely 24 hours had passed since he had slouched sulkily out of the Grands Lacs and headed home. London had told him they were tiring of the story, and he hadn't bothered arguing. He said that in any case he felt unwell, though the only things that really made him sick were Danny, and the remorse he felt for hurting Becky. He needed to get out.

He might as well have jumped into a time machine rather than a British Airways jet, for instead of dying Africans, he was surrounded by chubby shoppers waddling around his nearest Sainsbury's with overflowing trolleys. The kids cried like they did in Goma, but because they wanted sweets and ice cream, not because cholera was slowly killing them. It wasn't their fault, but he felt an irrational disdain for them. His soul needed more time to decompress.

'Yes, and get some burgers too, will you?' said Judith. He pulled them from a freezer and the cold air hit him in the face. He realised how much he missed the heat of Africa. Don't think about it, he told himself; don't even consider the insane idea that you'd rather be there, where there is only death and horror, than here, where there is everything. Everything and nothing.

For the next few minutes, he shopped in a daydream. He thought childishly about how he could get his revenge on Danny, and then about how he missed Becky already and how he wanted to be back in bed with her, with the fan whirring above them and the mosquito net to protect them from a disapproving world.

He was yanked back from the Grands Lacs by the shrill screams of a badly behaved three-year-old called – apparently – Jenny.

'Jen-*neeeee*!' her mother was shouting at her by the cold meat section. Jenny was writhing around in a tantrum, her angry little fists beating the shiny supermarket floor as if it were to blame for all that was wrong with her world. Together, the mother's shouts and Jenny's screams created a cacophony that assaulted Kaps' eardrums. The shelves behind them were a blur of colours and names: thousands of rival products jostled for attention, packed tight, high and wide in endless corridors – a maze in which this humble visitor from Africa had somehow managed to get lost.

The mother was verging on obesity and an example of Western over-indulgence, Kaps decided. She grabbed Jenny's hand and, having failed to pull her up, dragged her along the floor. The child looked like a suitcase being pulled along behind her. Jenny's screams reached a crescendo and split him apart until there was a third voice he could hear.

'Leave her *alone*, for God's sake.'

The woman dropped Jenny's arm and stared at him, trying to take in the enormity of his presumption.

'You *what*?'

'You're hurting her arm.'

'Why don't you mind your own fucking business, you fucking twat.'

Then she was calling out:

'*Daaaaave*.'

Dave arrived within a few seconds, this particular knight in shining armour emblazoned in tattoos with rings through both ears and – like his partner – overweight.

Once Dave had had the situation explained to him by Jenny's mother, he pushed his bloated face into Kaps'.

'Listen, cunt, you got five seconds to say sorry or I smash your fucking face in.'

The casual violence of Dave's words made Kaps draw back. He was used to feeling afraid in Bosnia, but not in England's green and pleasant land, and certainly not in Sainsbury's. It was a different kind of fear, more visceral.

'Bad man,' said Charlie, at his father's waist now. Kaps wasn't sure if the little boy meant his daddy or the fat, would-be assailant. Judith had appeared too.

'We were just going, weren't we, darling,' she said, taking Kaps' hand firmly.

'Not before he fucking well says sorry.' The tattooed man had clenched a fist and pulled it back, like a missile ready to be fired.

'You lay one finger on my husband,' said Judith with calm deliberation, 'and I'll call the police and then I'll call Social Services, and believe me you won't ever see that daughter of yours again.'

There was a second while Jenny's parents thought through their options.

'Fuck you,' said the man, spitting in Judith's direction, but missing hopelessly. He unclenched his fist and walked away, defeated.

Kaps looked at her. 'Sorry,' he mouthed.

Sorry about all this. Sorry about Becky. Sorry about still wanting to make love to her. Sorry about barely having touched you since I've come home. Sorry about always leaving you alone. Sorry for forgetting what an extraordinary woman you are. Sorry about wishing you would disappear.

That night he read to Charlie and Tom in their room. All three of them sat on the lower of the bunk beds, which was Charlie's. The book was called *Engelbert the Magic Elephant* and when it was over they begged him to tell them one of his made-up stories as well, because they liked those better. He came up with something about a ship that was attacked by pirates with swords and daggers, and a young boy like them who'd stowed away and who was the only survivor. Kaps was halfway through – describing how the stowaway ran from cabin to cabin, hiding from the pirates – when he saw from the boys' anxious eyes that his story was too frightening. He promptly made sure his hero escaped and rowed off to a desert island where, after a few Robinson Crusoe days, he was rescued and lived happily ever after.

'Daddy,' said Charlie, when he'd kissed them goodnight and was turning out the light, 'will you ever die?'

Kaps regretted again the initial darkness of his story.

'Well, we all die, one day. But not until we're about a hundred.'

'But I mean, will you die *soon*?'

'Of course not. Don't be silly.'

'But what about when you go to war?' said Tom. 'Because soldiers die, don't they, and you're like a soldier.'

Kaps wondered if they'd planned this together, the two of them deciding that now would be a good time to discuss with their father the important possibility of his sudden and violent death.

'Look, darlings, I'm not a soldier. I'm just a reporter. Soldiers die because they fight each other, but the reporters ... well, we just watch them. That's all.'

We just watch them. As a summary of his journalistic life, it was bleak but accurate. And to Charlie and Tom, it seemed a reasonable explanation of what their daddy did for a living.

'Can we sleep head to toe?' asked Tom.

Kaps said they could, but he was troubled: they only ever wanted to sleep in the same bed when they were scared, usually if there were a thunderstorm. He climbed in with them. It was an almost impossible squeeze in the narrow bunk bed, but he put an arm round each of his sons and held them both so tight he worried he might hurt them.

When Judith found all three asleep together, she smiled and was happy that he'd come home to them. Part of her wanted to climb in with them. She stood watching her children and her husband and decided that perhaps everything could work out after all. She needed to *make* it work out. Kaps was messed up – of course he was – and he'd been gone from her in so many ways, and now she had to get him back, if only for the boys' sake.

'Let's go to bed, darling,' she said softly, waking him as kindly as she could, pulling him up from in between them. Kaps felt stupid and apologised for dozing off. He followed her sheepishly into the double bed where he'd spent too many nights wishing it was Becky who shared it with him. As Judith cast aside her underwear, Kaps felt closer to her than he had for a long time. He could see in her face something that forgave him, for this one night at least. She was his wife, and his children's mother, and she deserved so much more than he had ever given her.

Still half asleep, he took off his clothes too and stretched out a hand to her in the half darkness of their master bedroom. To his amazement, she took it and began to kiss him hungrily, as though she had been waiting for him all her life. And then he was on her, writhing around with her and caressing her, and finally sliding into her. He moaned dutifully, but in truth it felt disappointing to be there when it should have been exciting, strange when it should have been familiar. He wanted to tell Judith he was sorry for all his treachery, but as he reached his climax, the only face he could see was Becky's and he realised she was the woman he was betraying.

23

Post-Liberation Iraq, August 2004

A few days after watching Lukas and Eliza on the video, Danny's opportunity comes from nowhere.

The toilet is no longer a lake of urine but an ordinary bathroom: cramped and dirty, but a bathroom nonetheless. There is even toilet paper of a kind, and a hand towel. To Danny, it could be a five-star hotel. One of Abu Omar's brothers has escorted him here and waits for him outside as usual. Danny urinates and washes his hands as slowly as he can, because he likes these bathroom visits: strange as it may sound for a hostage, he believes it's important to have some time to himself.

He splashes his face with water and it feels good, and when he dries it gently with the towel, that feels good as well. He looks into the small mirror on the doors of the bathroom cabinet. It's a different Danny, one he can hardly recognise: bearded, toothless and snapped in two. Broken, the way Lukas and Scar had always wanted him.

He turns the handle and comes back out as usual.

The guard has gone.

Danny looks up and down the corridor. At one end, he can hear raised voices in the kitchen, some sort of argument. At the other end is the front door, half open. Sunshine is gushing in through it, falling on the carpet as a triangle of light. It summons him. Is it a dream or a miracle, or just a fuck-up by the guards? Danny's heart thumps outrageously. Surely someone would stop him before he got there, or just a few yards outside? But what if they didn't and he could walk and walk? What if he could walk all the way back to the Hamra and into Rachel's arms? It is all too fast and unexpected: how can he possibly make a sensible decision?

Go on, he tells himself; swallow hard and breathe deep, just like you did the day you took that road. After all, this is how it was always going to be, a random chance that presents itself out of the blue, demanding to be seized, demanding courage.

Gingerly, he creeps along the corridor inch by inch, until he can almost feel the soft light on his face and smell the clean, fresh air of that other world outside.

Out of nowhere, she has moved into the doorway and is in front of him, little Aisha in her pretty white dress with a bow around the middle and her piercing eyes that seem so old. She is the sort of child who might once have been a heroine in one of his more harrowing stories, but now she is standing in his way, another jailer. Danny tries to smile at her but she looks at him with much the same contempt as all the adults in the house.

It is early evening when Danny hears angry voices shouting at each other. Abu Omar comes in to where he is sitting cross-legged on the carpet, watching incomprehensible Iraqi television.

'You go back now. Sorry.'

Danny is stunned, not only to hear him speaking English for the first time but also apologising.

'Go back where? Home? *Home?*'

Danny is lightheaded with elation, but when Scar follows Abu Omar into the room he sees how badly he's misunderstood.

• • •

This time the crate ride is not so bad. Danny is not seized by the same panic: he must be getting used to it. Within an hour, he's back in his old cell, lying on the same thin mattress, watching the same sliver of light prepare to die as dusk draws near. The green carpet, the sofa, the television – even little Aisha standing in his way – all seem like a lurid fantasy. Instead it is Scar who stands before him, and he holds a knife, its blade about ten inches long, and slightly curved. Its steel yearns to catch the light but it has almost gone and the metal is dull and grey, ordinary in its terror.

'Why … have you brought that?'

'Seven more days. This is what I like to use.'

Danny's throat feels dry and he swallows. A tremor runs right though him. He can see the first cut of the blade; it slices into the thin skin above his throat, a surgical incision that leaves a neat line of blood. Then the laborious sawing, through the gristle, bone and muscle of the neck. The novices among them may be surprised by the difficulty of their task but they will delight in it nonetheless, rejoicing that God's work is being done and that they are putting to death the American, the infidel. Each will clamour to have a go. Each will want Danny's blood spurting over them. After that it's Kaps who holds the knife. He saws for a while, then lets Edwin take his turn, then Becky, then Rachel. They're all smiling because it is work that's pleasurable and satisfying.

'Not the knife,' he says to Scar. He can hardly believe it has come to pleading about the choice of weapon, but it has started to obsess him. 'Please, I beg you, not the knife.'

In the desert it was sauna-hot again. Captain Jim Kolowski and the troops of B company had stopped to eat their MREs. They had parked up their Humvees and Bradley fighting vehicles, devoured the beef stew, peanut butter and biscuits, and dropped the brown plastic packaging into what Kolowski called the dustbin of Iraq.

Meals Ready to Eat; Troops Ready to Die.

Many times during his 15-month tour of duty, it had occurred to Kolowski that a lunch like this might be his last, that the next ambush or roadside bomb could be only a few minutes away. The Improvised Explosive Device was, in his opinion, an especially shitty weapon: you didn't stand and face the enemy but got blown up by them, anonymously and by remote control. IEDs could be hidden under a rock on the road, or inside a dead animal or even a piece of the US Army's own discarded, and ingeniously recycled garbage. An IED inside an MRE was too much for Kolowski to get his tired, dusty, sweaty head around. He had a vision of his wife receiving the news from the Pentagon in the porch of their little home in Idaho, clutching in her arms the baby daughter he'd never even seen. We think it was an IED, they would tell her, hoping the reduction of her loss to those three letters might reduce the pain.

It was why, when he saw the orange heap on the road ahead, Captain Kolowski's immediate suspicion was that it was some sort of trick. He brought the convoy to a halt about a hundred yards away and pulled out his binoculars. Now he could make out it was a body, dressed in a jumpsuit. There was blood around the head. Flies swarmed over it, blackening the red. Further down, around the crotch, there was another patch of blood, another feeding frenzy for the flies.

Kolowski would go no closer to the corpse than 20 yards.

'You squeamish, sir?' asked Hamilton, the driver.

'Yeah, but that ain't why we're stopping.'

'Uh huh?'

'I'm thinking whoever killed him, well, there'd be nothing easier than for them to stuff that poor fucker with explosives, like a big, fat Thanksgiving turkey.'

• • •

Within a few minutes, B company's radio operator had contacted divisional command, who in turn contacted headquarters in Baghdad, who contacted Adi at the US embassy.

'Sorry to be the bearer of bad news, sir,' said the young colonel on Adi's secure line. 'Looks like we may have found that reporter guy. Orange jumpsuit, the lot. Hell, they couldn't even wait until the deadline.'

Adi wondered how he'd break the news to Becky, and what impact it would have on his chances of further progress. He asked the colonel how Danny had died.

'Single gunshot to the head. But they used the knife on him too, sir. Cut off his … his genitals. Animals, fuckin' animals.'

Adi decided not to call Becky for a while. Perhaps he would go round to the hotel in person and offer to console her.

The body was waiting for them when they got to the hospital morgue. Adi, Munro and Harper were all there. They needed a relative to help with identification, and since Camille was the only family he had in Iraq, she didn't have much choice. Out of solidarity, the Junkies volunteered to go with her. The ordeal would be horrendous, but at least they'd see Danny one last time. It seemed important to say goodbye.

The place reeked. Even from several hundred yards away its stench grabbed you by the throat, all the circles of Baghdad's hell rolled into one. It reminded Rachel of Goma a decade earlier: too many corpses in too much heat.

Peering in through the bars of the perimeter fence were the relatives, waiting to identify their loved ones too; distraught if they found them, distraught if they didn't. Many of the dead would never be claimed. Before too long, they'd be wrapped up, numbered and dumped in a mass grave.

They came in four specific categories:

The favoured few, like first-class passengers, locked away in refrigerated compartments.

Those who had to make do with the concrete floor, but with the dispensation of a sheet to preserve their dignity.

The ones who lay uncovered on the spot where they'd been dumped, wide eyes gawping.

And finally the overspill, for whom there was no room inside: they had been deposited outside in the yard on a strip of sand to absorb the blood, Iraq's unforgiving sun beating down on them.

The morgue attendants, Raja and Nada, were two plump, matronly women who liked to take their minds off things by talking about their grandchildren or the cost of living or the endless power cuts. They wore gloves, and rubber boots for when they had to walk through shallow streams of blood. It was another busy day. Half a mile away a suicide bomber had just blown himself up in a queue of police recruits.

The main task for Raja and Nada was to keep count of the new arrivals, but Raja had somehow lost her pen amid the chaos, and now they had only a single biro between them with which to conduct their inventory.

Admissions frequently came in a batch, either from a bomb, a gun battle or a fresh rampage by the death squads. The victims of these marauding executioners were the worst, according to Raja and Nada, who graded their dead like a pair of quality-control inspectors. The hands and feet would usually be bound with plastic ties, the penis, tongue or ears sliced off, the eyes gouged out. Often the bodies would be bloated like fattened pigs after being left out in the heat or dragged from the bulrushes of the Tigris.

Danny himself had spent too much time in morgues just like this one. As the self-appointed representative of Baghdad's dead, he'd insisted on counting them himself, rather like Raja and Nada. He would publish his grim statistics, either to contradict those who insisted the violence was tailing off, or to remind his readers it wasn't only American soldiers who were dying in Iraq.

When Raja and Nada ushered the VIP visitors into their chamber of horrors, they entered like a funeral procession: Adi first, followed by Camille with Harper and Munro, then Edwin and Kaps, and lastly Rachel and Becky, who were quietly falling apart. There was barely room for them all.

Raja unlocked freezer 17 with a numbered key, as if someone might have wanted to steal its contents. She heaved open the thick steel door and slid out the slab. The procession had come to a halt, and they stood waiting in a semicircle. Adi, sopping with sweat, put his hand out for Becky to hold. It was a last-gasp piece of opportunism, an attempt at tasteless seduction – and in a mortuary, of all places. Denied Kaps' support – he had long since learnt to keep his distance – Becky grabbed Adi's hand and squeezed it so tight he couldn't help wondering if there might, after all, be hope for him. Her nails were digging into his damp skin. Next stop would be the funeral, he thought, a chance for further cautious progress and then perhaps the memorial service too.

A wall of cold air hit them. In any other place, it would have been refreshing, but this was rancid and repugnant.

Nada, standing at the far end of the white-draped corpse, lifted a corner of the sheet just below the twin-peaked outline of the feet. It wasn't often she had such a distinguished audience and she was determined to make the most of it, pulling the sheet off slowly, a magician ratcheting up the tension, building up the theatre, hoping for that satisfying gasp of disbelief.

Instead, there was a triumphant cry from Rachel.

'No no! Not him! It's not Danny. That's just not Danny!'

The others looked at her in astonishment. How could she possibly *know*? The sheet had been raised only enough to reveal his legs and the gory mess that lay between them.

'Don't you see? He's got trainers on! Danny always wore his boots – his lucky boots. Every day, everywhere. You know that, Becky, don't you?' She was shouting, in the hope her words might become truer if they were louder.

Everyone was bewildered, their heads fuzzy with the smell of formaldehyde. At first they assumed Rachel was in denial, but then it occurred to them she might be right: they couldn't think of a single time they'd seen him wearing trainers.

'Then who the fuck ...' said Edwin.

With another flourish, Raja and Nada yanked the remainder of the sheet, so that it floated up and billowed away.

Becky felt her knees begin to tremble, the bad leg first but then the good one too. Gradually they gave way and she folded, like a collapsible table, her sturdy body dropping on to the cold floor where so many of Baghdad's dead had lain before her. Adi let go of her hand. It summed up her luck with men, she would later think: even this sweaty reptile of a 'friend' had abandoned her the one time she needed him.

Rachel knelt down beside her and Edwin pulled out a handkerchief to mop her brow.

'What were those two witches playing at?' he asked. 'I mean, did they really have to make such a song and dance of it?'

They bowed their heads in a show of respect for the anonymous victim, who was hastily covered up again and slipped back into the fridge, still unidentified and unwanted, his brief appearance in the spotlight over.

After they got Becky back to the Hamra, they made her lie down for a while in the small side bedroom. Edwin put a wet towel on her forehead and gave her a sleeping pill.

'We should never have made her come. She's just not well enough.'

'What ... exactly is wrong with her?' asked Camille.

'Post-traumatic stress, if you must know,' said Rachel. 'Most of the time she's fine, but sometimes there are flashbacks, nightmares, hallucinations. Once she was in Regent's Park and thought it was a minefield.'

Camille looked confused.

'So what's she doing in *Baghdad?* Surely this is the last place in the world she should be convalescing?'

'She didn't have much choice,' said Rachel. 'They were offering her the Chelsea Flower Show and the Cannes Film Festival, crap like that. Stories like Iraq, they're her life. She needed to be here, with her friends.'

'Please don't talk about her when she's asleep,' said Kaps protectively, but Rachel ignored him.

'What happened to her, it could be any of us. We're all like the smoker who thinks he won't get lung cancer. Then there's one event, one trauma, one image that just gets to you. You can have the best suit of armour they ever made, but if there's one little chink and the arrow gets through – well, that's it, you're done for.'

'When?' asked Camille.

'When what?'

'When did it happen? When did the arrow get through?'

Rachel didn't answer for a while. She could barely bring herself to say it.

'The same year.'

'1994?'

'The best of years, the worst of years. Yes, '94, what else? Well, give or take a couple of days anyhow. Our Year of Living Dangerously.'

Becky emerged from the bedroom, drifting in ethereally. She was wearing only her knickers and a baggy T-shirt. Her pallid skin was whiter than ever, her hair a tangled mass from where she'd slept on it. She dragged her fingers through it, exposing briefly the few grey roots that had started to corrupt the red.

'What are you guys talking about?' she muttered drowsily.

'Nothing. Go back to bed,' said Rachel.

But Becky had overheard and she was already remembering when it had begun, the worst day of her life.

24

Chechnya, 1994

'If it's snowing, it really must be Christmas!' Rachel shouted as the cold, rushing air smacked her face. Her head was sticking out of the rusty Lada and the first flakes of the day were making tentative landings on her hair. 'God, it's good to be here.'

And God it most certainly was, thought Danny, holding hands with her on the back seat. Bosnia had started to bog him down: he wanted a war where he didn't have to spend days trying to get permission for a two-hour trip to the trenches.

'From everything I've heard, the only limits on what you can do are down to you and your own bravery,' he had told Rachel before they left Sarajevo for the long, convoluted journey via Split, Vienna and Moscow. She had nodded a little nervously and wondered – when it came to it – what her own limits might be: she had yet to discover them. She hoped she'd have the guts to do everything that Danny did, and maybe even a little more as well. Who said lovers couldn't be competitors?

Chechnya lay a thousand miles south of Moscow, nestling amid the mountains of the Caucasus. Much of the planet, including Rachel, had never even heard of the place but now it was all over the front pages – the world was officially worried about it – and for war correspondents, there was nowhere else to see in the New Year.

A surly Dagestani taxi driver had agreed to drive Rachel and Danny to Grozny for an exorbitant 500 dollars. As they approached the border, he gestured to a field where they glimpsed a sprawling Russian camp. Young conscripts traipsed around forlornly in the snow, their tanks nestling among the whitened tents and trees. A couple of teenage soldiers, one with a face full of pimples, stopped them to check their passports. Danny's was fat and battered and the guards leafed through it. Though they wouldn't admit it, they were curious about the world conjured up by his exotic array of entry stamps and visas. Rachel's, by contrast, was thin and more or less pristine: it was like her virginity had been once – an embarrassment, a reminder of how much more she had to do in life.

The guards waved them on with a sullen grunt. Soon enough these underfed adolescents would be taking on the wild, bearded warriors of Chechnya – men with Kalashnikovs, swords and daggers, and a hatred of Moscow written in their blood for generations. Chechen horsemen had fought the tsars for much of the 19th century, long before Stalin had tried to wipe them off the map by putting half a million Chechens on freight trains and deporting them to the wastes of Siberia and Central Asia. Now, in the chaos of post-Soviet, post-communist Russia, they were making another bid for freedom and the Kremlin was as determined as ever that they should be crushed. President Boris Nikolayevich Yeltsin might be the darling of the West with his free-market economic reforms, but when it came to Chechnya he was just another Russian tsar.

'Those soldiers are just kids,' said Rachel as they drove off. 'They should still be home with their families.'

She thought of her own family. Of course, she'd been right to escape from Billy Kelly's suffocating love, and she was proud of what she'd achieved since leaving him, but guilt hung over her as she imagined her father spending his first Christmas alone. For Billy, this time of year had always been about the Kelly family – enjoying together the roast goose that he always cooked and the pumpkin pie he made – but now it was about the pain of his solitude, a day of missing his wife and his daughter, and of wishing till it hurt that they could be with him.

Rachel tried to put out of her mind the picture of him sitting down to roast goose all by himself and focus on the landscape instead. The bleak, desolate villages they passed through would soon bear witness to battles and atrocities. Their Dagestani driver had a map but he didn't need it. There were plenty of signs to the city and only one road that seemed to lead there.

'Grozny,' said Danny. 'You know what the word means in Russian?'

Rachel shook her head.

'"Terrible".'

Their new home was on the outskirts, close to an abandoned factory. As they reached it, dusk was falling fast and the snow became more bountiful: great balls of cotton wool drifting in diagonally. Becky came out to meet them, still hobbling from her Bosnia wound. The winter cold had made it worse.

'What *is* this place?' asked Danny. 'Looks like a school or something.'

'A brothel, actually,' Becky said.

'You're kidding!'

'Nope. The pimps and prostitutes heard there was gonna be a war and just fucked off.'

He looked at the red-brick building again, smiling wryly, storing it up already for future anecdotes and a line or two of colour in the memoirs.

Becky led them inside. The power was down so they put on their head torches. It was a crucial piece of equipment she'd failed to take to Sarajevo, but almost twelve months later, she never left home without one. The three of them were like miners going down the pit as they navigated their way through darkened corridors, their beams criss-crossing each other as they illuminated a warren of rooms, each with a double bed and large mirror. Rachel could smell disinfectant everywhere and, she thought, the whiff of condoms and stale sex. Or perhaps it was her imagination.

'The way I see it, one lot of tarts have gone, and another lot arrive,' said Becky, the old familiar smile wrapped around her face. Danny went off to set up his satphone while Becky took Rachel into the kitchen and filled a blackened kettle that looked as though it dated back to the tsars.

'So who else is here?' Rachel was eager for a reunion – just as a mother hopes the whole family will come home for Christmas, just as Billy was hoping she would.

Not since Goma had the five of them worked together. Neither Kaps nor Edwin wanted to spend much time with Danny any more, while Becky and Kaps had accepted that they needed to be apart as well, if only for their sanity. But none of the Junkies could resist the lure of Chechnya, potentially the most violent, the most accessible war there'd been for years. The whorehouse was filling up.

'Most of the gang,' said Becky. 'Spinoza, Krontz and Dirk. There's that woman from MSF we met in Goma – Mariana, I think her name is. Edwin's here somewhere too, with poor old Alija in tow. Wanted to come and practise his Russian. You know, it's his 15th bloody language or something. Anyway, Edwin needs someone to hold his hand.'

Having watched him graduate from coke to crack, Becky had begun to worry about Edwin.

'I'm not sure he should be coming to places like this any more. He's taking crazy risks, like he's got this death wish.'

Rachel ignored Becky's diagnosis. She was enjoying this new war zone too much – and this new love affair – and she didn't want anyone spoiling the fun, not her lonely father and not Edwin either.

'Oh well, I'm sure we'll cheer him up. *And?* Anyone else?'

Becky told her Kaps had left a message saying that he might be here by New Year's Eve.

'It's all over with us, of course, so I don't really care either way.' Becky looked down forlornly. He was the other wound she was still trying to recover from. 'He's back with his wife and kids, which is a good thing, probably. I mean, it *definitely* is.'

'I'm sorry.'

'Don't be. Remember when you told me it was a mistake? I always knew I'd have to pay for it and … well, I'm paying now. I miss him every day, and every hour of every day. Every fucking minute, if you must know. Still, I'll bet he's happier. No more choices and dilemmas.'

'He loved you, Beck, don't ever forget that.'

'So now you're *defending* him?'

'Just defending what you had together, the memory.'

'Can't cuddle a memory though, can you, or kiss it or fuck it.'

After an hour, Danny came back in. He'd already filed a colour piece on the drive to Grozny and the pallid troops he'd seen at the border. It wasn't a classic, but it established that he was here ahead of most of his rivals. Casually, he put an arm round Rachel, who hadn't even thought of filing yet, and her glow lit up the brothel's seedy darkness. Becky retreated behind the jaunty, jolly face she always kept close by and squeezed out another smile, but all she could think about was that night in Goma, when Rachel had gained a lover just as she was losing hers.

'Oh, by the way, we have a landlady – Rosa. The madam of the house, so to speak, except I suppose you could say that now she's making her money from hacks instead of hookers. Same difference, when you think about it. Anyway, Rosa says there's just one rule: girls and boys in separate rooms. Very strict about that. Very *moral*.'

Danny looked disappointed.

'Terrific. Just our luck to get the only madam south of Moscow who's a prude.'

'Still, what a great place to be for Christmas,' said Rachel. 'I so *love* Christmas, don't you?'

Danny absolutely didn't and pretended not to hear the question.

Because he hated his father he hated religion, and because he hated religion, he hated Christmas. And because Christmas was when he'd been thrown out of his home, that was another good reason for hating it. Christmas sucked, Christmas stank. Come the festive season, he always liked to make sure he was in a war zone where people had more important things on their minds.

While he was at Yale, the star student, the campus heartthrob, Danny tried not to go back home during the vacations. In some ways it was a relief for Lukas and Eliza and Camille if he stayed away. He would only weigh them down again. But when it came to Christmas, when the Pittsburgh trees were twinkling and the carols were being sung, the whole family that was not a family had to be together.

The Christmas before Danny turned 21, Lukas had something he wanted to say to him. Eliza had begged her husband to leave it 'till New Year at least', but in Lukas' opinion it couldn't wait. The news was that he had a job lined up for Danny at Lowenstein Steel. Sure, they'd had their ups and downs, but he wanted him in the family firm, he *needed* him there. It was time to forget their differences and pull together. This job would put Danny on the first rung; Camille was already on the second, and the three of them could create a dynasty.

Lukas knew the love between him and his son had long since drained away, but surely every father was allowed to have a dream and in Lukas' case, it was positioning both his children in the business so they could run it when he'd gone – and after them their children and their children's children. One day they would dominate the city: the Lowensteins immortal, the Lowensteins of Pittsburgh. So what if they had their problems – which great American family didn't?

Danny tried not to laugh and it filled him with a certain sadistic pleasure to give his answer.

'Me – in Lowenstein Steel? You've gotta be out of your mind! You really don't understand *anything* about me, do you? I'm not going to be any kind of businessman. I'm not interested in making money, or making anything at all. I don't know a thing about steel, and frankly I don't want to. And when it comes to dynasties, perhaps Camille could create one on her own if she's such a fucking amazing daughter. Oh, and by the way – and just for your information – I'm going to be a journalist.'

Lukas should have been expecting it – if he'd been a better father to his son, he would have – but it felt like the final assault on all his values and everything he held dear.

'A *journalist*?' The idea was incomprehensible to him.

'Yes, a journalist. A reporter. I want to report, I want to write. Go places and tell it like it is.'

'That really is a joke, young man. Truly laughable. You'll always be poor, I just hope you understand that.'

'You know what? I'd rather be poor, if you're an example of what money buys.'

Lukas' mouth hung open. He stepped forward to slap him but Danny was a man now and the idea was suddenly absurd. For a moment, all the rage in Lukas was damned up: it had no place to go. When Danny saw him like this, hot and red with bulging eyes, he saw where his own anger had come from and it made him hate himself almost as much as he hated his father.

'Well then, you'll never need any of *my* money, will you?'

With these words, Lukas Lowenstein effectively disinherited his son. For good measure, he insisted Danny should leave the family home that night, before he could do anything else to 'sabotage the family Christmas'.

Danny, who was in shock for a while, managed to pull himself together before it showed: he couldn't *let* it show. Fine, he said, he was very happy to be going and he wouldn't be coming back. And he didn't need his father's filthy money either. He could get a scholarship to fund the rest of his time at Yale. They always looked at students from broken families sympathetically and, boy, was his broken.

As he walked down the stairs that night, all his belongings were packed into two suitcases and no one offered to help him with them. Instead Lukas shouted after him:

'Even if you make it as a journalist, Daniel, you'll never succeed. You'll always be a failure. I've seen your kind before. You've got failure written all over your face. You reek of it.'

Danny suspected that he might be right; perhaps it was why these last words from Lukas made his legs tremble and his hands shake. Tears were coming too, but he fought them off and convinced himself it felt good to be walking out of the house that had been a prison to him for so many years.

His mother cried beside the Christmas tree, while Camille stood there just as she always did, not arguing with Lukas, not pleading with him to change his mind. The way Danny saw it, she'd decided long ago that it was better to betray a brother than a father.

She didn't look up as Danny closed the door and set out into the frozen dark of that Pennsylvania Christmas where a cab was waiting to take him to another life. She didn't even say goodbye.

• • •

It was just after dawn broke across the gloomy Chechen sky when Rachel was woken by a crowing cockerel, though Danny snored on beside her. They had violated Rosa's rules and slept together on a bed that was saggy in the middle. Rachel imagined fat men on it hammering away at weary whores. It was also bare, without a sheet or blanket in sight, and so they'd snuggled up together inside a single sleeping bag. At first she found it erotic being packed against his naked flesh, her little breasts squashed against the bristling triangle of his chest hair, but he'd become a straitjacket around her and it was painfully cold, so they'd put their clothes back on and slept, unromantically, in separate bags.

The small bathroom reeked of piss. Rachel peed hurriedly, then turned on the tap to wash her hands and face. It spluttered like a sickly baby. Stumbling back down the corridor to Danny, she decided she'd wake him and make love to him again, just because she could, but then she heard a voice from one of the other rooms. It sounded like Edwin and she eased open the door that was already ajar.

'Oh, hello there, Rachel.'

He was mumbling to himself and busy preparing to smoke what she gradually realised must be crack, little chunks of it in a transparent plastic bag beside him. They reminded her of the vanilla fudge she used to buy at her local candy store in Arlington. He was wrapping a piece of cigarette carton round his crack pipe so he wouldn't burn himself.

'Hi, Ed. May I ask what the fuck you're doing?'

'I think that's reasonably obvious. Come on in and join me, if it's not too early for you. Just think of it as breakfast.'

He pulled out a cigarette lighter and started to heat his drugs, rolling the pipe around in his fingers.

'You don't think that stuff's a bit … well, heavy?' She said it without conviction. Having done dope and coke with him on several occasions, she was hardly in a position to moralise.

''Course it's bloody heavy – that's why I like it so very much indeed.'

'And there was me thinking you were a good Catholic boy.'

'More sinned against than sinning. In approximately ten seconds' time, it will hit my central nervous system and I'll have something better than an orgasm. The elixir of life. Just make sure you give it to me on my deathbed.'

She thought of him in Sarajevo, munching cannabis in the ladies', and wished that had been enough for him. Without his doomed love for Amra, it might have been. Now he sat before her, a shipwreck of a man, holed below the waterline. Rachel turned and left, closing the door quietly after her. She couldn't bear to watch him any more.

In the days between Christmas and New Year it was like the gathering wind that heralds a storm, laden with menace. Russia's defence minister boasted that a single division of paratroopers could subdue Grozny in a day. Abandon your dream of independence, the Kremlin told the Chechens, *surrender!* Danny said there was more chance of Boris staying sober, and besides, they didn't make white flags down here. The Chechens weren't so different from the Bosnians, he said; just fighting for their homeland and for freedom.

'God, Danny, why does it always have to be a cause with you, another bloody crusade?' Becky asked him one night. 'Can't it ever just be a story?'

Danny ignored her. He'd read two long histories of the Chechen people back to back and he was full of glorious indignation about Russia's crimes against them.

'You know, at one stage Stalin was deporting 80,000 Chechens every day,' he told her. 'Eighty thousand! Now *that's* ethnic cleansing. Puts the Serbs into the shade. But the Chechens have always hated the Russians. I was reading about this siege in 1830-something. The mothers killed their own children with their bare hands rather than let the Russians get hold of them.'

Becky was trying to imagine Danny writing up an atrocity like that. He'd have had a field day. Chechnya, she could see, had all the elements of a Lowenstein story: a complicated history, an underdog to champion, an aggressor to berate and an indifferent world to chide. He'd probably hang around here for months.

On the morning of New Year's Eve, the Grozny press corps prepared for Russia's latest onslaught on this tiny, troublesome republic. They stood in the old Soviet square of Minutka, waiting for battle to be joined, certain the fireworks show that night would be more spectacular than anything Sydney, Paris or New York had to offer. The sky would light up with tracer fire, Grad missiles and Katyusha rockets. Whole districts of the city would burn with an orange afterglow. Already Sukhoi bombers were swooping fast and low.

'Good people of Grozny, a very happy New Year to you all!' Danny announced in his cartoonish Russian accent as they watched the Russian warplanes set about their work. 'Citizens, we will rid you of these terrorist adventurists! We bring you freedom, we bring you bombs!'

Rachel laughed with him. In blissful ignorance of what would soon befall them, they were having the time of their lives.

An oil refinery erupted and a black cloud hung over the city. Day fast forwarded into night. Danny had a pair of binoculars which he shared with Rachel and they both filled pages of their notebooks.

Becky came across to talk to them, limping through the slushy, dirty snow, cameras swinging from her. She was worried about

Edwin again. Some of the other photographers had told her he wanted to stay the night in the Presidential Palace. He'd get unimaginable material, but the Russians were trying to shell it into dust, and when the elite troops of the Spetsnaz stormed in to mop up the survivors, they wouldn't bother separating rebels from reporters.

'There are risks and then there are *insane* risks,' said Becky.

Danny shrugged. If Edwin was playing poker with his life, that was his business. Danny didn't want people holding his hand, and he didn't expect to hold anybody else's either: risk went with the job, risk *was* the job, and this was one war where no one was going to tie you up with the red tape of permission slips. You had to make your own calculations, roll your own dice.

'He's a big boy now,' said Danny. 'I think he can decide for himself.'

'That's the whole point: I'm not sure he can any more.'

'Jesus wept, he's a grown man, isn't he?'

'And he's our *friend*. Or hadn't that occurred to you?'

The truth was it hadn't. Danny was more worried about whether Edwin might be about to scoop him with his sleepover in a building the Red Army was trying to obliterate. It would be an incredible story if he survived, but Danny didn't much like the sound of that 'if'. He considered himself to be a braver reporter than most, but not a headbanger. In Danny's book, there was an important distinction: headbangers usually ended up in coffins, if not in this war then the next. Months of coke and crack had turned Edwin into a headbanger, and Danny could no longer compete with him: it was like being up against an athlete on performance-enhancing drugs. On the other hand, he doubted Edwin was good enough to make the most of the story. The copy would be dramatic, but Edwin's writing style was too laboured and pedestrian – too damned *average* – to exploit it to the full. Danny had never feared him as a rival, any more than he'd feared poor old Kaps.

Danny, Rachel and Becky were stamping their feet to keep warm when two decrepit Volgas and a flatbed truck swung round a corner and skidded to a halt in front of them. They were packed with rebels, some dressed in Russian army combat fatigues they'd bought or stolen, extravagant bandoliers of ammunition slung across their shoulders. Others were just in jeans and sheepskin coats, green bandanas wrapped around their heads like bandages. Most had black beards of varying dimensions, and they shared a cocky, macho swagger that said they were going to have some fun this day – fighting for independence and, if necessary, dying for it too. If the headbangers were at the end of Danny's scale, these people were off it altogether.

'You want come to Palace with us?' The offer was from their leader, Ruslan. He said he'd take them there to see Dzhokar Dudayev, the former Soviet Air Force officer who was the leader of the uprising. They'd get an exclusive interview and he'd bring them out again an hour later. 'Safe,' Ruslan said. 'No problem.' He might have been suggesting a quick trip to the shops.

It was the sort of tantalising offer journalists both love and hate: it guaranteed both a story and an exit and it was full of promise; yet dangers lurked within it too. You could either choose to dwell on them or pretend they weren't there. Rachel and Becky looked at each other and waited for someone else to decide. Danny did it for them.

'Absolutely, we want to! What d'you say, ladies – you up for a quickie? Just an hour. If the Russians do move in tonight, we may never get the chance again.'

He liked to exude a casual courage even when he had his doubts. It was a way of driving himself on. If his words were daring, his actions had to match them: it was all about living up to his own bravado.

Rachel was clear she would stay with him, come what may. They were a partnership now, in bed and on the battlefield. Becky, though, was hesitant, unusually so: Kaps had knocked her so far off course that the old, swashbuckling confidence – when she did things without even thinking about them – had deserted her.

'I don't know. I don't like it.'

'Come on,' said Danny.

'I just need a minute to think about it.'

'Nerve gone?'

She gave him the long, withering stare she used to reserve for Kaps when she was angry with him. There were times she had nothing but respect for Danny, but equally times when she detested everything about him.

'Don't taunt me, Danny Lowenstein. Don't you dare,' she said, picking up her helmet.

Within five minutes, they were hurtling down the underpass from Minutka in a poor man's motorcade, exhilarated rebels hanging out of the windows, screaming wildly like little boys with new toy guns. Becky was in one car, adjusting the strap of her helmet and the Velcro of her flak jacket, checking and rechecking her cameras. Danny and Rachel were in the other, squeezing each other's hands. Rachel studied the burly fighters crammed alongside and in front of her, laughing and joking and slapping each other on the back. They didn't have a helmet or bullet-proof vest between them and wouldn't have worn them if they had. She couldn't help comparing them with the nervous, undernourished conscripts at the border. There were only a few hundred rebels pitted against thousands of Russians backed up by tanks and planes and helicopters, but she had no doubt who would win.

The underpass gave way to a sweeping, deserted boulevard. The bombing runs had left blast debris scattered along it; trees had been felled, branches snapped and scattered everywhere, trolleybus lines brought down. A gas pipe had been punctured, a steady flame licking out of it. Dead cats and dogs littered the road. A pig that had somehow found its way into the city was sniffing around two human corpses that lay uncollected by a block of flats. Nearby, beside a mound of rubble that used to be her home, an old woman in a headscarf sat on the street counting up the pots and pans which were the only things she still possessed. It made Snipers' Alley look genteel.

The Presidential Palace was a typical monstrosity of Soviet architecture that belied its name: more a dreary office block than a palace. It was not long for this world and would not be missed. When Danny, Rachel and Becky arrived, they saw it was packed with rebels whose welcoming faces and waving hands beckoned them to come in. Cautiously, they approached it. As well as fighters there were elderly men in fur hats and sheepskin coats and women stocking up on slabs of meat and jars of pickled fruit. They were preparing for a siege, but it could have been a party. Roll up, roll up for the great Chechen adventure, they seemed to say. Fight with us, die with us!

Some of the Palace was already in ruins. Its windows had all been blown out and its marble floors were glacial, but it was underground that the secret heart of the Chechen insurgency beat as strong as ever: a maze of rooms in the basement had become General Dudayev's headquarters. Uncertainly, the Junkies let Ruslan lead them ever deeper into the concrete bowels. They saw more volunteers stacking up not only piles of food, but also medical supplies. Becky touched random bits of wall.

'Let's not get trapped here,' she said, as she started burning off a roll of film. 'Don't forget there's a superpower army out there, and it's got us in its sights.'

'It's being in the heart of history,' said Danny.

'No, it's being in the fucking firing line.'

Becky wandered off to snap a straggling line of Chechens laden with a photogenic array of rocket-propelled grenades and anti-tank missiles, ceremonial swords and tribal daggers. They put down them down and started on the *zikr*, their traditional religious dance, clapping and stamping their feet frenetically, moving in an ever-faster circle. These were the *smertniki*; suicide fighters ready to be martyred for Chechnya and Allah. Behind them, framed in Becky's lens, Edwin had appeared like a ghost, bald, big-eyed and scrawny. Alija was by his side, trying to wipe the grime of battle from his professorial beard and glasses. He was clutching a volume of Proust, in the French, of course.

'Am I glad to see you!' said Edwin. 'You couldn't take out my copy, could you? Got some of the stuff of my life, but not a fucking phone in sight.'

'You're not seriously going to stay here?' said Becky. 'This place is a death trap. And' – she lowered her voice so that Alija couldn't hear – 'I'm just not sure you're very well right now.'

'Never better, girl.' He dismissed her anxiety with a flick of his bony hand and his eyes widened manically. 'Wait till you read my story. I tell you, I'm on fire!'

He was high on something, she could tell. She saw a man who was walking too close to the cliff. Some force was drawing him irresistibly to the edge and she had to shout out to him to stay away.

'Listen to me, Ed, this is just about the most dangerous place on earth right now. A notch up from Sarajevo – *several* notches, actually. You just cannot be flipping out and survive this. Alija, I'm right, aren't I? Tell him I'm right.'

Alija, the ever-faithful servant, said nothing.

'On the contrary,' said Edwin. 'You can't survive it *without* flipping out.'

He thrust his notebook into her hand with Jake's name and phone number scrawled on the cover.

'It'll take you ten minutes max to file this. And tell them they have to splash on it – front-page lead or I quit!'

'*You* tell them. Come out with us and file it yourself.'

'No can do,' said Edwin, talking faster, convinced that he was fascinating. Like the *zikr* he'd just watched, he was gathering momentum. 'Have to be here for the big one. It's going to be epic. Fuck the prizes and fuck the awards – but I'm going to win them all for this. In my penguin suit, gong after gong after gong, you wait and see. Danny will miss out for once, poor darling. Get this stuff across to London and it's the best thing you could ever do for me. It's the stuff of my life – did I tell you that? Did I tell you that I'm on fire?'

Becky rolled her eyes.

'And one other thing. Take Alija out with you, would you?'

She didn't see how he'd get by without an interpreter, but if she couldn't save both of them, she'd have to save one. There was no point in arguing. She hugged him like a child, kissing him on both cheeks while his new-found Chechen friends waited for him patiently. Becky wondered how many would still be alive to see in the New Year, and whether Edwin would be among them.

'I love you, you fruitcake. Just don't go dying on me, you hear?'

He shrugged.

'You really don't care, do you?' she said. 'Is it because of her? You want to join her?'

'Maybe. Yeah, if that's what the Fates decide.'

'They'll decide that if you let them.'

Edwin watched Becky leave with Danny and Rachel. He thought about how they'd been his friends, and how he'd grown apart from them as he'd gone in on himself in these last few months. Danny, of course, he could never forgive, but even Becky and Rachel were like characters from another time of his life entirely. It was as if he were swimming away from them, watching their heads bobbing in the water, becoming ever smaller until he could barely see them any more.

No sooner had they retreated to the haven of Minutka than Grozny exploded before their eyes. Anything and everything had become a target: blocks of flats as well as rebel bunkers, ethnic Russians as well as Chechens. Moscow seemed content to kill its own.

Inside the Palace, Edwin might as well have picked up a Kalashnikov and donned the Islamic green of the insurgency. He willed the men he was with to win. He ate, slept and all but fought with them. Paradoxically, without Alija to translate, the bonds between them became closer. He giggled, and so did they, when they failed to understand the semaphore of each other's sign language. One of them was shaven-headed too, and he and Edwin pointed at their respective scalps and laughed.

As the rebels ate bread – a last supper for some of them – Edwin crouched behind a mound of rubble and pulled out his bag of rocks. He did it discreetly, in case they disapproved. In Bosnia, he would have laid out a few lines on his notebook and snorted them through his pink straw, but the coke wasn't enough for him any more. The plastic shell of a biro served as his crack pipe, and Edwin dragged the sweet fumes through it. Even before he'd finished inhaling, the rush stormed through him. For a while at least, he was sitting on the roof of the world.

It might have been five minutes later or maybe five hours, Edwin wasn't sure, but word came through that the first Russian tanks were rumbling towards the Palace. If he'd been able to think about it, he might have concluded this wasn't the time to be on one of the best highs of his life; then again, perhaps it was the perfect time.

They raced out into the darkness without a flicker of hesitation, men anxious to meet their destiny, Edwin struggling to keep up. Occasionally, as they screamed their war cries, he would scream out too: he almost *was* one of them, a rebel fighting for a free Chechnya, fighting for something real at last, not like that desert war when it was just for oil and for America.

He was feeding hungrily on the dopamine that had flooded his brain. The way he would remember it later was that the volume on his TV set had been turned up to full blast, and the colour, contrast and brightness too: Grozny was being bombarded, but so were all his senses. Once in a while he would try to scribble something down, but the words looked like a child's scrawl and mostly he was happy just to live the night.

'Where are you now, Danny Lowenstein?' he yelled into the darkness.

The Chechens with him spread out and darted up and down back roads and side streets, hoping to sneak in behind the advancing T-72s. Most unsportsmanlike, thought the public schoolboy in Edwin. Like stabbing someone in the back.

Salam, their leader, had gold teeth, a Koranic verse inscribed on his bandana and pockets stuffed with hand grenades as though he'd just been picking apples. He fiddled endlessly with an anti-tank grenade on his shoulder before disappearing into a haze of smoke as he fired it, recoiling with the back blast. When Edwin swung round to see the tank, flames were already swallowing it. Then the ammunition inside detonated, like fireworks at a bonfire, and the crew spewed out, each a separate bundle of flames, young flesh melting before his eyes. He could see his own tank crew in the desert, and then the Iraqis they'd incinerated:

blackened skeletons half-buried in the shifting sands of the Kuwaiti border.

More pointless death. The world never learns. More lives slashed short. As Amra's had been. As he sometimes wondered whether his should be.

The Kremlin's burning children did not to have to suffer for too long: Salam's men were soon rushing from their hideouts, cutting them down with the mercy of their machine-gun fire.

An armoured personnel carrier trundled foolishly in the dead tank's wake. From the cold nowhere of the night, another horde of Chechens swarmed behind it, blasting its back doors with a rocket-propelled grenade. More teenagers tumbled out, not on fire this time, but making for the unfamiliar doorways and stairwells of a city they'd never been to and barely heard of. They were hunted, one by one, by Chechens who – unlike the conscripts – knew this city because it was their birthplace. They scurried around its basements and back alleys, even through its sewers.

Edwin watched a Chechen the size of a wrestler wield his sword above his head. The crack gave him a sensation of spinning back through time – spinning, spinning, spinning – till it was a 19th-century Chechen horseman that he saw, taking on the soldiers of the tsar. A wounded Russian conscript tried to make a break for it from his hiding place behind a wall. The rebel swung his sword and sliced his head off at the first attempt.

Tanks and APCs were coming and going in all directions, disorientated Daleks colliding with each other before they were destroyed. It was a rout. Edwin had never heard bangs that were louder or seen flashes that were brighter. The stench of cordite filled his nostrils. He hated war, and he hated what it had done to Amra, but tonight he felt he was falling back in love with it.

He knew it was the crack. He remembered the first time he'd fucked on cocaine, and decided afterwards sex would never be the same without it. He supposed war was similar: he'd never be able to watch it again without some sort of drug coursing through his bloodstream.

And eventually, inevitably, he began to crash. A heaviness descended on his limbs, and then an ache in his bones and muscles. He did his best to disguise it from Salam and his Chechen band of brothers, but Edwin knew he had to get back to the brothel. He needed to file and he needed to get wasted again, though in which order he couldn't quite decide.

It was almost midnight when Edwin stumbled into Rosa's whore-house, numb with cold. Somehow he had made it across town unscathed while Russians and rebels alike were falling all around him. His life seemed to be charmed and he wasn't certain he was grateful.

He managed to file 500 words of extra copy to follow up on what Becky had already sent for him. He hadn't written out his story, so he conjured it up as he dictated to the copy taker in London. He had no idea if it made any sense. She didn't comment either way, except to ask him – irritatingly – how to spell 'Grozny' and even 'Chechnya'. What the fuck was the point, he asked himself.

As soon as he'd put the phone down, he delved back into his supply and then, refreshed, he clambered up a ladder on to Rosa's roof where the rest of them were preparing to see in the New Year. Amid the swirling snow and red arcs of distant Russian tracer fire, they swigged cheap Russian champagne and danced in their coats and fur hats to Becky's ghetto blaster: 'Crazy' was playing yet again. By now, other journalists had started to descend on Rosa's whore-house and in all more than a dozen of them were on the roof, worrying vaguely they might fall through it.

Among the revellers was Kaps. His Aeroflot flight from Moscow had been delayed by 18 hours and he was convinced he'd missed the story, but Rachel had given him a fill, complete with quotes and colour from her visit to the Palace, and he'd hammered out a surprisingly convincing piece in less than an hour before joining them on the roof.

'I can't believe we're back together, and just in time for the New Year,' said Rachel, clinging to Danny for warmth. 'Must be an omen. Now then, who's got the right time? I mean *exactly*, to the second.'

Their watches, like their copy, all told slightly different stories, so Rachel went to fetch her shortwave. Throughout the year, the sombre voice of Bush House had been their saviour and on this, the final night, it was again. After holding the battered radio at various angles, twisting and turning it and wiggling its taped-up aerial, they found the reassuring tones of Lily Bolero and turned them up to ring out over Grozny.

In the brief silence before the first stroke of midnight, they paused for a moment to reflect on the year that had just died and the new one being born, and erupted into spontaneous applause. Quite what they were clapping, they weren't sure.

'*S Novym Godom.*' It was just about the only Russian that Kaps knew. Happy New Year. He was pleased to be seeing out the old one; in fact, he'd felt uncomfortable from the moment he arrived. The rupture in his friendship with Danny a few months earlier had not yet healed and he had no idea what to say to Becky: he could only assume she loathed him.

Everyone kissed and embraced, but after shaking hands with Edwin and putting his arms round Rachel, Kaps skulked off to a corner of the roof so he could avoid both his former friend and former lover. He'd thought about finding somewhere else to stay, but deep down Kaps had always known it would have to be the brothel. When he came to war, it wasn't just for the story, it was for the camaraderie. However awkward things had got with Becky and

Danny, he couldn't imagine being alone in a place like Grozny: what would be the point? Professionally too, he needed to be where the buzz was, to share information and analysis, gossip and tip-offs, not to mention resources and transport and alcohol. The relationship was healthily symbiotic – everyone sponged off each other.

He chatted to Spinoza and Mariana and only once or twice risked a surreptitious glance across the rooftop crowd, at Becky. He didn't even need to look up to see the smile or hear the laugh of the woman he should have been with. It was a combination of Seal and the bad champagne that persuaded him eventually to walk over to her. Though she had been affecting the studied nonchalance of a woman who'd moved on, nobody was fooled, least of all him.

He took her by the hand and kissed her on both cheeks before she had the chance to turn away.

'Happy New Year, Beck.'

'Oh. Hi. You too.'

'You okay?'

'Not really,' she said quietly, looking around to make sure none of the others were listening. 'You?'

'Nope.'

'It's shit, isn't it?'

'Shit, but for the best.'

She nodded and thought of Danny's Orwellian slogan in Goma: Worse is better. Now she had one of her own: Best is worst.

'Look, I'm just so sorry about …' Even though he'd rehearsed it a million times, he had no idea where the sentence might end, but Becky interrupted anyway.

'Don't be. You made the right decision.' She bowed her head before tears could betray her like the weasel informants that they always were.

'Right for my kids, wrong for you and me.'

Her eyes were fixed on the well-trodden snow that carpeted Rosa's roof. Another calamitous explosion rocked Grozny.

'It's like standing in the middle of a thunderstorm where there's no rain.' She felt the line was quite poetic, but Kaps, preoccupied, ignored it.

'It's killing me, you know,' he said, 'to be apart from you.'

'Good, I'm pleased.'

He touched her on the shoulder.

'Don't, Kaps. Please, just … don't.'

'I miss you. I miss your smile. I miss your hair. I miss your hobbly, wobbly leg.'

'Well, thanks a bunch,' she laughed, and he realised that was another thing he'd missed.

Rachel came over and grabbed them both by the arm. She wanted everyone to hold hands and belt out 'Auld Lang Syne', or as much of it as they could collectively remember, because they hadn't done so yet and it was already ten past midnight. They all joined in, even Alija, who'd given Proust a rare night off. The six of them, plus assorted late-comers, photographers and aid workers, formed a circle and moved with ever-greater speed until they were a merry-go-round in full flight.

'Look, we're doing the *zikr!*' Rachel screamed. She and Becky threw their heads back, children at the funfair, while Krontz and Spinoza drove them on. A refuelled Edwin laughed like the madman he was becoming and they forgot the carnage all around them. When the circle grudgingly broke up, Becky looked up to see where Kaps had gone, but he was back in his corner, hiding, afraid that if he kissed her again he wouldn't ever stop. A few feet away she saw Rachel and Danny slow-dancing with each other. Rachel was smothered in his chest and Becky wished it were her, swallowed up in the man she loved.

'Goodbye to '94,' Rachel was saying drunkenly, loud enough for the whole roof to hear. 'I wonder what the next one's got in store?'

By the time the New Year was two hours old, the Russian champagne and Chechen brandy had done for them. They had come down from their roof dance and crashed out in one of the brothel's bigger rooms. Becky was draped across a king-sized bed alongside Danny, while Rachel and Kaps lay on the floor, comatose and occasionally snoring. They looked like they could sleep all the way through 1995.

'I don't think I've been this *irretrievably* pissed since … well the last time I was irretrievably pissed,' slurred Becky. As she watched Kaps sleeping, she decided it was good to see his perfect face again, however much it hurt her just to look at it. Only six months earlier, she'd been making love to him two or three times a day and now she couldn't even touch him. There was as much pain in his presence as his absence, but at least the alcohol was an anaesthetic.

'That man down there, I adored him. Still do.'

'I know.' Danny had become her confidante while Rachel was indisposed. Unexpectedly he put a consoling arm around her, and unexpectedly Becky seized it, binding it round her belly. It was good to be comforted and have the feel and smell and strength of masculinity, *any* masculinity, and since Kaps had been so cruelly exiled from her life, Danny would have to do. In fact, she could almost pretend it *was* Kaps. She started to feel a little better.

Danny began tracing the index finger of his free hand up and down her jaw line. That felt pleasant too, like a massage: sensual and repetitive. Becky closed her eyes and dreamt of Kaps and when she opened them again, she was startled to see Danny looking into her. She should have smiled and thanked him, maybe made a joke about old times, said good night and turned her back on him. Then again, thought Becky, I should have done so many things.

When Danny moved his mouth to hers, she let him. Her tongue tasted his smoke and toxic alcohol but it was pleasing: his mouth was warm and wet and just the way she had remembered it from back when they were lovers. She told herself it might yet be a joke on Danny's part, a silly, drunken lark between old pals, but then she felt him hardening against her. Out of a clear, calm day, the champagne and brandy had created a tsunami that was sweeping away not just inhibitions but conscience and loyalty too, and everything else that was good and right.

She watched Danny casting glances down at Rachel on the floor. He was checking she was still asleep, but there must have been something else as well because he already knew she was too far gone to stir. Only when Becky saw him look and look again did she understand: the fact Rachel was in the room was titillating him, adding a frisson of danger and a vicarious thrill. And as he ripped open her jeans and pulled down his own, Becky watched him watching Rachel and was disgusted and delighted as he pushed his way in. He had become enormous and horribly excited. She closed her eyes once again and insisted to herself it was Kaps who was inside her, making love as he had done in Africa, the most beautiful sex she'd ever had.

Within a couple of frantic minutes it was over. A final, breathless thrust. A deep grunt from him, a suppressed moan from her. And then he was collapsed on top of her, asleep and shrinking rapidly inside, as fast as he had grown.

She looked down at Rachel, so pretty as she slept, almost childlike. Sometimes Becky had cursed her, but now she wanted to wake her up and tell her she was sorry and that she didn't know what she'd been thinking of and that she'd be her friend forever. Was this what her life amounted to, Becky wondered: stealing other people's men, even if it were only for a few minutes? She imagined Rachel waking up and seeing her, rubbing the sleepy dust from her eyes in disbelief

– How *could* you? – and then Judith watching too: You *whore*! No wonder you chose Rosa's place to stay in, it's where you belong!

Becky felt empty, a hollow carcass. And still Danny lay on top of her, unwanted now, crushing her, a dead weight she couldn't push away.

With her panoply of superstitions, it was no surprise that Becky would come to see what happened the following Saturday as an omen for the year ahead. The heavy grey clouds of that January weekend were pregnant with snow, overdue in fact; just waiting to deliver.

Danny, Rachel and Becky had taken Alija for the morning. Edwin, increasingly incapable of any work at all, grunted approval from his sleeping bag when they asked if they could borrow him for a few hours. Alija was depressed by the zombie his employer had become and glad to get away.

They were on their way to Yazhdnovskaya, a village that was a rebel stronghold and home to an especially ferocious Chechen clan. It lay to the east of Grozny, at the rim of a flat plain which gave way to wooded foothills which in turn sloped up towards the snow-crusted mountains rising mightily above. Yazhdnovskaya seemed as good a place as any to gauge the mood of the resistance.

When they got there, they found scores of rebels milling around outhouses with chickens, pigs and cattle: the animals looked like they too had joined the uprising. The Junkies quivered with the cold and watched the white breath that left their mouths every time they spoke. They came upon an elderly man with a twisting beard of grey who invited them into his farmhouse for some lunch, and they were grateful for the warmth. The meal was barely cooked lamb, but they were more interested in the low heat radiating from his woodstove and they gathered around it unashamedly with palms outstretched and fingers splayed.

Alija was, as usual, reading while the others talked and ate. He had traded the rigours of Proust for the soft cadences of Auden and every now and then he'd smile.

'What, is it funny or something?' asked Becky, who hadn't read a word of poetry outside school.

'Funny? No, not really. I suppose I was thinking how someone like Auden can create something so marvellous as this, and then you come here and see all these other men who just destroy things.'

'Yeah right, highly amusing.' Becky sometimes wondered what he was doing with them. He belonged in the reading room of an ancient university, not another frontline.

'No, he has a point,' said Danny. 'We're capable of so much – science, poetry, art – but we still fight like the savages we once were. Take these crazy Chechens and Russians. They could be cavemen, if you ...'

The whoosh of the first Katyusha interrupted him. It landed behind them somewhere in the hamlet, a pigsty or a haystack probably: the Russians wouldn't care, they were trying to make the Chechens flee. The instinctive reaction of the rebels in Yazhdnovskaya, however, was to stand and fight. Like cavemen.

Alija closed his book wearily, dragged back into the noisy inconvenience of another war. A second Katyusha came in, then two more in quick succession and ever closer. The Russians had brought in a multiple rocket launcher. No one was in any doubt what the barrage meant: a full-scale assault that would leave very few survivors.

'Can I suggest we fuck off out of here, very fast indeed,' Danny said.

They abandoned their elderly host and were out the door, running through the various farmyards of the village, snow-spattered mud and manure squelching beneath their Timberlands and up over their jeans. They hurdled a low fence, Alija the first to show it was easily surmountable. As a rule, he would trail behind, dawdling, stroking his beard, lost in his other worlds and centuries. Physical exertion often seemed beneath him. Today though his quiet bookishness was transformed into an unlikely athleticism and he was racing ahead. Only two more fields now lay between them and the car.

Incomprehensible Chechen voices came chasing after them through the winter air.

'They're saying we should stay with them, the crazy bastards!' shouted Danny, almost laughing. 'They never seem to get that we might want to stay *alive*.'

'No, no. Wait.' Alija had stopped about 30 yards in front of his three colleagues. 'It's something else, they're saying something else. *Mini*. Yes that's it: *Mini* – mines. They're telling us this is a minefield. They probably laid it to keep out the Russians.'

'Oh fuck,' said Becky. 'Fuck, fuck, fuck.'

They all stopped statue-still.

The daunting crack of sniper shots added themselves to the sound of the Katyushas, like percussion joining in the rhythm as the band picks up its swing.

'Shit, snipers too.' There was no longer excitement in Danny's face, only fear.

'So what do we do now?' said Rachel. 'Keep going or head back to the farm?'

'Back,' said Becky decisively. 'We'll take cover in that shed over there till things calm down.'

'But what if this *is* a minefield?'

'Well, we can't just stand here like this. That sniper will pick us off, one by one.'

In a split second, war and all its deadly choices had come to them. To go on, or go back: which way lay disaster?

'Come *on!*' Danny shouted. Someone had to make a decision, right or wrong. Warily, they retreated towards the shed. At Walsingham, the teachers had shown them how to escape from a minefield, using a knife or even a pen to probe each square inch of soil with agonising care. 'Take all the time in the world,' the instructor had said. Strangely, neither Katyusha rockets nor a sniper had been part of the scenario, nor had numbing cold, and they could think of no alternative but to run to the shed and hope for the best. Its four walls, part brick, part wood, part corrugated iron, represented some sort of shelter, however flimsy. They represented a plan.

Heads down as they sprint. Trying to make footsteps feather light, as if it might make a difference if they tread on one. Cursing the sticky mud from the field accumulating on their boots, great clods of it, making them too heavy. Vaulting back over the same, low fence, Danny in the lead this time – the commander – Rachel just behind and Becky – cruelly handicapped by her Sarajevo limp – in third position. Alija, furthest ahead on their way out of the village, now last on their return to it.

Almost there, just a few more yards. The shed that will be their sanctuary. Dive in through the door, slam it shut and draw breath. Then think of another plan and maybe say a prayer.

A bang, different in texture from the cracks of the sniperfire and whooshes of the Katyushas. It seems to violate the air. Low shockwaves ripple out. It is only now that they are here at last, within the shed's dubious protection, panting and sweating, that they realise he is not among them, that the crumpled heap in the field they've just escaped from is their Alija, writhing around like an animal trapped in a snare.

The anti-personnel mine was small, but powerful enough to cripple him. Blood seeps into the snow from his right foot and a red halo surrounds it. This has been the device's cunning ambition: not to kill but to disable and draw in others.

Alija is a mere 20 yards short of the fence. Becky says nothing but unwraps the cameras from herself, dumping them on the floor of the shed before starting to run back the way she has just come.

Three whistles around her head – mortars now too, flying through the cold, dank air.

She dives into the brown-white slushy snow just outside the shed, showered by clumps of earth from the explosions all around. They have her in their sights. She thinks of Dragan back in Sarajevo. Are they enjoying their sport as much as he did? Or just obeying orders, conscripted kids, scared stiff, dragooned into Chechnya and wanting only to get out again as fast as possible.

She is up once more, and it isn't until she feels the muscular arms around her waist, halting her momentum, pulling her back, that it dawns on Becky she can no longer move. Like a cartoon character, her feet are still in motion, but going nowhere. He drags her back inside the shed.

'Danny, get your *fucking* hands off me! We have to get him, we have to bring him in here.'

'There are mortars and snipers and a minefield out there,' Danny shouts back. 'Leave this shed again and you're dead too.'

'He's not dead, no one's dead. He's wounded. Look! There! He's still moving around, can't you see?'

'It's the first rule of a minefield, you don't go in there to rescue casualties. If you're out, you stay out.'

She looks at him incredulously.

'*What?* This is not some fucking training-ground exercise, we're not working from a manual here. That's our friend, in case you hadn't noticed, the guy we've spent the last two years of our fucked-up lives with, remember?'

'I'm sorry. You want all of us to die here? We have no choice.'

'Of course we have a choice. There's always a choice. Between courage and …'

'Yes? Say it, Becky.' He is in her face, pumped up and yelling. Rachel, who has retreated into a corner of the shed, watches the two people she loves most in the world tear each other apart.

'All right then. Between courage and *cowardice*.'

'No, actually; between living and dying.'

'And what if that was me lying out there now, or Rachel. What would your choice be then?'

'I … Don't be dumb, this isn't the time for hypotheticals.'

'You're damned right it isn't.'

Becky struggles to break away from him but the running has tired her out. She's frozen and frightened and he's too strong. He has hold of her wrists, so tight it's hurting like a Chinese burn, but in the months and years of remorse that lie ahead, she will often wonder if there were something else that prevented her from going back out to Alija.

A long, ululating moan emerges from the field, like a woman in labour. It rises and falls on the frozen breeze. Then his first words carry to the doorway of the shed.

'My leg, please, my leg.'

A whiteness descends on Becky like a veil.

Another cry from Alija, this time with more determination.

'Help me! I am bleeding. I'm bleeding so badly.'

Becky looks at Danny once again. She no longer has the energy to fight him or to run. All she can do is beg him the way she imagines Alija's eyes are begging her.

'Please, Danny. Please. I can't let him die out there like a dog in the road. I can't ignore him, I'll never live with myself. He's one of us, for Christ's sake.'

And then he says it, with all his cold, clinical brutality.

'No, he isn't. Of course he isn't one of us.'

Her mouth hangs open. She looks at him with bewilderment followed by withering contempt. And she hates him, almost as much as she hates herself for having fucked him.

He lets go of her arms. She is free to run and save him now, but her feet seem nailed to the splintered timber floor. They won't move: she wills them to, but stubbornly they refuse. Blame them! Blame Danny! Blame anyone but me!

At first, the desire to rescue had been instinctive. Not doing it never crossed her mind, but now Danny has filled her head with doubts. She starts to see mines lurking everywhere, sharks in the sea, ready to gobble up the easy flesh of trailing legs. Perhaps he is right: *nowhere* outside this shed is safe.

Another pitiful wail from Alija.

'I'm bleeding away here. You have to … to help me.'

Her head boils with the frenzy of the moment. There are a dwindling number of seconds in which to decide, a tiny handful. *Courage or cowardice.*

'We need a map of the minefield!' she shouts back at him. It sounds weak, almost bureaucratic. Yes, we'll save your life, but first there are certain procedures to be completed, papers to be consulted, meetings to be held.

'Becky, please, for the love of God, I'm losing all my blood.'

Why does he have to use *her* name? Why her, why not Rachel or Danny? And 'for the love of God'? Why does he have to demonstrate, yet again, his mastery of English idiom?

She pictures his extraordinary brain being drained of its lifeblood, the bundle of tissue and cells that can speak four languages fluently and contains unfeasible quantities of information. Like a library, its shelves are stuffed with thousands of dusty volumes, from Cicero and Aristotle, through Chaucer and Shakespeare, to Byron and Keats and Steinbeck and Hemingway. Could it really just shut down?

She thinks of New Year's Eve, and how happy they had been together. She remembers him abandoning his books for once to join the midnight dance, that stupid *zikr* they all did. Why couldn't they be back there now, making different resolutions and different plans?

Everything lies in ruins. Like a pile-up on a pleasant afternoon, the routine of just another day has turned into catastrophe. The wrong foot on the wrong patch of ground. The wrong amount of pressure. The wrong friends making the wrong choices.

He has become quieter, whimpering. The final seconds drag by, Becky stranded in the prison of her confusion. Someone else has locked her in, but even now escape is possible, she knows it is: she just doesn't want it quite enough.

From somewhere in the village two burly, bearded Chechens appear, in the snow-white overalls that camouflage them. They are jabbering to each other, walking straight past the shed, not even running. If a sniper's bullet drills through their skulls and out the other side, so be it. It will be God's will and all for the cause of a free and independent Chechnya. *Smertniki.* They share not a scintilla of Becky's doubts.

Onwards they march to the fence, onwards Chechen soldiers, moving with so much ease. No more shots or mortars. Why? screams Becky to herself. Why does it have to stop *now*?

Even when the Chechens jump the fence into the minefield, they seem careless of where they tread. Courage or cowardice? In their case courage, raw and undiluted. They've never even met him.

One of them picks up Alija as she has yearned to do, as she *should* have done, as she *would* have done if Danny had not stopped her with his policy of strict non-intervention. The Chechen throws him over his shoulder, carrying him back into the farm like a sack of potatoes, blood from Alija's wounded feet running down the back of the snow suit, daubing its pristine white with violent streaks of red like some urban graffiti artist.

Becky watches. Maybe he's asleep. Maybe he's unconscious and when they bandage the leg and raise it up, the lifeblood will flow back to him. Just like when Edwin saved that pregnant woman in Sarajevo. Just like when Kaps saved those kids in Goma. Another miracle for the Junkies. Please God, just one more miracle, I beg of you, and then we'll ask no more.

He is on the shed floor where he should have been 20 minutes earlier. The Chechens rip up their whites and tourniquet his leg. They talk quickly to each other, confident and resolute, and Becky cannot help but admire their expertise. They are skilled at saving life, she senses, as well as taking it. They will perform the miracle. One kneels and puts his mouth to Alija's. Becky is remembering how she always struggled with those plastic dummies at Walsingham in the artificial respiration class. Alija is in better hands than hers. The Chechen works away at him, the two men's beards enmeshed.

Becky looks for a rise and fall of Alija's puny chest, and now she's certain she can see it – shallow like a baby's, so shallow, but most definitely there. And surely that's his breath, faint white wisps of it exhaled into the icy air? Oh praise the Lord!

'Look, he's still alive!'

Rachel, at her side, grips her hand; the other friend she's betrayed, fucking him in front of her.

'Beck, I don't …'

'No, look, he is. He's breathing.'

She forms a picture. The attack will abate and they'll drive him to a hospital in Grozny; the hard-pressed doctors will do their best but probably he'll have to lose the foot. So what, she'll joke with him: now we'll both walk with a limp! When he's stronger he'll be flown to Moscow, and then air ambulanced back to Britain. The good old *Telegraph* will come up trumps. He won't go back to Bosnia till the war is over, minus one foot, of course. Oh well, he'll say philosophically, it could have been worse, it could have been both. And I've always got my books!

One of the Chechens finds an oily blanket in the corner of the shed and lays it over him with as much dignity as he can muster in the circumstances.

'What the fuck are you *doing*?' Becky shouts. 'You've just covered up his whole face, you're going to suffocate him.'

Rachel tries to put an arm around her, but Becky pushes it away and screams at them again:

'I told you, he's still breathing. Look!'

She kneels by his side, and puts an ear to his chest.

'Yes, yes, *yes* he is!'

The Chechens shake their heads with big brown melancholic eyes that say, We're sorry for your loss. They're wise enough to know that for people not like them, not *smertniki*, death can be hard to accept.

25

Post-Liberation Iraq, August 2004

Danny suspects the fever is amoebic dysentery. He has had it once before, in Sumatra, when the doctor discussed it with him in graphic detail, announcing with relish: 'the amoebae have taken up residence in your intestines, Mr Lowenstein.' Now, as then, he's doubled up with stomach cramps and his diarrhoea is bloody, seeping from him all the time. It's as though he can see his body shrink in front of him: near the place where Scar branded him, his wrist bones are beginning to protrude. He yearns to be back with Abu Omar and the mad bombers, and the television pictures of his parents, and the carpet that made him think he might still be human.

He has no appetite but a rampant thirst, and yet when Slow arrives with his daily rations there is no beaker. Once Danny would have accepted it, but today he's seized with moral outrage.

'Where the *fuck's* my water?'

The anger feels good, a release.

Slow lumbers away to find out. Five minutes later it is Scar who comes in, heaving a yellow bucket into the cell. Water laps wastefully over the sides and Danny gawps at it. He could down its contents in one go, or duck his head in it. It's the most perfect thing he's ever seen.

'*Shukran*,' Danny mouths. Thank you.

Graciously, Scar nods. Danny concludes it's strength that they respect.

'Look, I'm sick. I need doctor.' He points to his stomach.

Scar nods again but says nothing in reply.

'I said I need a *fucking* doctor. I'm seriously ill here, can't you see?'

Scar carries the bucket over to him, one shoulder dragged low by its weight, his body lopsided. He puts it down and Danny prepares to plunge his dried-out, aching face into the water. Cold, sweet water to wash it all away: the dirt, thirst and pain; the memories and the dreams; the past.

At the last moment, Scar snatches it from him. He lifts the bucket high and pours it over his own head, which he shakes like a dog so that his soaking hair sprays Danny with fine droplets. He cackles. It's the funniest thing in the world to him, a hilarious schoolboy prank. Then, after checking to make sure the bucket is empty, he hurls it into Danny's face with such velocity that its metal handle cuts him, slicing open the skin just above one eyebrow. A stream of blood runs down his face and flows fast into his tears.

Now that he is back with Scar, the bad dreams are more frequent. Each evening he waits for them to ambush him, afraid to sleep.

It's the Toyota at al-Talha again, but this time it's not his friends who are pressed against the windscreen, taunting him: it's the dead. Mohammed is behind the wheel, the bullet holes in his chest still bleeding after all this time. Next to him is Amra, her face dusty from the hospital that's collapsed upon her. Then Alija, his shredded leg resting on the dashboard, blood gushing out of him as well. He's waving to Danny: 'Keep driving,' he says. 'Don't be scared! Come and join the dead! I may not have been one of you, but now *you* can most certainly be one of *us*.'

'Yes, come on, Danny,' say the others. 'Do the brave thing! We did, after all.'

Camille was dreaming too. Her bed at the Hamra was comfortable enough, but the night was almost as sticky as the day and her sleep, like Danny's, was fretful. A sheet was tangled around her legs, wet with sweat. She would have given anything for the aircon of her swanky apartment in Dubai, its cool oxygen so abundant.

All night she struggled to see Danny's face. She was locked into the strangest of anxiety dreams where she would catch his eyes, his mouth, his hair, but each time she thought she could put them all together they would slip away.

Until 12 years ago, they had met occasionally for lunches or coffees, and endured stilted long-distance conversations. It was 1992 when she put the phone down on him for the final time: he was in Sarajevo – he was *always* in Sarajevo. The call had started pleasantly enough. She was worried about him, she said. She kept seeing terrible pictures of Sarajevo on TV. Was he safe? Was he getting enough to eat? He told her he was fine and that it looked worse than it was and she said she hoped so, but when she raised – yet again – the idea of a family reconciliation, it started an argument that slid out of control with alarming speed.

'You did *nothing* for me, Camille, and you know why? Because you'd always rather have been a daughter to him than a sister to me.'

It was with some relief that she was woken by the call to prayer. It reminded her of the church bells on a Pittsburgh Sunday, ringing in the next round of the long fight between Danny and Lukas Lowenstein. Religion, she thought; it's been waking me all my life.

Camille lay there for a while, until the morning light began to glow. She put on her glasses and walked naked to the window, pulling apart the thin gauze curtains that only half kept out the

Baghdad dawn. An enormous sun had divided into layers: a rich band of orange at the top, then ever paler strips of yellow lower down. Helicopters floated back and forth across it, the occupiers already hard at work. The messy sprawl of Baghdad lay before her, waking to another day of horror. She saw the jumble of beige boxed buildings whose windows sometimes twinkled when they caught the day's young light. She looked too at the hotel's ever-growing fortifications: an open prison of blast walls, barbed wire and sentry boxes where the Hamra's security contractors stood guard, cradling Kalashnikovs around their midriffs. It made her wonder where Danny might be incarcerated now and what he might be doing. Had he slept as badly? Did he have the same trouble conjuring up her face? Did he even want to try?

She opened her handbag and took out the small picture of Danny she kept there, feasting on every detail, trying to learn it like a piece of homework. As she looked back out across the skyline, a blurred figure emerged into the corner of her vision, in the courtyard down below. She brought it into focus and saw the familiar curve of his spine, a fresh white dishadasha hanging over it. Jamail was by an outhouse, unpicking a padlock and easing himself through a gap between its double doors. From her window, she had seen him shuffling around here before, but it was what followed that interested her. Edwin and Kaps walked up to the same building. Then, looking even more anxious than they had in the tea house, they slipped through the double doors Jamail had just unlocked.

After she had showered and dressed, Camille flicked on the television. No news of Danny, not even a mention. She went downstairs and found Jamail busy on the phone at the reception desk, engrossed in a conversation. She mouthed a casual 'hi' as she walked past him. Distractedly, he half-lifted a hand to acknowledge her.

Having strolled down the main steps and into the front yard, she headed for the outhouse. The double doors had been padlocked up again. She felt faintly ridiculous as she peered through the slit between them. When her eyes adjusted to the gloom, she could see the darkened blur of several shapes: three cars, she realised. Her vision improved still further and she could tell they were two GMCs and some sort of saloon, bundled up tight in a brown tarpaulin. Big deal, she told herself. It was a garage.

Most days Camille would join the Junkies for breakfast in the café, but this morning she found them chatting at a table for four. She hovered awkwardly nearby before Edwin invited her to squeeze in next to them – a little late, she thought, and without much enthusiasm. It meant going to find herself a plate, a napkin and some cutlery. She did it without fuss but wondered all the same why they couldn't have chosen a bigger table in the first place: they knew she liked to sit with them and discuss the day ahead.

Edwin poured them all some dreadful instant coffee, lukewarm and tasteless. The bread rolls were stale and brittle, and the pot of jam had specks of old butter from other people's knives. The omelettes, when they eventually came, needed paper napkins to dry the oil from them. It reminded the Junkies of their breakfasts at the Holiday Inn and all the crap hotels they'd ever stayed in.

'You guys look like you slept better,' said Camille.

Becky nodded but her face was as drained as ever.

A couple of journalists from the *Baltimore Sun* and the *Times* drifted over to ask if there was any news, but the rest kept their distance, nervous of causing unnecessary distress with questions to which there were no answers. Jamail had no such scruples. He came up to them and expressed ritual concern for Danny and they talked to him politely. There was none of the hostility Camille had witnessed the day before; the whole tea-house incident seemed to have been forgotten. She supposed it had probably been some misunderstanding about a bill.

'I'm going to clean my teeth,' said Camille. 'See you guys a little later.'

'Actually, we'll be out all day,' said Kaps.

'Oh really? Something going on?'

Camille assumed there must have been a fresh atrocity they were heading out to cover.

'No, nothing. Just some stuff to do.'

The implication was that they didn't want to talk to her about it and she felt excluded. Perhaps it was why they had chosen a table for four, not five.

She was left kicking her heels all day. She tried to push on with the Henry James novel that had been lying around the suite, but read entire paragraphs only to discover she had no idea what they contained. She made futile phone calls to Munro, Harper and Adi. Let's talk tonight on the conference call, they said. In other words, there was nothing to report. Finally, she decided to go down for a swim to work off her frustration. The lift was working for a change and, just as the doors were closing, Melissa, the eager producer from NBC, squeezed in.

'Hey! How are you?' Camille was glad to have someone to talk to as they descended through the Hamra.

'Good, thanks.'

Melissa felt guilty. With only a week until the deadline, she was busy setting up coverage for the day of Danny's death. New York had said they'd go 'really big' on it with three packaged reports and a couple of live interviews with correspondents. They'd devote half the *Nightly News* to it, maybe even anchor from Baghdad.

'You should know we're all thinking of you.'

'Thanks.'

They talked for a while and Melissa said if there was anything she could do – anything at all – Camille must let her know.

'It's just so awful,' said the young producer. 'That morning we all heard, God I think that will stay with me forever.'

'Me too.'

'Poor Rachel sobbing. Just running through the breakfast room, and sobbing, sobbing, sobbing.'

It wasn't till after dark that they returned. Camille had done the evening conference call without them, but Edwin offered to cook them up some ratatouille for supper. The wine flowed and then the whisky and then the dope. Edwin surprised Camille by producing a little bag of it, the first time any of them had done their drugs in front of her. It was as though, having excluded her, they were admitting her to their circle. She felt strangely honoured.

'Did you have a good day?' It was her discreet invitation for them to explain what they'd been doing, but they sidestepped it.

'Yeah, good thanks,' said Kaps. 'And you?'

'Mmm. Not too bad.'

Camille decided to be more direct.

'So, what have you guys been up to?'

'Oh, just this and that, you know,' said Edwin.

'Uh huh?'

'Really, nothing much. We do have jobs you know, employers. Bureaux to look after, contacts to talk to. Can't mope round here all the time.'

'So, filing?' she persisted.

'Not exactly.'

'What then?'

'Camille, chill out,' said Rachel. 'It really doesn't matter. We're journalists. Life goes on, even if it's life without Danny.'

Edwin assembled the joint with the same meticulous care he put into his cooking. Camille admired the dexterity with which he rolled the paper and mixed the tobacco and tangled strings of cannabis: he could have done it with one hand tied behind his back and both eyes closed. He handed it to her first. Perhaps he thought she needed to relax and stop asking so many questions.

She took it from him and inhaled more deeply than she meant to. Nothing happened for a few seconds. She wondered if the chemicals ceased to work after a certain age, or the menopause negated them. She was about to give up on it when the dope hit her hard, rushing through her head, flooding every corner of it. It was the best thing that had happened to her all day, partly because it was the only thing that had happened to her all day. She floated round the room a few times and it occurred to her she was floating into Edwin's world.

Danny, squatting over the toilet, looks up at the ceiling. Two lengths of black flex hang down where there used to be a light fitting. He's seen them plenty of times before; now though he studies them in a new way. They are coiled up, but if he could unfurl them and tie their ends together, they might just be long enough. Not only that, but there's a rusting drum in the corner he could move and stand on. There'd be just enough time, but only if poor Slow were on duty. Slow never likes to look when Danny's in the toilet.

Once it would have been unthinkable. Danny loved to boast how rich his life was and how fast he lived it, and now here he is, contemplating ending it – and yet there's a logic. Wouldn't it be so much better than the knife? There would be a softness to it, a calm, with none of those terrifying screams, from them or him. Why not make death come a little easier? And doesn't he deserve it anyway? Hasn't he visited it upon enough others, all those poor wretches in his dreams?

He imagines Slow discovering his body, swinging gently. Slow will shout for Scar, who in turn will come running in, cursing the fact he's been denied his moment with the knife.

Short of being rescued, it's the only way Danny could hope to defeat him.

26

1995–2004

Alija had always said he didn't want to be buried in Bosnia. Too noisy, he told them with a twinkle in his eye. He'd prefer Highgate Cemetery, so he could be near George Eliot and, of course, Karl Marx. 'It's where they put all the interesting people,' he said. 'That's so weird,' Edwin had replied. 'Because I'd like to be buried in Sarajevo. Maybe we could arrange a swap.'

With some help from the *Telegraph*, Becky organised everything; she wrote his obituary, which the *Telegraph* ran unedited and with a big picture of Alija alongside Edwin in Tuzla. She arranged for his body to be flown to London. She booked the undertakers, the service, the invitations, the flowers and the choir. The music was to be Bach, his favourite, and the readings literary rather than religious: the Bible and the Koran were just about the only books he'd never read. His friends recited a poem each, an eclectic mix of Sassoon, Keats and Goethe. They imagined him inside his grave, beard still neatly groomed, a furrowed brow behind the glasses, listening with delight. The editor of the *Telegraph* turned up, along with several other foreign correspondents and even an MP for whom Alija had translated in Sarajevo. You see, Becky felt like telling Danny, he *was* one of us after all.

But Danny didn't make the funeral. He sent a wreath, and a message saying he was ill.

After Chechnya, nothing was ever quite the same again. They were undone by Alija's death and for a while they couldn't face another war. In any case, all of them knew there'd never be another 1994.

When the funeral was over and Becky had nothing left to organise, she started to go in on herself. There were nightmares first, followed by insomnia and a loss of appetite. Gradually it got worse, with spasms in her legs and anxiety attacks if she heard loud or sudden noises. The bosses at Sigma paid for her to see a Harley Street psychiatrist, who diagnosed post-traumatic stress disorder. He told her what any sensible person could have done: that she should stay away from war zones. She tried taking pictures of things that were nothing to do with death or violence, but they held no interest for her. She saw a life ahead that was desolate – without her career, without her lover.

Rachel suggested it might help if Becky talked things through with Danny: 'You're good enough friends to be honest with each other; I think it could be therapeutic for both of you.' Becky said she wasn't sure they were good friends at all and that she couldn't face him yet, not after what he'd done in Yazhdnovskaya.

'But he didn't *do* anything,' Rachel pleaded with her. 'You can't keep blaming Danny. God, it's not as if he killed him.'

'Isn't it?'

Becky could have gone further. She could have told Rachel: 'And what about you, Rach? Aren't you culpable, too? Okay, so you didn't stop me, but you didn't exactly play the hero either, did you? Hiding in the corner of that shed, hoping no one would see you.'

It was why, when she thought about fucking Danny in front of Rachel, Becky didn't feel so bad.

• • •

For the rest of the 1990s, Kaps tried to make things work with Judith, but when he weakened, he sent Becky texts and e-mails. Sometimes she ignored them, sometimes she was polite: *Doing fine, thanks – much better. Not sure meeting up such a great idea.* And sometimes, when he pressed her, she was firm. P*lease, Kaps, you have your life and I have mine.* Her strength surprised her, but really it was just self-preservation.

Half of him, the half that loved her and wished her well, wanted her to find another man. The other half, which still yearned for her, would have been devoured by jealousy if she had. When Kaps was in Brighton, he'd cuddle the boys at night and his sacrifice would seem worthwhile, but as he got into bed with Judith and turned out the light, he'd long for Becky and the glory of her flesh and the fullness of her smile, and the life she injected into him.

The next time they saw each other wasn't until two years after Alija's funeral, and it wasn't in some failed state but in London after Labour's election victory of 1997. He'd been up all night and felt like shit. Becky was taking pictures of the victorious young leader and his toothy grin outside the Festival Hall, and Kaps was writing it up for Reuters. It was almost daybreak when the new Prime Minister arrived to thank his loyal party workers. Amid the dazzling glare of television lights and flash guns, Kaps' eyes somehow found hers in the frantic media crowd. She was hard at work, racing around to get the best angle. She had never seemed so beautiful.

They both found the moment overwhelming, as though *they* should be the story of the day, not the start of some new government. But as dawn lit up the Thames, the old lovers only skimmed along the surface; they didn't dare go any deeper.

'He was good, wasn't he? Impressive.'

'Always is, and takes a good photo too,' said Becky.

'Quite a night.'

'Yeah. Really glad I was here. Historic. Just goes to show, history isn't only wars.'

They danced around each other until finally, like a nervous teenager, he managed to squeeze out the invitation.

'Um, listen I was just wondering … d'you want to get some breakfast? There's a café I know round the corner. Best egg-and-bacon bap in town.'

It hardly qualified as a date, but he might as well have suggested dinner in a candlelit restaurant and Becky knew it.

I can't start all this with you again, Kaps. It might just kill me.

'Better not,' she said. 'I need to get these piccies back to the office. You know how it is with history.'

'Oh, okay then.'

He was despondent. She'd walked back into his life and walked straight out of it again, and he couldn't help thinking this would be the last time he'd ever see her.

'I'll e-mail you.'

'Sure,' he said. 'Let's keep in touch. Bye, then.'

'Bye.'

They exchanged the safest kiss, a brief, dry peck that signalled the end of something rather than the beginning. Both were careful to make sure it fell well wide of the other's mouth. Then she turned away from him, towards Parliament and the tube station. Each step felt as if she was defying gravity. She didn't want to be walking to the tube at all, or even to his little café. She wanted to run off with him to some cheap hotel where he could hold her like he used to, and they could make frantic love for the rest of this new day, or new era, or whatever it might turn out to be.

As the decade rolled on, Edwin's addiction became an open secret at the *Telegraph*. The paper's new breed of bean counters, who'd already given him one official warning, were determined to get rid of him. His name kept cropping up in management meetings, but every time, Jake loyally defended him.

'We owe the poor bugger, simple as that,' he'd whisper, while the ruthless young Turks around the table shook their heads in disbelief: what *was* it with these fucking journos? Why did they always have to stick together?

Jake did his best to keep him out of the way, despatching Edwin to the furthest corners of the globe: Somalia, Burundi, even Eritrea. But when there was nowhere for him to go, Edwin stalked the office or festered in his flat off the Kilburn High Road. It was squalid and full of the paraphernalia of his various habits. Dirty dishes were stacked high by the sink, last night's half-eaten fish and chips sat on the table, cold and limp, and the rubbish bin was overflowing.

A relationship might have saved him from himself, but after Amra he doubted one were possible. The closest he got was Mimi, his dealer, a crack and smack addict well on her way to oblivion. Edwin would meet her under the railway arches at King's Cross. This was his new world, surrounded on rain-soaked London nights by prostitutes, pimps, dealers and tramps. One night, as he was scoring from her, Mimi grabbed his hand and dragged his sodden face to hers. He felt nothing when he kissed her, only a vague hope it might do them both some good. If he couldn't screw a saint, maybe he should try a sinner. It was only when they went back to his flat and stripped that he realised she was as gaunt as he was, snow-white skin stretched too tight over bones never meant to be so visible. They fucked a few times, mostly to assure themselves they were still alive, usually in his flat but once under the arches when the tramps were sleeping and the tarts were all with clients. Her flesh said nothing to him, except to tell him what he already knew – that life's purest pleasure had become laced with pain.

Edwin never heard from Danny, and neither did he try to get in touch. He would meet Becky for a drink occasionally, in Covent Garden or Camden Town. They would tell each other, in the nicest possible way, that they looked like shit, and then they'd talk about the good times.

Now and then he saw Kaps too. Once, as they sat at a bar in Dean Street, Edwin asked his old friend if he thought this was how death might be: not a sudden, dramatic end but a gradual decline into nothing much at all.

By the time the century began drawing to its exhausted close, only Rachel and Danny could say that they were happy, and even then for just some of the time. They argued too much, split up twice and dated other people for a while, but when they were together, they criss-crossed the world in search of the wars that were getting harder to find.

It was after the *New York Times* lost an associate editor and senior columnist that people started touting Danny's name as a replacement. He scoffed at the idea – how could he even think of coming off road? – but Rachel persuaded him it was a compliment and a new platform for his talent. It showed how much they loved his writing. He'd no longer need to slip his opinions surreptitiously into stories, they'd be *expected* of him. What was more, they'd be read and respected in the White House and around the world. It was the new millennium: anything seemed possible and Danny was seduced.

Rachel asked the *Washington Post* if she could come home too. The only job they had for her was a junior reporter on Capitol Hill, but she took it anyway because she wanted to be with Danny; she couldn't not be. She was abandoning the dream, but when she mulled it over, she saw it was a dream she'd lived already. Five years on the road had felt like 50 and she was thinking about a family.

They split the rent on a swanky apartment in Georgetown and moved in together. Overnight, Danny's life became a warren of corridors instead of trenches, briefings instead of battles. At the same time every morning – ten past eight – he put on a collar and tie. His body, starved of adrenalin, began to suffer withdrawal symptoms. Why had he imprisoned himself in suburbia? Why had he let her convince him to come off the road when he'd been so happy there? Danny began to blame Rachel and resent her. She wasn't a true Junkie, after all, but an impostor, the fly-by-night he'd originally suspected when he first met her in Sarajevo.

The metronome of their relationship started swinging in wilder extremes, until one autumn evening in 2001: Mohammed Atta and his friends had been and gone, and America was about to wreak its revenge on the Taliban in Afghanistan. Danny had been reading copy from Kaps and Edwin on the frontline outside Kabul. They were waiting for the city to fall, for the moment they would wrap themselves in glory and Danny felt physically sick he wasn't there. After 9/11, the planet was re-ordering itself but Danny had been left out: it was going on without him and he needed to be somewhere, anywhere but here.

He trudged home through swirling snow that reminded him of Bosnia and Chechnya. Instead of sitting in a trench watching US bombers in the sky, he'd spent the day at a policy institute watching a power-point presentation on America's probable stand at the next round of WTO trade talks. He thought of double physics at high school and decided this was worse. When he walked into the apartment, he was tired and grouchy and ready to take on anyone who got in his way. Naturally it was Rachel.

He pulled a can of Budweiser from the fridge, threw himself on to the leather sofa they had chosen together for their new home, and flicked on the expensive plasma screen that dominated the living room. Even buying it had caused a row. She told him it was 'gross'; privately, he accepted she was right but wanted to prove a point by getting it, and then watching it all the time. Quite *what* that point was he couldn't say exactly, but proving it had felt damned good.

Rachel threw herself down to join him as he watched the *Evening News*, featuring an unusually powerful report from the old poseur Todd Diamond, complete with his carefully combed scouring-pad hair and his 'wanker jacket' as Danny called it, a khaki, quasi-military waistcoat full of pockets. He and his cameraman had got caught in some crossfire between the Northern Alliance and the Taliban. 'I've been reporting war for 30 years,' a breathless Diamond was saying to the lens, 'and I can tell you I've never been in the middle of gunfire like this, not since Vietnam.'

'Oh yeah,' said Danny. 'Go ahead, why don't you, and remind us you were in good old Nam; tell us one more time about the glory days!'

To show he wasn't exaggerating, Diamond kept uncharacteristically quiet for a few seconds so the viewers could hear the bullets whizz around the camera. The microphone picked up their high-pitched whistle, sickening but exhilarating, and something in Danny's brain was reactivated.

'Now *that's* where I want to be.'

There! He had made his confession, said it out loud, and it felt good. He sipped the cold beer and slumped further into the sofa. At first Rachel ignored him – it was usually the best way when Danny was in this sort of mood – but he was desperate to provoke an argument. He couldn't let her just appease him, he was a nation trying to push its peaceful neighbour into war.

'That guy is such a dick.'

'But a dick who's where the story is,' said Rachel. 'Which I guess makes him a dick worth listening to.'

'My point exactly. I should be there.'

It was so puerile, she couldn't let it pass.

'Why? You think the world can't get its news without you? You think you have some God-given right to be at the heart of every event that ever happens? You've got more awards than you can count, and you still need prove yourself?'

'You're as good as your last story.'

'Oh, please tell me you're not that insecure.'

He watched the rest of the report with a scatter-gun rage firing off in all directions. It was how he used to feel at home in Pittsburgh, when he'd denounce religion and the Republican Party and rise of global inequality. Now his anger was being sprayed over Todd Diamond, the superficiality of television news, Rachel, his own weakness in ever listening to her in the first place, and the quaint charms of Georgetown.

'Looks dangerous as fuck, but sure beats the hell out of this life.'

'What d'you mean, "this life"?'

'This life that's so grey, just a washed-out shade of grey. Think about all those colours we used to see … the reds of blood, purples of courage, yellows of cowardice, blacks of death, whites of surrender. We saw all the colours of the world.'

Rachel could have let it go, but this was an assault on the life they were trying to build here – an assault on her dreams.

'That's the most pathetic thing I ever heard.'

'I mean it. We go to work at the same time every morning, say hello to the same people on the way to the same desk, and eat the same damned sandwiches for lunch. The only danger is crossing the road to get to and from the office. Oh, and maybe slipping on the snow.'

'You know what, there are some people out there – I mean, admittedly, total fucking freaks and weirdos in need of urgent psychiatric help – who might think that's a *good* thing.'

'Yeah, well, I must be wired up differently, because I can't do this shit any more.'

'It's not shit. In my obviously perverted view of the universe, it's actually bliss. Okay, we fight a little, but who doesn't? We're together and most of the time we're pretty happy. Or perhaps I'm wrong. Perhaps you don't think we are?'

'Well we were "together" in Goma and Grozny, and I'd take both over Georgetown. And right now I'd definitely take Kabul.'

After all their skirmishes, the decisive battle loomed. Both armies braced themselves.

'You've got it all – a great job, a great woman, if I may say so, a great place to live – and you want to be in some shithole of a hotel where there's no power, no heating and no glass in the fucking window?'

'Sounds like heaven. Never felt so alive as when I was in those places.'

'And so now you feel – what? Dead?' She was shouting at him, but he could shout louder. It was just like when he used to shout at Lukas, and Camille would cover her ears. Shouting was as much a relief to him now as it had been then, letting blow all that pent-up fury that bubbled up within him.

'It's what *you* wanted once, you were desperate for it – or have you forgotten that? Look, it's not just that office life is tedious, it's that anyone can do it. It's ordinary. But us … we've been something else. We've been *extra*ordinary, don't you see?'

And she did see, but she also felt it would be extraordinary to have a family and that was the difference between them. Danny was like a little boy who wanted to play his war games for ever and never grow up. Peter fucking Pan. 'Yeah, I did want that life,' yelled Rachel, 'and yeah, I loved it, but I've moved on and got myself a home.'

'Well, maybe it's a home I don't fit into any more.'

She wanted to cry when he said that, and for him to hold her and say he didn't mean it and admit he'd gone a few words too far. If he'd reached out to her at that moment, she would have run to him and they'd have probably tumbled into bed as they did so often after they had fought. Fighting and fucking, it had become the dangerous pattern of their life together. Instead he turned his back on her, defying her, willing her to retaliate.

'No, Danny, maybe you *don't* fit in. Maybe you should just go find yourself another crappy war.' It was then that she launched the most destructive weapon in her arsenal, the one she'd never turned to even in their darkest moments. 'Who knows, you might even get someone else killed.'

He turned back round to her slowly, a wounded beast, staring at her, narrowing his eyes, scarcely able to comprehend what she had said. He was tempted to hit her, except that Danny had never hit a soul, not even his father in their darkest moments, and so he decided to deal her a harder blow.

That night he walked out of her world.

In the wilderness years that Danny was gone from her, he was still everywhere around. To see his ghastly, gorgeous face, all she had to do was pick up her papers from the doormat as she had done in Arlington, read his copy and linger on his picture byline.

She tried dating some DC men – hacks, policy wonks and even a struggling actor who she was surprised to discover swung both ways but was predominantly gay. Reluctantly she kissed them all, but their tongues always felt wrong in her mouth. They seemed to be invading her. They were too smart or too stupid, their chins were too scratchy or too smooth, they wore too much aftershave or too little. One by one they fell away and each time it was relief she felt, not disappointment. She had been dating for the sake of it. Of course she wanted a family, but not with anyone.

Occasionally her mind ran through the days she'd hated him, from the Karadzic kiss to the moment he announced he could no longer share her life. More often though, she picked over the good times, when she'd loved him unreservedly and in full knowledge of his multitude of sins. Arrogance, pomposity, self-obsession: she had accepted them all, because for Rachel they were merely the downside of the most wonderfully addictive man she had ever known. In the post-9/11 world, the post-Danny world, she wanted him as she'd been wanting him for so much of her life. She wondered sometimes if she'd wanted him before she even met him.

It wasn't until 18 months later – 9th March 2003 – that she saw him again. America was about to rain its bombs down on Baghdad and Danny had decided he'd very much like to be under them. He had a new book deal that depended on it. Afghanistan, and now Iraq: he'd missed one but he was being offered a second chance by a President generous enough to lay on his wars in pairs. Becky, Edwin and Kaps were there too – no self-respecting war correspondent could fail to be – and when the *Washington Post* cast around for volunteers, even Rachel found it irresistible. She kept telling herself it was the story of a lifetime, a one-off, but inside she knew that part of this assignment was the search for a missing lover: it was a dangerous reason to be going back to war.

She arrived in Baghdad ten days before the bombing started. It was the first time she'd ever been to Iraq, and she half-expected Becky to offer her a bottle of Ballantine's and a water heater. Everybody had crammed into the Palestine, right beside the Tigris. They were all there, the cast of characters from her former life, schoolfriends reunited: Shark, Spinoza, Lacroix, Dirk and Krontz, and even Todd Diamond himself, pontificating from the roof, on the hour, every hour. The Palestine Hotel was like a throwback to the Holiday Inn, the centre of the universe, for a few weeks at least.

Rachel was relieved to find a Becky who seemed convinced her traumas were behind her, an Edwin who insisted he was doing nothing more than dope, and a Kaps who was just happy to be on the road again: even Judith had to admit the invasion of Iraq was unmissable and that he should be there.

What was wonderful about Shock and Awe, the blitz of bombs and cruise missiles America unleashed on Baghdad, was that it brought back all the old intensity of Sarajevo: for the first time since 1994, they were frightened for their lives and the feeling was welcome. It helped to heal their wounds. Becky seemed to have forgiven – or forgotten – what happened in the shed in Yazhdnovskaya, and Becky and Kaps were talking to each other with civility. Pretty much everyone was talking to Danny: whatever he had or hadn't done was ancient history.

One night when the bombers stayed away they gathered in the gloom of Spinoza's seventh-floor room and laughed louder than any time since New Year's Eve in Grozny: they were the Junkies once again. Becky had replaced her ghetto blaster with an iPod docking station, but the songs remained the same, *Songs of Sarajevo*. Even Seal's 'Crazy' got another spin and they danced till they were too exhausted to continue, losing their petty rivalries and niggling jealousies in the fog of their latest war.

When everyone else had either closed their eyes or staggered off to bed, only Rachel and Danny were left. Rachel, having been exhilarated, became uncomfortable. She was tempted to feign sleep or get up and go like everyone else. They hadn't been alone together since the day he walked out on her in Georgetown, and the words they'd exchanged in Baghdad so far had been perfunctory, brief exchanges between professional colleagues, rather than a man and woman who needed to return to each other. How strange it was that Rachel could know every intimate thing about him – the birthmark on his left buttock, the shape and the taste of his penis – and yet here she was, unsure how to start a conversation with him. And how strange that Danny, who was easily able to visualise her little breasts and how one was slightly smaller than the other, had even less idea what to say.

'I'm … I'm glad you came.' She pretended not to hear him and swallowed hard, willing herself not to cry. She looked in the other direction where there was nothing to see but blackness. 'I suppose what I wanted to say was that I'm sorry. And that I've missed you.'

'You left me.'

He walked over and knelt before her, forcing her to look at him.

'You and me, Rach, we were it. I know that now.'

'You never called, you never even wrote.'

'I'm sorry. I wanted to ask if we could …'

'What? Try again? How d'you know I'm not involved with someone? Or married.'

'Are you?'

She flipped through her back catalogue of doomed dates and romances.

'No, but I might be. I don't like your assumptions.'

'Look, Rach, you fill the room when you come in, it's empty when you go: I've come to realise that.'

'Bullshit. You want someone to hang out with on the road. Someone to keep you company, to check your copy, someone to …'

She was going to say hump and dump, but she knew his face well enough to see the loneliness that disfigured it. It was like looking in the mirror.

'I need some time,' she said eventually. '*We* need time.'

• • •

They both knew getting back together was as inevitable as Iraq falling apart and a few days after the President declared that major hostilities were officially over, they were back in each other's beds. Rachel and war, war and Rachel: Danny had everything he'd ever wanted.

The days bled into weeks, and the weeks bled into months. People like Todd Diamond pulled out soon after Saddam and his statue were toppled, but Danny insisted history would dwell much longer on what followed. He sensed the real war was just beginning. He and Rachel explored each other as well as every corner of Iraq, from Basra to Kirkuk, from Najaf to Ramadi, watching it implode. From the earliest days, Danny had warned of the chaos an invasion would unleash. One piece in particular, 'Iraq: The Carnage We Could Create', was lambasted by the White House neocons but now seemed spookily prophetic. Sunni insurgency, Shia extremism, sectarian murder, Iranian interference, a tripartite disintegration of the state – he had foreseen them all. The doyen of Bosnia had become the doyen of Baghdad.

They moved from the Palestine to the Hamra and, in their downtime, they frolicked with Saturday-night parties round the poolside, laid on by Marla the effervescent aid worker. They would drink until the early hours and often end up in the water, fully clothed or occasionally stark naked.

Danny was relaxed enough to take long breaks in the Georgetown home he had previously despised. He'd slob out in front of his plasma screen with an obscenely large pizza, and if Rachel were curled up with him, so much the better. Together they would watch bad soaps and game shows and go for long walks by the Potomac, astonished they could wander wherever they liked in this parallel universe without thinking through the safety implications.

They still fought; they wouldn't have been Danny and Rachel if they hadn't, but they did so within limits which were well defined.

She never mentioned marriage, let alone children. She couldn't contemplate either without Danny and yet she knew they were anathema to him, the locks on a cell door that would imprison him forever. One day he might change his mind, but by then it would probably be too late. She was already into her thirties and even for a Sandstealer, time was running out.

So when the accident happened – as they made love one evening on the carpet with empty pizza boxes scattered around them and the monster TV set on mute – it seemed to Rachel the best, the most miraculous accident the world had ever known. She was even sure of the date; 14th June 2004.

27

Post-Liberation Iraq, August 2004

'You're having his *baby*?' said Becky. 'Why the hell didn't you tell us before?'

Outside the hotel there was the shriek of sirens from a nearby street. In Baghdad, where everything was an emergency by definition, they faded into background noise.

'I was going to, I swear. Then all this happened.'

'Oh, Rachel, what have you done?'

The bad taste of jealousy was back in Becky's mouth. A lover – albeit a kidnapped lover, about to die – and now a child. And she had neither.

'Well, congratulations. I suppose,' said Edwin. 'Does he know? I mean, did you tell him before …'

'Of course I did.'

'Well, well. Another little Lowenstein running round the world. I'm not sure this planet's big enough for two of them!'

The joke hung limply in the air and the room was hushed again. Though the bump was barely perceptible, Camille could scarcely take her eyes off it. Her brother was going to be a father, she was going to be an aunt, her parents were going to have their first grandchild. She thought of Lukas' dreams of a dynasty at Lowenstein Steel, and almost laughed, but perhaps it could be the glue her family needed. She felt suddenly protective towards Danny's unborn child, her niece or nephew. 'It can't grow up without a father,' she announced, as if she had decided that were that.

It is the day before his execution.

Danny is thinking about his career. What has it really amounted to? A few stories that may have caused a stir for a day or two but were laid to rest in a graveyard of yellowing, curled-up back editions. A few awards, soon to be forgotten by almost everyone but him. Ephemeral. Fast food for a greedy ego. A tome on Yugoslavia, overlong and far too rushed to be as definitive as it had claimed. A book of memoirs, now never to be completed and possibly just as well, since, if he were honest with himself – and what better time for honesty – the world could do without another 400 or 500 pages of flaccid self-aggrandisement. Everything that used to be so important to him – worth using and losing friends for – is suddenly valueless and his pride has given way to shame.

He thinks about Becky, Kaps and Edwin, and wishes they were with him to say goodbye.

He thinks about Rachel and sees those uneven, bee-sting breasts, that boyish bottom, that freckled nose. He remembers that raw enthusiasm – naive but beautiful, a first flowering of talent – and how, barbarically, he tried to crush it. As he pleads for the pain to go away and the fever to cool down, and for the shitting and the bleeding to please, *please* stop, he hugs his blanket as if it were her, long legs locked into his, soft arms wrapped tight around his battered back, cool skin soothing on him, lips touching his just like they did on that first night at the Grands Lacs.

He thinks about the President and wonders if he's in the Oval

Office, deciding whether to release the prisoners and save his life. Or is he on the golf course?

He thinks about his father, just standing there in the video, wordless, motionless, expressionless. Why couldn't he have *said* something, anything? Why couldn't he just have said sorry so that Danny would have known before he died, and then he could have left a note or a letter saying that he was sorry too?

Give me a reason to love you, Daniel.

How many reasons did he want? For a start he was his son, for Christ's sake, wasn't he? Well, *wasn't* he?

In his cell now, Danny can see his cousin Jackson so clearly he might have been chained up next to him. The huge mop of the 11-year-old's hair, the braces on his teeth, the strutting, cocky swagger he had about him. Jackson, the only son of Eliza's brother, loved telling people things they didn't know. In another life, Danny sometimes thought, he'd have made a good reporter. The thing he had to report that weekend he came to stay in East Allegheny was so sensational, so spectacular, that he could barely contain himself. Jackson's only worry had been finding the best time to drop the bombshell. He couldn't just come out with it; he needed to weave the conversation around it, and let his terrible secret seep out into the gentle sunshine of the early summer's day.

They had returned from a bike ride around East Commons, and were lying by the gnarled apple tree that formed the centrepiece of Eliza's garden. Danny was the same age as Jackson; they weren't exactly friends, but as cousins they got on well enough. Fallen fruit lay around them in the long, unmowed grass. Some of it was ripe and juicy, and both of them took a few bites as they stretched out in the sun. Some was rotting and squishy brown, with wasps crawling over it and tunnelling their way in.

The conversation came round to their parents, because that was the way Jackson had steered it.

'I heard my folks saying some strange shit the other day.'

Jackson swore as a matter of routine, the young Danny almost never. Just the word was enough to unsettle him.

'Oh yeah?'

'They were talking in the kitchen and I heard them. Guess I wasn't supposed to be listening, but I did.'

'Listening to what?'

'Oh, about your ma.'

Danny had a bad feeling straight away. He had no idea what was coming, but whatever it was, he didn't want to hear it. Still, he couldn't just run away or put his hands over his ears. That was probably just what Jackson would have wanted.

'Uh-huh. What about her?'

'About just before she had you. About the other guy she was with when she split up from your dad for a while.'

Danny's eyes had narrowed in confusion until they were squinting. *With?* What did that mean: *with*? He couldn't ask any questions because he needed to look like he didn't give a damn what Jackson was trying to tell him, like he knew it all anyhow. He lay on his side, chewing a blade of grass and watching the wasps as they burrowed away and devoured the fruit's bad flesh. His head felt as though it was exploding.

'Sorry, Dan. Maybe you didn't know …?'

'Sure I did. It's no big deal.'

'Oh right. Of course. So how d'yah feel about it? Not being your dad's kid, an' all? Must be kinda weird. I mean, I know he brings you up like you are, but doesn't it ever *bother* you?'

Danny would remember for the rest of his life the way he bit into another apple when Jackson said that, bit so hard his teeth sliced straight through it and into his tongue, where it drew blood.

He could taste it flooding through his mouth. He would remember the way the pain was a relief – he was actually glad of it – because it distracted him from the news that Jackson had just reported, which wasn't news at all, of course, because – as Danny kept insisting – he'd known about it for years.

It was never spoken of again, not by Jackson, nor Danny, nor his parents. Danny had told himself a hundred thousand times that perhaps it wasn't even true, just a piece of mischief-making by his mischief-making cousin. He could easily have invented the whole damned story just to get himself some attention. But the long years in which Lukas had loved Camille over his son spoke of another truth, and as Danny sits, hunched up against the wall looking at his little pool of light, he wants to bite his tongue all over again, and this time cry out with the pain.

In the toilet that night, he has managed to roll the rusting drum so that the two lengths of flex are just above him, coiled up on the ceiling. Slow is outside but not watching. Why would anyone suspect he's taking this trouble to kill himself, when they're about to do it for him anyway?

Danny only has to undo the coil, knot the ends together and form a noose. He's rehearsed it in his mind so many times, but his hands are shaking as he starts his work. It makes the simple task harder than he'd imagined, but finally it is done and a loop is formed, just big enough for his head. He hears a noise outside: Slow pacing up and down the corridor. Danny pushes his head in, crown first, and then the rest.

When he is in and the shiny black flex is tight around his throat, he wonders if it could strangle him to death all by itself without a jump. He teeters on the edge of the drum and looks beyond his feet, blackened toes curled around the corroded edge. The drop from the drum will be enough to kill him. It isn't far, but he may as well be standing on a cliff.

He would like to leave a note. If only Scar allowed him a pen and paper, he'd write to his friends and his family. Thoughts of what he'd say run through his mind but he decides one sentence would suffice: 'I wasn't who I thought I was.'

It is all futile. He knows now he cannot do it, just as he could not escape even when there was a half-open door and only a little girl in his way. All his life he has revelled in the role of journalist-as-hero: people have marvelled at the courage of this reporter who gets shot at as he brings a hungry world its news. His bravery has been saluted at awards ceremonies and in the book reviews, where one admirer even wrote: 'If there were a Purple Heart for journalism, surely it should go to Lowenstein.' Danny had glowed, while dismissing it all with obligatory modesty: 'Of course I'm not brave, I'm the biggest coward on God's green earth.' Now at last he can be sure he really is that coward. It's why he couldn't save Alija or let Becky save him either.

Danny isn't even brave enough to kill himself.

Scar will have to do it after all.

When they come to take him from his cell, he can tell it is daybreak from the drops of dawn's weak light dripping from the tiny hole in the ceiling. Scar is at the front, the long, curved knife in his right hand. Danny wonders if it's from a kitchen, or something they reserve for the sacrificial slaughter of goats and sheep. The others, who've been so sullen for the last few days, begin waving around their Kalashnikovs and screaming 'Allahu Akhbar' as they'd done on the day they first seized him, another choreographed show. A blindfold is bound unnecessarily tight around his eyes. He is pulled to his bare feet and dragged along the corridor. His bare toe catches something sharp – a nail or shard of glass – and he squeals, a pig being led to slaughter.

Up the staircase, banging into walls, tripping over steps. Through a door. Through another door.

A voice, Scar's inevitably.

'This is your last journey.'

The boot is opened and he is pushed inside.

28

Post-Liberation Iraq, August 2004

They were eating in the Hamra's Chinese restaurant when Jamail approached.

'Good evening, how are you all?'

Danny's friends ignored him, which Camille found strange and rude, so she spoke on their behalf.

'We're fine, thanks. How are you, Jamail?'

'I need talk with you, while you wait for the food?' He inclined his head gently towards the four journalists, beckoning them to follow as he left the room. Camille realised that, once again, she was not included.

Becky, Kaps, Rachel and Edwin exchanged glances, a private language of their own, and to Camille's astonishment, pushed back their chairs. They had been so reluctant even to greet Jamail, yet now they traipsed out of the dining room after him, as if he were the Pied Piper of Baghdad and they were its children walking to their doom.

'Be back in a sec,' said Kaps. 'Start without us, if it comes.'

They gathered in his office, a small room just behind the reception desk cluttered with paperwork. Some tatty photographs were pinned up on the wall: Jamail as a soldier many years before, Jamail grinning in a suit, shaking hands with Tariq Aziz, Saddam's debonair henchman. It had pride of place: personal recognition by the old regime still appeared to be a badge of honour a whole year after liberation. He sat in the handsome chair by his desk, red leather and mahogany, pivoting around on it, the Junkies crowded in front of him.

'So sorry to disturb your eating.'

'Just get on with it, Jamail,' said Kaps. 'What the fuck d'you want now?'

'Want? *Want?* No, is not want. It is kind request.'

'Okay then, what are you requesting?' But Kaps and the others could already guess. Their appetite was disappearing fast.

'I request … fair payment.'

Edwin squared up to him just as he had in the tea house, and this time the others thought he might throw a punch.

'You've had fair bloody payment – more than fair.'

'Look, we agreed yesterday,' said Kaps, more reasonably. 'You looked after the car and we paid up. Not a penny more, you said. You promised.'

'But I start to think, Mr Kaps. Maybe is not fair price. Maybe ten more thousand, and then I am happy, then I say nothing to no one. Not ever.'

Edwin grabbed him by the lapels and lifted him until he was almost off the floor.

'You said not a penny more, and believe me, that's exactly what you're going to get.'

Becky and Rachel held hands. They wanted Edwin to beat him to a pulp, but they also wanted to give Jamail what he was asking for and finish it for good, however much it cost.

'Okay, guys,' said Becky. 'Enough. We'll pay. But this is the end. You do this to us one more time and we go to the police and the Americans and then, believe me, you'll be well and truly fucked.'

'And you too, Miss Becky. Or maybe not.'

Edwin threw him against his desk, so that Jamail scattered bills and invoices everywhere, his ample buttocks narrowly missing a spike that skewered some of them together. He was frightened, but when he realised no more violence was imminent, he grinned inanely.

'That's the trouble with blackmailers,' said Edwin. 'They never know when to stop.'

Jamail brushed himself down, straightening out his dishadasha as if it were a Savile Row suit. Edwin tried breathing slowly to calm himself. He picked up a box of matches from Jamail's desk and carefully lit a cigarette.

'Well, tonight you've just pushed your luck that bit too far.'

He spun round and walked out of the office, inhaling hard, dragging the nicotine into him, as far as it would go. At first the others were confused, but then, almost simultaneously, it dawned on them what he was about to do. All his years of pain had been leading up to it.

'Ed!' Becky yelled after him. 'Come back!'

'Let's talk about this!' shouted Rachel. 'We can still sort it out with him. There has to be a compromise.'

He wasn't listening to any of them.

For an hour, maybe more, Danny's body bounces up and down in the boot. His back feels like it's broken. Where are they going? North, south, east or west, or round and round in circles, just to complete the destruction of this particular prisoner's mind?

The car stops. Voices again, but no sound of Scar. Doors open then slam shut. The creak of the boot being lifted up. Light creeping back into his blindfold. Air, thank God, some air. Then other noises he has not heard since he was kidnapped: traffic and beeping horns. Hands grab his body, hauling him out like a sack of rice, swinging him back and forth two or three times before letting go so that he flies for a few feet before landing painfully on what feels like bumpy waste ground. He rolls until he comes to rest. In a ditch perhaps, or some sort of culvert?

Footsteps approach. Something said in Arabic. Is this to be the coup de grâce, a bullet to the brain? Yes, please, the bullet rather than that blade. Just do it now, please. *Now!* Instead, another kick, in the testicles again. The pain splits him in two. White. Electric.

His hands are untied. More footsteps, but becoming quieter now, moving away. Voices and laughter gradually disappearing like the end of a record that smoothly fades away. Car doors open and close again, the engine starts. The revving of the accelerator and an ostentatious screech, a boy racer showing off.

Silence.

Gone.

My God, can it actually be over?

No, Daniel, do not dare to even think it.

Silence still.

Is it an elaborate trick to fuck him up for good? Have they stayed behind, giggling as they gesture to each other to keep quiet? Are they looking down with knowing smiles, ready to finish it at last?

How long to lie there? No sounds at all, only the traffic's distant hum. Should he risk provoking them by ripping off his blindfold? His aching crotch cannot countenance any further punishment. On the other hand, if he's been dumped here and they have left, he should move before they change their minds and come back for him. He listens again, straining his ears for their car, their voices. Nothing. No one.

A count. Ten … nine … eight …

He removes the gaffer tape and grabs himself a great mouthful of air. Then he takes off the blindfold tentatively, a bandage stripped away from a painful wound. Nice and easy now. His puffy eyes take several seconds to adjust. He blinks into the ferocious, unforgiving sun. It is more glorious than it has ever been, the sky a richer blue and far, far bigger than he remembered it. Nobody around him. He's in Anywhere, Iraq. It could be Iskandariya, it could be Baghdad, but he is free, oh sweet Jesus he is free! But where to go and how to get there? Who to ask? What if someone else wants to kidnap him all over again? Or take him straight back to them?

Some women and children are walking down the road. They catch his eye but hurriedly look away and carry on past him as if he isn't there. A Westerner wearing a straggly, unkempt beard and an orange jumpsuit, sprawled in the dirt and bleeding badly: in Iraq there is enough shit to steer clear of every day without all this. Best not get involved. Best pretend it was just a ghost you saw, and who knows, perhaps it was.

Edwin strode back into the restaurant, brushing against a garish painting of an unspecified Arab on a horse, almost knocking it from its hook. He swept up Camille and bundled her back upstairs to the Presidential Suite.

'I take it supper's off, then,' she said, bemused.

'You could say that. Camille, there's something I want you to hear.' Edwin was gabbling as though he might change his mind if he didn't get his words out fast enough. 'Something I should have told you right at the beginning.'

'Don't!' Rachel was breathless from the chase. She pressed the palm of her hand against his chest to stop him talking, but he brushed it away and carried on.

'We've behaved badly, and I've decided you have a right to know.'

Becky, Rachel and Kaps looked at him, willing him to change his mind.

'A right to know *what*?' asked Camille.

'Before anyone else tells you, I need you to understand that it was me.'

'No, this is madness!' Rachel was trying to shout, but her voice had become too weak. 'Please don't say any more. Not another thing. And, Camille, please don't listen to him, he has no idea what he's saying, he's been doing too much weed again. And coke.'

Edwin, however, had rarely looked more together. The Junkies gawped at him, then her, then him again. They were like bewildered bystanders, watching a dreadful accident unfold, powerless to prevent it.

Camille was frowning. With a slight readjustment of her glasses and a gentle upward tilt of her head, she beckoned Edwin to continue.

'*What* was you?'

'Me in the other car.'

'Stop it right now.' Rachel's voice was still strangulated, pitifully ineffective. 'Just shut the fuck up. You're stoned out of your mind.'

'Me who let him go on into the ambush. We got shot up, just like that shepherd boy told the Americans. By some miracle we managed to turn around and we got the fuck out of there, and that's when we saw him. I could have stopped him, I *should* have stopped him. All I had to do was say something, anything. I … I still can't explain why I didn't. It was that grin on his face; so smug, so self-satisfied, so damned competitive. He was on his way to another exclusive. Hoo-bloody-ray! He didn't even ask if we needed help. It was all about him, whether the road ahead was safe for him. I'm sorry, I know it's horrible for you to hear it about your own brother, but it's the truth. He only ever thought about himself.'

Camille leant against the table and shook her head. Day after day she had been sitting here with him, hearing his pain, eating his curries, smelling the smoke from his Marlboros and even smoking his dope.

'I don't believe you,' she said quietly.

The Junkie walked out to the balcony and its insufficient summer breeze. It was time for one last look at Baghdad before the curtains closed across it. A pair of Apache helicopters were flying north, following the course of the Tigris, and there was the familiar thud thud thud of their rotor-blades. They fired off white flares to distract heat-seeking missiles. In a home nearby, a woman didn't even look up at them. She was too busy hanging out her washing while her children played hopscotch in the yard, both valiant attempts to pretend Iraq was something better than a daily torment.

The moment was close at hand. Soon everything would be lost: a career, a reputation and a lover.

The Junkie stepped back into the suite, only to find that Camille had just disappeared down the corridor, running towards the offices of NBC.

'Listen, Melissa, I really need to see that tape now.' Camille was flushed and out of breath. Melissa was editing a spot for that night's news. She said she was sorry, but could she find it later because she was really up against the clock.

'Please. It's important. I have to see it now.'

Melissa wanted to let out a sigh of irritation but stopped herself in time. If anyone deserved humouring, surely it was Danny Lowenstein's poor sister.

'Sure. I guess our edit can wait a few minutes.'

She looked along a shelf and quickly found the tape. Camille wondered why, if it were so easy, the young producer couldn't have come up with it when she'd first been asked.

Melissa pulled the small Betacam tape out of its box and slipped it into an empty edit machine. The picture rolled into life on two tiny monitors. A medal-spangled general was mouthing words, the white numerals of the time code ticking away beneath him. Melissa started spooling backwards so that he disappeared into a blur. As she did so, Becky, Kaps, Edwin and Rachel walked in uninvited, to watch what she was doing.

'Oh, hi guys,' said Melissa cheerfully. 'Just helping Camille here with something.'

Together they stared at the miniature screens.

'So you wanna hear what he says from the beginning?'

'Actually, I'm not really interested in him at all.'

Melissa frowned, a look of pained confusion sweeping across her.

'I don't quite …'

'The people I really need to see are the reporters. The press he's talking to.'

'Oh. Really? Um … okay then.' She began spooling forward instead, until it became clear the cameraman had grown weary of filming a head and shoulders any longer. He had darted behind the podium and was taking wide shots of the assembled media, 'cut-aways' for editing. Perhaps 30 journalists were listening intently – or pretending to – plus a few other camera crews and photographers.

'*There!*' said Camille triumphantly. 'Could you pause it there, please?'

Melissa hit the button, and Camille bent forward to study the frozen image. Melissa offered to put it on a bigger monitor, and connected up a couple of cables. Thirty seconds later, the image had been transferred to a normal-sized television screen. There for all the world to see was Becky crouched on the floor in the CPIC, cameras beside her, looking bored. Just behind, in the second row from the front, were Kaps and Edwin, notebooks on their laps. Next to them was an empty chair. It looked as though they'd been saving it for someone who'd never come.

Camille dialled Adi's number, her finger trembling slightly.

'Hey, Adi, I just needed to check something.'

'Shoot.'

'What time was it when you first called Danny's friends about what had happened?'

There was a long pause while he thought about it. She guessed he was trying to work out why she wanted to know.

'Around one thirty, I think. I'd just finished lunch.'

'Lunch? You're sure about that? Not just after breakfast?'

'Sure I'm sure. How in the world would I forget?'

Back in the suite, Rachel tried to quantify what she would have left. Her loyal friends, she hoped. Becky, Kaps and Edwin, who had already done so much for her and lied so hard. Her baby. And of course her freedom from the reptilian Jamail.

'Poor, sweet Edwin couldn't hurt a fly,' she said. 'He's too damned nice. An officer and a gentleman to the end.'

'So what happened out there?' demanded Camille. 'What did you do?'

'*Do*? It wasn't a question of *doing* anything.'

Rachel opened a tin of pineapple juice and eased herself down into the sofa with Becky's arms around her. She looked better now that she had been unburdened. Camille no longer saw the gaunt, hollowed-out face of the last few days but that of the pretty, precocious 23-year-old who had first arrived in Split with a rucksack full of dreams.

29

Rachel's Story

I decided to tell him while we were in bed together. I was so excited, I've no idea how I had kept it secret for so long.

The night was overheated as usual and neither of us could sleep. We both knew we'd be exhausted in the morning and that Danny needed to be up early. He couldn't stop talking about his meeting with Abu Mukhtar, he'd been working on it for days.

I asked him if he was worried it might be a trap.

''Course not,' he said, 'Asmat fixed it up, and he'll be there to introduce us. He's never let me down before. Don't worry.'

He kissed my belly. He was so close to our child, snuggled up inside me but just an inch away from him. I'd been running through all the pros and cons of telling him, but now a feeling overwhelmed me: that he had a right to know, whatever my opinions on the subject. We were a family, a family of three, a marvellous triangle of love. We hadn't exactly planned it, but he'd come round, of course he would, and he'd make the perfect dad. A little older, sure – but wiser too. I had a vision of him carrying our baby in his arms, and pushing our toddler on the swings, and helping our child with homework after school. There'd be more children – at least two, maybe three.

'I'm pregnant, Danny,' I announced. It felt so good to say it for the first time out loud.

His eyes were closed, as though he was finally drifting off to sleep.

'What?' he asked me. He sounded so drowsy.

'I said I'm having your baby. A little Daniel Lowenstein. Or maybe a Daniella.'

There was no reaction. Not a word, not a movement. It was as if he was paralysed.

'Are you awake?' I said. 'Did you hear what I just told you?'

I knew he had and I began to dread his response.

'Yes, unfortunately I did.'

'What d'you mean, "unfortunately"?'

'What d'you think I mean?' he said. 'It's unfortunate, isn't it? Unfortunate you didn't talk this through with me. Unfortunate you didn't bother to ask whether I might want kids, which unfortunately I do not.'

I could feel my love for him flip over into hate, the way it had done too often.

'You bastard,' I said.

I got up and put on a T-shirt and my knickers. I couldn't have this row and be naked with him. He stayed in bed, wide awake now, his head propped up against the pillow.

'Why?' he said, 'because I don't want kids?' He was suddenly so angry. He said we'd discussed children in Georgetown and that he'd told me how he couldn't be tied down and was never going to be a family man. He was so fucking patronising, like I hadn't understood him properly and he was tired of having to repeat himself.

'Well, tough luck,' I told him, 'because whether or not you want to be a father, you are one now.'

He looked at me as though I were a stranger and said, quite calmly: 'Get rid of it.' At first I wasn't sure I'd heard him properly, but he'd already come up with a plan. I couldn't be more than a few weeks, he said, it didn't even show. I should fly back to Washington and book myself into a clinic. He'd pay for everything, if that's what I was worried about.

I sat at the desk, shaking my head. How could he think so little of me?

'You know what my biggest mistake has always been?' I asked him. 'To ever think we really knew each other. You just con the world, don't you, Danny? All that compassion, and inside you're a … monster.'

I picked up the book he'd been using to take notes for his memoirs. It was the size of a photo album and surprisingly heavy. I threw it at him and hit him square on the side of his head just below the ear. And then, although I was trying so hard to stay strong, I started sobbing. I remember looking into the mirror and watching the mascara run down my cheeks.

He got out of bed and, still naked, he walked over and put a hand on my shoulder.

'Look, it's my fault,' he said. 'I should have made it clear from the beginning. I mean, take tomorrow: odds are it'll all be fine, but sure, there's a chance it won't, there's always a chance. How do I take a gamble like that if I have a family to think about?'

I told him I couldn't believe how scared he was. He just laughed.

'Scared!' he said. 'Scared of Abu bloody Mukhtar?'

'No, you dick,' I said, 'scared of settling down.' Then I really went for him. 'Look, here's the news, Mr Lowenstein, the real news: you're freefalling towards fifty. Those bits of grey around your ears? Sure, they're distinguished, but they're also nature's way of whispering very quietly that you're getting older. It's time, Danny. Time for a home. Not just a base, not just a flat: a proper home, with stairs and a garden. And yeah, time for kids. You're changing. I can see it in your eyes, watch it in the way you move. You're tired. Exhausted, even. You've been to every country, covered every war, won every prize, but are you happy? Or actually, have you had enough? Done enough and seen enough?'

But I knew that while he was looking at me, he was also looking at the other life that beckoned if he agreed with me: a return to the desk job in DC, more columns, more analysis. Sensible dinner-party friends. Babies and bottles and diapers. The school run. Mortgage payments and pension plans. No more Junkies to do drink and drugs with. No more jumping in and out of bombed-out basements, or racing along that narrow ridge that runs between life and death. Who was I to deprive him of all that, he was thinking, who was I to steal his soul?

He gave me the coldest look I'd ever seen and his eyes were empty.

'I don't want to be anybody's father,' he said. 'I told you: get rid of it.'

Only four hours later, he showered while I was half-awake. The most calamitous day of both our lives was just beginning. He dried himself, dressed and tried to slip out of the room as softly as he could. I would have probably gone back to sleep, but he'd forgotten the door creaked so loudly. I guess both our futures might have been quite different if anyone had ever oiled it.

With the morning, his words seemed even crueller. How *dare* he? He'd made me mad so many times, but now I knew there was a darkness to my anger. He had threatened my child and I needed to protect it.

I jumped from the bed and threw on the clothes I had worn the day before; they were still in the pile where he had ripped them off me. At his desk I found the same book I'd thrown at him. He'd taken care to put it back exactly where I'd picked it up from: he cared more about his fucking memoirs than our child. I thought about tearing it into shreds or even setting fire to it, but that would have been too petty and predictable. I needed something more.

On the other side of the desk was his small reporter's pad, a scrawl of jottings across the page. *Asmat Mahmoud/Abu Mukhtar. Al Suqlahat bridge, al-Talha. Nine miles from Iskandariya. 8 a.m.'* Underneath, in block capitals, Danny had written *EXCLUSIVE!* and drawn some doodles around it.

'Asshole,' I said aloud.

I looked at my watch. It wasn't even seven yet. There was time. I could gatecrash his rendezvous and steal his story, the same way he'd stolen Kaps' in Goma.

Fuck him, I thought. Fuck him and all his patronising crap about paying for a clinic. Fuck his childish boasts about 'exclusives'.

I'd show him. And then I'd leave him.

I grabbed the notebook and went downstairs. I caught a glimpse of him going for an early breakfast with Mohammed. Danny looked like he was laughing. What the fuck was so funny about aborting our child?

I turned away and walked towards reception where Jamail was hunched over some paperwork. I knew him well: he'd been my driver after the invasion, until the Hamra hired him as duty manager. The two of us used to cruise around Baghdad, sniffing out stories in his battered red Toyota. I much preferred it to a showy four-wheel drive. In the end we fell out over money: he wanted higher wages, I couldn't afford them.

'Good morning, Miss Rachel,' he said to me, 'you wake so early.'

I told him I had to get on the road to Iskandariya right away but that Zaid, my usual driver, wasn't around yet. I needed someone now, that minute. He smiled.

'Perhaps you drive yourself!' he said.

It was a crazy, crackpot scheme. I knew I should give it up, go back to bed and sleep it off, but the fever wasn't letting go.

I said to him, 'Jamail, I've got a huge favour to ask – for old times' sake. Could you take me?'

He did this belly laugh, loud enough to wake the whole hotel. I told him to name his price.

'Is not money,' he said, 'Iskandariya very dangerous. Too, too dangerous.'

I hadn't even mentioned that we'd be meeting insurgents.

'Not Iskandariya itself,' I said, 'a little village on the way there, called al-Talha. I'm meeting Asmat Mahmoud – you remember him? We interviewed him a few times.'

'A thousand dollars,' he said. I told him that was extortionate and five times the going rate.

'Up to you,' he said. He just returned to his books, making out he wasn't bothered either way, like a shopkeeper in the bazaar.

I turned away, waiting to see if he'd call after me with a lower price. Nothing. I didn't have time to haggle. Danny would be finishing his breakfast soon and hitting the road.

'All right then,' I said. 'Done!'

I followed him out to the hotel garage and he undid the padlock on the double doors. I waited impatiently as he threw the tarpaulin off his old Toyota. Mohammed's car was already parked outside, but if we left now, we could beat them there. We'd be on the bridge with Abu Mukhtar when Danny arrived. He'd be apoplectic.

Jamail's old saloon made this wonderful, throaty roar as we drove out of Baghdad. Abu Mukhtar might not know we were coming, but he'd certainly hear us.

I was pumped up.

'Come on,' I told him, 'can't you go a bit faster? Doesn't a thousand bucks buy a bit of speed?'

I sat in the front passenger seat, occasionally dozing off, then waking and crying a little as I played back Danny's words. Their violence seemed to be reflected in the burnt-out cars we passed along the way and the endless convoys of American armour, heading to the latest hot-spot. A wall we drove past had *Death to USA* daubed on it, and a little further on *Kill Bush, kill Blair*. Everyone wanted to kill someone, I remember thinking.

I suppose, despite everything, I'd always thought Danny and I were going to make it, and it was Becky and Kaps who wouldn't. Their love had this congenital defect: from the start, it wasn't right – 'inappropriate', as I'd so patronisingly put it. Now I saw that, actually it was ours that was all fucked up. Danny had shown his contempt for me from the moment we first met. The relationship should have been terminated there and then.

Jamail raced towards Iskandariya. At that time of the morning there was hardly any traffic and we were waved through checkpoint after checkpoint. He just wanted this trip to be over, to get home with a big stash of bucks in his back pocket, and we were there in no time. Jamail spotted a couple of women in abayas leading a cow through the date palms. He asked them the way to the Suqlahat bridge. '*Al Sahafi*,' he explained to them. Journalists. He nodded his head in my direction.

'*Ahlan wa sahlan*,' they said. Welcome.

'*Ahlan bekum*,' I replied.

We pushed on another mile or so and I looked up at a young shepherd standing on a hill. He was no more than 12 or 13, I guess, and curious. For some reason, he made me think of my own child and I imagined it growing up to be his age, running off to school, scampering through the fields, playing with his friends. Danny's demand that I get rid of our child was murderous. I wanted to tell him he'd 'got rid' of everything we'd ever shared.

'Bridge up here,' said Jamail. Of the two of us, only he was nervous. I could hear it in his voice. 'Close now,' he said. 'Very close.'

I looked at my watch. We'd made good time, but Danny and Mohammed wouldn't be far behind, only ten or 20 minutes.

Looking back, my vision of how it would unfold was horribly clear; there was no other way it could turn out. Abu Mukhtar would be delighted that a young female had come to interview him. Danny's face would fall when he found me there, scribbling away. 'Hey, Danny,' I would say. 'Wasn't sure you were going to make it. But, seeing you're here now, we could split this one 50-50.'

Halfway through this daydream, I heard shouting and looked up to see gunmen on the bridge, covered up in fat sunglasses and different-coloured kafiyehs, some waving Kalashnikovs above their heads, some pointing them at us. I wound down my window and held out my laminated press pass, to show I was a journalist. When the first bullet cracked through the air, I just dropped it. Instinctively, I hit the floor of the Toyota and felt my stomach leave my body as Jamail threw the car into a spin. It wheeled around 360 degrees before I heard a second shot, only this time it was from behind us because we'd ended up facing the opposite direction. Jamail stabbed his sandal on to the accelerator and zigzagged back down the road. After a couple of minutes, when I dared to raise my head and look out of the window again, I saw the same shepherd on the hill, still standing there, still watching. I asked Jamail why we'd stopped. 'Tyre, Miss Rachel,' he explained, 'bullet hit tyre.'

'Shit, can you fix it?' I asked him. I apologised for getting him into this mess.

'It's okay,' said Jamail, 'they only want frighten. If they want kill us, they can, no problem.'

He got out and started changing the driver's side front tyre, spinning off the wheel nuts and cranking up the jack. He was impressive, like those guys in the pit-stops. He told me to stay in the car.

When Danny and Mohammed drove up to us, I knew they'd recognise the Toyota right away. Danny wound down his window and so did I. This was not how it was supposed to be: I wanted him to find a smug smile on my face, not the same old tears. He shook his head.

'I just don't believe it. What's your fucking problem, Rachel – can't get a story of your own?' I hadn't seen him so angry since the day he walked out on me in Washington. The way he saw it, I'd tricked my way into getting pregnant and now I'd tricked my way into his exclusive too.

'I … Danny, listen … you mustn't go—'

'You went through my things, didn't you?' he said. 'You found my notebook and you thought you'd just go ahead and help yourself. I mean, how much lower can you sink?'

'Listen to me for …'

'And stop *crying* for once, will you? I don't want the fucking baby, all right? Get over it.'

'You bastard,' I said.

We looked at each other for a deadly fraction of a second, both of us drowning in mutual resentment. He couldn't bring himself to ask if I'd already met up with Abu Mukhtar, he wouldn't give me the satisfaction.

'Anyhow, I'm pushing on,' he announced. His tone had changed, he was quieter now. There was so much to discuss, and yet so little we could say. 'How's everything up there? Okay?' He asked it casually, as though I was just a passer-by.

I sat there dumbstruck. He could see I was in tears; why wasn't he getting out to help us? Sure he didn't want the baby, but couldn't he even comfort me, the woman he was supposed to be in love with?

If I had been going to stop him, this was the moment. Anything would have done it. I could have shaken my head quietly or screamed at the top of my voice or jumped out of the car and flung myself in front of his. Or, of course, I could have just said no – no, it really isn't okay up there at all.

I couldn't move. I couldn't speak.

Anyway, they only wanted to *scare* people, that's what Jamail had said, and if anyone needed scaring, it was Danny. If they could shake him out of his self-obsessed complacency, maybe he'd think about other people for a change. About me. About our baby.

In that split second, Danny was persuaded by my silence. He ordered Mohammed to drive on. When Jamail finished the tyre change and got back into the car, he couldn't believe I hadn't stopped them. I can still see his eyes now, so wide with surprise and trepidation.

'Miss Rachel, why didn't you say ...'

'Let's go home,' I told him.

'But we cannot just ...'

'Do what I tell you, please, Jamail. Go home.'

30

Post-Liberation Baghdad, August 2004

Camille knew that everyone was watching her to see how she reacted. She supposed she should probably scream abuse at her brother's would-be killer, and swear vengeance on behalf of Mohammed's widow, but it would have been a manufactured anger. What she really felt was a mix of pity and curiosity.

'What happened?'

'What happened to what?' said Rachel.

'To that sweet girl who flew in to Sarajevo. I just don't understand, what did he do to her?'

'I did it to myself.'

Rachel had her head in her hands on the sofa. Edwin poured her a large Scotch, the doctor administering his medicine. Then, with the help of Kaps and Becky, he pulled her up till she was standing and all four of them embraced. Camille couldn't help admiring their solidarity: whatever they'd been through, the bonds between them were unbreakable. At the same time though, they had colluded in deceiving her. She felt a fool and this was the one thing she was genuinely angry about – the fact that she'd been humiliated.

'You *all* knew, didn't you? Right from the beginning.'

'Well, almost the beginning,' said Becky. 'I'm sorry, we haven't been fair to you.'

'Damn right, you haven't.'

'We needed to protect her.'

'You covered up for her.'

'We helped a friend, that's all.'

'By lying to me?' Camille's question floated, unanswered, in the paralysing heat. A maid hoovered outside in the corridor and, while no one spoke, its droning filled their ears until it stopped abruptly and the cleaner knocked. She wanted to turn the bed. Edwin opened the door to her.

'Thanks so much but would you be an absolute angel and fuck right off for me?'

Camille couldn't help but smile, albeit briefly. She wondered if, in the same position, she might have sheltered Rachel in her storm the way that they had done. Camille thought of the expat friends she had in Dubai, at least the people she called her friends: the bankers and diplomats and construction engineers, and all of their bored wives. Not one of them would have done this for her.

'So who was Saddoun?'

Even as she asked it, the answer came to her.

'A figment of Jamail's febrile imagination, I'm afraid,' said Kaps. 'He wanted you to know a bit, but not too much. He needed you to suspect one of us had been up there, so we'd get scared and pay him off. Which, I'm ashamed to say, is precisely what we did. He played us beautifully.'

'He's such a snivelling little creep,' said Becky. 'He said what Rachel did was a crime and he'd tell you the whole story if we didn't pay him.'

Edwin was sitting back on one of the kitchen chairs, inhaling hard on another Marlboro and forming his lips into a perfect O before slowly blowing out the bluey smoke so that it made a ring.

'Rachel was doing a pretty good job beating herself up about it all, without everyone else beating her up as well. We just didn't see any point in the whole of Baghdad finding out. It would have been in all the papers, plastered across the TV and the Internet. Imagine the headlines: *Star Reporter's Lover Sends Him into Kidnap Horror*, or something like that anyhow. They'd have crucified her. I mean, look at the state she's in as it is. I'm not sure she'd have survived. But you're right: we've lied to you, and for that I'm truly sorry.'

Camille didn't want their apologies or explanations. She was too busy trying to piece everything together. She felt frustrated. Confused. Stupid.

'I want to know it all!' she shouted, startling them with a thunderclap of temper. 'No more lies, no more secrets and cover-ups. Whatever happens to my brother , I want the truth and nothing but the truth.'

Edwin told her that after they'd paid Jamail his first 5,000, he demanded 20,000 more. They argued about it in the tea house, but then they'd given him that as well. Still it wasn't enough, and they had begun to doubt it ever would be.

Camille got up and paced around the room.

'The list at the news conference – you forged her signature? You went to that much trouble?'

'It seemed a sensible precaution,' said Edwin.

She was starting to focus on things she'd seen, small things that had meant nothing at the time.

'The garage. I saw you creeping around there with him.'

'Did you really? Well, it was where he kept his car. It had the bullet hole in it. It was his proof, he said; he was threatening to show people his precious Toyota if we didn't pay up. After we gave him the twenty, we told him to get rid of it.'

'And?'

'When you kept asking what we were doing, we went with him to the other side of Baghdad and he set fire to it. Said it wasn't worth a dinar, anyway. But it didn't stop him asking us for more.'

Camille screwed up her eyes and kept wiping her spectacles even though they were perfectly clean. She was thinking hard, like a child who's almost finished the puzzle but can't quite make the final few pieces fit.

'And that day we were up at al-Talha. I saw you picking something up, Kaps. That's always bugged me.'

'Rachel's press pass,' Kaps explained. 'We couldn't take the risk someone would find it.'

Camille shook her head. She was starting to see the clinical efficiency with which they'd covered Rachel's tracks for her.

'There's something else, isn't there?'

'No, that's it, Camille. You have it all.' Edwin looked relaxed now that the confessional was over.

'I mean, another reason you protected her.'

'I'm not sure I ...'

'It wasn't just that you felt sorry for her. You could imagine doing the same thing, couldn't you? Hating him so much that you'd let him walk right into the arms of a bunch of killers. I think you *sympathised* with Rachel.'

Becky shrugged.

'Who's to say what anyone might do if they get mad enough.'

'The trouble was, we all loved and loathed him,' said Rachel. 'I think it was always like that with me and Danny. Even in my very first week on the road, when he shot me down in flames for hanging out with Karadzic – that's when he first taught me how to hate him.'

Naturally it was Adi Duval who called them with the news. The military liaison people had heard it from the local Iraqi police chief in the Doura district of Baghdad, a Sunni stronghold. A Westerner thrown out of a car there. Alive. Battered, bruised and disorientated, but very much alive.

'We're still waiting for confirmation, I really gotta stress that, but it sounds like Danny,' Adi told Camille.

'Oh my ...'

'Look, it's really not a hundred per cent –'

'But why would they just let him go?'

'You know those talks Munro and Harper were having with the tribal elders? We have some intelligence they were making progress. Seems these high-up guys were kinda embarrassed Danny got invited out there, only to be kidnapped.'

Camille realised she'd misjudged Munro, just as she'd misjudged everyone else – Jamail, the Junkies, and no doubt Danny too. Munro might have been sullen and unfriendly, but he'd been working hard behind the scenes to get her brother freed. She rang her parents, but told them not to get their hopes too high. She repeated what Adi had told her – that nothing was confirmed, but things looked like they were moving. She was calm, calmer than she expected to be.

She watched the four Junkies stand in a circle again. This time they held hands, their eyes closed. They would not celebrate yet: if the man in the morgue had been someone else, this one could be too. They were giving each other more strength, and Camille was happy to let them have some time.

It was less than half an hour before her phone rang again. Adi was back on the line, enjoying his role at the centre of an international drama which was nearing the final scene of the final act: it beat working on the infrastructure reconstruction programme.

'He's made it to the embassy,' he announced. 'It's definitely Danny. He's home!'

This time they all cheered in unison. Kaps punched the air. 'Yes!' he shouted, before charging to the broken fridge and pulling out a bottle of warm champagne they'd kept there, waiting for this moment. Like all of them, relief cascaded off him, but some of his celebrations were for show, just as they had been at the Hilton. Now, as then, there was resentment. Danny had got away with it the way he always did. His ordeal would take him to another stratosphere of fame. He'd no longer just be a great reporter but a legend. There'd be interviews, a book, maybe even a movie.

Part of Kaps, the part that disgusted him and that he tried to hide even from himself, still wished that Danny had never made it out alive. These were thoughts that were obscene to him, like some depraved sexual perversity, but there was nothing he could do to stop them. He shook up the champagne and fired the cork into the ceiling. Spurts of white fizz shot out across the room.

Rachel jumped up on to the sofa she had been slumped across for so long, bouncing up and down on it until its springs twanged in protest. Her child still had a father, Camille still had a brother, his parents still had a son. What *she* had, she couldn't guess: would he even talk to her? Rachel's knees began to buckle as she imagined the moment when she would come face to face with him again. She thought about the one last secret she had kept clutched tight to her bosom; soon she would have to give it up and then, surely, Becky, Kaps and Edwin would wonder why they'd gone to all the trouble of protecting her. They would denounce her, as they should have from the start.

Adi came to pick up Camille and take her to the embassy so she could see Danny straight away. His friends would have to wait a while, Adi said: Danny was having a preliminary medical and the medics needed to get some high-protein food and drink into him. The poor guy had wasted away. 'Believe me, he needs everything from a dental check-up to a new wardrobe, and you can imagine they *all* want a piece of his ass: the ambassador, the general, the spooks, the Hostage Crisis Group, even the President – best thing that's happened to *him* in a while. Oh, and then there are your pals in the press, of course.'

There was a news conference planned because – according to Adi – 'Danny has something that he wants to say.' He'd catch up with them after that. Rachel and Edwin gave each other a look that said the day of reckoning had arrived, and Edwin walked into the kitchenette where he'd cooked so many meals for them. He lit himself yet another Marlboro, cupping his hands as if there were a wind from which he had to shelter its hesitant flame. He flicked on the news. A garish red ticker was already running along the bottom of the screen: *Breaking News – US Hostage Lowenstein Released*. He switched from channel to channel, English language and Arabic alike. Danny's mugshot was everywhere, like some Orwellian dictator.

As Adi drove Camille back across the Tigris, they found traffic had strangled the bridge that would take them to the Green Zone and to Danny. Up ahead someone had been sniping at an American patrol from a window. The troops had strung a line of Humvees across the street to block it off. They were running around in a frenzy, darting in and out of doorways, screaming at shopkeepers and passers-by, swinging their guns, pointing them at whoever was nearest to them, even women and children. Anyone could be the enemy in Iraq, anyone and everyone, and the soldiers had sweat trickling down their reddened faces. They were counting down time till they got home: this was one more scary Baghdad day to be negotiated and put behind them.

'Shit,' said Camille. 'Shit, shit, shit. I can't believe it. This day of all days.'

It gave her more time to think about whether he would even recognise her when she walked in. What if he needed to be told by someone – in hushed, embarrassed tones – that this was his estranged sister who stood before him? What if he decided, at the last moment, he didn't even want to talk to her? And even if they spoke, how would it end? With each of them begging the other for forgiveness, or a polite exchange of platitudes and a swift return to their separate worlds?

An hour later they had crawled through the gridlock and Green Zone security checks until they were back amid the fake splendour of Saddam's Republican Palace, now the strangest American embassy in the world. She walked through an imposing set of doors, past furniture, statuettes and works of art that wouldn't have looked out of place in Versailles. There was another kind of royalty lounging around them now: the diplomats who'd been promised by their masters they could have the pick of any other posting on the planet – as long as they did a quick stint in Baghdad.

Adi showed her into the meeting room he had found for the reunion.

'They say the old man used to hang out here,' he told her. On the walls, two long, gilded mirrors faced each other, and between them a fireplace, its mantelpiece covered in artificial flowers that made no serious attempt to convince. The centre of the room was dominated by a long, mahogany table: the President had used it, apparently, for talks with visiting diplomats, businessmen and arms dealers. Perhaps this was where he had even bought the weapons of mass destruction he turned out not to have.

With every minute Camille had to wait, she grew more nervous, her teeth tugging on a wick of dried skin beside a fingernail. She heard a noise outside and watched the door's golden handle turn and knew that he was here at last. When she saw him, she wondered why she had been so terrified: before her was a creature who was pitifully frail and who winced with pain as he shuffled his feet forward, just a few inches at a time. To help him walk, he held on to the arm of a nurse from the embassy medical team, like a patient in a geriatric ward. Camille thought about running over and embracing him but decided not to in case she hurt him. Or perhaps that was just her excuse.

At the Green Zone's state-of-the-art hospital, the Ibn Sina, they had treated the infected burn on his hand and put his arm in a sling. There were two squares of bright white cotton gauze on his forehead, held in place by narrow strips of plaster. The front teeth, however, were still a gaping absence and the hostage stubble, whose last appearance had been in the kidnappers' video, had grown into a full beard. Camille wasn't sure if he didn't want to shave it off, or if he hadn't yet had time, but parts of it were speckled grey and they made him look entirely different. Now she didn't feel so bad that she hadn't been able to picture him. She guessed that, if he'd looked in a mirror, he'd have barely recognised himself.

He'd had a shower – his hair was moist and combed – and Adi's people had found him some clothes, a baggy striped shirt that looked like a pyjama top and a pair of jeans that were far too wide around the waist. Danny, normally so conscious of his appearance, was oblivious. Whatever he had on, it was better than an orange jumpsuit.

Adi and the nurse sat him down in a high-backed chair and then left the room so they could be alone together. Camille saw his eyes focus on her and try to take in this face he hadn't seen in so many years. She felt all the moisture in her mouth disappear, and hoped her voice wouldn't crack when she spoke to him.

'Welcome back, Danny. It's good to see you. How are you?'

The question was nonsensical, of course. He looked like a man who'd been hit by a train. In the video he'd seemed broken, but now she could see it was worse than that: he was shattered, into a thousand pieces.

'I've been better.' His dried-out, scabby lips barely parted from each other when he spoke. 'Thanks for coming all this way.'

'It was the least I could … I mean, I wanted to be here.'

All she could hear was a conversation between two strangers that was struggling for life. She feared it would flicker away and die, and searched desperately for something else to say – anything. All this time she'd had to prepare, and still she had no ready-made thought or sentence on hand. Then she realised she didn't need to worry: he'd got used to silence over the past few weeks, and when she appreciated this, the quiet between them was no longer uncomfortable. It was calming, in fact; a time to reacquaint themselves with each other's presence and get used to sharing the same space again.

'Mom and Dad are so happy you're free,' she said eventually.

'They're not here as well?'

She laughed nervously.

'God, no. But we could call them, when you're ready.'

She thought he might scoff at the suggestion, even in his shrunken state. Instead he nodded.

'I'd like that.'

'I think it's time. Time for all of us.'

'I know.'

The cocksure arrogance, the Lowenstein swagger had ebbed away from him, every drop. She looked into his face and part of it was deadened, but somewhere in there she could still see that little boy she used to play with. She wished Lukas could have just loved him for what he'd been, and cherished his intelligence and even admired his anger with the world. She wished she could have too.

She walked towards his throne-like chair and knelt in front of him. Again she thought about putting her arms round him and sinking her head into his bony ribcage, but still she dared not touch him. Instead, the tears that had been damned up so long began to flow, a trickle at first and then a torrent. She cried like Rachel and Becky had done, and it was the most marvellous release. She gave thanks, as a farmer in a drought gives thanks for the rains. Danny watched her back rise and fall, and heard half-stifled cries of anguish. Nothing could surprise him any more.

'I should mention something, before you see anyone else,' she said when the spasms of her crying had started to die down. She was looking up at him, her face sweaty with strands of hair across it. 'I know about Rachel. No one else does, only her friends. Danny, I have to ask: will you tell people?'

The imposing, high-ceilinged room where the press conference was to take place was packed. Becky sensed Rachel's trepidation, and rather than just hold her hand, she gripped it hard, the way Rachel had once gripped hers at Heathrow.

They'd squeezed in at the back, drawing a few sanctimonious tut-tuts from those who had reserved their places long ago. It was strange for them to be at a news conference where they had come to watch rather than to report. They sandwiched themselves awkwardly between the live cameras of the BBC, CNN and Al Jazeera, just some of the lenses through which a fascinated world would get its first glimpse of Danny Lowenstein. One cameraman – a lanky Texan – was chatting to another: 'Not too often there's a good-news story out of this place. "American Citizen Held Hostage, Lives to Tell the Tale" – that's gotta make top slot tonight, right?'

'Beats another car bomb,' said his colleague. 'One live Yank must be worth at least 100 dead Iraqis; 200, if it's a Yank with a Pulitzer!'

The low hubbub of the waiting press corps stopped abruptly, as if someone had flicked off a switch. A respectful, funereal hush replaced it. Danny was making his entrance and no one could take their eyes off him. The idea of being kidnapped haunted every journalist in Iraq and here was their nightmare, right in front of them: no longer the well-worn television image of the prisoner in orange, but a human being they could reach out and touch, resurrected from the dead.

'Welcome to you all and thanks for coming,' said Adi at last. 'And welcome home to Danny Lowenstein.'

The entire press corps burst out into emotional, unprofessional applause. Their spines tingled and they felt good to be here with him. Rachel, languishing at the back and hidden behind the battery of cameras and tripods, put her hands together weakly.

Danny managed a tired smile of gratitude and dozens of flash bulbs exploded simultaneously as the snappers caught the money shot, a blaze of white light that made him blink. He looked to see if they were out there somewhere, his fellow Junkies. Becky and Kaps waved but he was dazzled, like an actor blinded by the footlights.

The barrage of questions came thick and fast: about the food, the fear, the guards; whether he had really thought he might die, why he'd been released and if a ransom had been paid. People would be putting the same questions to him for the rest of his life. *What was it like*? they would demand over and over, and each time he would try to tell them but never quite succeed. From now on he'd be known not as 'award-winning journalist, Danny Lowenstein', but 'former hostage, Danny Lowenstein'.

Once Danny would have revelled in it, regaling the world with jaw-dropping stories of his captivity. After all, they'd be watching in the White House, Downing Street and the Élysée Palace and millions of homes in every continent. Once he would have told it all. Now though he wanted to get it over with. He was proud of nothing he'd just been though, and nothing that he'd done.

'I'm really not sure what to say,' he muttered, so softly they could barely catch it. 'I mean, how d'you describe walking through the gates of hell and thinking you'll never come back?' The rich, East Coast timbre had vanished. Now it was a rasping whisper with a whistle because of the gap in his front teeth. The raconteur, the speechmaker, the passionate campaigner for a better world, sounded as though he had a speech impediment.

The questions flowed easily but not the answers, and after less than ten minutes Adi announced that Danny needed to get some rest.

'I'm sorry, guys, you can all see how tired he is. I promise you'll get another chance to talk to him in the coming days, but for now I'm going to take just one last question please.'

It came from the same French reporter who had thrown Camille at the end of her press conference at the Hamra.

'Mr Lowenstein, there has been a persistent rumour that another journalist was there when you were kidnapped. The story is, they were in a second car that got away. Perhaps even someone that you knew. Can you tell us anything about that?'

Rachel felt dizzy. *Danny has something he wants to say.*

'Please, no,' she said under her breath. 'Please God, not now, not here in front of all these people.' Instinctively, Becky reached across and put a hand on her knee.

The Junkies searched his battered, patched-up face for some clue about how he might reply. There was so much damage he could do with just a sentence. His pause was unbearable but eventually he shook his head, the way Rachel knew she should have done that day.

'Sorry,' he said quite firmly, and louder than he'd been till now. 'I really have no idea what you're talking about.'

They met him in the room where the reunion with Camille had taken place earlier. Kaps was the first to offer an embrace. He had none of Camille's qualms about physical contact and hugged him hard. Danny flinched with pain.

The man Kaps saw in front of him no longer looked like a rival but a dried-out husk of who he'd been. The long years of Kaps' jealously suddenly seemed to him infantile and ridiculous. His suspicion that Danny might somehow profit from his ordeal was equally absurd. Now that Kaps could feel that withered body, he knew instinctively that Danny would never report again. He suspected that meant he wouldn't either, for there would be no one to spur him on, and it filled him with warm relief. He could reclaim a friend from the past. He could try to love Danny all over again.

Edwin and Becky embraced him next. They too carried the guilt of everything they'd been thinking about Danny for the last few weeks, and all their toxic memories. Becky peppered his cheeks with kisses and wondered if he already knew how they had colluded, treacherously, to hide the truth about what had happened to him.

Rachel approached him last, as reduced as he was. She dared do no more than stand in front of him.

'Oh, Danny. Thank God you're alive,' she said. 'Thank you God, thank you, *thank you.*'

'And there was me thinking you were an atheist,' laughed Edwin, who had just unscrewed the cap of his whisky flask and was searching the room for glasses. Everyone smiled, hoping Danny might as well. Perhaps they could all pretend nothing bad had happened to any of them and that they were back in the good old days of Sarajevo. Perhaps they wouldn't have to discuss anything at all. But laughter had not yet fought its way back into Danny's life and he sat before them in an unfamiliar pose, back straight and knees together, sipping straight from Edwin's flask. He looked as though he was drinking tea with strangers.

Rachel thought about sitting alongside him and putting her hand in his, but she couldn't face the possibility he might fling it back at her. She had no idea what to do next, so she merely retreated to the other side of the room. It felt as though she was running away from him and all his unspoken accusations.

Then Danny started to talk – as best he could, with four teeth missing.

'I had to see you.' His voice became more audible as the whisky gave him strength. 'I had to get some answers.'

Without asking, Rachel grabbed one of Edwin's cigarettes from the packet that lay on the table and stuffed it in her mouth. She longed to light it, but for the baby's sake decided not to.

''Course you do,' Kaps said. 'But there'll be plenty of time for all of that. Don't you think you should take some time to … decompress, or whatever they call it?'

Danny wasn't listening. He had a speech prepared, ready to be delivered in the unlikely event of his freedom, and no one was going to stop him delivering it.

Every one of them knew what the coming words would mean for Rachel. They tried not to stare at her, just as those in a courtroom try not to stare at the defendant in the dock, but it was impossible to look away.

'You get a lot of time to think, when you're chained up in a cell like that, day and night. We've all had close shaves, near-death experiences. I used to like to boast about them – I guess we all did. You couldn't be a real war correspondent without them. But this thing, it was on another level. Not fearing you might die: being absolutely certain that you would. Just waiting for it. Does that make any sense?'

'Of course,' said Becky. Like the others, she had assumed that if he ever came back to them, it would be the Danny they had always known, bristling with indignation and bursting to file on his story of a lifetime. This one seemed like an impostor.

'Well, it was when I was waiting that I got to thinking …'

For a moment he said nothing more, adrift in Scar's cell and Abu Omar's house.

'Uh-huh?' Edwin prompted him. 'Thinking about what?'

'About what Rachel did to me on that road.'

She was light-headed again, closing her eyes and wishing she could take a drag on Edwin's cigarette. She thought she might expire without it. 'Oh, Danny, I'm so sorry. I'm going to be saying sorry to you all my life and it still won't be enough.' She wanted to run over and throw herself upon his mercy, to smother his shattered mouth with kisses so that he could talk no more. Something held her back though. He had a force-field around him and it frightened her.

Becky put a protective arm round her and spoke up in her defence, a character witness giving evidence in mitigation.

'Look, you'll never know how broken up she's been about what happened. She's absolutely devastated. She just can't get over that she ...'

'That I did nothing to stop you,' said Rachel.

'Is that how you remember it?' Danny said quickly and in a detached, deadened voice they were beginning to find unnerving. 'That you did *nothing*?'

'I ... well, yes.'

'Are you sure?' His bloodshot eyes were fixed on her, they had no interest in anyone else. Saddam himself could have walked back in to reclaim his seat and Danny would not have shifted his gaze. 'A little more than nothing, wouldn't you say?'

It was the secret she had kept from them all, even Becky, perhaps even from herself.

So he *had* seen. He *had* remembered. Of course he had, fool. How could he possibly not have done? It was the wildest flight of fancy to ever think he might forget. He knew and he wanted them to know, yet even now she couldn't bear anyone else to hear it.

'I'm not quite sure what …'

'Tell them, Rachel. Please tell them what you did.'

Even if she had been willing, the muscles around her mouth would not form the words and she shook her head from side to side as Becky held her. But Danny's stare was still upon her like a searchlight.

'When I asked you if it was okay on the road ahead, what was it you did?'

'I …'

With hot blood pounding around her head, she looked at Becky for some guidance. None came. How could it?

'I … just didn't do anything. I should have, I know, but I did nothing.'

'No, *not* nothing. Don't you remember? When I asked if it was safe up there, you nodded your head, didn't you? You gave me the green light to go on. You wanted me to …'

'Don't say it!' Rachel put her hands over her ears. She was sure she could deny the existence of this truth if only it were not said aloud. *Nod*: such a short, innocuous word. *You nodded your head.* Perhaps they wouldn't have heard it properly, or grasped its significance. But she closed her eyes as well because she couldn't bear to see the shock on their faces – Becky, Kaps and Edwin, the dear friends who'd held her hand and lied for her and paid a blackmailer.

Danny slugged down some more whisky. It was like a fireball in his shrunken belly. He was reflecting, more concerned with working out what he'd become than denouncing Rachel. He had laid bare her crime, but he didn't want her punished for it. He didn't even want to talk about it any more.

'You know, I remember covering some other hostage who got released once. When the guy got back to his family, he kept saying one thing to them, over and over again: "I'm the same," he said.

"I'm the same. I'm the same." He wanted to reassure them, I guess. Well, here's the thing. I'm *not* the same. I've changed.'

'Of course, that's understandable,' said Becky. 'You're bound to have.'

'All that time to think in there, and you know what I thought about most of all? How someone I loved so much could wind up hating me that much, enough to want me dead.'

They'd been waiting for him to complete the charges against her, but instead he wanted to accuse himself.

Rachel became calmer. Her storm had passed. Finally, she could bear to look and listen.

'And what was it?' she asked him, in a voice as quiet as his. 'The answer you came up with?'

He hauled himself out of his chair and shuffled over to her, each step full of pain, and without asking, he took one of her small hands. It was the first time they had touched since they made love before al-Talha, the night neither of them should have ever interrupted.

'I went back over everything we'd done together, everything we'd said. I realised that, if you behaved badly, it was because I'd behaved even—'

'No, you couldn't have,' Rachel broke in.

After all, he had not killed one man and very nearly killed another. This was what she had to live with now, whether the world knew about it or not. It was a burden of guilt that would be with her till the grave.

'I killed Mohammed. A silly temper tantrum, and I killed him.'

'No you didn't,' insisted Danny. 'If anyone did, it was me. He was scared and I pushed him on. I wasn't interested in his opinions that morning; I just wanted to get my story. I always wanted to get my story.'

Perhaps that was how it would be, she thought: both of them sharing the guilt for the rest of their lives, and making it bearable for each other. It would be their bargain. She put her flushed face closer to his, battered and bearded, but neither of them sought a kiss, not yet.

'What do we do now, Danny? What's left for us?'

She looked into the same eyes she'd been watching all these years. She'd never been sure about them, not since she'd studied them when he picked her up on that first day in Sarajevo. At last though, she could be certain: they were good eyes, and all the hardness and the cynicism had gone from them, and all the bad things had been washed away with his tears these last few weeks.

When they emerged from the Palace and the pleasure of its air conditioning, the blast of Baghdad heat hit them hard. Some of the press were still there, waiting to ask what Danny had said to them in private, and how they thought he'd coped with his ordeal. Their response was that he was their hero and they were proud of him. He would need some space, they said, but of course he'd be back on the road in his own good time. The journalists seemed pleased enough: the quotes, heartfelt and optimistic, would make good copy. Readers loved a tragedy, but they also loved a happy ending.

As they finished talking to the press, the Junkies saw the nurse emerge with him, shepherding his fragile frame towards an ambulance. Adi and Camille followed close behind. Rachel hoped he might look up and wave to her, but those new eyes she'd seen trailed along the ground, lost in an ocean of thought.

'Should I be staying with him?' she asked Becky.

'Just give him a little time.'

Instead of Danny it was Adi who waved – to Becky, naturally – and in return she smiled the last smile she would ever give him. 'Fuck you, dickhead,' she said beneath her breath.

They watched the crew of the ambulance open up its doors and prepare to drive Danny back to Ibn Sina.

'Only the best for our Danny,' said Kaps. 'That's where they treated Uday when he got himself shot up in that assassination attempt.'

The words made Rachel shiver: she wondered if what she'd done could be considered an assassination attempt too. Again she thought about the enormity of her crime. She started walking, then running, to the ambulance, ignoring Becky's advice, and was surprised to find herself standing back in front of Danny. Having got there, she could think of nothing more to say to him, and so he spoke instead, lifting his fragile head towards the sun.

'I love it now, you know; the heat of it, the power. There were times in that cell I thought I'd never see it again.'

'You can get as much of it as you want,' said Rachel. 'Spend the rest of your life on a beach, if you like. Slap on some cream and lap it up.'

'That morning before they took me, I hated it, I cursed the way it made me so feel so goddamned tired and sticky. Took it for granted, I guess. Can you believe that? The best thing in the world, the most *necessary* thing in the world, and I took it for granted.'

He'd have stood there all day, basking in its light, but Adi and the nurse stepped forward and took him by the arms again, guiding him into the back of the ambulance as half a dozen photographers snatched some more pictures, jumping out in front of him, pushing their lenses back into his aching face, knowing there was nothing he could do to stop them.

For a while, a few of the journalists from Danny's press conference dawdled outside the Palace on its green and pleasant land, reluctant to leave this fake Baghdad and return to the real one. The Junkies hung around too. What was there to do except report on Danny's release, and since they could never tell the true story, what would be the point? And where was there for them to go except the Hamra? They'd be happy if they never set foot in the Presidential Suite again: for the last month it had been their own cell.

It was 20 minutes later that the distant rumble of an explosion vibrated gently in their ears. They looked over the tops of the palm trees and soon they could pick out the telltale pall of smoke, a grim signal to the city that yet another martyr's day had come.

'Shit, that one wasn't too far away,' said Edwin with a weariness in his voice where once there would have been excitement. Still, it was a story, he supposed: the bloody waves of the Red Zone lapping ever closer to the hushed shoreline of the Green one.

Becky looked pale and, without caring who was watching, Kaps held her hand.

'Should we go and check it out?' he asked.

'Not me, thanks,' said Rachel. 'Not me ever again.' She remembered her headlong rush to her very first Sarajevo massacre a decade earlier, her brain split in two. Now she watched the new generation of wannabes dashing forward. Did they have hangovers as well? Did they have to borrow a helmet from a friend who turned into an enemy and a lover?

Becky smiled because she was remembering too.

'You know what they say: there's always another story. Always another war-zone virgin to go and cover it, too. I vote we send for more volunteers, all bright-eyed and bushy-tailed like you were, Rach, the day I met you.'

Around them, the last of the camera crews and photographers were running towards their vehicles and heading for the scene. Rachel wanted to be with the people running away from it.

'Fuck it, let's go back to the hotel and have a swim.'

Lethargically, the Junkies climbed into the car, but Rachel stood for a moment with the passenger door half open, her face inclined to the sun the same way Danny's had been a few minutes earlier.

She made herself squint at it through half-closed eyes and loved the way her skin tingled in its heat.

That night the scream came from down the corridor: it was Becky's room and Kaps ran there, though it was well past midnight and his legs were leaden with fatigue. When he pushed the door open, he found her sitting up in bed, her eyes wide, her mouth trying to draw breath. He placed the wide palm of his hand on her forehead.

'Okay, it's all okay now. Nothing to be afraid of, just a bad, bad dream.'

She stared at the bare white wall in front of her.

'Sorry. I was there again. The bullets, rockets, everything. So loud … his screams …'

Kaps stroked her cheeks. They were burning up, hot beneath his fingertips.

'And then he was on a precipice calling for help, and I was trying to get to him, but someone had tied me up …'

'Shhhh, it's over now.'

It felt good to be caring for her again, the way he had done in the Kosevo hospital when the mortar had torn her leg apart. That first, sweet bedside kiss.

She closed her eyes to signal that her nightmare or panic attack or whatever the shrinks might classify it as was over.

'It's been a decade, near enough; how can it still fuck me up like this?'

'You're damaged, Becky. It's what it's done to you. Who knows, maybe what *I've* done to you as well.'

When she looked at him, she realised nothing had changed: she still hadn't seen a more beautiful man in her life and she never would. She wasn't sure she could endure this dreadful passion any longer.

Kaps looked at her as well, so vulnerable, so in need of being cared for, and all he saw were the years he'd wasted. He took his hand from her forehead and replaced it with his lips. And when she sighed, he let them trace a path that travelled down, through the gap between her heavy eyebrows, along the ridgeline of her nose, until they reached her mouth where they kissed her the way they always had. He pulled up the sheets and climbed in next to her. He had on a pair of shorts and a T-shirt, but she was naked and he let the clothes fall from him until he melted into her overheated body. It became an extension, once again, of his. She was soaked and slippery with sweat, as she had been when they'd danced in Sarajevo, and for a moment he pretended he was back there, ten years younger, the love of both their lives just beginning. They barely blinked as each held the other in their gaze, still kissing, wondering if it was all too late.

'Tell me something, Kaps, will we ever be together? Properly, I mean. I just need to know, that's all. I have this sense that somehow one day everything turns out right for us. A completely crazy fantasy, but I'm not sure I could survive unless a little part of me believed it.'

It was the same fantasy he'd indulged in so many times and, like her, it had kept him alive. But even now he could not say the words. He kissed her again and answered her with the same silence she'd been listening to for all those years.

31

London and Sarajevo, October 2004

Irony, Danny would always say, was one of the most overworked concepts in journalism. As in, 'ironically, the man was robbed on his birthday,' when in fact it wasn't so much irony as vaguely interesting coincidence. Miracles were another bugbear; they should stay within the pages of the Bible, he would insist, which was all a fairy story anyhow. Still, it didn't stop people calling his release 'miraculous', while even Danny had to admit it was 'ironic' that barely two months after the Junkies had been waiting for him to die, they were visited by another death instead.

The morning he was found, it was a blustery, drenching London day when those who ventured out cowered beneath umbrellas and struggled to hold on to them. He was not one of those who had braved the elements; he never even made it out of bed. His latest on-off girlfriend had got herself together sufficiently to dial 999, and when the paramedics found him, he was naked. A pool of his own dried-out vomit was spread around his head like a halo and his body was lying prone, arms and legs spreadeagled across the sheets. 'Looks like bloody Jesus on the cross,' said one of the ambulancemen. They cleared his airway and tried to resuscitate him with CPR and a cardiac defibrillator. He was breathing but unconscious. 'Another day, another junkie.'

When they got him to St Mary's Hospital, the doctors said it was not drugs but an overdose of painkillers and sleeping pills he'd been prescribed: they couldn't tell if it was accidental or deliberate, but the combination of temazepam, oxycodone, hydrocodone and doxylamine had overwhelmed his body.

His friends, emotionally spent after their premature grief over Danny, had to wring themselves dry again. They had lost so many who were close to them – Amra, Alija, Mohammed – but now, as Danny would once have said, it was one of them. They converged on St Mary's, a setting that seemed to them altogether too drab for such drama. Where was the driving snow? Where was the chaotic influx of wounded soldiers and civilians, the cacophony of shell-fire? Instead, all they found when they arrived was rain dripping from the gutters, elderly people grumbling in green gowns, and the terrifying quiet of the intensive-care unit. Edwin lay there amid a spaghetti of tubes fastened to his disappearing body.

His head was lolling to one side, eyes closed but mouth open with a dribble of saliva rolling out of it, like an old man who's fallen asleep in his chair. There was already that sheen to his skin, that unmistakable look of the death that had fascinated him for so long.

Danny wanted to be there, even though he was still convalescing himself and – they all agreed – only a hint of the man he'd been. The four of them kept a vigil by Edwin's side, establishing a rota so that at least one was with him. They were all he had: his parents were dead, there were no siblings, and the few distant relatives he had were frankly not that interested in whether or not this particular druggie pulled through; after all, when in his fucked-up life had he ever shown any interest in *them*?

The doctors waited three days before agreeing at their morning case conference that he was lost. 'By our criteria for brain activity, there is no hope, I'm afraid,' one of them told Rachel and Kaps. He was young and kind with a voice that was deep and posh. He could have been from the same public school Edwin went to, Rachel thought. 'In layman's terms, he's brain dead. It's only the ventilator that's keeping him alive and we feel any further treatment would be futile. We'll be asking next of kin for permission to turn off the machine, but we wanted to consult you as well. To find out what your feelings were.'

Rachel looked at Kaps with sagging, watery eyes which asked him how it had come to this – that a man who'd lived a life at war and survived it all could now die on the say-so of his closest friends.

'Should we get someone in to give him the last rites?' Becky was staring out of a grimy window at another day of gales and drowning rain. No one had thought of a priest till now and instinctively they all looked to Danny, seeking special dispensation from the atheist.

'Of course,' he said amenably. 'If we think that's what he would want.'

Rachel stroked Edwin's scalp, her fingertips scratched by the stubble allowed to grow on it at last, thriving on it even as he died his dawdling death.

'He sort of gave up on God after Amra,' she said. 'Then again, I don't suppose it would do any harm.'

The Lord's servant came in the shape of a young man called Liam who arrived on a scooter, soaked by an irreverent London downpour. He couldn't have been more than 30 and when he walked in with his helmet under his arm, bedraggled, Edwin's friends were surprised to discover that this was what Death should look like: so much younger than them, so fresh-faced and helpful. In his soothing Irish lilt, Father Liam chatted easily to them for a while, then he produced a small silver pot of oil and began his business. He dipped a finger into it and anointed Edwin's forehead with the sign of the cross.

'May the Lord who frees you from sin save you and raise you up.'

Becky would say afterwards that it felt she could almost see Edwin's soul rising from the skeleton his body had become, and it was this that they took as the final moment, rather than the switching off of the equipment, which came a few minutes later – a curiously mechanical action, like turning off a lamp or a computer before you leave the room. They had envisaged many deaths for him – a bullet, a shell, even a war-zone car crash – but not this one.

When Father Liam uttered the words 'raise you up', they tried hard not to cry – not to make a sound, in fact. Danny in particular struggled with his tears, sniffing and snorting them back because he thought they were an intrusion, coming from him especially. After a minute or so he couldn't fight them any longer and he threw himself on Edwin's chest. He wrapped his arms around it, buried his face in its jutting ribs, and kissed it as he cried. He had an overwhelming conviction that it was the wrong man who was about to die.

Just as Alija wanted to be buried in London, Edwin needed to go home to Sarajevo. Some thought it outlandish, ghoulish even, to fly a corpse all the way from Heathrow to one of the world's discarded war zones, and it was fraught with bureaucratic and logistical difficulties. But where else could anyone say he truly belonged? Certainly not England.

This time his friends didn't fly on a Hercules firing flares to protect itself, but a British Airways Airbus with hot towels and tasty snacks. The airport they arrived at was no longer a frontline battleground. It boasted a new, gleaming terminal, paid for with sackloads of European Union euros. There was no need for Bessie;

instead a Mercedes taxi drove them down Snipers' Alley, where they had to stop at traffic lights and parking wardens were on the prowl. Shop windows were festooned with designer labels, and affluent Sarajevans in chic clothes and sunglasses sat outside cafés texting each other or working away on laptops.

But it was still their Sarajevo. *His* Sarajevo. The four of them held on to each other hard as they stared out of the Mercedes at the city sweeping by and thought about him here. They chuckled again at the story of his armoured Land Rover sliding into the poor old lady's living room, and they cursed when they thought about the things he'd said: *We tell ourselves we'll get away with it, that we're a protected species.*

Rachel gazed up as they passed the Holiday Inn, rebuilt in all its ugly yellow glory. She was no longer thinking about Edwin, but about the heady thrill of arriving in its bunker car par and picking up her room key. She supposed she ought to wish she'd never come, never met Edwin or Danny or Becky or Kaps. They had brought her horror, but then again, that was what she'd wanted at the time; they had also filled her life with love, filled it to the brim, and there would have only been long years of emptiness without them. She felt the light flutter of her baby kicking, and wondered whether he or she would ever want to be a war correspondent. Despite her nostalgia, the thought of her child in that situation – gambling with the odds, daring death to come and get it – was suddenly repugnant. Billy had been right to try and stop her. She had been horribly selfish in abandoning him. The baby kicked again and, protectively, she put both hands on the gentle slopes of her rising bump.

Danny was next to her in the Mercedes, his face pressed against the window too. He watched the passing blur of hills and red rooftops and minarets, and saw a city he'd never wanted to leave. He should have eschewed the temptations of Africa and Chechnya:

this was the only place he'd really belonged and when he'd strayed from it, pain was all he'd brought with him.

People kept telling him he'd be back on the road one day soon, but Danny knew it was over now. It wasn't only war he could never face again; he couldn't do another story or write another word.

When they reached the cemetery, it felt odd that they could just stand there and not worry about planning which open grave they'd jump into if they needed cover.

Their memory of the place was that it had been busy and muddy and makeshift, fresh mounds of earth springing up each morning from the new graves that were like shellholes on a battlefield. Now the grass had grown and there were flowers and proper tombstones instead of wooden markers with plastic letters or even pen scrawls to name the dead.

They were relieved to discover there was just enough space for Edwin next to Amra. A lapsed Catholic next to a lapsed Muslim: it had a certain symmetry. Only a few inches away from her name and dates, his were inscribed as well: *Edwin Christopher Garland, 1966–2004.* They imagined him reaching out a hand, underground, and holding hers – tentatively, without presumption.

Rachel put an arm round Danny, and he held on to it as if he were a drowning man. Becky rested her head on Kaps' neck and wished she could leave it there forever.

The four of them were remembering Edwin's anguished howl at this very spot. For a moment it haunted them anew, but then it faded in their heads, so that the only sounds left in the Lion Cemetery were the blackbirds and some fallen leaves rustling in the wind, the sweet nothings of peace.

It was as if history had never happened.

Author's Note

This novel is set against the backdrop of recent history. I've been to all the places the Junkies went to and stayed in all their 'crap hotels'. However, the characters are plucked from my imagination and some of the events they're involved with are fictitious too – for example, the particular massacre that Rachel covers early on in Sarajevo. The more minor places in my story, such as al-Talha and Yazhdnovskaya, are also my creations. Where I have described actual historical events – in 1994 and 2004 – I have tried to be as accurate as any conscientious BBC reporter would be. In this endeavour, I'm enormously grateful to the following people for their expertise and memories: Jon Jones, the brilliant war photographer; Kim Sengupta of the *Independent* and a veteran of Baghdad; Madeleine Lewis, my first producer in Sarajevo. Any mistakes, of course, are mine not theirs.

Thanks too to those who read early drafts of *Sandstealers*: Laura Heberton, Nancy Miller, Fehmina Ahmed, Alan Lewens, Joanna Gosling and Emily Maitlis. In their different ways, they all helped shape this novel. I'm hugely indebted too to my agent, David Miller, for having so much faith in me, and Arabella Pike, Annabel Wright and Anne O'Brien at HarperCollins for their insights and patience.

Finally, my everlasting love and gratitude to my darling wife Geraldine, who insisted this was the book that I should write; to Ella, Grace and Gabriel for letting me hog the family computer; to my mother Sheila for all her encouragement and support, and to my late father, Antony Brown, who urged me to write and is still my inspiration. I miss him every day.